For Allyriane

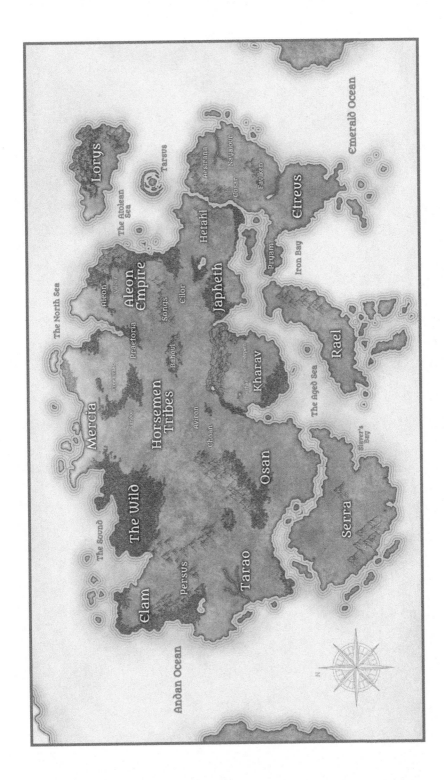

SHADOW QUEEN

CHAPTER ONE

Time was of the essence now. Collective footsteps echoed through the halls of the Kharavian castle. The sun hadn't yet reached its peak, but Soren worried the day was too far gone. The queen had fled, and every moment counted in recovering her.

He strode quickly, and his men followed in unison. Artem strode beside him, like an equal.

But he was not.

Soren waved his men and Artem to wait as he turned into the alcove of Mikael's study, and he paused as he took in a deep breath before letting it out slowly. He had never felt anxious about delivering bad news. But today was different. This was different. Mikael was different now.

He pushed open the ash-wood door and found the king at his desk, mulling over a letter. Mikael lifted his head on hearing him enter, and leaned back in his chair, tossing the letter to the edge of the desk for Soren to see. "Aleon has sent additional forces to their borders. Nearer to Japheth, and nearer to us."

Aleon had long been the North's ally. Now, with an alliance between the North and Kharav, the North Queen would have Mikael believe Aleon was a friend. But Kharav was still allies with the Aleon king's brother, the king of Japheth, and the conflict between the brothers would be resolved only when one of them was dead. Aleon would never be a friend.

Soren picked up the letter and read through it. His uneasiness grew. The Bear was in Aleon now. It was as they feared. The Bear was bringing Aleon against them.

The king sighed, unsettled. "They're preparing. But whether it's with intention of—"

"The North Queen is gone," Soren interrupted him. No sense delaying.

Mikael stopped in his words and looked up in surprise. "Gone where?" he asked as he rose from his desk. "What happened?"

"She went riding this morning and"—Soren paused—"went through great lengths to escape the Crest. This isn't a coincidence."

Mikael rested the knuckles of his closed fists on the smooth hardwood of his desk as he stood, and he leaned his weight forward. "If the North plots against me, she's promised she has no part in it."

Soren's jaw tightened as he fought his irritation. The king's love for this woman blinded him to reality.

Mikael moved to the window and looked out across the city. "Was Artem with her?"

The mere mention of the Crest captain's name irritated him. "He was."

"Where is he?"

Soren sighed. He'd already gotten the details from Artem and needed to leave now to catch the queen. This was a waste of time. "He's in the hall."

Mikael drew in a breath of what Soren knew was forced composure. "Bring him in."

Soren opened the door and summoned the captain, and Artem strode in, bowing low. "Salar," he said with a smooth but needling voice.

A quiet growl rumbled in the back of Soren's throat as he tried to not show his annoyance. Artem—always seeking to be at the top, yet always over the top.

Mikael stepped back to his desk. "I'm told Salara's gone. Evaded you."

"Yes, Salar. She rides for the North."

Mikael nodded. He calmly stacked the parchments on his desk, but Soren knew the storm below the surface. "Tell me, how is it possible for her to slip the elite soldiers of the Crest and their captain?"

Artem shifted uncomfortably. "Salar, this is the same woman who stole the lord commander's horse from under him at the base of Bahoul."

Soren bristled. Artem was a pisspot coward who did whatever he needed to do to deflect from himself. Soren's father, Tyrhar Nazim, had once been captain of the Crest, and Artem defiled the honor of the position. Artem had taken over as captain under Mikael's father when the former king charged Tyrhar to look after Bahoul. Artem had no principles, and Soren couldn't stand a man with no principles.

"She led us to the overlook at Hava Lake," the captain continued. "When we reached the top, a madness took hold of her, and she jumped."

Mikael shifted back in surprise. "Into the water?"

Artem gave a nod. "Yes, Salar. She swam to shore, and by the time we got back to the horses, she was gone."

Mikael stood silently for a moment. He reached down and moved the bottle of ink in line with the parchments. "Madness, you say?"

"Yes, Salar."

"And you didn't jump in after her, Captain?"

Artem hesitated before shaking his head. "No, Salar."

The corner of Mikael's mouth twitched. "Then she's not mad. She's clever."

The captain gave a reluctant tilt of his head. "Perhaps, Salar."

Mikael swept the top of his desk in a rage, flinging the items on top to the floor. "Not *perhaps!*" he roared. He gripped the corners tightly—no doubt to keep from flipping it over. His cold calm returned. "Yesterday, she told me she needed to speak to me, that she could no longer tolerate you." He straightened and walked around his desk to stand in front of Artem. "Tell me, Captain, why would she find you intolerable?"

Artem's breath came unevenly. The captain was nervous. He should be.

"She wants to do as she pleases, without restriction," the captain answered.

Mikael lunged out and grabbed the captain by his breastplate, slamming him backward, up against the wall. "She is *salara!*" he said from between his bared teeth. "She *will* do as she pleases, without restriction. You are the captain of the Crest! You keep her protected *as she does as she pleases, without restriction!*"

"Yes, Salar," Artem said quickly. "I understand."

The king's nostrils flared with rage. "You no longer answer to me, you answer to Salara. When you find her, you'll swear your sword and beg her forgiveness. You'll keep your position if she sees you fit." Mikael released him.

"Of course, Salar," Artem said, bowing low again and not daring to look up from the floor.

"Get out of my sight."

Artem bowed even lower before quickly leaving the room.

Soren didn't find moments of joy often, but he did now. Perhaps this wasn't a waste of time after all.

Mikael turned back to him. "Find her. I want her here. I want her safe."

His silent joy evaporated. He gave a stiff nod and turned to leave, but Mikael stopped him.

"Has her captain returned from the North? Caspian is his name."

Soren didn't like where this was going. "I believe this morning."

"Take him with you. He may be of help."

A Northman wouldn't be of help, but Soren forced another obedient nod.

The king gave a regretful grimace. "I wouldn't hear her," he said bitterly. "I was so seized by the visions that I couldn't even speak to her. Now she's out there alone."

Anger rippled under Soren's skin. Mikael couldn't see it, even when it was right in front of him. "The Bear is bringing Aleon against you. The North Queen—"

Mikael's eyes flashed. "I urge you caution if you have an accusation," he warned.

"You would have me do you a disservice? Who else can make you see?" Soren pressed.

"Careful, brother."

But Soren wasn't one for care. "She goes to meet her original betrothed."

Mikael ripped his sword from its scabbard with a shaking fury and swept it to Soren's neck, his nostrils flared.

Soren stood, unmoving. He saw Mikael's offense, but this was what he feared. Mikael was blinded to the danger he welcomed. He was turning a deaf ear to those who loved him, those who would give everything for him. The North Queen would bring his end, and Mikael harbored her, defended her, bent to her, even in the face of her betrayal.

Slowly, Mikael lowered his sword, but his warning was clear. Without another word, Soren took his leave.

Vitalia sat quietly at a small table in a stone, terraced home, mending a pair of her gloves as Serene read a book. For their own safety from Captain Artem, Salara had sent her maids to the house of the Crest guard Kiran, which he shared with his mother. Vitalia wished she could have stayed with the queen to help her. Salara carried the weight of the world on her shoulders.

"Do you think she'll return?" Serene asked quietly. The queen was obviously on her mind as well.

Vitalia looked up from her sewing and smiled reassuringly. "Of course she will. She wouldn't leave us alone here."

"What if something happened to her?"

It was a question Vitalia asked herself over and over—with the answer she feared most—but she forced a smile. "If there's one thing I know about Salara, it's that she can take care of herself." She nodded to the book Serene was holding. "What are you reading?"

"It's a book of poems, a favorite from home. It always brings me comfort." Serene held it out for her. "Would you like to read it?"

Vitalia swallowed. She felt so inadequate as a queen's maid sometimes. She didn't have a proper education, as the Mercian maid had. "I'm not able to read," she said with a flush of embarrassment in her cheeks. She would forever be indebted to Salara for giving her the opportunity for a better life, in a respected position, and for treating her as more than a slave. She only wished she could do everything expected of a maid, all that Salara needed of her, all that Serene was able to do.

"Oh," Serene said softly. Then she gave a warm smile. "Would you like me to read it to you? I could even teach you, with time."

Vitalia let out an unexpecting breath, and she smiled. "I would like that very much."

Serene opened the book again, but a banging outside made them stop.

"Open the door!" a man's voice called from the street below.

Serene looked at Vitalia with her eyes wide. With Salara's disappearance, they knew they'd be sought for questioning. And likely worse things.

"Guards," Vitalia whispered, hurrying to the large armoire against the wall. "Get in. Hurry!"

Serene ducked inside, and Vitalia followed in after. They pulled the doors closed. Unable to stand fully, they crouched, holding hands. It was difficult to hear over the sound of their nervous breaths.

They waited.

Time stood still.

Outside fell quiet. Had the guards gone?

The front door of the home opened and closed, and footsteps traveled up the stairs to where they crouched in hiding. Serene clutched Vitalia's hand until it hurt. Vitalia ignored it. They peered through the misalignment at the bottom of the doors but could see only the legs of the table where they had been sitting. A man entered the room; just the black of his breeches and boots were visible. He picked up Serene's book that she'd dropped on the chair, and Vitalia cursed under her breath.

He turned toward the armoire and stood in front of it for a moment, then pulled open the doors, making Serene gasp.

A breath of relief escaped her when she saw it was only Sonal. "You scared the piss out of us," Vitalia said to Salara's Crest guard.

"A book from the North. You can't leave things like this around," he told Serene, tossing it at her.

"I know, I'm sorry," the Mercian maid said as she fumbled to catch it. "We just heard the guards, and I guess I panicked."

They moved to the window and looked across the street to Kiran's home, watching guards depart. Salara had sent Vitalia and Serene to stay with Kiran's mother before Sonal moved them across the street to his own grandmother's house.

"I knew they'd come for you," he told them. "It's not safe to return to Kiran's. Stay here. They're leaving now, but they might come back. He's ordered a search for you."

"Salar?" Vitalia asked.

"No. Artem."

The thought made Vitalia's stomach turn.

CHAPTER TWO

Alhilat. That's what Kiran had called the sudden wave of warmth. The earth's great trick, a false spring. Norah was grateful for it. Its warmth in the harsh of winter had given her the break she needed, the opportunity to escape Artem—an opportunity she'd been desperate for—but it would last only a few days. She had to find this seer, this mind traveler. If he truly was the most powerful in the four kingdoms, maybe he could help her get her memories back.

And she needed to see the visions. She'd seen the images painted by the Mercian seer; she knew the vision Mikael spoke of—Alexander killing him on the battlefield. But everything should have changed when they wed. The vision *had* to have changed. A marriage meant no war, which meant Mikael should be safe.

She wanted him safe, this man who had once been her enemy, whose kingdom had warred against hers for ten years. This man who had captured her, and a piece of her heart—she *needed* him safe.

Yet he wasn't.

And if he wasn't safe, Alexander wasn't safe.

Alexander. What was he doing? She was barely holding peace between their kingdoms, and he'd traveled to Aleon without telling her. Of course

Mikael would see it as a plot against him. She needed to find this seer and figure things out before Alexander returned to Kharav. If it was true the vision hadn't changed, she needed to figure out how to change it. She needed to see this traveler, not just for herself, but to save both the men in her heart.

Her mare of the Wild carried her east, toward Odepeth. Norah knew nothing of the city, only the name and a general direction based on poorly remembered maps she'd seen in Mikael's study. At least she hoped she was riding in the right direction. It certainly wasn't the most thought-out plan, but then again, she hadn't really planned this.

Norah rode until her legs were numb and her hips stiff. Finally, when she came upon a small stream, she slowed the mare to give them both a rest. Not that the mare needed it—a horse of the Wild was no ordinary animal. Norah still wasn't sure what her connection was to the horse, but for now—especially now—she was grateful for it. Captain Artem would be unable to find her, unable to track the mare, and she inhaled a rich breath of freedom. However, her relief was short-lived as she turned her thoughts to the challenge ahead. She couldn't trust anyone to help her. In fact, quite the opposite. If she was discovered, they might return her to the lord commander or, worse, Captain Artem. She shook her head. She'd figure it out, she told herself. She just needed to rest for a moment and gather her wits.

She slid from the mare's back and let the animal drink her fill at the creek's edge as Norah scooped the cold water to her own lips. It tasted good, and she drank deeply. She closed her eyes and let her mind settle. When she opened them again, she saw a young man standing a small distance away, looking back at her. He'd startled her, yet he didn't look startling.

Norah put him at sixteen or seventeen, not quite a boy, not yet a man. His hair was short and black like his clothing. A sword hung at his side, but his look wasn't that of a soldier's.

"Hello," Norah called out to him, rising to her feet. "Who are you?"

He didn't answer.

"Who are *you*?" a voice said behind her, and Norah whirled around to see a young woman between two trees. She was dressed like the boy, only she carried a bow instead of a sword. Her dark hair was pulled back into a thick braid, and her face closely resembled his—likely his sister—but a little older. She had a fierceness to her, one that Norah liked.

"Why are you here?" the girl pressed. "What do you want?"

"I'm just passing through."

"Outsiders don't just pass through Kharav. Where are you going?"

Norah paused. She had told herself she couldn't trust anyone, but they might point her in the right direction if they were eager for her to move on. On the other hand, they'd also be able to divulge where she was headed to anyone who happened along behind her. But merely knowing the name of her destination wouldn't get her there, and time wasn't a luxury she had. She needed help. She had to take the risk. "Odepeth," she said cautiously.

"You speak the common tongue," the girl said. "Where are you from?"

A benefit to the Northern language being the common trade tongue between kingdoms—it didn't immediately give her away. The girl obviously didn't recognize her, and Norah wanted to keep it that way. "Very far," she said. "It would be a great kindness if you could point me in the right direction, and I'll gladly be on my way."

The girl eyed her skeptically, then looked over Norah's shoulder to her brother. She made a small motion with her hand by her cheek. Norah turned to look at him as he gave a small hand motion back to his sister.

"You talk to him with your hands," Norah said. "Can he not speak?"

The girl's eyes darted to Norah with an intense defensiveness. "What of it? He's not stupid, if that's what you're thinking."

"Of course not. I have a friend who's deaf," she said, thinking of the young boy that worked in the sparring field back in Mercia. "I've never met another like him, that's all."

The girl's face softened. "Can you speak with your hands?"

Norah shook her head. "No, I can only say hi," she said, trying to remember what she'd been shown so long ago and holding up her hand. "And thank you," she added, cupping her fist and then extending her fingers.

"Hi is the same," the girl told her, holding up her hand, "but thank you is"—she brought her fingers to her lips and made an arc downward. "But Cohen can read your lips, in both the common and Kharavian tongue."

"That's amazing." *Cohen.* It didn't sound like a Kharavian name, not that Norah was an expert in Kharavian names.

The girl smiled. "I'm Calla," she offered, her defensiveness forgotten. "Short for Callamine."

That also didn't seem like a Kharavian name. Norah smiled back. "I'm Norah."

"You should keep east for Odepeth," Calla told her, pointing to her left, "but you won't make it there tonight."

"Oh," Norah said with a sigh. *Damn.* "Well, that's all right. I'll see how far I can get."

"Come to our house. You can rest there tonight and leave for Odepeth in the morning."

That was the opposite of what she should probably do. Norah could name more than one person who'd chide her for trusting strangers, including herself. She eyed the girl. Hells—she knew a good spirit when she met one. "I think I'll actually take you up on that offer. It's incredibly kind, thank you."

Calla smiled again. "This way," she said as she started down a trail through the trees, waving for her brother to join.

Norah followed Calla and Cohen down a trail that opened into a meadow. A small homestead sat in the sunset. She smiled at the cobbled farmhouse as they approached. It was humble but well cared for, with boxes of thick-stemmed flowers hanging under the windows. Evergreen shrubs lined the graveled walkway to the front door, and dark flagstone on the side led to a large garden. "Do you and Cohen live here by yourselves?" she asked.

"With our grandparents," the girl answered.

"How will they feel about a visitor?"

"I don't know," Calla replied. "We never have visitors."

That was a good sign. She should be able to keep to herself if she wasn't on a path well traveled.

"You can hobble your horse on the side if you'd like."

"That's all right," Norah said, pulling the saddle from the mare. "She won't go anywhere."

Calla gave her a doubtful look. "She's really pretty. Would be a shame to lose her."

"It would be, but she's fine."

Calla shrugged. "C'mon," she said, tipping her head toward the garden.

"Apah! Amah!" Calla called as she walked.

A head rose from between the thick rows of green and yellow, and a man stepped out into the pathway. He was an older man, his long hair tied back and grayed by time, but there was no mistaking the evidence of a warrior. The inked skin on his arms told her he'd seen his share of battles—he still looked like he could manage a few more, but a heavy limp slowed his walk. He carried a small bucket and tossed a handful of pulled weeds into it, not yet aware of Norah. He replied to Calla in the Kharavian tongue, brushing his hand on his apron.

"Apah," Calla called again for his attention. "We have a visitor."

The man looked up and stopped. He stared at Norah as he slowly set down his bucket. He was darker than the children, and the lines on his skin told his years. His eyes moved to Calla and then Cohen. He looked at the mare, then back to Norah. She could feel his unease.

"I don't mean to impose," Norah tried to assure him. "I'm only passing through."

"Marta," he called over his shoulder.

A woman stepped out of the flora to join him, equally wary of their visitor. Norah looked over her with curiosity. Her skin was light, like her own. And despite the gray of her hair, it hadn't been black in her youth. This woman wasn't from Kharav.

"We don't have many visitors, but you're welcome here," the man said.

"Thank you. I mean to stay for only the night, and then I'll be on my way in the morning."

He eyed the mare again, distracted, but then pulled his gaze back to Norah. He glanced around. "You're traveling alone?"

She supposed it did seem odd that a lone woman would be traveling across a foreign kingdom. She hoped that was the only thing that seemed odd to him. "Yes."

He looked at his wife, quiet, but then gave Norah a nod. "I'm Hamed," he said, then gesturing to the woman, "and this is my wife, Marta. Come. Let's go inside."

Marta placed her basket full of leafy greens on a preparation table, and Calla started washing them in a large bowl of water.

Norah watched, fascinated, as everyone busied themselves with dinner. "You have a full garden in winter?" she asked, trying for polite conversation.

"While it's cold, it doesn't freeze here in the valley," Hamed said. "We can get away with a good variety of winter vegetables. It's one of the many reasons we like it here."

Cohen quickly set bowls on the table and then went to fetch water in a pitcher. Hamed stirred the coals on the fire, fueling the heat under the pot that hung from above. Calla added her chopped vegetables and smiled at her grandfather as he held the lid for her.

"So, you just live out here by yourselves?" Norah asked.

Hamed gave a nod. "We lead a simple life, but it's ours." He looked over and smiled at Marta lovingly.

Norah's heart warmed. They seemed content. Happy. She wondered how they came to be together.

"Japheth," Marta said.

"What?" she asked.

"It's what you are wondering, yes? Where I'm from?"

Norah looked at her in surprise. "No. I mean, yes. You don't look like you're from Kharav." Then she eyed Hamed with a raised brow. "Well, you do, obviously. But I was mostly wondering how you two came to be together."

"Apah was a warrior," Calla said proudly. "He saved Amah's life, fell instantly in love with her, and then wooed her with his charm."

A warrior. Her eyes traveled back to the markings on his arms. Yes, he had definitely been a warrior.

The old man gave a chuckle.

"All true," Marta told Norah. "I was taken by Japheth soldiers and brought to their camp for entertainment. Fortunately, this was at the border of where Japheth and Kharav meet. Hamed saw from his border post and intervened. Can you imagine? A Kharavian soldier taking a Japheth woman from the Japheth army on Japheth land? This was back when Japheth was still part of the Aleon Empire, before being allied with Kharav. Almost started a war in the process." She smiled at her husband. "I couldn't return after that, so he brought me to his mother, who took me in."

Calla grinned. "Then he discovered she liked flowers and wove a bracelet of white lacies for her every day until she agreed to marry him."

Hamed grunted. "I suppose I was charming."

"Still are," Marta said with a smile.

Norah laughed. She would be fortunate to have a life like this.

Marta took the bowls and filled them with stew from the hearth. Calla carried them to the table as Cohen poured cups of water. Hamed motioned for her to sit, and they all took their places. He poured some tea from the pot Marta placed in front of him and calmly took a drink.

16

"Forgive me," he said, "but I can't help but ask the most troublesome question of why you're traveling on your own, in such a state. Are you fleeing? Do you need help?"

Norah shifted uncomfortably, looking around the table. How would she explain her situation? "I'm not fleeing," she replied, then mumbled to herself, "although I'm sure Artem thinks otherwise."

Hamed raised his brow. "Captain Artem?"

Norah stopped and cursed herself, realizing her mistake. A weight grew in her stomach. Hamed had been a warrior. Of course he'd know who the captain of the Crest was.

He stirred his stew in his bowl, silent.

Norah's heart pulsed in her throat. "You know him?" she asked, trying to hide the disquiet in her voice.

Hamed sat back in his chair. But he didn't answer.

"Artem thinks my brother's an abomination," Calla spoke up angrily. "Like being deaf makes him not fit to live."

Norah's eyes widened as she shifted her attention to the girl—it wasn't the response to Artem she'd been expecting, but neither was it surprising.

"Calla," Hamed scolded, trying to restrain her, but the girl ignored him.

"He wanted my father to leave Cohen at an orphanage, to throw him away, like he was nothing. Well, my brother wields a sword better than anyone in the Crest, including Captain Artem!"

"Calla," Hamed warned, stronger this time.

Cohen looked at his sister and gave her a small smile.

Calla gave him a wink. "If they'd had a warrior like Cohen, maybe Kharav would've already taken back Bahoul from those Northern cowards."

"Callamine!" Hamed snapped.

Calla's head jerked toward her grandfather in confusion. "Apah! You know—"

"Hold your tongue!" He looked at Norah with an uneasy eye. "She doesn't know what she says."

He feared for his granddaughter. Norah's pulse quickened.

"Why would you say that?" Calla persisted.

A silence fell over them.

Norah's heart hammered against her ribs. "Because he knows who I am," she said. She didn't take her eyes from Hamed. "Don't you?"

The old man shifted in his chair. "Yes, Salara," he said finally.

She was pleasantly surprised that he didn't call her the North Queen like so many others. Calla and Cohen gaped at her in astonishment.

"How did you know?" she asked. "Did Artem give it away?"

"You're clearly not from Kharav. I've heard of the North Queen with winter hair, and"—Hamed paused—"your horse, the Wild one. I've seen only one other like it before, ridden by the North King."

Norah's heart leapt into her throat. "My father rode a horse of the Wild? You saw him?"

Hamed nodded, taking Marta's hand. "Years ago. In battle. The day my son died"—his eyes moved to Calla and Cohen—"and their mother."

Norah's heart fell. Calla and Cohen's parents had both been warriors, and both died in the war. It had claimed so much from so many on both sides. She suddenly became aware that perhaps her presence brought them pain. Her father had led forces against them in war. "You don't have to offer the Mercian king's daughter your hospitality," she said softly. "I understand the pain I must cause you."

"I offer my hospitality to my salara. You honor us, and our home."

Norah forced a smile as her eyes brimmed with tears. How could people continue to be so kind after suffering such loss?

"So, if you're not fleeing, what are you doing? What's in Odepeth?" Calla asked her.

Hamed cast his granddaughter a look of disapproval, but Norah found herself appreciating the girl's boldness.

"There's a man there. A seer. I'm hoping he can help me."

"You want to see the future?" Calla asked.

And the past, but Norah would keep that to herself. She only nodded.

"Going by yourself—that seems like a lot to go through just to see a vision," Hamed said.

It *was* a lot to go through. "There are so many things that don't make sense. I'm just trying to find answers." She hoped that was enough of an explanation. It was all she could give. "Anyway, I just need to get there."

"We could go with you, Cohen and I," the girl offered. She turned to her grandfather. "We could help her."

"Your kindness has helped me more than you can imagine," Norah said quickly, already feeling indebted to them. "But it's probably best if I go alone."

"You can't really think that," Calla challenged. "The North Queen, traveling without protection." The girl quieted, then shrugged apologetically. "Salara, I mean."

Hamed nodded. "Lone travel isn't safe for an outsider, even you, Salara. I can't ride to see you there myself with my ailment, but you'll find Calla savvy of the city, good with a bow, and Cohen skilled with a sword. I've trained them myself."

"You've given enough already," Norah said. "And I worry about attention coming to your family for your part in my transgressions."

"You're salara, you have no transgressions," Hamed said, surprising her. "And to be a member of the Crest is a great honor for a soldier. It would bring great honor to our family to serve in their stead."

This family amazed her. "How can I refuse?" she said finally.

They all let out a laugh. Even Cohen was grinning. Norah's heart was full and grateful.

CHAPTER THREE

Caspian stretched his travel-worn muscles as he rode. He had just returned to Kharav from his journey to Mercia, and had been back only a couple of hours before he found himself thrust into a journey to find Queen Norah. It was a situation he'd never imagined—tracking his queen in partnership with the Destroyer through the Shadowlands—yet he couldn't say he was entirely surprised. Nothing surprised him when it came to Norah. He just wondered what she was up to.

The captain of the Crest joined them, Captain Artem. He wasn't the kind of man Caspian could relate to, or the kind of man he could imagine leading the Crest to protect Norah at all costs. He was the kind of man Caspian knew to watch.

And then there was the Shadow commander, the Destroyer. This was the man Caspian needed to be the most wary of, be the most cautious of. Regardless of whether the stories of the Destroyer were all true, he was certainly the most dangerous—he moved with an unnatural power and had eyes that saw right through a man, into his soul. He fed off fear, and he knew how to make people afraid. And he seemed in a particularly foul mood.

But regardless of the company, Caspian was appreciative to be part of the search. He'd rather be doing something than simply waiting for the queen's return, although he wasn't keen on the thought of bringing Norah back to the Shadow King if her intent had been to leave. He told himself he'd find her and take her wherever she wished to go.

"She rode north," Artem said as they passed through the gates and out of the capital city of Ashan. "We can head toward the Canyonlands and hope to pick up her tracks there."

"You can't track a horse from the Wild," the commander said. His voice held an edge of annoyance. "But we'll start there, with the Uru."

Caspian didn't know what he meant by *a horse from the Wild*, but he was more focused on the icy air between the captain and the commander. This was going to be interesting.

They spurred their horses northwest, riding in silence. Caspian found himself curious about the western pass and the Horsemen tribe that watched over it. Previously, he'd only traveled the eastern pass, taking the route through Bahoul.

Kharav fascinated him. For a kingdom viewed as being so evil in the eyes of men, it seemed to hold the gods' favor. It was protected by the earth itself, with its mazed canyons on the north side and sharp cliffs on the south and eastern sea sides. With the addition of their Urun friends, who stretched from the north canyons and partway down the western borders, the Shadowlands were positioned favorably. It was a kingdom not easily breached.

Aleon had once tried to take the Shadowlands. King Mathias, King Phillip's grandfather, had moved against them when he overtook the eastern kingdoms to form the great empire of Aleon. It was an infamous battle, but in the end, the Shadowlands stood strong. Caspian had never imagined himself within its borders. Now that he was, he had to give it due respect.

Despite the unpleasant company, they moved fast, and time passed quickly. The Destroyer pushed on mercilessly, not allowing them to slow. The sun set as they rode, and they continued on. As darkness fell, the moon sat full in the sky, and they easily found their way in its light.

Finally, the ridges of the canyons loomed dark against the moonlit sky, and they slowed their mounts. The night lay quiet, save for the chitters of wildlife in the distance.

"Is there a village?" Caspian asked. "Where are these Uru?"

The commander didn't answer, but Artem gave a dark chuckle. Caspian couldn't help the tension growing in his shoulders, and he kept his hand on the hilt of his sword.

They reached the base of the canyons, and all lay still around them. As they rode into the shadows of the narrow slot canyon, the pit in his stomach grew heavier. The commander pulled up his mount and slid down.

"Why are we stopping?" Caspian asked as he swung down from his own horse.

"We're here," Artem said.

Caspian was just about to ask more when a movement behind him made him spin and draw his sword. Shadows shifted around them—a man, Caspian realized. Then more. Many more.

The commander spoke in the Shadow tongue, and the man answered. Their exchange was brief, but there was no mistaking his respect for the commander. The mysterious man barked orders into the night around them, and he gave a low whistle with a chitter into the dark of the canyons. Caspian realized it hadn't been animals he'd heard.

They followed the Uru farther into the canyons, deep into the narrow slots of earth. Caspian knew the dangers of these mazes, where a man could easily lose himself. But the commander knew his way, and Caspian followed. The narrow canyon opened back up to the sky, and he was thankful to again have a little more sight.

They rounded a corner, and a village appeared. Houses of rock, stacked and layered, sprawled wide. He paused and momentarily stared in amazement at its sheer size. He was no stranger to Horsemen tribes—they spanned the vast lands beyond Mercia's outer reaches—but he'd never seen one this large.

They continued. The hour was late, and few fires remained, although a large central fire still blazed bright. As they drew closer to the light, Caspian could better see the man they'd been following. The Horseman was covered in twisted strips of leather and fabric, with ghostly coloring spread over his face and the bare-skin areas of his chest and back.

As they reached the central fire, a woman emerged from the darkness. She had long dark hair, interwoven with braids and feathers, and beautifully wild. Black paint striped her brow and cheeks. Her eyes burned fiercely. There was a strength about her. Caspian had never seen anything like her, and it was as if he'd been struck.

"Soren," she greeted as she approached. Interesting that she would address the Destroyer by his name. Caspian realized he hadn't even known his name. She gave a wry smile. "I wish I had known you were coming. I would have come to meet you properly."

"Tahla," the commander said with a nod.

Tahla. Her name was Tahla.

"Aleon places additional forces along the borders," Soren told her.

24

Caspian glanced at him. King Phillip was moving forces south along the border? He hadn't known that information. It unsettled him further, with Norah out alone.

The Horsewoman nodded pensively. "Salar sent word, but we've seen nothing. Regardless, we've called our men in the hills back to the canyons. We'll spread them east for more eyes."

"Good," he replied.

Tahla eyed Caspian suspiciously. "You ride with a Northman? Surprising."

"Is it?" the commander replied. "Our kingdoms are joined. It should be no surprise our forces are joined as well."

"You command him?" she asked the Destroyer, not taking her eyes from Caspian.

"The commander leads," Caspian cut in. "But I answer to my queen."

"What about your salar?" she challenged.

Caspian knew he was being tested. "Queen Norah would expect my obedience to him, and so I give it."

Tahla looked him over, seeming not to have made up her mind about him, but her eyes were curious, and he waited patiently as they explored him. "How is Salara?" she asked. "I trust you're keeping my sister safe."

Caspian noted her fondness for the queen, and that she obviously hadn't seen her. "Keeping her safe is what I've dedicated my life to," he replied honestly.

"Good." She turned back to the commander. "Stay. We'll see you rested and fed."

"We need to keep going," the commander replied, "but we're in need of food and fresh horses."

"Of course." Tahla nodded as she turned and motioned them around the large fire.

"You didn't tell her about the North Queen," the commander said to Caspian, low so that only he could hear.

"She obviously hasn't seen her. And the fewer people who know of a lone queen roaming the open, the better."

The Shadow commander gave the slightest tilt of his head. "You surprise me."

"In that you agree with me?"

"In that you seem like a smart Northman. A rarity."

Caspian gave an amused puff of breath at the complimentary insult. And he didn't so much think himself smart as just... not stupid.

It was quiet at the late hour, but people emerged from their stone houses to eagerly greet the commander. They seemed not only to respect the formidable Shadowman, but also to genuinely like him. *Quite peculiar.*

A large woman handed Caspian a bowl of soup and a loaf of bread. "Thank you," he said as he accepted it.

He took a seat on a rock not far from Tahla and watched her in the firelight. She laughed as she talked to a man beside her, and Caspian sat, fixated on her beauty. The paint on her face did little to hide her high, chiseled cheekbones or the slender slope of her nose. This was a dangerous woman, he could tell right away, but it made no difference. He saw only her eyes, the shape of her face, the graceful way she moved in the flickering light of the flames.

And then her eyes found him. They burned brightly, seeing into him. Through him. His skin prickled over his arms, across his neck, and down his back. Inside, he twisted and fought the strange hold taking over.

26

The commander kicked his boot, bringing Caspian back.

"What has you?" the Shadowman asked with a hint of annoyance. "Finish and get a horse. We've a long ride still ahead."

Caspian forced his senses back. "Where?" he asked. "Did you get an idea of where she might be?"

"I know she's not here. And she didn't come this way. Perhaps she flees to Aleon through the eastern pass." The commander let out an irritated sigh.

Flee? "She wouldn't flee, not now," Caspian said. "She doesn't just give up; she's too intent on bringing peace. Knowing Norah, she's probably searching for answers, or a way to solve whatever problem is in front of her. And Aleon is the last place she would go."

The commander looked at him with a skeptical eye.

"Aleon's forces must be quite worrisome if this calls for a joint effort," Tahla called out to the commander from where she stood by the fire. "Maybe I should go with you? Or send warriors?"

"I'll take you up on a couple men," the commander said.

"Will more men not slow us down?" Caspian asked him quietly.

The Shadowman shrugged. "If I said no, she'd just come herself. We'll cut them loose when we're clear from the canyons."

Caspian suppressed a chuckle. "Just like the queen. There's no telling her not to do something."

The Shadowman stopped. He stared at Caspian with a strange stillness in his eyes.

"Commander?"

"If she's not fleeing, then I think I know where she's headed."

Caspian furrowed his brow. "Where?"

"Get your horse."

Caspian's pulse quickened as he saddled a horse from the Uru. It was a larger beast than he was used to, and he couldn't help but admire the quality of the stock. He gave the animal a light pat on the shoulder and turned, nearly colliding with Tahla right behind him.

The corners of her mouth turned up in amusement. "You're a long way from home, Northman."

Her voice held a smokiness, and it lingered in his ear. His mind told him to step back from her, to put space between them, but his body refused. She held him with a force unseen to the eye. He had a task at hand, but he could no longer recall it. What was this power?

"Are you an enchantress?" he asked her.

Tahla laughed, leaning closer. "Do you find yourself enchanted?"

"Enchanted, bewitched," he said. "What other explanation?"

"Do you wish to be free?" she asked in a low voice.

He didn't answer, gripped by her nearness.

Tahla's smile softened. "Can I ask something of you?"

"Anything." He meant it.

She held out a soft leather sachet of scented gifts. "Will you give this to Salara, with my well-wishes?"

The mention of the queen brought him back, and he let out a breath, freed temporarily from the trance. "That seems like hardly an ask at all," he said. "But I'll deliver it to her hands myself."

Tahla smiled. He couldn't get enough.

She cast a wary eye toward the commander and then back to him. "You should be on your way. Soren won't be too keen on me giving a handsome Northman my attention."

Caspian leaned back, glancing at the commander, then back to her. Of course she'd be taken, a woman like this. "My apologies. I, uh... I didn't know you two were..."

Tahla laughed as she shook her head. "No. We're not. But Soren is protector of the Uru, and our family."

Strange to think the Destroyer protective over anyone, but his pulse quickened, and he gave an encouraged nod. "Well... did I hear correctly that you found me handsome?" Then he cursed himself silently. *Stupid thing to say.* This shouldn't be the topic on his mind, but how easy it was for her to pull his attention, to make him forget even his name.

"Hair of the sun. How can I not?"

He smiled. "Then I can't let you meet another Northman."

She let out another laugh. Then, growing more serious, she asked, "Will I see you again?"

"I'll make certain of it," he promised. And he meant it.

CHAPTER FOUR

His destrier moved anxiously underneath him with an uneven gait, as it did just before the charge into battle. No doubt it felt the tension in its rider, and Alexander was indeed in the midst of a battle, a battle of mind and heart.

He dropped his hand to the thick neck of the beast, patting it underneath the silk of its white mane to settle it, or maybe to settle himself. It had been a difficult journey to Aleon, in more ways than one, and while he wasn't eager to return to the Shadowlands, he was eager to return to Norah. He ignored the beauty of Aleon's capital city, Valour, with its manicured gardens and fountains that wound through the silver-stone structures that seemed to reach to the sky, its patinaed domes that covered the hills in additional layers of green. None of it mattered.

What mattered was that Norah would be safe here.

And out of the clutches of their enemy.

He urged his mount down the mainway, under the blue banners of the lion. Once past the front gates and posted city guard, he turned and headed south, back to the Shadowlands.

Alexander hadn't wanted to come to Aleon, but the council's task had been clear, and one he couldn't refuse. Not just because of the council's authority. He knew he had to come.

Norah wanted peace so badly—enough to sacrifice herself for it. But he wouldn't let her. It was only a matter of time before the alliance fell apart, and he wouldn't let her fall with it. It wasn't easy choosing between what she wanted and what she needed, what was best for her and what was best for Mercia. But he'd made a vow. He'd sworn himself. And more than that—he loved her, and there was nothing he wouldn't do for her, nothing he wouldn't give, even if it broke him. It was already breaking him, over and over again, as Norah was taken from him. He'd lost her, and he kept losing her. Over and over again.

He would bear it, and continue to bear it, so long as she was safe.

But she wasn't safe now. He cast a last look over his shoulder at the Aleon capital as he rode out. He would do what he had to. No matter the cost.

CHAPTER FIVE

The journey was long but relatively peaceful, save for Calla's continuous conversation. Norah didn't mind. She found herself growing quite fond of the girl, who was confident, proud, and fiercely loyal. She noticed Cohen's smile as he watched his sister talk, and his admiration for her.

By the end of the day, Odepeth loomed into view. The city stood like an ancient oasis, a stark contrast to the barren high desert around it. Stacked stone formed the foundations, but it wasn't dark like Ashan, Kharav's capital city. It was bright, golden even, and it glistened in the sun. Not at all like she'd expected.

Calla pointed to the temple in the center. "That's where the seer is."

Norah frowned. "That's it? He just spends his days in the center of a small city in the middle of nowhere?"

Calla shrugged. "Pretty much. How are you going to get in? Only Kharavian royal blood may enter the temple."

"Well..." She hadn't thought it through entirely. "I was just going to walk in."

For once, the girl was speechless.

"What does the seer look like?" Norah asked.

"I don't know. I've never seen him." Calla wrinkled her face. "Old, I bet. What are you going to do about the guards? They won't let you in, even if they know you're salara."

Norah puffed a breath through her lips. She really should have thought this through. "What do you propose?"

Calla was silent for a moment. "I can distract them in the front by trying to enter there. I'm good at making a spectacle." She grinned mischievously. "And you and Cohen can slip inside from the back. But I've never been inside, so I can't tell you what you'll find there. More guards, likely."

Norah moved her hand to the hilt of the sword at her side. She was thankful that Hamed had lent it to her. She looked at Cohen. "How good are you with a sword? Really?"

He shrugged and gave a flat wave of his hand.

That wasn't comforting. And she wasn't entirely sure how good *she* was with a sword. She supposed she'd find out on both accounts.

They left their horses in an inconspicuous hitching area. Norah worried the mare might draw attention, but there wasn't much she could do about it. It wasn't easy to hide a horse. They split up, Calla curving around and making her way through the streets to the temple from the front, and Norah and Cohen approaching from the back. Although small, the city was dense, with the buildings mostly connected to one another. The structural faces of the houses varied, making it easy for Norah and Cohen to slip stealthily from corner to corner. They reached the point where the structures ended, and a long sweep of stairs started to the temple. Two guards stood at the top. Norah looked at Cohen from his hiding place across the walk, and they waited.

True to Calla's plan, her exaggerated attempted entry from the front of the temple pulled the attention of even the rear guards, and they left their posts to aid their fellow guardsmen. Norah and Cohen moved quickly, racing to the top of the stairs. They paused outside a set of large double doors.

Norah struggled to listen over the pulse of her heart pounding in her ears. This was it. She had risked a lot to come here. And what if they couldn't find the seer? What if the seer refused to see her? Worse, what if she was caught and turned back over to Artem and the Crest?

Cohen put his hand on her arm. While he was deaf, he seemed to *see* everything. He gave her an encouraging nod. He wasn't asking her if she was all right—he was telling her. All without words. And her strength returned.

They pulled open one of the oaken doors and slipped inside, finding themselves in a hall that ran along the perimeter of the temple's base. High arches made up the inside wall that opened to a large center, filled with delicately carved stone pillars. Norah followed it around, with Cohen close beside her.

The temple seemed empty. They turned a corner, and a man surprised them. A guard. He wore a crimson robe and was armed with a bladed staff. "Halt," he said to them.

"I've come to speak to the seer," she told him, as confidently as she could muster.

"You're forbidden," he answered angrily. "Leave this place."

She pulled back the hood of her cloak. "I'm salara," she said firmly. "I'll leave after I speak to the seer."

"You'll leave now," he answered.

Norah bit the inside of her lip. She really had imagined this differently.

The guard pulled up his bladed staff. "Do not make me remove you."

Barbs of anger prickled along her back. "You can try," she challenged as she pulled her sword from its scabbard. Then she cursed herself—probably not the wisest reply, as she was pretty sure he *could* remove her. *Easily.*

Cohen stepped forward with his own blade in hand.

The guard started toward them, and she cursed again under her breath. She had hoped for a more tactful approach, but she wasn't faring well.

The guard rushed Cohen with an overhand swing, and for a moment, fear flashed through her. The guard was twice as large as Cohen and surely doubly as skilled. But the boy used the arc of the guard's swing to his advantage, stepping left and delivering a blow that steered the man's momentum to the side. Cohen spun and swung outward in a move that hooked the guard's helm and flung it from his head. Then he lunged, whipping up his elbow and catching the man under his chin. The guard dropped to the floor.

Norah stood, shocked at the extraordinarily short fight she just witnessed. Then her eyes narrowed at the young man. "Cohen, I don't think you've been entirely honest with me."

He gave a sheepish smile.

Footsteps sounded behind her, and she turned to see three more guards running their way. *Great.* Norah readied her own sword. She glanced at Cohen, and he nodded.

Norah clenched the handle of her sword, calling to it, and it answered with familiarity. The first guard thrust his staff forward, and she spun along it, bringing her blade down and cleaving it in two. He tumbled forward, off balance, and she sliced her blade into his thigh. Not bad, she pepped herself.

Norah met another guard with a counter swing as he lunged at her. The sound of steel rang in the air. To her left, she heard Cohen's sword working, but she couldn't peel her eyes to look. The temple guard lunged forward again. She swept up her sword to respond, but the power of his strikes beat her back. She wavered. He was too close. Dangerously close. Mikael's words came back to her. Her strength was speed, and she needed to protect it with distance. But she had no distance. She stumbled backward, but the temple wall stopped her retreat. The guard grabbed her sword arm. She tried to push him off, but she wasn't strong enough.

It had been a terrible idea to come here.

Just then, the guard's head bounced forward from a blow from behind. He released her and crumpled to the ground. Behind him stood Cohen.

Norah's eyes darted around the hall. There were more than four wounded guards that lay on the ground. She hadn't even realized two more had come. And Cohen had managed them.

She feigned a scowl. "Now that's just bragging."

The corner of his mouth turned up, but it was too early to celebrate a victory. He grabbed her hand and pulled her down the hall.

When they rounded another corner, they skidded to a stop.

In front of them stood more guards, twenty at least. Footsteps rang behind them, and Norah jerked her head to see more. A lot more.

Her spark of hope was quickly snuffed. There were too many guards, even with Cohen's skill. This was definitely a terrible idea. Now they were caught. She was caught. No doubt she'd be in Captain Artem's hands again by nightfall, with nothing to show for it. In fact, she'd be in a more precarious situation than before.

Her heart hurt. She'd gotten Cohen into quite a mess, and Calla too. She wondered where the girl was. She couldn't let them get hurt. They had only been helping her.

The guards closed in around them, and Norah reached back and clasped Cohen's arm, stilling him.

It was over.

"Let them be," a voice called, bringing them all to a pause.

Norah jerked her head to see from where it came. The guards parted, and an elderly man walked through. "It's not very often I'm surprised," he told her.

Norah looked at the guards. They reluctantly withdrew a few paces but watched her closely. She turned back to the man. "You're the seer?"

He gave a single nod. Calla had been right, he *was* old. He wore a simple brown robe, modest and unpretentious, not at all what she had imagined of the head of a highly guarded temple. His head was shaved bare, or perhaps he grew no hair, but his white beard hung long and straight.

"I'm sorry," she started. "I don't mean to intrude... or cause such a mess... but it's very important I speak with you." She needed to see these visions he'd shown Mikael. Maybe she could make better sense of them. And if he could unlock her memories...

"It must be important if it brings the North Queen to my temple," he said.

"You know who I am?"

"It's also not very often I meet the subjects of my visions," he told her.

"Your visions are why I'm here. I need to see them."

He frowned. "You want me to tell you of them?"

"No, I want you to show me."

He shifted back in surprise. "I do not conjure them in the air," he said stiffly.

"But you're a traveler, are you not?"

The briefest look of surprise flashed across his face. "How do you know such things?"

"You are, then."

He didn't answer; he only turned and started deeper into the temple. "Follow me," he said over his shoulder. "The boy waits outside."

Norah turned back to Cohen. "He's agreed to see me," she told him. He hadn't seen the seer's lips to read them. "But he asks that you stay outside."

Cohen gave a reluctant nod, sheathing his sword.

"Thank you, friend," she mouthed, then turned back to the seer.

Norah followed him through the pillared room, to a door, and down a narrow hall that opened into a smaller room. Lit candles stood in each corner, with sitting mats in the center.

"So, the North Queen returns," he said. "How did you escape my sight for so many years? What power do you have?"

Norah shook her head. "I don't have power. And I don't know."

His aged eyes narrowed.

"I tell you the truth. In fact, it's part of the reason I'm here. My memories were taken from me, or locked away, rather. I was hoping you could help me get them back."

She took a seat on one of the pillows in the center of the room and waited. He stood for a moment before he finally took his seat on the pillow across from her. He eyed her skeptically.

Norah still waited, resisting the want to urge him along.

The seer reached to a thin mat near his cushion and took a cup in his hand. Ink markings trailed his forearms to the rolled cuffs of his sleeves. These were different from the patterned markings the Shadowmen bore. Their dark bands with rune images in between looked more like a written language.

Norah leaned forward. Nemus, the Mercian traveler seer, had similar markings, but he had penned them on. The markings of this seer were permanent, like Mikael's markings. The thought of Mikael brought a twinge to her stomach. He'd know now she was gone. Did he think she'd betrayed him? The pain in his eyes when he saw that she wanted to leave...

She couldn't think about that right now, and she forced the hurt in her heart down, turning her attention back to the seer. "You've permanently inked the spells onto your skin?" she asked.

The seer pulled back. "Easier than drawing them on each time. And they're not spells."

"What are they?"

The seer pursed his lips.

She leaned back, giving him space as he poured wine into the cup. "What's your name?" she asked.

He paused, and for a moment she thought he might not answer. "Bhasim," he said finally. "But I've not been called that for a long time."

The lord commander had said only those with Kharavian royal blood were permitted in the temple. Was Bhasim all alone? Besides his guards, was there no one else who spoke to him?

Bhasim sat with a cup of wine in his hand. "They're not spells, they're staves," he said.

39

"What are staves?"

He eyed her warily, obviously not used to conversation about his power, or perhaps not used to conversation at all. "The power of the Gift is not easy to wield. It can consume the body. One must protect himself, and the staves give this protection. The more powerful the Gift, the more protection required."

Bhasim bore more markings than Nemus, which meant he was a more powerful traveler than the Mercian seer. Mikael had said he was the most powerful seer in the four kingdoms—which four kingdoms, she wasn't certain. But her excitement grew. He might be able to help her where Nemus couldn't.

Bhasim breathed a silent spell into the air.

"Why do you need the blood?" she interrupted. She didn't think his lips could get any thinner, but they did. Was he annoyed?

"You seem to already know quite a bit about seers." But where she expected a dismissive reply, he only asked, "Do you know of the Eye?"

She searched her mind of her visit with Nemus in Mercia, but he'd only mentioned that he had no control of what the Eye showed him. "It's what shows you the future?"

He frowned, as if somewhat disappointed in her awareness. "To get to the Eye, one must step into the Aether, the place through which all energy flows. The Aether connects us all, but it's a place of chaos. It is easy to find the Eye, but to *travel* to others, we need the blood spell to find our way, and to connect. Our blood calls us and lets us in." He paused, eyeing her. "May I continue now?"

She swallowed and nodded.

He breathed his spell again. Then he pricked his finger and squeezed a small drop of blood into the goblet and held the cup for Norah.

She took it and drank it, then closed her eyes and tried to relax. Even though she knew what to expect, she still jumped with a start when he came to her. Bhasim kept his current form, unlike Nemus, who'd shown his younger self.

In her mind, they stood in the same temple, only it was dark, with long cloths that draped from an endless sky, creating rooms of memories between them. She turned, seeing all around her, almost overwhelmed by it all. With Nemus, there had been almost nothing.

They walked slowly, in silence, from memory to memory: seeing her grandmother for the first time, Alexander showing her through the castle, meeting with her council, talking to Adrian.

Norah paused.

A pain gripped her heart.

In front of her was the moment when Alexander found her in the forest. She watched him realize who she was. Now she understood the emotion in his face: the elation, the fear, the sting of her not knowing him. She wished she could touch him now, but he was only an image.

Another memory pulled her attention from Alexander.

Mikael.

The day of their wedding. His eyes were on her. Always, his eyes were on her. She smiled sadly and was surprised at the longing that pulled deep inside. She suddenly remembered she wasn't alone. "I'm sorry," she said, turning back to the seer.

He looked at her curiously, and they continued through the memories.

Suddenly, Bhasim stopped. "So, this is how you know of travelers."

She turned to see the image of her with Nemus.

He lingered at the memory, looking at it intently. "I've never seen another," he said quietly.

"Another traveler?"

He nodded. "Those of us with the Gift of sight have a shield—a shield that protects us from others with the Gift. It hides us from visions. I cannot see others, and they cannot see me. But to see in a memory..." He smiled. "I'd never thought of that."

"It must be very lonely," she said softly.

His eyes met hers, surprised. "It is."

"His name is Nemus," she said, realizing the significance to him.

"Nemus," he repeated back to himself.

Just then, something drew Norah's eye. Her pulse quickened.

The door—the door that had been locked and that Nemus couldn't open.

This was what she had come for. This was it. Nemus hadn't been strong enough to help her, but Bhasim could be.

Norah left Bhasim and moved to it, her heart racing. She reached out and grasped the knob, giving it a turn.

It clicked open.

It was so unexpected that it almost made her jump.

That was it? So easy now? Without even a struggle? Her breath shook as emotion swelled within her. To have her memories back, to have everything back—she couldn't even imagine.

She pushed it open. So easily.

And stepped inside.

The first memory she saw was one she was already familiar with—her and Alexander lying on their backs on the hill, in the summer sun. Where they'd made their plans. Where they'd dreamed.

And then the memory that had broken her—them under the tree before her father had taken her away, and Alexander telling her goodbye. It still tore her heart. Tears threatened, but she pushed them back. She wasn't here for this memory. She was here for the others.

Except there weren't others.

Norah stepped forward, but only darkness hung in front of her. "Where are they?" she breathed. "Where are the others?"

"There are no others," Bhasim said from beside her.

She shook her head. "No," she said, her voice shaking. "They have to be here. This is the door that wouldn't open. They're here. They have to be."

"There's nothing more here," he said.

Norah turned and ran back into the stone-columned hall of memories. Maybe she'd been mistaken. Maybe it had been another door that had been locked. "There has to be another." She charged the hall, searching, praying, pleading. There had to be another door.

"North Queen," Bhasim said, "there's nowhere in your mind I cannot see. There's nothing else of your past here."

That couldn't be. There couldn't be nothing. *No.* She felt the threads of desperation weaving their way into her being—growing, spreading, taking over. But she stopped and swallowed back the hopelessness. This wasn't defeat. This wasn't the end. It couldn't be.

He wasn't powerful enough, she told herself. She would find a way to get her memories back, just not here. She forced her mind to calm—she'd find another way. She told herself that over again. It was the only thing keeping her from the edge of complete defeat.

Then, an image caught her eye, and she stepped toward it. It was her, sitting on a bench in a garden. She didn't recognize the place. It wasn't

Kharav, or Mercia, and it wasn't a memory, she was sure. "What is this?" she asked.

"Sometime in the future," Bhasim said. "Not all visions are of significance. Some are beautiful. Quiet. Peaceful. These are my favorites."

Norah watched herself as she sat on the bench. Her image held out her hand, and a butterfly landed on her palm. She smiled as she studied it, then she let it flutter into the air.

It brought her back to a place of calm, and she appreciated his showing it to her, but she shifted her attention back to the present, to visions that *were* of significance. "Will you show me what you showed the king?"

Bhasim gave a nod, and the image of her in the garden faded. The rooms fell into darkness. After a moment, a faint light came from one, and she drew closer to it. Something moved in the distance and started toward her. Norah squinted her eyes against the light.

A horse.

Horses.

Horses galloping toward her.

Norah stumbled back as a wave of mounted soldiers flooded past her. Their numbers were in the thousands. Blue—the color of Aleon. The soldiers held their weapons high in attack. She whirled around to see them clash against a sea of green—Japheth.

The scene changed. The same battle? A different battle? White mixed with blue, Mercia joined with Aleon. To her right, Kharavian forces battled another army she didn't recognize.

Norah turned back against the tide of war and saw herself. Riding beside her—the Aleon king. *Phillip.* They rode side by side, battled side by side.

Her heart beat in her throat as she staggered backward. She'd seen this image before. She knew what accompanied it. She spun around, her eyes combing the clash of death. She searched for him. *Alexander.*

And she found him. *No.* Norah ran toward him.

He slid off his black warhorse, his sword in his hand. But something was different about him, there were things she hadn't noticed when she'd first seen the painting of the vision in Mercia. His hair was cut short, his golden locks gone. Malice dripped from his skin. His black leather-plated armor was trimmed with the color of old blood, and on his shoulder, bladed pauldrons—not the head of the great Northern bear.

This wasn't right. This couldn't be Alexander.

His eyes were locked on the figure of a man downed by an arrow in front of him—a large, armored man in a horned helm. *Mikael.* Alexander stalked toward him as Mikael tried to pull himself backward and away. Mikael held his sword in his hand, but he didn't lift it. He didn't even try to fight—why wasn't he trying?

"Get up!" she cried. Why wasn't he fighting? "Mikael! Get up!"

Alexander swung his sword above his head.

"Alexander, no!" she screamed, but he couldn't hear her. "No!" she screamed again as he brought the blade down, severing the helmed head from the king's body. A cry ripped through her throat; the feeling of loss as real as if it had truly just happened.

The image faded and fell away, and Norah dropped to her knees on the marble floor with a sob. This couldn't be the future. It should have changed when they wed. This couldn't be Mikael's fate.

She wouldn't let it.

"How do I change it? Please," she begged, "tell me how to change it."

The seer shook his head. "You cannot change fate."

"Of course you can! My father saw me captured by the Shadow King and hid me away."

"Yet you were still captured," he said.

A chill rippled through her. How had she not realized it before? Her father hadn't seen the senior Shadow King capturing her. He'd seen Mikael. Her father took her away for fear of a danger that wouldn't come until years later.

He'd changed nothing.

What if she could change nothing?

Her emotion threatened again. What had she done to warrant a fate so cruel? Did the gods hate her? Did they even exist?

Well, damn the gods. Damn Hammel himself. They could curse her. They could take from her, but if they thought they could break her, they were wrong. If they thought she wouldn't fight, they were wrong.

Norah forced the despair-filled air from her lungs. She needed to pull herself together and figure out what to do next. She gathered her strength and stood.

"Thank you for seeing me, Bhasim," she whispered.

He gave a small bow of his head.

She turned to go, then paused. "What did you show the lord commander?" Mikael had said the commander wouldn't speak of it, even to him.

The seer hesitated. "That you must ask him."

How strange he'd share what he had shown Mikael, but not the commander. She didn't have the strength to press him for it, though.

She left the temple feeling like the air's weight would crush her. The vision of Mikael's fate seared her mind. It haunted her.

Calla ran to her as she stepped outside, with Cohen right behind her, and Norah was relieved to see them both safe.

"What happened?" the girl asked. "Did he refuse you?"

Norah shook her head.

"Then you saw? The visions? Did you get your answers?"

Norah shook her head again, the despair returning. Suddenly, her breath caught in her chest. The lord commander stood at the bottom of the temple stairs, axe in hand.

Waiting for her.

CHAPTER SIX

The sunlight hurt her eyes. Norah walked slowly down the stairs of the temple of the seer. The lord commander stood at the bottom, waiting. Her stomach churned. How had he found her? Behind him stood Captain Artem and four other soldiers: two of Artem's men and Bhastian and Javed from her own Crest guard. She hadn't expected to see Caspian, but he was a welcome surprise.

Cohen stepped in front of Norah and Calla and drew his sword.

"You don't want to do that, boy," the commander said from under the wrap hiding his face. He fixed his grip on his axe in warning.

But Cohen didn't move.

"I'll tell you only once to step aside," the commander warned.

"He can't hear you," Norah said as she put a hand on Cohen's shoulder to settle him. "And they're in my service, seeing me safe."

The lord commander snorted. "You put your safety in the hands of children instead of your captain? All for a seer who won't see you." He was so smug. *Ass.*

"The captain cares nothing for my safety, and you know it," she snapped. The commander looked over his shoulder at Artem. There was a strangeness between them, as if the commander were waiting for

48

something. But no matter. "Have you come to escort me back, Lord Commander?" No point avoiding the obvious.

"You're most perceptive," he said with an icy edge in his voice.

The bitterness of disgust wormed its way up her throat. She had almost forgotten how much she hated this man. But as her eyes found Caspian, she managed a small nod. At least there was one man she could trust here. "Caspian," she greeted him.

He bowed with his fist to his chest as she drew nearer to him. "Queen Norah, I'm relieved to see you safe." He stepped closer, dropping his voice so that only she could hear. "While I've come on this mission to find you, it's not my intention to take you back if that's not what you want."

She didn't want to be taken back, but there was no avoiding it now. She would only endanger those she cared about. "Thank you, Caspian. But I have to go back. I need to repair things with the king." And she needed to find a way to change the vision.

Her mind turned back to Mikael, and guilt bubbled up inside her again. She wasn't sure what she would say when she saw him.

She turned to Calla. "I suppose this is where we part. I'm so thankful to you, and to Cohen and your grandparents. I wouldn't have made it here without you, and I'm in your debt."

Calla smiled. "It's been our greatest honor serving you, Salara. I only hope we have the fortune to see you again."

Norah reached out and hugged her tightly. "You will. I can promise you that."

She turned to Cohen, and he gave her an awkward bow. She handed him Hamed's sword and pulled him into a hug too. Then she stepped back so he could read her lips. "Thank you, master swordsman. You honor yourself and your family. Your father would be proud."

He gave an emotional smile.

"Take them back to their home," Soren said to the soldiers. Javed stepped forward.

"Caspian," Norah called, and he gave a nod. "I want you to go with Javed and see that Calla and Cohen return home safely." She didn't trust anyone else. Not after what happened to Bremhad, the greenskeeper and Kiran's father.

He started to object. "Queen Norah—"

"Please," she said softly. "They're very important to me. You know I'll make it back to the castle just fine."

Caspian sighed, giving a reluctant nod. "I'll see them safely home."

"And then I'll see you back at the castle." With one last look back at Calla and Cohen, Norah mounted her mare and turned toward Ashan.

The commander led the way, and Artem followed with his two soldiers and Bhastian. She rode between them. An anxious ache rolled in her stomach. Artem would find a way to punish her for slipping him. The commander would too. Had it been worth it? She had no more answers than when she'd started.

The lord commander set a fast pace, no doubt eager to get back. They traveled against the wind, and Norah had to hold the front of her hood while riding to keep it from blowing back. Her arm grew tired, and she let it go. It wasn't like she was trying to hide herself anymore. She'd been captured.

Hours passed, and a stitch grew deep in her stomach. She pressed her hand against the scar to allay the cramp. Finally, she could go no longer.

They reached a small stream, and Norah slowed her mare to a halt. She slid to the ground. It felt good to stand again.

"We'll take a moment here," the commander called to the men as he reined his destrier nearer to her and dismounted, probably wary of another escape attempt. He pulled a skin of water from his saddlebag and held it out for her.

Norah eyed it. She would rather drink from the stream, even if it was a muddy stream, but she took it. She was thirsty, and as much as she hated to admit, it was good. She drank her fill and handed it back to him, and he pulled down his wrap and took a drink as well.

"You were wrong, you know," she told him. "He did see me. The seer."

The commander stilled. His face darkened as he put the stop back on the waterskin. "What did he show you?"

"Everything."

A silence hung between them, and Norah could feel the rage under his calm—a rising, fearful rage. Whatever the seer had shown him—whatever he was hiding—he was afraid of it.

He looked over his shoulder at the men and then back at her. "What did he show you?" he asked again. There was a threat in his tone.

She moved to step past him, but he grabbed her arm, pulling her close with a tightness that hurt.

"Let me go!"

"What did he show you?" he hissed.

"What are you so afraid of?" she cut back.

His shoulders relaxed, and he released her arm. She could see it in his eyes—his relief. He knew she didn't know, and she cursed herself for speaking too quickly.

Norah couldn't help the frustration, the hopelessness that suddenly washed over her. She found a large rock to sit on and gazed blankly out at the uneven terrain. She came all this way, and for what? She'd married the Shadow King, and for what? The visions still held. While there was peace, it could break at any moment. She held the title of salara, but she could do nothing.

The commander looked at the sky. "Winter's returning, and a storm's coming. We need to go."

Let it come. She didn't care anymore. The hopelessness was overwhelming.

"North Queen," he called to her again.

She sat, not letting him push her to leave. "Why do you still call me that?"

"Are you not the North Queen?"

The hopelessness gave way to anger, and something snapped inside. "Am I not your salara?" she knifed back.

A rumble came from his chest. "Of course, *Salara*," he corrected himself, his voice thick with agitation.

She stood and faced him, all care gone, all caution gone. "That's what you'll call me from now on."

He snorted. "Surely you don't seek to quarrel now."

"What quarrel should I have with *my* commander?" she snapped. "You're *mine*!" Norah stepped forward, drawing close enough to touch him. A shaking fury rippled through her. "I'm salara! And Salar has committed to me everything of Kharav. Everything and *everyone*. He said you're a loyal man. Does he lie? Because all I've seen is your opposition to his promise at every turn. You *and* your men." She shot a daggered glance at Artem.

Black pools eddied in his eyes, but she refused to let them drown her. She returned his gaze with a dark intensity of her own. She had nothing more to lose.

"I am loyal to my salara," he said slowly, "as are the rest of my men."

Norah didn't believe him. She snapped out her hand, snatching the dagger from his belt and whipping the cold steel to his neck.

He didn't move.

Artem and his two soldiers behind him drew their swords. "Release him," Artem demanded.

Her Crest guard Bhastian stood unmoving, his eyes on the commander. He looked at Artem and then drew his sword slowly. That hurt her. She had started to think he was one of the few she could trust.

Norah tilted her head, bringing her eyes back to the commander. "Ah, yes. I see they're so very loyal to me."

His face twitched in a burning fury. Slowly, he reached up and curled his hand around the dagger in her hand. She wouldn't kill him, and he knew it. Defeat tethered her spirit. She let him pull it from her fingers, and he stepped backward, toward his men.

Her strength left her.

She wasn't salara.

She wasn't queen.

She was a prisoner.

But then the commander turned, letting out a growl, and drove the dagger into the soldier to his left. Bhastian swung his sword out, slicing open the throat of Artem's other man. The commander recoiled, then grabbed Artem by his breastplate and pushed him to his knees, onto the ground. "You fail Salar," he seethed.

"My lord!" Artem cried out, but he wasn't able to finish his plea before the commander pushed the point of the dagger into the front of his neck and through to the back.

Norah stumbled backward in shock and gulped a startled breath.

The commander pulled the blade out slowly and held Artem by the hair, watching the dying captain choke on his own blood. Artem flailed his arms, grasping for life as it left him. When his struggling gurgles stopped, the commander let his body drop to the ground.

Norah gaped at him, wide-eyed and speechless.

The commander turned back to her, stepping forward and sinking to his knees. He held the dagger by its bloodied blade, offering it to her. "If you doubt me." But his voice still betrayed his hatred.

Of course she doubted him. Did he think this would absolve him? Her breath shook, but she forced it quiet. She could no longer let him go unchallenged. "Killing your men doesn't remove my doubt."

"Only one man here is mine, and he still stands."

Bhastian.

"The others were not," he added. "They take up arms against you and are traitors to the crown. Let me share their fate if you judge me the same."

She took the dagger slowly. The commander pulled down his wrap farther and let his head fall back slightly, exposing his neck. She clutched the handle tightly. It was warm from his grip, and she pressed it against his skin at the base of his throat. He sat motionless, except for the rise and fall of his chest.

She wanted to kill him, or rather, she wanted to want to kill him. She wanted to rid herself of him. But she couldn't. That wasn't what strength was to her. She sighed, lowering the knife. "You already know I won't kill you. But just because I won't doesn't mean I'm weak."

His voice came low. "I've never thought you were weak."

"Why do you hate me?"

He clenched his jaw with a twitch of irritation. "Because you'll be the end of Salar. You'll be the end of all of us."

"You really believe that?"

"It doesn't matter what I believe," he seethed. "I told you I'm loyal, and I am."

"Hate pours off you. Is that really loyalty?"

"I am, nonetheless. I have been, ever since Salar wanted you for his salara. In Aviron, he made me swear myself to you, even after he's gone."

Norah stopped and swallowed. *Even after death?* Why would Mikael do that? She eyed him warily. He said he was loyal. How could she believe a man she knew hated her? Yet, for some ungodly reason, she did. "Get up."

He rose.

"If he dies, what does it matter to you, then?"

His eyes burned into her. "Because I made him a promise."

And he loved the king. Norah let out a deep sigh. She let her eyes drift back to Artem's body.

"Bhastian told me what happened, all that he's done," Soren said.

Norah glanced at Bhastian in surprise. The guardsman gave her a small nod. She wanted to hug him.

"It's important you know those things weren't on my orders," the commander added, "nor were they done with my knowledge."

Her eyes narrowed. "If you had known, would you really have done anything?"

"I would have," he said angrily, as if offended.

Freezing droplets of rain hit her cheek, and she looked to the sky. "The storm," she said.

"There's a hillside house," he told her. "We'll take shelter there and continue to Ashan in the morning."

The thought of staying with the lord commander even longer soured her stomach, but she supposed she didn't have a choice. She looked at the bodies of the fallen men.

"Leave them," the commander called back to Bhastian. "Bring only the horses."

Mounted again, Norah followed the commander, with Bhastian behind. She shivered as the freezing rain soaked through her layers. They hurried their horses, but the biting wind made Norah want to slow.

She followed the commander down a trail and through the crag of a mountain. The rain fell harder, and the trail became slick.

"Careful," he called back to her.

Around a turn, the crag narrowed with barely enough room for their horses to pass through. It didn't seem like a path to shelter. They wound upward until the crag opened wider, revealing a hillside looking out over the mountains. Norah straightened in surprise. A quaint house sat carved into the side stone.

Soren dismounted and led his horse to cover under a recess in the rock, and Norah slipped down, off the mare. They were drenched by the time they reached the door.

"Does anyone live here?" she asked through her chattering teeth.

"No. Almost no one knows it exists. This is a royal safe house, and it's stocked." He led them inside and motioned down a small hallway. "There's an armoire in the back room. You'll find clothes there."

She turned toward the back room but paused. "I'm sorry about Artem."

"He didn't deserve mercy," he said angrily. "Or your sympathy." He turned toward the fireplace. "I've wanted to kill him for a long time."

Norah had wanted him dead for a long time. Well, days. But it felt like a long time. Now that he was, she carried a twinge of regret. Not that she felt sympathy for Artem, but the end of any man's life held a great sadness.

She took to the back room to see what clothes might be available and was surprised to find the armoire filled with a variety of options: riding gowns, sleepwear, underclothes. And beside garments for her hung those for Mikael. She reached out and drew her fingers across them. In a way, she was glad to be returning to Ashan. She'd missed him, but her stomach turned at the thought of facing him again. She'd said straight to his face that she wouldn't betray him, yet she'd left. Would he understand?

She settled on a navy, front-fastening riding dress, the only one she could manage herself. There was no denying it was good to get into dry clothes again, although her body still shook with cold.

When she returned to the front sitting room, she found the commander tending the fire. His cloak hung nearby to dry, but he still wore his damp breeches. As usual, he was without a shirt, wearing only his weapons strappings, and she watched the inked flesh of his arms work as he fostered the growing flames. It was silly he hadn't worn his heavy tunic, given the return of winter. She hoped he was cold. Very cold.

"Where's Bhastian?" she asked.

"Outside. He's not permitted in. No one is."

She pursed her lips. "Except *you*."

"I'm permitted everywhere."

"You're not *wanted* everywhere," she cut back, sharper than she'd intended.

He paused. "Do you want me to leave?"

She gritted her teeth. She did want him to leave, but she also wanted him to tend the fire. Norah saw a wine bottle on a small side table, and she walked over and poured herself a cup.

"I know you hate me," he said.

She took a drink and closed her eyes, savoring the sweet taste of berries on her tongue as she sank into an armchair by the fire. She was tired, tired of the constant fight. Her shivering stopped, but she wasn't sure if it was from the flames of the fire or the warmth of the alcohol.

"That's what you want, isn't it?" she asked. "You try to intimidate me. You stand against me on everything."

"I say what needs to be said."

Norah sighed. She couldn't win this argument with him, not with his hatred running so deep. She swirled her wine in her chalice. "Why would Mikael have you swear yourself to me?"

He shifted the wood on the fire with his sword. "To keep the peace. That's what you want. And as with everything else you want, he gives it to you." There was a hint of bitterness in his voice.

"But you don't want peace," she said. It wasn't a question.

"It doesn't matter what I want."

Norah felt a small sadness, not in the way he yearned for war, but in the way he cast all his desires aside, how he gave without expectation. He really did love the king. She sighed, thinking. "Surely the army wouldn't follow you and continue to be allied with Mercia if the king fell."

His brow dipped. "They would," he said, taking offense. "They would follow me anywhere." He leaned his sword against the stone of the fireplace. "It's the nobles that wouldn't. That's why you need an heir."

An heir—it was a topic she dreaded. Mikael hadn't brought it up again since their wedding night, but she had expected it would surface eventually. She just hadn't expected it from the commander. Norah took another drink of her wine. "What would the nobles do if I didn't have an heir?"

"Try to take the throne."

"What would you do, then?"

Soren stood and stepped back from the growing fire, taking a chalice and pouring wine for himself. "Kill them," he said blankly. Then he brought the cup to his lips.

Norah frowned. So much death. "Is that what you were worried about when Mikael absolved his marriages? The nobles? Did you think they'd do something?"

"They did. And they still might."

She hadn't forgotten the attempt on her life. A knot tugged in her stomach—it might not be settled still.

"Salar needs to satisfy the nobles to keep his crown," he said. "You do *nothing* to help him."

She wanted to. She wasn't sure she was ready for a child yet, but she wanted to help Mikael. She cupped her chalice in both hands, letting the brim rest on her lips. The alcohol warmed her cheeks. "Do you have any children?"

He snorted. "No."

"Have you been with a woman before?" she asked, surprising even herself. Her cheeks grew hot. Why had she asked that?

"Of course I have." He balked at her question, insult heavy in his voice.

"Oh," she said awkwardly. She had just thought with his preference...
What was his preference? It was none of her business, that's what it was.
She pursed her lips and then mumbled, "That was rude. I'm sorry."

"Don't apologize," he said irritably. "You're salara, you don't
apologize."

That hardly seemed the criteria for whether an apology was owed.
Norah took another drink of her wine. "Do you have anyone? A lover?"
she asked. Yet another question that surprised her. What was wrong with
her?

"You said you wouldn't speak of this again."

Their pact... "This is different." *Kind of.* And here she was again, deep
into not-her-business territory.

His eyes seared into her. She forced back another apology that sat
on the tip of her tongue. Another intrusive question. She should stop
drinking the wine.

He surprised her when he actually answered. "If I let myself care about
another, my enemies will hurt them to hurt me. To pull me away from
Salar."

"You mean that's what *you* would do."

"It's what any cunning foe would do," he said sharply. A tension hung
in the air, and he exhaled. "No one can take me from Salar. No one, save
for you, as he's made me promise."

"And here I was hoping it was because you were starting to like me,"
she mumbled sarcastically.

"I *don't* like you."

She pursed her lips. *Yes. Precisely.* And she took another drink of wine
as he went outside to spend the night on guard with Bhastian.

CHAPTER SEVEN

The storm was a long one, and the commander finally yielded to Norah's demands that he and Bhastian take refuge inside the house. They set their post just inside the door while she took the back room to sleep.

She woke occasionally through the night to the sound of the fireplace in her room being tended. She knew it was the commander. Part of her stiffened under the quilts in annoyance that he would come into her room so freely. Closed doors meant nothing to him. The other part of her secretly appreciated she didn't have to tend the fire herself.

When the morning came, they continued on their way. The commander set a slower pace, seeming to have found some compassion, but he sent Bhastian ahead to inform the king of their arrival. The air was easier between them now, the quiet not so intimidating.

"What did you name her?" the commander asked, breaking the silence.

Norah frowned. "What?"

His eyes twitched in annoyance at having to repeat himself. "The mare. What did you name her?"

Strange. "Oh, um... she has a name. Savantahla."

The skin between his eyebrows wrinkled. "Savantahla's not her name. It's what she is."

She hadn't thought of it like that. Norah tilted her head and brushed her fingers through the mare's mane. "All right, I think I'll call her... um, Cloud... no... Spirit."

The commander rolled his eyes.

"What? You don't like it?"

"It's a terrible name."

Was he serious? "What would you name her then?" Not that she cared what he thought.

He looked straight ahead as he rode, absolutely no help. She should have known. He didn't have anything less terrible. A terrible person, he'd only have terrible names to offer.

"Sephir," he said finally.

And she paused the mutterings in her mind. She silently rolled the name along her tongue. *Se-FEER.* "What does it mean?"

"It's just a name," he replied, annoyed.

She hated that it wasn't a terrible name. Norah bit the inside of her cheek in annoyance. It was actually a nice name. She might call the mare Sephir.

It wasn't long before Ashan loomed in the distance. Norah grew more anxious as they neared the capital city. How would Mikael react with her return? It had hurt him when he thought she wanted to leave, and surely it had hurt him when she actually did. Would he be angry? Would he mistrust her now?

"Your cover," Soren called to her as they got closer. "Put it on. Conceal your hair."

They'd hidden her disappearance, she realized. She'd expected the entire kingdom to be looking for her, but of course, the king had put his faith in his commander. She tempered her irritation. The king had trusted him, and again he delivered. He'd tracked her like a hound, even though she'd been on a horse of the Wild.

The guards let the commander through without a word, and they rode to the stables. After leaving their horses, he didn't take her through the front of the castle. Instead, he led her into a small stone building. She followed him out the back and into a small side street, then through a maze of alleys. They entered another small structure, and inside found a stairway leading downward.

He led the way through narrow halls and back up a small staircase with a door at the top. The door opened into a sitting room. She made mental notes, trying to remember as much as possible. The doors to the sitting room led to another hall, and then she knew where she was. They were making their way to Mikael's study. Her heart beat heavily in her chest. She couldn't escape the feeling of being captured once again.

They entered the room, and her breath came unevenly at the sight of Mikael. His armor was piled on a side chair, as if he'd taken up residence in the study. His hair hung loose around his shoulders. He rose slowly from the desk when he saw her.

The commander stepped forward with a bow of his head. "Has Bhastian made it to you?" he asked.

"Yes." Mikael's eyes were locked on Norah. "Leave us."

The commander glanced back at her before leaving the study, then closed the doors behind him.

Mikael's eyes pierced hers, and she waited, her mind tumbling for what to say. But the anger she expected from him didn't come. She searched his face, not sure of the emotion behind it. Hurt? Concern?

"You didn't flee to the North," he said. His voice was soft, uncertain almost.

She shook her head weakly. "No."

"Or to Aleon."

"Why would I go to Aleon?"

"Why would you go to Odepeth?"

Really? For the same reason he went to Odepeth. "Because I wanted answers."

"Did you get them?"

Not as many as she wanted. "I discovered my father rode a horse of the Wild, the same as I do."

Mikael shifted back in surprise. "How? What does this mean?"

She wished she knew. "I don't know."

"The seer told you this?"

Norah shook her head. "No, someone else I met along the way." She frowned. "The seer couldn't help me."

"We told you he wouldn't see you."

Patronizing. "Well, he did see me," she cut back, and his eyes widened. "I saw the visions. Bhasim showed me everything."

"Bhasim?"

She narrowed her eyes. "You go to this seer, and you don't even know his name?"

He didn't have an answer for her.

Now who was being patronizing, she chided herself. She looked to the ground, drawing in a deep breath and letting it out slowly. "I asked if he could unlock my memories."

He stilled, so still it seemed unnatural. Like he wasn't even breathing. Was he afraid of her getting her memories back?

"He couldn't," she said.

Mikael's shoulders loosened. But his face... it held... a disappointment. A sadness. Was he sad for her that she didn't get what she was searching for, even though he was afraid of it? Her chest tightened. At least now he knew she hadn't fled back to Mercia—she hadn't just left him.

"But he showed me the visions," she told him. And now it was her turn to feel sadness for him. "I won't deny that they're... terrifying. I understand what you fear. And to be honest, I fear it too. But Mikael, something's wrong. That isn't Alexander." She shook her head. "I don't know who that man is, but it isn't him."

He didn't speak; he only stepped closer.

Her eyes welled, and she cursed herself. Why was she getting so emotional? Maybe it was the exhaustion, the frustration, the fear that she wouldn't get her memories back. Maybe it was the fear that the vision of Mikael would be true. But she knew in her heart it couldn't be.

He lifted her chin so that her eyes met his. "After the seer, where would you have gone? Back to the North?"

She didn't know where she would have gone, but she knew she couldn't run. She wanted to go back to Mercia, but if she returned in flight, she risked war. She couldn't do that. And if she was completely honest with herself, she didn't want to leave Mikael. Slowly, she shook her head.

"Why?"

"For the same reason you swore the commander to me." To protect the peace.

His brows drew together. "He told you this?"

She nodded. "He said you made him promise in Aviron, when you wanted to make me salara."

The corner of his mouth twitched.

"What?" she asked.

"I wanted you for salara well before Aviron."

She drew her brows together.

He pulled open his shirt, revealing the crown marking from the ink mastera, Salta Tau, on his chest. "Battle. Blade. Blood. Crown."

She hadn't understood when they'd gone to Salta Tau, and she didn't understand now. What did that even mean?

He reached and curled his hand around hers, and her heart beat faster.

"It was the day you cost me Bahoul. The day you threw my commander from his horse, cut my spear from my hand, and stabbed me with my own dagger."

So much had happened that day she could barely recall it, but she couldn't help the smile that came to her lips. "That sounds more magnificent than I remember."

Mikael pulled her even closer. "You are magnificent." He took her hand and pressed it over the marking on his chest. The nearness of him...

And then she knew—this was for more than peace now. It was for more than her people, or Mercia. It was for her. He had to see it—the power he had over her, not as an ally, not as a king. Just as himself.

His voice dropped to a whisper. "I'm sorry I didn't listen to you. I'm sorry I wouldn't hear you when you tried to speak to me. I wasn't there when you needed me."

She shook her head. "I know what compelled you. But you have to know I wouldn't betray you, Mikael. I know words are just words, but I—"

Her voice fell as he lifted her chin and covered her lips with his own. His tongue tasted of want and fire, but it was tempered. Most of all, he tasted of remorse. Of safety. Of promise.

He pulled back and looked at her. "I believe you and your words. Let's find the truth then. You can start with your lord justice when he returns from Aleon."

The thought made her stomach knot, but she nodded.

The afternoon sun hung high, and Norah wrung her hands as she walked quickly back to her sanctuary from Mikael's study. Worry writhed in her stomach, twisting and thickening, eating up the space for her heart to beat and her lungs to breathe. Alexander's business with Aleon could be dangerous for everyone.

She pushed open the door of the sanctuary and gasped when she saw her maids, Serene and Vitalia. Her gasp turned to an emotional laugh as she rushed forward, hugging them both. "Thank the gods, you're safe!" she breathed. While she'd sent them into hiding, Artem was cunning, and she'd still feared for them.

"And you!" Serene exclaimed. "Queen Norah, we were so worried."

"I was worried about you both! You're supposed to be with Kiran. What are you doing here?"

"Bhastian came and told us you returned just this morning," Vitalia told her. "He brought us here."

Serene nodded. "Artem's soldiers were looking for us when you left. Sonal told Kiran they were going to search Kiran's house, and he brought us to stay with his grandmother."

"Sonal?" Norah felt her eyes well as she nodded. He was one of her less favored Crest guards. Perhaps she'd judged him too harshly. There were good men in this place.

"And"—Serene paused—"Bhastian told us Captain Artem was dead. But all he said was treason."

Norah nodded, hesitant at first. "I threatened the lord commander, and Artem and his soldiers pulled their swords on me."

Serene gasped. "What did you do?"

"I didn't do anything. The lord commander and Bhastian killed them."

Vitalia raised a surprised brow and shook her head. "Well, despite my loathing for him, he does seem to have his priorities in order."

Norah sighed. "Maybe." He was a difficult man to understand.

"How did you even get away from Captain Artem to begin with?" Serene asked.

She hesitated. She didn't really want to recount her overly dramatic escape. "I just found an opportunity to slip from sight, and then he couldn't follow me on Sephir."

"Sephir?" Vitalia asked.

"Oh, I named the mare. Apparently Savantahla's not her actual name."

"You gave her a Kharavian name?" Vitalia grinned at Serene. "It means *spirit*. It's so perfect."

Norah paused. Sephir meant *spirit*? But the commander—

"Where were you?" Vitalia asked her, not giving her an opportunity to mull over the difficult man.

Norah pushed out a breath. "I went to Odepeth, to the seer. He showed me the visions. In every way it appears Alexander kills Mikael, but there's something not right about it."

"Why not?" her Mercian maid asked. "He's been battling the Shadow King for years, trying to kill him. Mercia feels Kharav is still a threat. And, if I may be so bold"—Serene shifted uncomfortably—"the lord justice obviously cares for you a great deal, and he's very unhappy with this current arrangement."

Norah felt a flash of anger at her maid's words, but how could she be angry at the truth? She pushed it down and gave them both a small nod. "I know." Serene was right, but she knew the visions weren't.

"You'll figure it out," Vitalia said. "You'll find the truth."

Their eyes were on him. Even in the darkness of night, he could feel them watching. Alexander strode from the stables toward the castle, keenly aware of the Shadowmen who stalked his every move. And the Destroyer was there—unseen, but Alexander knew he was there. No doubt the Shadow commander knew the moment he'd crossed back into the Shadowlands. Did the commander know where he'd been? It was possible. His chest tightened. Alexander needed to find Norah and give her the news himself.

He expected word of his return had spread to her quickly, and that she'd be looking for him. It wouldn't be good for her to meet him outside under prying eyes, and prying ears. He crossed the threshold inside. Alone, he settled slightly.

The hour was late, and the castle, quiet. The torchlit halls were wrapped in shadows. As he strode the long corridor, a shift of light came around the corner, and he slowed.

Norah stood like a flame, bright against the night, against the darkness that surrounded her—the darkness that always surrounded her now.

"Lord Justice," she said when she saw him. There was a weight to her voice. A hesitation. A worry.

She knew.

His chest tightened, his heart feeling the pressure as he continued toward her. "Norah."

Even in the dimly lit hall, the blues of her eyes pierced through him. "Where have you been?" she asked softly, but it wasn't meant softly.

He heard it, her fear, and he stepped closer. "On a task. From the council."

"What kind of task?"

His mouth moved to speak, but he paused. She would see this as a betrayal. She wanted peace so badly, it blinded her. But Alexander knew—more than anyone—wanting something couldn't make it so.

When this all fell apart, and it *would* fall apart, she would need options. "A task of building options," he said.

"What does that mean? Where have you been?" Her voice begged him not to say it.

He could hear the silent plea for her suspicions to be wrong, and it clawed at his heart. But she needed a way out of this world that was breaking her. It *was* breaking her. More than that—when this alliance crumbled, it would kill her. And wasn't this his duty—to protect

Mercia? Protect her? To save her, even if she didn't know she needed to be saved? "Aleon," he said finally.

She let out a shaky breath. "Why didn't you tell me you were going to Aleon?"

"I wanted to fully understand the situation." And come to terms with it himself.

"No," she said sharply. "You didn't tell me because you knew I wouldn't let you go." She was upset.

So was he. It had been a hard journey—traveling to the man who still had intentions for Norah, the Aleon king. It had been torturous to look at his face and negotiate her hand. "The offer for marriage still stands."

Shock stopped the obvious argument on her tongue. "What?" she breathed.

He could barely get it out the first time, the second cut even deeper. "Phillip's offer for marriage still stands."

Norah shook her head, her brows stitching in confusion. "I'm already married. *To Mikael.*"

"For how long? Even if this all doesn't come crashing down, there are many who seek his fall."

She shook her head again. "Mercia stands with him."

"Norah, the council will never support the Shadow King." He hadn't intended to be so direct, but she needed to understand.

"He's *their* king! I wed him!"

"In name only!"

She stopped. But it wasn't the stop that suddenly gripped his heart. It wasn't the abrupt quiet. It was the small catch of her breath—so faint that it was barely noticeable.

But he noticed.

The catch of breath she gave when she was caught...

"Welcome back, Lord Justice," the Shadow King's voice called from behind them.

Alexander spun to see the king and the Destroyer step out from the shadows. How much had they heard? He almost didn't care, his mind was still on Norah's reaction.

"Interesting news from Aleon," the king said calmly. "Does it come with a proposal of how to be rid of me?"

The scraping of the Destroyer's giant axe on the stone floor as he stepped toward Alexander made Norah step closer to him, but that was the opposite of what he wanted her to do. He needed to get her away from here, away from the danger of this situation, and away from this king.

"There were no such discussions," Alexander said stiffly. His mind replayed the catch in her breath, and heat rippled over his skin.

"Then a little premature for a marriage conversation. Don't you agree?" the king asked.

Alexander didn't agree, but he said nothing. His pulse thrummed deafeningly in his ears.

The king pulled his sword, and Alexander put his hand on his hilt.

"Alexander," Norah pleaded. In normal circumstances, he might have listened.

His mind swirled—the catch in her breath...

He pulled his sword.

Her head jerked to the Shadow King. "Mikael, wait." She was trying to calm the tension, but there would be no calming. She looked back desperately at Alexander. "Go to your chamber."

He wouldn't need his chamber after this.

"If I didn't know better"—the Shadow King took another step toward him—"I'd think you were a man of Aleon."

Insult to injury.

The catch in her breath...

"I'm a man who will see your end," Alexander bit back.

The Destroyer let out a roar and raged forward, swinging his axe with a fury.

"No!" Norah cried as Alexander charged forward to meet him. The clash of their weapons echoed through the halls. Footfalls sounded, soldiers fast approaching. They swarmed into the hall and surrounded them.

"Don't!" the Destroyer snarled at the Shadowmen warriors. His eyes of night found Alexander. "He's mine." And he attacked again.

Alexander fought him back with equal skill.

"Mikael, stop this!" Norah cried, but the king wasn't listening. None of them were.

Alexander's own fire of rage burned. He broke from the Destroyer once again, and they circled each other, each looking for an opening.

Suddenly, Norah rushed forward between them and grabbed Alexander, forcing him to look at her.

"You'll stop!" she cried. "Stop this!"

He gaped at her in surprise, and the commander saw the opportunity for distraction. He swung with a forceful blow, barreling by Norah and striking the sword from Alexander's hand.

The king called to her, but she was too entangled in the attack. The Destroyer delivered a lunging kick, taking the wind from Alexander and dropping him to his knees. Then he raised his axe to deliver the fatal blow and brought it down with all his weight.

"No!" Norah screamed as she threw herself forward, wrapping herself around Alexander to shield him.

Too quickly for him to stop her.

A loud clang rang through the hall as the Shadow King's sword met the Destroyer's axe, sending the commander stumbling back. He caught his balance, stunned, and looked in shock at his king.

The king staggered back, his eyes on Norah.

Tears streamed down her face as she clutched Alexander.

Alexander reached up and threaded his fingers into her hair, pushing her back to look at him. All was quiet. "Why would you do such a stupid thing?" he said between his teeth, not able to keep the anger from his voice, not able to hide the fear, the horror of what had almost just happened. "Do you know what you could have done?"

"I can't let you die," she cried softly, shaking her head. "I can't."

He brushed her cheek with his thumb, his emotion too thick for him to speak. If anything happened to her...

Norah looked up to see the king, who held his sword low. Their eyes locked, and the king grimaced.

And Alexander realized. She'd revealed herself, her heart.

"Out," the Shadow King ordered the soldiers, and they quickly filed out the way they had come. He looked at the commander. "You too."

"You can't mean for me to leave you here," the Destroyer hissed.

"Go," the king said sternly.

The commander's eyes tightened with a bitter rage, and he reluctantly drew back with his axe, disappearing into the shadows.

The king looked back at Norah with an expression Alexander knew all too well.

"Mikael," she started.

But he shook his head. Then he turned and followed after the commander.

"Mikael!"

Norah followed after, leaving Alexander alone.

His body shook. He'd lost himself and endangered Norah. He'd lost control. And he wasn't sure if he could get it back again, as his mind reeled back to...

The catch in her breath.

CHAPTER EIGHT

Norah sat on the bench in the conservatory, grasping the quill tightly in her hand and looking at the page of blank parchment. Words wouldn't come. There was so much she wanted to say, but she struggled for a way to say it. Every sentence she tried sounded ridiculous. Maybe what she wanted to say was ridiculous. Maybe trying to say anything was ridiculous.

"I didn't think I'd find you here." Mikael's voice startled her.

For two days, she hadn't seen him, not since what had happened with Alexander. Her breath knotted in her throat, and she stood quickly. Had he not wanted to find her here? Did he not want her in the conservatory anymore? It was a place that was special to him, meant only for people who were special to him. She wasn't sure she was considered so anymore.

He eyed the quill and parchment.

"I'm just writing a letter," she said. *Or trying to.*

"To?"

Norah looked down at the blank parchment. She wasn't sure her voice would come. "You," she said finally. "I... wanted to explain myself in a way that made sense, but"—she paused—"I'm having difficulty starting."

"What's there to explain?" he asked, strangely calm.

His composure scared her. Had she lost him? Norah opened her mouth, but she still couldn't find the words. Her chest tightened, wringing the air from her lungs. "So much" was all she could manage.

A long silence sat between them. He only waited, watching her. She had to say something. *Anything.* But nothing came.

She had nothing.

Except for how she felt. She focused on that. "If I'd tried to guess my future when I woke in the forest of the Wild," she started, "I would never have imagined this for myself."

It felt like an understatement. *Never in the wildest of dreams*, she should have said.

"So haphazardly life seems to have been thrown at me," she continued, "like the gods cared nothing, planned nothing." How could the gods have planned this path? She couldn't even call it a path. "I doubted there even were gods."

Mikael only watched her.

She sucked in an uneven breath. She couldn't hold back the tears now. "But now there's no doubt. This path isn't haphazard, it's purposeful. The gods are there, and they're angry with me, and they're cruel. And the more I care for you, the more they use that to hurt me too." They knew how to hurt her the most. *Damn them. Damn them all.*

Norah looked down at the stone floor. Mikael stepped to her and drew her face up to look at him. But she couldn't read his eyes. She couldn't understand his face.

"How much?" His voice came barely above a whisper. His hands clasped her arms just below her shoulders. "How much do you care for me? Am I in your heart?"

"Do you not see it?" She knew it wasn't enough. Why couldn't she say the words?

But he nodded. "Yes," he said hoarsely. "But I see there is also another. And not just any other."

She had no excuses. She couldn't deny it. She wouldn't lie.

He brushed her hair softly from her face. "It's important you speak the truth to me," he said in a low voice. He hesitated, seeming to fear his words. "He stays in my kingdom. Have you been to his bed?"

"What?" Did he really think—

"Please," he said, his voice softer. "These past two days, I—" He shook his head. "My mind is weak. I need to hear you say it."

She wanted to be offended, but she knew how easily the frenzy of jealousy could poison the mind. She shook her head, looking into his eyes. "No. I've not been to his bed."

He closed his eyes, seeming to calm before opening them again. "But you love him." It wasn't a question. "It's why you wouldn't give him to me."

She said nothing. She couldn't deny it. Now he knew why she protected Alexander so fiercely. What would he do?

Alexander was still in Kharav.

What would he do?

His face held no emotion now, no hint of his thoughts or of his intentions. He dropped his head beside hers, and his breath danced across her ear. Alexander's fate lay on his lips, and she feared it—more than feared it. Terror trembled through her. Surely he wouldn't let him live now.

But instead, he whispered, "Tell me the heart is not finite. Must you love one less to make room for another?"

Norah's heart raced. Was he telling her he would do nothing? A tear fell down her cheek. She whispered the only thing she could. "The heart is not finite."

He nodded, taking the parchment and quill from her hand, and dropped them to the ground. Then he pulled her close. "You don't need to explain anything else," he said softly.

They stood in the light of the morning sun. Everything should have felt perfect, but there was still something that lingered, something that weighed heavily on her mind. She had to ask him. "When you asked me to marry you, did you really believe it would change your fate?"

"I wanted to believe."

She pulled back and looked up at him. "Did you, though?"

He shook his head. "Not truly, no."

Her heart hurt. "But you still married me. Why?"

"Because I needed you." He threaded his hand back into her hair. "I still need you."

His words caught her in the most beautiful way. Her lip trembled. "And I need you."

"Then we need each other, and we'll have each other."

She smiled as she sniffed.

"Can I walk you back?" he asked.

"Of course," she whispered. "I'd like that." There was nothing she wanted more in that moment.

He pulled her arm through his and led her from the conservatory, back toward the castle. "You still stay in the sanctuary," he said as they entered the castle and walked through the high-arched halls.

This conversation again. "It's comfortable."

"But not fit for the quarters of salara."

"It has everything I need." Would he press her to stay in the villa? She couldn't stay there. She *couldn't*. "I like the sanctuary, really," she tried to assure him. "And it looks north."

"As does my own chamber," he said, stopping as he turned to her. He reached up and ran a lock of her hair through his fingers. "Maybe you'd like to stay there from now on?"

"In your chamber?" she asked in surprise. "Where would you stay?"

"With you."

Oh. "I see," she breathed, feeling foolish. Of course with her.

She looked down the hall, toward her sanctuary, and then back toward a hall that led to the king's chamber. He pulled her hand gently, asking.

Should she give him what he asked? No—not what he asked, but what she wanted. She did want to stay with him, be close to him. He was her husband, who—surprising even herself—was stealing her heart.

Norah threaded her fingers between his, giving her answer. He smiled and led her back toward his hall. They walked slowly. When they reached his chamber, Mikael stopped in the doorway. "If there's anything you'd have differently, you only need to say it," he told her.

"I've seen your chamber, and it's perfectly fine."

"Not just the chamber. Anything."

She knew.

He stepped forward and caught her in a kiss, and she kissed him back. His lips were soft, yet firm.

Claiming.

He reached behind her and opened the door to the room, using the frame of his body to push her backward and inside without breaking their kiss, then swung it closed behind them. His hunger—she could feel it in him, loosely leashed. He made no effort to hide his want. There was no reserve, no mask. And she loved it.

The scent of him was intoxicating, and she breathed him in. All of him. He moved her backward, toward the bed, the hunt in his eyes and his intentions clear. She could stop him, slow him, she knew. But she didn't want to.

He laid her back on the bed, as gently as the storm inside him would allow, then he stepped back and away. She watched him as he reached over his shoulders and pulled his shirt over his head. The muscle rippled under his skin in forced restraint, and a warmth pooled in her stomach. His need fueled hers. He kicked off his boots and unbuckled his belt, pushing his breeches down and off, and stood naked in front of her.

Norah drew her bottom lip in between her teeth. She loved his body. She'd always considered herself a somewhat modest woman, but just the look of him made her want every inch of his flesh. And she'd have him. She brought out her foot from underneath her dress and held it for him. He reached out and slipped off one shoe, then the other. Her heart beat faster.

She pushed herself up, onto her knees, and turned around, her back to him. A shiver ran up her spine as he stepped closer. He pulled her jacket from her shoulders and tossed it to the side, then set his attention on the fastenings down her gown, so many fastenings. He pushed apart the backing and pulled loose the lacing from the corset underneath. Then she turned back to face him.

The thought of inviting him back to her bed before was always *just* beyond the reach of her confidence. Perhaps it was the shyness of convention, or the pervasive voice in the back of her mind telling her she couldn't love this man, she shouldn't want this man. But she did want him. He'd said he thought of her inviting him into her sanctuary, often. She did too. But only in the darkest corners of her mind did she let herself think of his touch, and of his body. But tonight, she wouldn't let herself be confined to only thoughts.

Slowly, Mikael pulled the gown from her shoulders and down. They both paused for a moment, breathless. Then he pushed the fabric down farther, over her hips, sweeping her undergarments with it, and she rocked to the side as he stripped it down her legs and pulled the dress free. Her skin prickled, but not from the cold.

Mikael pushed her onto the bed, prowling over her, and drew her back into a kiss. He wrapped his arm around her and pulled her to the pillows as he drank from her lips. She could taste his want and responded with her own. He nipped along her jaw as she let her head fall back, giving him her throat. He trailed hungry kisses down her neck and bared his teeth against her shoulder. She wouldn't have minded if he'd bitten her; she wanted to bite him.

Mikael followed the line from her shoulder to the base of her throat, letting her feel the warmth of his breath across her skin. She knew his breath, his mouth, his touch, and she needed it all. He brushed his lips over the side of her breast, and she arched her back, wanting more.

Norah pulled him up, opening her thighs, begging him to come to her, and she felt his body respond. Mikael loved with a strength, not one that overpowered her but one that fueled her, made her stronger.

He positioned himself and moved slowly. But she needed him now. She rocked forward, taking him inside her and joining them together. Deeper, then deeper still. The full length of him, until he filled her completely. The pleasure that rippled through her stole her breath.

He groaned as she moved her hips against him, bringing him almost all the way out and then sheathing him fully again. Pressure built within her core, and she quickened her pace.

Mikael gripped her waist, slowing her. Every fiber of her body protested—she needed him. She needed them to be one, not just in body, but in mind and heart. They had to be one to overcome the world against them, their own kingdoms against them, the gods against them. Mikael was hers, and no one would take him from her. He was hers, she told herself again as she gave in to her own desires. And he let her. There was no reservation with Mikael, no shame. Only freedom.

Norah pulled his hand down between her legs and guided him to touch her. She angled herself to feel him more, to take him deeper, and he gave himself to her. She let the fire build within until she thought she would burn, and then they both writhed in the inferno of their release.

As they descended, he collapsed, dropping to his elbows over her and panting. Slowly, he calmed, nuzzling into the warmth of her neck. She loved his tenderness—something so many thought he was incapable of. But she knew him.

"Mikael," she breathed. There was no reason. She just needed his name on her tongue.

He drew up to look at her. "You're the only one who calls me that."

She bit her lip. "Do you not like it?"

He smiled. "When you say it, it's the most beautiful sound in the world."

She smiled back, and he brought his mouth to hers.

CHAPTER NINE

Norah woke to Mikael sitting in the chair by the window and pulling on his boots. He'd already donned his clothes. His black hair fell loose on his shoulders, a way she didn't often see. She loved his hair, thick with a silky curl. He noticed her watching him, and he stopped and smiled.

"What are you doing awake so early?" she asked as she propped her head up on her elbow. "And where are you going?"

"I have to go find the lord commander," he said.

Of course.

"I won't be long, though," he added.

She bit her smile in her teeth. "I suppose I should take a bath, anyway."

"Vimal will draw you one and fetch you some breakfast."

She nodded.

Mikael rose from the chair and stood beside the bed. She pulled the sheets around herself and sat up on her knees, and he pulled her close as he leaned down to kiss her. "I'll return soon," he said.

When he'd gone, Mikael's servant, Vimal, stepped inside the chamber, careful to avert his eyes. "Salara, a bath is ready for you. I'll get breakfast and have your maid bring a new dress."

"Thank you," she said appreciatively.

Vimal left, and Norah padded into the bath chamber. She slipped into the tub. The heat from the water made her skin tingle as she submersed herself. It felt wonderful. Vimal had put salts in the water, and she closed her eyes as she breathed in their scent.

This was what happiness felt like. *Finally.* Things were right between them. For the first time in a long time, she felt like she could persevere—more than persevere, she could make a life. She could love this life.

Remembering Vimal would return soon with breakfast, Norah quickly finished washing. She wrapped a towel around herself and stepped out of the tub. Through the hanging panels, she found the dressing room. Surely there would be a robe she could put on. But the dressing room had only Mikael's clothes: shirts, breeches, boots, and a wide variety of leathers and armor. She reached out and touched a shoulder shield. It was thin, smooth, light, but strong. Its polish hadn't removed the wear of war. How many battles had it seen? Battles against Mercia?

Suddenly, the hair on the back of her neck stood on end. She felt a presence from behind, and she spun around as the commander plunged through the panels with his sword ready.

Norah gasped and stumbled back a few steps before catching herself. "Hammel's hell! What are you doing?" she asked angrily.

His eyes widened in surprise. He pulled back, slowly lowering his sword.

"What's wrong with you?" she snapped. "I could have been Mikael, or a servant!"

"Salar's sword isn't here," he said between his teeth, "and Vimal's in the kitchen."

Norah sighed, shifting uncomfortably under his eye. Her near nakedness didn't seem to bother him. But her presence did. It didn't matter—she had no fear of him now.

"Why are you here?" he challenged.

"I live here," she spat back.

"You know what I mean."

"My answer's the same. I'm to stay here now, in the king's chamber."

His nostrils flared. "You were in his bed last night?"

"No, I just run about random rooms with no clothes on." She rolled her eyes. "Obviously I stayed here last night."

He made no effort to hide the fury inside him.

"Can you at least give me my dress, by the bed?" She would put on her old dress until Vitalia came with a new one.

"There is no dress," he said coldly. "Otherwise, I would've known it was you."

She pursed her lips. Vimal must have taken it. "You mean otherwise you wouldn't have hesitated before running me through," she mumbled under her breath.

The commander reached out and pulled one of Mikael's shirts from its hanger. He threw it at her, and not kindly. She clenched it in anger, wanting to throw it back at him. But she didn't. It was better than a bath towel.

She scowled at him. "Can I have some privacy?"

He walked out to the bedchamber, and Norah pulled the shirt over herself. It was large, more of a short gown.

"Where's Salar?" he called from the bedchamber.

"Looking for you."

"I'll wait here for him."

"Of course you will," she muttered. There really was no getting rid of him.

Norah raked her fingers through her damp hair, trying to look as regal as a woman could in an oversize man's shirt and without a hairbrush. Then she walked back out to the bedchamber.

The commander had sheathed his sword back in its scabbard and stood by the window.

She forced herself calm. She couldn't fault him for his anger. Undoubtedly, the seer's vision of Mikael's death haunted him, as it did her, and her defense of Alexander on his return from Aleon would still be fresh in his mind. But she didn't want things to be like this between them. "I understand your concern—"

"My concern?" he snarled as he spun to face her. "You don't. Because it's more than concern. You lead Salar toward death, but I won't let that happen."

"You think that I would? I care for him!"

"Then you'd give me the Bear!" he raged. "Or at least send him back to the North. If you cared for him, you'd protect him!"

Just then, Mikael entered. There was no mistaking the high tension in the room, and he looked at his commander with a warning eye. "Wait for me outside," he said stiffly.

The commander gave Norah one last glare and left the room without a word, closing the door behind him.

Mikael's eyes moved back to her, and he softened. He stepped forward, reaching out and pulling her close to him. "I'm sorry. I meant to tell him first. That was my intention this morning. But I'll deal with him."

She sighed as she swept her locks behind her ear. "Don't be angry with him," she said. "He worries for you. He doesn't understand, after all that's happened. And my being here caught him by surprise."

He looked down at her, and the faintest smile touched his lips.

"What?" she asked.

"You defend him."

Then he looked down at his shirt on her.

"Sorry," she said, glancing down at the shirt and shrugging. "I don't have a dress yet."

Mikael brushed her hair back from her shoulder. "I was just remembering what I felt the last time I saw you in my shirt."

Norah swallowed, remembering the night he had saved her from the Horsemen's attack. "What did you feel?" she whispered.

His eyes moved back and forth between hers. "I wanted to hold you. I wanted to put my arms around you." He pulled her closer. "I was already falling for you."

She remembered that night well. Too well. It still haunted her—what had almost happened. She covered the emotional scar with jest. "Took you long enough."

He smiled, dropping his head, and caught her in a kiss. She needed his kiss. She opened her mouth to him, and his body responded. He picked her up and carried her back to the bed.

But as much as she wanted to continue, the commander was angry enough with her. "The lord commander's waiting for you," she reminded him as he laid her on the bed and nipped at her breasts through the linen shirt.

He growled in protest before rising and pulling her back to her feet.

There was a small knock on the door, and Vitalia appeared. She held a dress and a tray of cheese and fruit.

Norah smiled at him as she shimmied her shoulders. "Perhaps I'll put it on for you again this evening."

"I'd prefer to see you taking it off," he said. Then he kissed her once more and left to join the commander.

Mikael found Soren in the hall. His commander watched him approach with a steely gaze. They had much to talk about.

Soren's nostrils flared. "You're a fool. You welcome your death."

"Watch yourself," he warned.

Soren snorted. "Are you just going to ignore what happened with the Bear? What you've seen? What you've heard?"

Mikael's anger grew. "We talked about it. The matter's over."

"You mean your rutting has bewitched you."

Mikael grabbed Soren by his weapons strap and slammed him against the wall. "Be very careful of your next words," he said between his teeth. "I have no more tolerance for you, brother."

Soren shook with fury but yielded, quieting.

"Salara's joined me in my chamber," Mikael told him. "She is my wife and rules by my side, and you'll respect her as such."

"And what of the Bear?" Soren demanded.

"I've committed to her his safety."

Soren's eyes blazed. "He plots against you!"

"If you engage him, there will be consequences." Although, when had Soren ever cared for consequences? "Severe ones," he added.

Mikael released him, then turned and walked away. But he didn't head back to his chamber. He had another matter to address.

He had promised Salara the Bear's safety, but he couldn't tolerate treason.

Mikael found the lord justice with the Mercian captain and several Northmen outside by the forge, looking curiously over the hearth. No doubt they found it far less advanced than the forges of the North that produced Mercian steel. Mercian steel would advance his army to near invincible heights, and it was something Mikael needed to speak to Salara about. He should have bargained it as part of their marriage arrangement, but he hadn't, because the only thing he'd been focused on getting was *her*. He'd deal with it later. He had more pressing things to focus on now.

The Northmen stiffened when they saw him. "Northmen," Caspian called, and led them away for Mikael and the justice to speak alone.

Mikael watched them leave, noting the captain lingering a distance away should he be needed. He didn't mind. Caspian struck him as a man that would equally stop the Bear from doing something stupid as much as he'd give his life to save him. He was a respectable man, and Mikael had no intentions of doing unrespectable things. Not yet, anyway.

Mikael spoke first. "Let's not bother with courtesies," he said as he eyed the Bear.

The justice puffed a small breath in amusement, clearly never having intended to.

"You're not welcome in Kharav. I tolerate you because it's Salara's wish, but this is my realm, and regardless of whether you see me as your king, I am. And there will be rules."

The Bear snorted.

Mikael used every ounce of his strength to temper his rising anger. "You think my rules don't apply to you? Well, they apply to everyone, and if you wish to discuss it with your queen, you'll find her in my chamber where she's taken residence."

The Bear showed no emotion, but Mikael knew he'd wounded him.

"You'll cease your work of division. Kharav and Mercia are united. *Salara and I* are united. If you seek to divide us again, there will be no one to save you, not even Salara. If you engage my lord commander again, there will be consequences, and as I've told him, they'll be severe. While you're in my realm, you're subject to *my* rule. You are *mine.*"

Then he turned and left the justice in the wake of his anger.

CHAPTER TEN

"Another!" Alexander bellowed as a Mercian soldier picked himself up off the ground of the sparring field. He didn't usually participate as the army practiced their drills, but he desperately needed an outlet for his anger. It had been two days since his confrontation with the Shadow King, but time had done nothing to temper his frustration, his disappointment in himself. He was failing. Failing himself and Norah.

And his challenge with the Destroyer had almost killed her. He'd been blinded by his emotion, the fear that her marriage to the Shadow King wasn't in name only.

And the king had practically confirmed it.

He waited for another soldier to step from the ranks. He had lost count of how many men he'd tested this morning on the field. His body was tiring, but he'd take a few more to help ease his troubled mind.

Another Northman stepped forward with his shield and sword.

But Alexander's mind swirled—the Shadow King had said she resided in his chamber. Did she do so willingly? It was beyond his comprehension. Did she want this marriage to be more than in name only? And worse—what turned his stomach and haunted his dreams—had she given herself to him?

He pulled up his sword again, and let the soldier make the first attack. The Northman lunged forward with an overhead swing, and Alexander met it with an upstroke of his blade. The steel echoed through the early morning. Alexander pivoted, throwing his shoulder against the chest of his opponent, and sent the man stumbling backward.

His thoughts drifted. This alliance would fail. He could understand her logic that a marriage to the Shadow King would stop the war between their kingdoms. And it had temporarily, but it wouldn't last forever. Successful alliances were formed by those who shared common goals, held common values. But the Shadowlands warred against everything Mercia stood for, against everything they believed in. And if her marriage to the Shadow King truly was complete, it would be hard to exercise any other options in the wake of a fall.

The Mercian soldier launched another attack, and Alexander found himself having to focus to counter against the well-coordinated maneuvers. His soldiers' training was coming along nicely in the Shadowlands. His men made good use of the advanced practice stations, and they had learned a few things from watching the Shadowmen run their drills. He felt both pleased and irritated, but he forced his irritation aside—if his men were improving, it was a good thing.

As the Mercian soldier broke from his attack, Alexander's mind shifted back to Norah. Did the Shadow King require her to share his chamber? Despite his loathing for the man, the king did seem to genuinely care for her. He didn't deserve the benefit of the doubt, but Alexander had seen him yield to her. If what the Shadow King said was true, if they now shared a bed, he couldn't get past the thought that this was Norah's decision. And he would want it to be her decision, yet...

His Northman launched another assault, driving him back a few paces. Alexander's body begged for rest, but his mind begged for distraction. He charged forward and locked his grip on the soldier, giving his arms a reprieve from the swing of the sword. Then he shoved the soldier back.

Had she come to have feelings for this man? He'd watched how she looked at the Shadow King—not with contempt or disdain, but he hadn't taken it for love. However, one action lingered on his mind—the way she took the king's arm. Most of the time it was the proper way, her arm scooped under his with her hand resting on his forearm. But then, sometimes, she'd curl around and clasp his upper arm, as if wanting to hold him close to her—the way she used to hold Alexander's. Before he'd lost her.

The Mercian soldier stopped and straightened, halting their bout, and Alexander followed his gaze to see the Destroyer approaching with his own warriors. The Shadow commander came in his usual fashion—darkness and depravity personified. Alexander hated that he couldn't see his face.

"Enjoying our amenities, Bear?" the Destroyer rumbled as he approached.

Alexander didn't answer. The Shadowmen invested in death; of course their practice stations were superior to those of the North.

"A friendly spar?" the Shadow commander asked, pulling his sword.

Alexander knew the invitation was anything but friendly, but he had to fight the desire to accept it with every fiber of his being. His blood burned with the want to sink his sword into the Destroyer, to cut limb and life from him. Yet it wasn't the king's warning that made him pause.

He cared nothing about the king's orders, or his threats. But Norah needed more from him. Expected more. He was already failing her.

He flicked his gaze over his men. "We're done here," he said, giving them a slight nod to leave the field. "To your duties." His men pulled up and stowed their weapons and turned to leave.

"Well, isn't that just like the North," the Shadow commander growled out. "Avoiding the fight. And you wonder why your men are so poor at it."

Alexander paused. The Destroyer was goading him, he knew, and he sent back a daggered insult of his own. "Were we so poor at it during the Battle of Bahoul? When we took the mountains from you?"

If a shadow could grow darker...

"You had Aleon," the commander snarled. "Now you're alone. And do you forget, Little Bear, it was your father who helped the North King take Bahoul. You think you're half the warrior he was? You think you're worthy to wear his armor?"

Alexander's chest quaked under the taunt that hit at his core. But he couldn't let the Destroyer see. "Yet you still fear me," he cut back. "So obsessed you are with trying to kill me."

The Shadowman gave a dark chuckle. "Fear? It's *you* who runs away at a mere suggestion of a spar. Does your queen know her commander is a coward? Does she really believe you can protect her?"

His blood heated to near boiling. Alexander cast aside the protest of his weary muscles and tightened his grip on the hilt of his sword. A spar, then, to show this Shadow beast his place.

The commander's eyes smiled as he read Alexander's acceptance, and he advanced, delivering a few basic blows.

They were easy enough for Alexander to deflect, but there was a force behind them, and he knew the commander was playing with him, testing. Their men backed up to give them more space.

The Destroyer launched another attack, and Alexander countered. Their swords came together with a force that shook Alexander up his arms and to his shoulders. While the Shadow commander stood only half a head taller than him, he carried a muscled frame almost twice his size. Alexander wasn't a small man, but damn it if he didn't feel small in the wake of this giant. Their blades cross-caught as they each pitted their weight forward, but Alexander was no match in strength, and the commander pressed him backward. Their eyes locked, their faces close.

The commander chuckled.

"Show your face, coward," Alexander spat.

"What will my face show you that my sword won't?"

Alexander shoved him back and away. They circled one another, each looking for an opportunity to strike. Alexander's body moved numbly from exhaustion, but anger fueled him and kept him on his feet.

The Destroyer lunged forward, and their weapons came together in a deafening clang. They locked again, and he drove Alexander back all the way to the fence along the weapons' hold. The Shadowman used his weight as he crushed Alexander against the railing.

"But I don't think it's my face that bothers you," the commander sneered quietly so that only Alexander could hear. "I think it's your queen in Salar's bed."

The Destroyer's eyes smiled. Rage rippled through Alexander, searing the need for blood inside his heart and lighting a burn across his skin. He ripped his dagger from his belt and plunged it into the side of the

Shadow commander. But his range was limited, and it wasn't a fatal strike. Regrettably.

The Destroyer stumbled backward, his eyes dropping to his side as he held his hand to the wound that now streamed blood over his hip and down his thigh. The morning came alive with the sound of swords pulled from scabbards. The Shadow commander's eyes blazed, and a snarl ripped from his throat as he charged Alexander again.

And hell broke loose onto the field.

The days came easier with Mikael's love, and Norah found herself loving in return. She could be happy here, she knew, and she started to dream about it. But with that dream came the darkness of fear, and of worry. The vision of Mikael's death haunted her. The search for the truth—and to change fate—had become even more important to her, and not just for Alexander's sake, but for her own and for Mikael's.

She walked solemnly through the main hall, but her thoughts were interrupted by a sight out the window—two soldiers helping the lord commander up from the field, shouldering his weight between them. Blood poured from a gash in his side.

Norah ran outside to meet them. "What happened?"

"I just caught a blade—it'll be fine," he said between his teeth.

Norah followed them to the healer's workroom.

"I said it's fine," the commander snapped as the healer poked at him.

Blood still poured from it. It didn't look fine. It didn't look fine at all.

"How did this happen?" she pressed. "Who did this?"

"Your Bear," he snarled.

No, she didn't believe that. "Alexander did this? I don't understand. What happened? Where is he?"

He eyed her darkly.

If Alexander had been harmed... "Where is he?" she demanded, anger swelling inside her.

"Salar has him."

Norah's breath caught in her throat. *No.* She spun for the door.

She raced through the castle, outside, and toward the courtyard. Panic filled her. There would be no wounding the commander without consequence. She stumbled but didn't slow. When she reached the courtyard, a wave of horror washed over her. Two soldiers dragged Alexander toward one of two posts erected in the center. His hands were bound.

Mikael looked on, with a crowd growing around to see the commotion.

She raced toward him. "What's going on?" she demanded as she reached him.

"Salara, go back inside," Mikael told her.

She shook her head. Did he really think she would leave? "I won't! What are you doing? Release him!"

"Bring the lord commander," he bellowed as he waved to the second post beside the one Alexander was being tied against.

"Wait. What?" She reached out and clutched Mikael's arm. "He's injured! He's with the healer!"

"It won't keep him from punishment," he said, his voice solemn.

Her fear grew to desperation. "What punishment? What's going on?"

Mikael turned to another guard. "The lash," he said in a low voice.

"No!" she cried. "No!" She ran to Alexander and struggled with the rope around his wrists.

"Norah, stop," Alexander said. "There's nothing you can do. Go. Please."

"Take Salara inside," Mikael ordered.

The guards tried to take her gently, but she twisted away from them.

"Don't touch me!" she spat.

"Norah," Alexander pleaded again. His voice stopped her, and her desperate eyes found his. "Go," he said. "I don't want you to see this."

"Whatever this is, it's not going to happen!" she seethed through her tears. She wouldn't let it.

"Norah," he said again. "Please. Go."

The commander was brought out and bound to the post beside Alexander. The wound to his side was wrapped, but the blood had already started seeping through.

"No." She gritted her teeth, rising up to Mikael. "They're the heads of our armies!"

"That's why they are getting my lenience."

"*For what?*" He called this lenience?

He frowned. "They started a fight between our men."

Was that all? "Men fight all the time!"

He looked at Norah with a fury she hadn't yet seen. "They drove dissent within our armies. We lost twelve men—North and Kharavian men. I've already warned them, and I've promised severe consequences."

"The lord commander isn't fit for punishment!" she argued. "Look at him!"

Again, the king glanced at the guards. "Take her inside."

"Wait!" She reached forward and clutched Mikael's arm, her mind racing for anything else to stop him. "Mercy! I beg you, mercy!" She looked up at him, pleading. "Husband, please. I'll do anything for your mercy."

He grimaced. "This is my mercy."

The guards took her by the arms, but she wrenched away. "I said don't touch me! I'm not leaving!"

Mikael nodded to the guards and then looked at her with sadness in his eyes. "Leave her, then."

"Queen Norah," came Caspian's voice behind her, and she turned with a start.

"Caspian! You have to stop this!"

But he shook his head. "Queen Norah. I can't."

"You have to! This can't happen!"

Caspian caught her arms, pulling her still. She looked on in horror as the punisher walked toward Alexander and Soren with the lash in his hand. Their shirts had been pulled off, and their bare backs were exposed.

"Courage," Mikael called to them.

The punisher struck Alexander first, who grunted at the lash, but held fast. Again he drew the lash across Alexander's back. Purple welts sprung up across the skin. On the next strike, Alexander cried out, pulling against the rope.

"Stop!" Norah screamed, but Caspian held her tightly. She clasped her hand over her mouth to hold back a sob. That she could be married to a man who could do this—no, not a man—a monster.

Again, the lash hit across Alexander's back, and he twisted. Lash after lash. Norah didn't know how many. Alexander's legs gave way, and he lost consciousness. She sobbed as his body swayed on the post.

The punisher looked at the king, and Mikael gave a nod. Then he turned, delivering a stinging lash to the commander, who flinched but let his body hang against the post. The commander was still, almost lifeless, only tensing when the whip hit. Another lash opened the skin, and blood spilled down his back. Another lash made him cry out, and finally, after a sickening number, unconsciousness came for him too.

Norah wept with fury as the two men hung from the posts. Mikael motioned the finish and for the soldiers to collect them. Caspian released her, and she ran to Alexander. He hung limply by the binding around his wrists.

"Help me!" she cried. Caspian and another Mercian guardsman stepped forward to cut the rope.

"Careful!" She looked back at the commander. "And him."

Kharavian soldiers stepped in to help, pulling him off the post.

"Take them to my sanctuary," she said, her voice shaking.

Mikael stood, watching her. She stopped and glared at him, tears streaming down her cheeks and rage seeping from every pore.

"Salara—"

"Don't speak to me," she hissed, and she turned and followed the beaten men into the castle.

Serene met them in the room.

"Lay them both across the bed on their stomachs," Norah ordered the soldiers. "And get another bed for the commander. They won't be happy if they wake beside each other. Where's the healer?"

"He's on his way," Serene said.

The soldiers brought in another bed and set it up along the opposite wall. They moved the commander to it.

The healer came and mixed a salve while Norah washed their backs. The cleansing would be painful, and she wanted to do it while they were still unconscious. When she was finished, she took the mixture from the healer and sat on the bed next to Alexander. She bit her lip as she spread the salve across his broken skin. She'd never forgive Mikael for this.

Alexander stirred.

"Be still," she said softly. "I have only a little more to apply."

He tried to turn his head back to look at her.

"I said *be still*."

"I'm sorry," he said faintly.

She drew in a shaking breath. "I'm sorry I couldn't stop it."

"Twelve men died because of me, some of them our own Northmen." His voice cracked with guilt.

She set the bowl of salve down on the small bedside table. Men had died today. North and Kharavian men. All her men. "What caused this?"

His eyes settled on the commander on the other bed. "Only words, and they're best left unsaid."

"What words?"

He inhaled and let his breath out slowly. "I have to ask you—do you share the Shadow King's bed now, Norah? Do you love this man?"

She tried to swallow, but her throat was dry. She couldn't love a man who would do this. Because what did that make her?

The healer returned with a bowl of milky liquid. "Poppy," he told her as he offered it. "This will take away the pain and make him... unaware. Sleepy."

She took the bowl. "Drink this," she said as she held it to his lips.

Alexander drank and lay his head back down on the bed.

"Rest now," she whispered as she brushed her fingers through his golden locks. This man... If anything happened to him, if he was hurt—

She stopped. Something *had* happened to him, and he *was* hurt. Gods help Mikael when she left this room...

Within a few moments, she could see the fog roll into his eyes. They closed, and he fell into a deep sleep.

The commander was just waking as she walked over to him. The healer had almost finished coating the bleeding welts with the salve.

"I'll do the rest," she said, taking the bowl.

The healer motioned to another bowl on the table. "The poppy."

She nodded. She looked back at the commander and stared at him for a moment, before cautiously taking a seat on the side of the bed. He said nothing. He didn't snarl at her, and his eyes didn't seem to will death in her direction. Had this broken him as it had her? Did he feel betrayed, as she did?

He lay in silence as she spread the mixture over the rest of his wounds. His skin was hot to the touch. "Your side required stitches," she told him, "so don't move about." When she finished with the salve, she held the bowl of poppy for him, but he turned his head away.

"It'll help with the pain," she said.

"I want a clear head."

"Well, you're beyond that," she snapped. Then she bit her lip. She'd wanted to take a different approach with him—a kinder approach. Maybe she shouldn't care; he didn't respond to kindness.

The commander snorted in irritation.

"What happened?"

A deep rumble came from his chest. "Send the Bear back to the North."

"Why?"

"You know why," he snapped. "He shouldn't be here. And I can't trust him with Salar."

"Alexander wouldn't hurt the king. He knows I stand with Mikael."

His eyes blazed. "Have you lost your mind?"

She sighed. She didn't want to fight with him. He was as loyal to Mikael as Alexander was to her. But he didn't understand. "I need him," she whispered.

"Why?"

Filled with sadness, she looked out the window and swallowed back the threatening tears.

"Salar didn't want to do this," the commander said. "We left him no choice."

Anger flashed inside her. "How can you say that?"

"He would never choose to hurt me."

Norah scoffed. "You can't believe that. He made a choice—this choice!"

"What else should he have done? I should lose my head, and so should the Bear. Our soldiers need to see accountability. But Salar—he loves me. And he loves you. So he gave us pain over death, and I'm grateful."

Grateful? Norah didn't know what to feel, but she certainly wasn't grateful. She couldn't imagine a world where pain like that was necessary.

"Why did you defend me?" he asked.

Norah stared at him for a moment. Why *had* she defended him? "It's a character flaw," she mumbled.

She finished with his wounds and wiped the salve from her fingers, but she didn't move to stand. Their conversation wasn't over, and she gave it time.

"I'll serve you," he said finally. "Send the Bear home. You know it's best. And I'll serve you as I serve Salar."

It wasn't about service, and it was hard for her to think of being without Alexander. She needed him. She loved him. But the commander was right. It *was* best. She needed to send Alexander back to Mercia—he wasn't safe in Kharav.

And Mikael wasn't safe.

She took a deep breath, trying to quell the emotion. "Drink the poppy," she said, holding the bowl out, "and it will be done."

The commander drank deeply and let sleep come.

CHAPTER ELEVEN

Whispers all around her—a voice that flowed not through her ears, but directly into her being.

She knew this voice.

Alexander's voice, but words she couldn't understand.

Then she saw him.

He stood over a weathered trestle table layered in parchments. Maps. He spoke as he marked paths with a pen, as if to people around him, yet he was alone. Who was he talking to?

His golden locks were gone, shaved off. He was dressed in a loose black tunic and leather breeches.

"Alexander," she called.

He stopped.

He looked up from the table, but the eyes looking back at her were not the brilliant blues she knew so well. They were dark sapphire, and angry.

They locked with hers, and his lips peeled back in a chilling smile.

Norah woke with a start to Vitalia gently nudging her. She sucked in a breath and stumbled up from the chair she'd been sitting in.

"Are you all right, Salara?" Vitalia asked.

Her racing heart slowed as she realized she'd fallen asleep watching over Alexander and Soren in the sanctuary.

Slowly, she nodded. She looked at the men. Thanks to the poppy, they were still asleep, their chests rising and falling slowly with their breaths.

"You should go wash and get some rest," Vitalia whispered. "I can stay with them until you return."

Norah looked down at her dress, with its golden fabric crusted in browning blood. She wasn't sure if she could go back to sleep, but she did need to wash. Norah brushed her hair out of her face. She could trust the men to Vitalia's care for a time.

She walked stiffly to the chamber she shared with Mikael. He wouldn't be there, not after what had happened. He was most likely in his study. She caught her reflection in the hall mirror and noticed a dried smear over her temple. Alexander's blood.

Would she accept this? She thought she knew herself, but she could barely recognize the woman looking back at her. Her hands shook as she pushed open the chamber door. The image of Alexander stung her over and over, and she couldn't breathe. Her stomach twisted at the memory of his beaten body hanging limply from the post.

As she stepped inside, she stopped. Mikael's sheathed sword leaned against the wall.

He was here.

A madness swept around her, crawling up her body and searing itself into her mind. She reached down and wrapped her hand around its hilt and then pulled it from the scabbard. Her skin burned with a fury, and her vision tunneled as she moved around the linen panels.

As Mikael stepped out of the bath chamber, she met him with his blade to his neck. He stopped abruptly. Norah pressed the point of the sword against his throat and walked him backward to the wall. Her arms shook—whether from her rage or the weight of the weapon, she didn't know. She dug the tip of the blade farther into his skin. Could she really hurt him? She wanted to.

"Salara," he breathed.

Did he expect her mercy? When he had none? She gritted her teeth as her eyes welled.

Slowly, Mikael reached up and curled his hand around the blade.

But still she held him. She could make him pay. Except her body wouldn't let her. She couldn't move.

Mikael guided the tip away from his neck and then pulled the sword toward him. She trembled as she surrendered and let it slip from her hands.

And she hated herself—she hated that she couldn't hurt him, like he had hurt her. She hated that he could see her weakness for him.

He stepped closer, his eyes burning into her. She couldn't meet them. He reached up to touch her cheek, but she turned her face. He pulled her closer still. "I know you'll bring death to me, but it won't be today," he whispered before he kissed her head somberly. Then he moved to the door and left her to her heartache.

Mikael found the Mercian captain on the wall, and the captain straightened as he neared. Mikael leaned forward against the stone, looking out over the city. He was curious about this man. Caspian—the only Northman that Soren didn't seem to completely despise, and who held the Bear's trust. A rare combination. Perhaps the rarest. He was also the man who managed to contain Salara as Mikael punished the commanders.

"I believe her heart's filled with hatred for me now," Mikael shared in a burst of openness.

"It's very possible," the captain answered honestly.

Mikael could see why Soren tolerated him. His commander valued candidness, no matter how brutal. He did too. "I knew it would come," he said somberly. "But I didn't think she'd try to take my head. She threatened me with my own sword. But then, I'm not sure I'd expect anything less."

Caspian's eyes widened, and he shifted in surprise.

Mikael sighed. As painful as her rage toward him was, he couldn't even muster anger over it. "She loves so fiercely." He had hoped he had won some of that fervor. But after today, he was sure that anything he'd won in her heart had been lost.

The captain was quiet.

"Perhaps you can reason with her," Mikael said. "She seems to listen to you."

Caspian hesitated. "I'm not sure she'd see that as my place. And I'm not sure she'd hear me. Not on this."

Mikael nodded again—it was as he'd feared. "Is it beyond repair?"

Caspian gave a reluctant tilt of his head. "I don't know."

Mikael crossed his arms and brought his fist to his lips. "I can't lose her."

"Give it time, then, Salar. I won't say that she'll forgive, but I don't think she can lose you either."

Mikael looked at the captain curiously. "Why aren't you angry with me, Northman? Why don't you hate me? For what I've done to you, your men, your kingdom. And now to your justice, whom I can see you're close with."

He watched as the captain drew in a deep breath and let it out slowly. "I have been angry. Sometimes I still am. But I know war makes men no longer men. And we've warred for so long that none of us should recognize ourselves, including me. I don't like your decisions. They wouldn't have been my own, but I don't wear the burden of the crown."

"I don't know what to think of you, Captain," Mikael admitted. He looked out over the wall at the city. "I have to travel to the Horsemen tribes of Caan. I won't be gone long, but perhaps long enough that Salara may settle a bit. Will you tell her, tell her that I'll be eager to return to her?"

Caspian nodded. "Of course."

Mikael gave him a nod in thanks and left the wall.

Washed but not rested, Norah made her way back to the sanctuary. She worried Alexander and Soren would try to kill each other again, or disappear to tend to themselves. But in peeking through the door, she saw them still resting on their beds.

She tried to enter quietly, but Soren was awake and turned his head toward her. She glanced over at Alexander, who was still asleep.

"You're still here," she said softly, drawing close to the commander.

He gave an annoyed snort. "I thought you might see me lashed again if I left."

She couldn't help a small smile. Norah picked up the bowl of salve on the table and sat carefully on the bed beside him. She touched his back gently, testing the wounds. The lacerations had started to scab over, but they still needed care. She dipped her fingertips into the healing mixture and spread it across the torn skin.

"You don't have to tend me," he said.

She shrugged. "Well, I'm here, you're here, and you need it, so that's how this works."

Norah finished applying the salve and wiped her hands on a cloth. She picked up a rolled strip of clean linen. "Can you sit up?"

He pushed himself up, wincing.

She held the end of the linen roll against his chest, and he raised his arms, letting her wrap it around him. She looped the wrap over his shoulder and pinned it, then picked up another.

"You'll send him back to the North?" Soren asked as she worked.

She knew he would press her to send Alexander back. It was the right thing to do. It was what she should do, and she had agreed. Why was she struggling so much with it?

He grabbed her hand, stopping her. "You'll send him back?"

Reluctantly, she nodded. She pinned the second wrap, then pulled some fresh clothing for him from a side chair.

Soren rose gingerly from the bed. He pulled on his breeches but eyed the shirt she held for him.

"You should keep covered while you heal, and not let the wounds dry out," she said, stepping close. "Let me help."

But he pulled away. "I don't need help to dress myself," he said sharply.

She knew he felt vulnerable, and that it unsettled him. "I know you don't," she said back, with her own sharpness, trying to keep from sounding too caring. "But I don't want you messing up my bandaging."

He stood a moment, then yielded grudgingly, letting her pull the back of the shirt down as he pushed his arms through one at a time. Then he put on his boots. Dressed, he stopped and looked at her quietly. Silence—his means of thanks.

"Go on." She nodded to the door. "And have that bandage changed daily."

He gave an obliging nod and then glanced over at Alexander, who still slept, before letting himself out of the room.

Norah sighed heavily and made her way to Alexander. His eyes were closed and his face peaceful, but his back still bore the harshness of the day before. She sat on the bed beside him and brushed her fingers along the curve of his shoulder and down his arm.

His eyes opened at her touch, and he gave a small smile. She reached and swept the blond locks from his forehead. "How do you feel?" she asked.

"Sore, but better than I expected."

Norah checked the scabbed welts. She spread salve over his wounds again, as she had for Soren. He grimaced as she touched a particularly nasty abrasion.

"Sorry," she whispered. Her heart hurt. This was her fault. She should have sent him home sooner.

He watched her from the corner of his eye as she finished and wiped her hands on a clean cloth. He waited patiently, always so patiently. She reached her hand out and ran her fingers through his hair. He closed his eyes again under the feel of her touch.

"Do you miss Mercia?" she asked.

He opened his eyes and gingerly rolled onto his side to look at her. "All the time."

"Me too."

Alexander winced as he sat up.

"Easy," she told him. His eyes burned a brilliant blue. They were beautiful, and they brought a wave of emotion she hadn't expected.

"Hey, hey," he whispered as he took her hand. "What's the matter?"

Everything was the matter. She shook her head. "You have to go back. To Mercia."

He balked slightly, his brow creasing in objection. "I'm not leaving you."

"You have to," she insisted.

"You need me."

"I'm a queen with two kingdoms now, and both my military heads are here. Mercia needs you. Grandmother needs you."

"I can send Caspian," he argued.

"Alexander, I'm sending you."

His face twisted. "I dishonored you, I know, but—"

"I'm not sending you back because you dishonored me!" She couldn't fight the tears that threatened. "You could have been killed. So long as you remain in Kharav, it's my constant fear. Simply being here puts you in danger, and it puts the king in danger."

"I swear to you, Norah, I swear to you I won't bring harm to the king. You have my word."

And she believed him, but—

"It's not enough," she whispered. She stood and picked up a strip of linen. She pressed the end against his chest, but he reached up and covered her hand in his, making her pause.

"Norah," he said softly, looking up at her. "Come with me." His eyes bore into hers, begging.

Norah's heart ached. *Go with him*—how she wanted to. She brought her hand to his face and grazed his cheek with her fingertips. She felt her eyes well as she gave a sad smile. "You know I can't," she said. "Plus, I left things... harshly with the king. I..." She paused. "He'll be back before the moon wanes. I need to stay and settle the division of our kingdoms."

"He left?"

"He had to meet with a Horsemen tribe." Norah bit the inside of her cheek. "You need to leave before he returns."

Just the thought of his absence left her with a gaping hole. To not be able to hear his voice, to not see his smile, to not feel the warmth of his touch or to have his nearness. It stole her peace and crushed her heart. But she needed him to leave. To keep him safe. To send him away from this Shadow King—this Shadow King she loved.

The cold morning air gave away the unsteady emotion of her breath. Norah watched as the Northmen finished preparations for the journey to Mercia. Caspian would escort them back and return with a new unit of soldiers. Only her Mercian guardsman Titus would remain with her.

She stood in the courtyard to see them off. Alexander mounted his white destrier, and she stepped close, running her hand up the animal's neck and under the warmth of its thick mane. She looked up at him and gave a sad smile.

"How long?" he asked her. "How long will you let yourself be kept here?"

She didn't answer. She didn't know. She might not ever be able to leave, but she couldn't think about that now. It would break her.

The thought of not seeing him again—it was already breaking her. She needed him to leave before she couldn't let him go. "Goodbye, Alexander." She gave his mount a soft pat and stepped back.

His jaw tightened as he gave her a longing look of goodbye, then he reined his destrier around and urged it forward with his men following behind.

She walked back to the castle and found Soren waiting for her out front. Her heartache turned to bitterness. "I hope this satisfies you."

"Salar will be obsessed with your forgiveness when he returns."

"It's not to be had." She pushed past him and continued toward the castle. It was all she could do to make it back to the privacy of her bedchamber before the tears came. Alone, she sank to the cold stone floor and let the sadness take over.

CHAPTER TWELVE

The Northmen set a quick pace en route to Mercia, and Caspian could feel the army's spirits lifting as they set their thoughts on home. But an uneasiness sat in his stomach. They would ride through the western Canyonlands instead of east and through Bahoul as they normally traveled. While it was a faster route, it wasn't preferred. The route through Bahoul passed through the allied outreaches of Aleon. Safer lands—at least, they used to be safer.

With Mercia and Kharav now united, they would travel through Kharav's allies, mostly the Horsemen. The first test would be the Uru.

But Caspian was looking forward to one thing—seeing Tahla again.

It took almost three days to reach the Canyonlands. The army traveled much slower than Caspian and the lord commander had traveled before. He found himself growing impatient, but his frustration fell away as his attention shifted to his friend riding beside him.

Alexander rode lethargically, but not from his wounds. Caspian knew the justice was not looking forward to returning to his cherished Mercia, for he had left his heart in Kharav. They hadn't talked about what had happened—the lashing—and they wouldn't. Pain of the flesh was temporary. Caspian worried more about Alexander's spirit, which seemed to die more with each step farther from Kharav, each step farther from Norah.

"She worries for you," Caspian told him, breaking the silence in unusual form. "That's why she sends you back."

Alexander shifted from his thoughts. "She shouldn't."

"Yes, she should," he corrected him. Alexander wasn't thinking straight. "You don't generally threaten the life of a king like she did with no consequence. Especially the Shadow King."

Alexander's head jerked up and his brow furrowed. "What?"

Caspian gaped at him in surprise. Alexander hadn't known. "I'm sorry. I thought you knew."

"Norah threatened the king?"

Caspian nodded. "That's what he said, threatened him with his own sword."

Alarm grew in his eyes. "And what does he plan to do?"

He shook his head. "Nothing. He seeks her forgiveness."

Alexander looked back at him in disbelief. "Her forgiveness?"

It had dumbfounded Caspian too. But he saw something in the Shadow King he hadn't thought possible—he loved the queen. Surely that was the only reason Alexander was still alive and permitted to come and go from the Shadowlands as he did. Alexander was the Shadow King's greatest threat, yet he remained untouched. But for how long?

"She needs to take care," Caspian warned his friend. "And you do too."

It was almost dark when the canyons came into view. Caspian knew the unease that rippled through the army, the same unease he'd felt when he had come before. He'd be lying if he said he didn't feel it again. While he didn't think Tahla and the Uru would attack them, he wasn't sure they'd welcome them either. Not like the Shadowmen.

"Where are these Uru?" Alexander asked him. "And the village?"

"They are watching us, I'm sure," Caspian said as they reached the base. "They'll show themselves soon. Our men should wait here. Let us go to meet them."

Alexander cast a skeptical eye. He bid the men to stay at the base, and he and Caspian set into the canyons on foot.

Darkness layered the canyons, and Caspian found the footing difficult. He heard Alexander struggling as well. How did the Kharavian soldiers find their way so effortlessly in the night?

"It doesn't appear these Uru are going to show," Alexander said after a time.

Caspian looked up into the darkness. "They're here. I know it."

"Then what do they wait for?" Alexander asked. "Let's make camp with the men. We'll find our way through in the morning."

"We won't find our way through the canyons without their help."

"Then we'll go to the eastern pass and go through Bahoul."

That would take even longer than originally going the route through Bahoul. No. The Uru were here. "Tahla!" he called.

But there was no response.

Caspian combed the peaks of the canyons against the starlit sky, looking for movement. But all was still.

"Tahla!" he bellowed again.

Again, silence.

Alexander gave him a hearty pat on the shoulder and turned back the way they had come. Caspian sighed and finally followed.

But a woman's voice stopped them. "Is the North so bold to assume the Uru friends now?"

Caspian spun to see a shadow drawing close.

"Queen Norah would think so." He knew it was Tahla, and although he couldn't see her face, he knew she was smiling.

A torch was lit, and Caspian stepped back in seeing the Uru had surrounded them. Alexander put his hand on his sword, but Caspian held out his arm to settle him. Then he looked back at her, and his heart raced. She was just as he remembered, perhaps even more beautiful.

"How is my sister?" Tahla asked.

"She's well. She sends us back to Mercia for an exchange of men and goods. We hoped"—he hoped—"that you would see us through the canyons."

"I might be persuaded." Her lips curved into a sly smile. Then her eyes found Alexander. "Who's this?"

"The Mercian lord justice."

She drew closer to Alexander, and Caspian gave him a small nod of reassurance. "This is Tahla. Daughter of the Urun chief. The Uru are close friends of Salar and Kharav," he explained.

"And Salara," Tahla added, and Caspian smiled.

"And Salara," he echoed.

"Tahla." Alexander gave a respectful bow of his head.

"The Mercian lord justice," Tahla said curiously. "That sounds important. Are you an important man, Lord Justice?"

"He is the queen's right hand," Caspian told her. "Her commander."

Tahla exhaled a breath of realization. "The Bear." A smile peeled across her lips. She stepped closer. "I never thought I'd actually meet you."

Tahla took a torch from the Urun warrior next to her and moved even closer to Alexander. She circled him, running her eyes over him, studying him. "You don't look like a bear."

The corners of Alexander's mouth turned up. "I hope I don't disappoint."

Her smile returned. "Not at all."

A pang of jealousy coursed through Caspian, but he leashed it. He wasn't blind to seeing Alexander was an attractive man and drew the eyes of many women, but Tahla seemed mostly curious. And who wouldn't be curious about the famed Mercian justice?

"Have your men make camp where they are," she told them. "In the morning we'll provide passage. But you both, we'll host you this evening."

"We can stay with the army," Alexander said.

But she cut him a sharp eye. "I said we'll host you."

"We would be honored," Caspian interjected, and Tahla gave him a wry smile.

They made their way back to the small army and had the men set camp, while the Uru waited just inside the canyon.

Alexander eyed him warily. "Are you sure about this?"

"I'm not sure of anything," he replied.

After their men were settled, Alexander and Caspian followed Tahla through the narrow slot canyons until they opened up to the sky, then around to where the village appeared, just as he remembered.

People gathered as they approached.

"My father's away," Tahla said. "He's visiting another tribe. He'll be very disappointed to have missed you."

Caspian knew she was talking to Alexander. Of course the chief would want to meet him. Everyone always wanted to meet Alexander, but

Alexander was a man who kept to himself, and didn't particularly enjoy the attention. Caspian wouldn't have either in his place. The life of the justice was one he didn't envy.

When they reached the village, Tahla waved toward a small house and looked at Caspian. "You'll find your quarters there," she told him. Then she turned back to Alexander. "Bear, you'll come with me." And she led the lord justice toward the center of the village.

Caspian looked at the small house, then back to Alexander and Tahla disappearing around a corner behind a row of small houses. He sighed, disappointed. His return hadn't been as he had expected. But what had he expected? He chastised himself. He shouldn't have expected anything. He'd had only the briefest of exchanges with Tahla. She'd already forgotten, as he should.

Caspian made his way to the house provided to him and stepped inside. It was comfortable, with a prepared bed and a fire. He pulled off his sword and armor, laying them by a small table, and sat on the edge of the bed. His body ached, but he wouldn't complain. The queen was cared for. Alexander was leaving Kharav with his life and on his way back to the safety of Mercia. The Shadow King seemed committed to the peace the queen sought. War no longer loomed over the kingdoms. With this, he would be content.

A knock on the door pulled him from his thoughts, and he rose to answer. He opened it and then stepped back in surprise.

Tahla stood with a small plate of food. "May I?" she asked.

She didn't even need to ask. "Of course," he said as he swept the door wider and motioned her in.

"You delivered on your promise, Northman," she said as she put the plate down on the table.

He hoped his nervousness didn't show. "And what promise was that?"

She turned back toward him with a slight smirk. "That I would see you again."

She had remembered. His pulse quickened. "Were you looking forward to it?" he asked.

"Perhaps I was." She drew closer to him. "I wondered if, perhaps, you were looking forward to it too."

Caspian swallowed. He didn't find himself a particularly shy man, but with this woman, he couldn't think—not enough to trust his words. "Perhaps," he answered back finally.

"Is that all?" she prodded.

He stepped closer to her. She was playing with him. "You would ask a man to bare his soul?"

"Among other things," she said mischievously. She closed the gap between them, looking up, her dark brown eyes drawing him in. "Is that all?" she asked again.

In a move that surprised even himself, Caspian reached up and pushed a lock of hair back over her shoulder. How did she have such power over him? He would give her whatever she asked. "Perhaps I thought of you every day since I last saw you," he admitted. "Perhaps on the journey here, I was consumed with the thought of being able to see you again. Is that enough?"

She raised a brow with a wry smile. "If it were true." She didn't know how true it was.

"Do you think it's not? Enchantress?" He lowered his head closer to hers.

Tahla lifted her chin, bringing her lips to where they almost touched his. "Do you want to kiss me, Northman?"

"You don't even know me. You shouldn't let me kiss you."

She grinned. "I know you well enough. And that doesn't answer my question." She put her hand on his chest. "Do you?"

Was it an invitation? He brought a hand to her cheek, threading his fingers around to the nape of her neck and pulling her closer.

Just then, an Urun warrior called to Tahla from outside, interrupting them.

She answered, then gave Caspian a mischievous smile. "You're a dangerous one, Northman."

But Caspian knew he was the one in danger.

She slipped away and stepped toward the door. "Will you be returning?" she asked him.

He straightened, pulling himself back together. "Yes, I'll be returning to Kharav with a new unit from Mercia."

"Then I'll expect you to return through the canyons."

With certainty.

"And you owe me a kiss," she added.

Caspian's pulse thrummed in his throat, and he gave a shy smile. "On my return, then."

"Rest well, Northman," she said.

Caspian let out a breath as he watched her go.

CHAPTER THIRTEEN

True to Caspian's message, Mikael wasn't gone long. Only a week had passed, and the horns signaled his return. When he'd left, Norah thought it would be hard to face him again, but as she stood looking out the window of the chamber they shared, the flutter in her stomach surprised her. She pushed it down quickly. This wasn't a man she could let herself love. She'd move back into the sanctuary tonight.

Norah checked herself in the mirror and headed down to the courtyard. She walked into the square and took her place next to the lord commander.

"I didn't think you'd come," he said without turning his head.

She'd surprised them both, then. "I didn't think I would either."

The returning soldiers brought with them a new herd of horses, and Norah watched as they drove the animals toward the corrals behind the stables. These weren't the normal working horses that she often saw around the castle and city. They were giant beasts—destriers—like Soren's. Like Mikael's.

Mikael rode through the gates. Her heart pulsed painfully in her chest. She shouldn't have come, but she'd missed him. She hated herself for it.

He looked up at the castle, to her sanctuary window, expecting her to be there instead of in the courtyard. She wished she could see him underneath his helm. As if hearing her wishes and answering, he pulled it off. His gaze moved to her sanctuary window again. But she wasn't there. Melancholy hung from his face. Her heart hurt more. His eyes moved through the crowd until he found Soren, and he gave a nod.

Then his eyes locked on her.

Norah almost smiled at him but stopped. She couldn't let herself forget. The thought of Alexander being beaten brought back the wave of anger.

He urged his mount nearer to them, not taking his eyes from her. When he reached her, he swung his leg forward and over, and slid to the ground.

She stood, unmoving.

"Salara," he said softly.

"Salar," she replied. She'd never used his title, and it felt strange on her lips.

He closed the space between them but didn't touch her. "Have you been well?" he asked.

That was a relative term in this kingdom. She hadn't died. "Well enough. And you?"

"Not well enough," he said, even softer.

His words thrummed a chord within her, but she quieted the song that called. She couldn't be so quick to forgive him. He offered her his arm, and she stared at it. Had they been in the castle, in a more private setting, she would have refused it. But in the courtyard, in front of everyone, the slight would be noticed. He would deserve it, she told herself.

He didn't press her. He only stood, waiting.

She yielded. But instead of sliding her hand underneath and taking it, she simply laid her hand atop his vambrace, letting him feel her distance.

He led her through the throngs of people who had come to greet their salar, and into the castle. Behind the latch of the heavy wooden doors, she dropped her hand as they made their way through the great hall.

Mikael glanced at Soren. "We'll meet later. There's something I have to tend to," he said, shifting his gaze to Norah.

He meant her. So much for avoiding him. She led the way to their chamber, hoping to reach it before he said anything. Confrontations in front of others unnerved her, and she'd need all her strength for this. They swept inside, and he closed the door behind them.

He unfastened his belt and leaned his sword against the wall. He would be smart to leave it on, she thought to herself.

"You're still angry," he started.

She'd never stop being angry.

He stepped closer. "You hate me now, then?"

"I hate you," she jabbed. The words slipped out before she could stop them. They weren't entirely true; she hated herself more. She hated that she wanted to forgive him.

He stiffened. She'd wounded him. Good. He'd wounded her.

"I knew it was only a matter of time," he told her, his voice low.

"How astute," she knifed back, "that you can expect me to hate a monster."

His jaw tightened and anger flashed in his eyes. "I had no choice."

"You always have a choice!"

Heat radiated from him now as his own fury grew. "You're right," he snarled. "I should have killed him. If this is what it cost me, I should have killed him."

She struck him across the face, a stinging slap that hurt her too. She tried to strike him again, but he caught her hand. Norah twisted sideways, almost breaking his hold, but he spun around behind her, caging her with his arms and holding her close.

"I should have killed him, and I should have done it sooner," he hissed in her ear. She sank her teeth into his wrist, stunning him enough to wriggle loose and catch him with her elbow. He grunted and pulled her tighter, using his size to overpower her. "I should have taken his head when he first arrived," he said through his teeth. "When I was stronger. When your hate might have been bearable."

"Get off of me!" she cried. She struggled against him.

"But I was a fool," he said, "and I let myself love you. The seer showed me my fate, and I gave not the slightest resistance. The Bear will take everything from me. Even you. He doesn't even acknowledge me, in my own realm, so smug he is under your protection! He refuses my rule, refuses even to present himself at my return!"

"He's not here!" she screamed through the tears that had started to fall. "I sent him back!"

He stopped. He loosened his hold but did not release her. "What?"

"I sent him back to Mercia," she said between uneven breaths. Norah wept as he turned her to face him. She tried to shake him off, but he still held her. "I couldn't look at him. To see the wounds *you* gave him!" She hit his chest with her fist. He didn't bother defending against the blow.

She stilled, spent with emotion. "I sent him away because I can't protect him." She took another sobbing breath. "And because I love you, and I can't face him." Those were words she hadn't intended to speak.

The heat of his fury faded. They stood in the quiet, him watching her. She put her face in her hands. Mikael pulled her to him and held her. His touch was gentle now, and it only brought more tears from her. She cursed her emotion.

Mikael lifted her up and carried her to the bed, where he laid her down atop the cover of black silk. Then he crept up and lay beside her. He waited for her to calm, then he spoke. "Is it possible?" he asked softly. "For you to love me?"

Norah drew in a ragged breath of emotion. "It's impossible for me not to," she whispered. She hadn't wanted to admit it, but it had been true for a long time. That scared her. Regardless of what he'd done—and perhaps more frightening, what he might do—she loved him.

He moved over her, covering her body with his. The dark pools of his searching stare swept over her face, as if not quite believing. But she'd meant what she said.

And he saw it. The faint flicker in his eyes—she knew he saw it. He bent his head to hers, but she reached up and gripped him at the base of his jaw, making him pause. "But if you touch him again..."

Mikael's face grew serious. "I know," he said softly.

And she pulled him down to seal her promise with a kiss.

Chapter Fourteen

Cheers rang through Mercia as the Northmen crossed the bridge and entered the courtyard of the castle. Families met their loved ones with hugs and tears. Alexander should have been happy to return, yet he wasn't. He doubted happiness would find him again. Regardless, he covered himself with a smile as he nodded to the throngs of people who had come to greet them.

He dismounted and turned his horse over to a stable hand, then strode up the stairs of the castle judisaept to where he knew the council awaited him. As he made his way through the great hall, he stopped.

Catherine stood, alone in the hall, waiting, for news of Norah, no doubt. While she was regent in Norah's absence and concerned with the health of the queen, she was also Norah's grandmother, and she feared as a grandmother would.

He walked to her.

"Does she not come?" she asked when he reached her, her eyes brimmed with worry.

He shook his head. Norah hadn't come. She *wouldn't* come.

"Grandmother," he said softly. He didn't know what made him call her by the name he had used for her as a child, or what brought the crushing heaviness of emotion down on him, but it came suddenly and without warning. He couldn't say any more.

"Oh, my dear boy," she breathed, and pulled him into a tight embrace.

He clung to her and gave himself a moment—a moment to suffer his loss, to grieve, to feel the weight of hopelessness and defeat. So many feelings he denied himself, but he let them come this once.

And then the moment was over. He collected himself and pulled back.

"How is she?" she whispered.

"She's all right," he told her.

Catherine let out a long breath as she clutched her chest. She seemed to find the relief that escaped him.

It was true Norah was safe, but for how long? He'd been forced to leave her alone in the kingdom of a false ally, unable to see her, to protect her. Every day he faced the risk of losing her. Forever.

Catherine searched his face. "Why doesn't she come home?" She clutched at the ruffled collar of her gown as she stepped back and cast her gaze to the floor around her. "Did she not read my letter?"

It was a rhetorical question, and one he didn't answer. He wasn't sure he could answer. He hadn't seen Norah read it, but surely she wouldn't have ignored a letter from her grandmother. He had placed it in her hands almost two months prior, seemingly a lifetime ago.

"I told her to come urgently. She must come home." Catherine looked out the windows of the hall as she wrung her hands. "Why doesn't she come?"

He offered the only explanation he could. "The peace between Mercia and the Shadowlands hangs in a delicate balance. She stays and works to sustain it."

"She can't sustain it! Foolish girl. The council won't stand for this." Catherine's breaths became labored from her worry. "Phillip amasses troops at Aleon's southern borders. He intends to advance. She can't be there. She needs to come home, where she's safe. I told her to come urgently." She wavered slightly.

He grabbed her arm to steady her, but his mind reeled and his pulse quickened. "Phillip intends to advance against the Shadowlands?" With Norah there...

"No, against Japheth."

Alexander settled, but only slightly. If Phillip moved against his brother, the Shadow King's ally, the Shadowlands would join. No doubt that was the intent.

Catherine gripped his hand tightly, catching herself, then she released him. "We must go to the judisaept," she said, straightening. "The council awaits."

The council remained a governing body in the queen's absence, even though Catherine was regent. If they had a unanimous decision on a matter, they could override her, and even Alexander. Alexander didn't detest the council as Catherine did, but there were only a couple he deeply trusted, primarily James, who was more like a father to him.

Alexander strode alongside her to the judisaept, where the council was indeed waiting.

"Welcome home, Lord Justice," Edward greeted him as he stepped inside.

He bowed his head. "Thank you, Councilman." He almost added that it was good to be home, but he'd be lying.

The councilmen looked past him, then at each other.

"Where is the queen?" James asked.

Alexander swallowed. "She didn't come."

Edward looked at Catherine. "You were to convince her to return home in the letter."

"I tried, but she doesn't understand there's a larger plan at work."

Plan. Alexander stiffened. There was a difference between knowing Phillip would move against Japheth and planning with him. Planning with him would be... treason. Alexander curled his hand around the hilt of his sword. That, he wouldn't allow.

"You didn't tell her?" Edward asked.

Catherine scoffed. "I wouldn't put such words into enemy hands!"

Alexander's heart thundered as he realized—he'd helped them. He was also guilty, but his intentions were to make sure Norah had options. That she wasn't forced to stay in a situation that wasn't her choosing.

But this... She wasn't choosing this...

His eyes met James's, Mercia's most loyal adviser. Norah's father had trusted him. Alexander's father had trusted him. Alexander trusted him. James wouldn't tolerate treason, and James's eyes told him to settle.

"Our priority is keeping Queen Norah safe," James said, not taking his gaze from Alexander. "Protecting her and protecting Mercia."

Was it treason when they worked to protect her? And Catherine—for years she'd worked relentlessly to hold Norah's throne, in the face of uncertainty and doubt. She'd never betray her blood. Alexander settled, dropping his hand from his sword.

"We have to proceed cautiously," James said. "If the Shadow King discovers—"

"The Shadow King knows," Alexander said. "He knows I went to Aleon. He knows of Phillip's offer."

Catherine put a hand over her mouth, and the councilmen looked at each other in fearful surprise.

"They have eyes everywhere," Alexander said. "Tensions are escalating. It's why the queen bid my return." He left off the lashing. That wouldn't help the circumstance.

"Is she in danger?" Catherine asked, her voice barely a whisper.

"She's always in danger there," he cut back, sharper than he'd intended. He softened his tone. "But the Shadow King"—he paused—"he seems to... have a great affection for her."

"We could use that," Henricus said.

"Time is against us," Edward stressed. "Whatever we do, we must do it now, while her marriage remains unconsummated."

Alexander's chest tightened. He stayed silent. He wouldn't speak of what he suspected, what he feared. He wouldn't say that Norah returned the king's affections. That she now shared his bed. As far as the council was concerned, the marriage contract had not been fully executed. An alliance to Aleon was still an option—one that he would let them believe if it helped get her back to safety. But his skin still rippled with unease. They walked a fine line here.

"Tell us of the attack, the stabbing," Catherine said. "Who's to blame?"

Alexander's mind reeled back to the attack on Norah, and he stiffened. But he chose his words carefully. "A disgruntled citizen, offended by the marriage." The topic of the king's previous wives would only fuel the fires, and despite Alexander's desire to build a wall between Mercia and the Shadowlands, and between the Shadow King and Norah, he found himself pulling back.

"We need to get her out of there," Catherine breathed. She turned to James. "What do we do now?"

Edward looked at Alexander. "We must find a way to get you back to the Shadowlands."

"He can't return," Catherine argued. "It's too dangerous for him there, now that our efforts are known. And the vision of the Shadow King's fall shows the lord justice on the battlefield with Aleon, who is not yet by our side. We must trust the gods and wait. You can't force the hand of fate."

"I lean the same," James said.

Edward pursed his lips. "Send word to Aleon, then. Phillip must know the queen is still there, and to hold. We wait—for the Shadow King to be drawn from his shadows."

Alexander's hand rested on the hilt of his sword again.

His feet fell heavy through the hall as he made his way to his chamber. Alexander's mind was chaos, warring with his heart. The comfort of home should come as consolation, but it didn't. He found himself wishing he were back in the Shadowlands, with Norah. He would follow her anywhere, even into the fires of hell.

Jude came quickly as Alexander stepped into the chamber. "My lord." He bowed. "It's good to have you home."

"Good to see you, Jude." He greeted his servant with a friendly nod. Jude had worked for him for well over twenty years, and Alexander was fond of him. "I hope you've been well."

"I have, my lord."

"How's my brother?"

Jude raised his brows. "Asks the council about you incessantly, but he's well."

Alexander couldn't help a smile. "Send for him"—he held up his fingers—"actually, let me wash first."

"Of course, my lord." Jude heated water for the tub in the side bath chamber as Alexander sat in a chair and pushed off his boots by the heel.

He stood and pulled off his travel-worn clothes and then stepped wearily to the tub and into the bath.

Suddenly, Jude stepped back in alarm.

Alexander had almost forgotten—his back. It was a few weeks healed now, the pain gone, but no doubt still evidenced on his skin. "Not a word," he said as he sank into the steaming water. His servant nodded obediently and left him to wash.

Alexander bathed quickly. He wanted to see how Adrian fared. His body ached, but he'd have to muster the strength to spar as well. His brother loved showing him his progress with the sword. He had become quite good, rivaling even Alexander. Any day now he might overtake him. That would be a proud day.

He stepped from the bath, drying quickly, and pulled on the clean breeches Jude had laid out for him. The water seemed to have returned some of his energy. He stretched his arms out, enjoying the prickle across his skin from the chilled air. Then he pulled the clean linen shirt from the hook on the wall and stepped out of the bath chamber and back into his room to the vanity.

"Jude, I—"

"Gods' mercy!" Catherine's voice rang out.

He stopped, and his chest tightened. She'd seen his back. He turned to face her. Her lip trembled in horror.

Alexander glanced at Jude in the corner of the room, who shook his head fervently that he hadn't betrayed him. "You may go," he told him, and Jude slipped out of the room.

"You've been tortured," Catherine breathed.

It wasn't entirely different from how he expected she might react. "I wasn't tortured. I was punished. By the king."

"For what cause?" she demanded.

"I'd prefer not to discuss it." But he knew that wouldn't be the end of it.

"And what makes him think he has the right to punish the lord justice of Mercia in such a way?"

"He's the king of Mercia," he snapped. As much as he hated to say it, it was true. He took a breath, drawing back his patience. It was out of concern she was reacting in this way, he told himself.

"You'll tell me what happened," she pressed.

"I said I don't want to talk about it."

"You'll tell me, or I'll convene the council to address the matter of your torture."

His nostrils flared. He didn't think she would take it that far. And the council was already walking a line he wasn't comfortable with. "I said I was punished. Not tortured."

Catherine stepped to him, her cheeks shaking. There was real fear in her eyes, and it sobered him. He calmed himself. Slowly, she moved around him. There was no use trying to hide it from her. He stood silently. Her breath hitched behind him, but she said nothing. Then, slowly, she came back around to face him. Her eyes were large and rimmed red.

"You'll tell me what happened," she insisted.

"A crime against the crown," he said finally. "I engaged with the Destroyer. It created chaos in the ranks, and twelve men died, Northmen included. It's my punishment."

Catherine shook her head. "How could Norah allow such a thing?"

"Did you not hear what I just said?" he asked, his voice sharp and angry now. "I was guilty. The Destroyer was charged the same, and he bears the same marks I do."

"Norah should have stopped it!" she said through her tears.

"She tried!" he thundered back. "She begged him for mercy. But we'd already been given mercy in keeping our heads. Caspian had to hold her."

Catherine gaped at him in horror.

"She threatened his life that night," he continued. "She threatened the Shadow King."

"What?" Catherine's voice shook.

There was no hiding his rage now. "If she'd have done that to a Mercian king, she would have been guilty of high treason and her fate much worse, even as queen. I'm sure it's the same in the Shadowlands, except... the Shadow King loves her." He forced an icy calm back to his voice. "So, no, she didn't *allow* this to happen."

Rage steamed from his skin. "It's so easy for you and the council to judge her, to question her. But you have no idea the sacrifices she makes. She bears the burden of our people the best she can, this burden you like to remind her of so frequently." Alexander's anger left him breathless. "And you've abandoned her in it. Everyone has. And now she's all alone."

Catherine stood, speechless, whether by his words or by her regret, he didn't care. He pulled on his shirt and boots and left her to the afternoon.

CHAPTER FIFTEEN

The morning air hung cold and wet, heavy enough to drown a person, but it didn't matter. Nothing could dampen her spirits. Norah pulled on her gloves and mounted Sephir, looking back at the soldiers who were preparing to depart. It seemed the entire Crest was to travel with her, but she wasn't going to complain. It had taken a great amount of convincing for Mikael to allow her to visit Hamed and Marta and their grandchildren who'd helped her to the seer, and even more convincing to do so without him escorting her. It didn't require a king to see her visit friends. Apparently, it did require the commander of the entire Kharavian army, who had nothing more important to do. Soren insisted on going, and of course Mikael had agreed. At least her Mercian guardsman Titus was accompanying her as well—not all her travel companions would make her want to jump off another cliff.

Mikael stood in the courtyard to see her off. He eyed the large wagon that accompanied them. "What is all that?" he asked.

She smiled down at him from atop Sephir. "Gifts. And I'm very excited to give them."

He raised an amused brow and nodded. "Here," he said, pulling a purse of coins from his belt and holding it out. "Add this."

She leaned over and pulled him close. "Who is this kind soul?" she teased him.

"This family took care of my salara," he replied. "I'm in their debt."

She smiled and kissed him. "I'll return tomorrow."

"I'll do my best not to come out after you before then."

She feigned a scowl. Then she straightened and urged Sephir out from the courtyard, starting her way through the hills and toward the valley.

The journey was quiet but enjoyable, and Norah let the daydream of seeing the small family again entertain her mind. She wondered what Calla kept herself busy with, and how Cohen fared. She hoped Hamed and Marta's garden was coming along nicely, and she was excited for them to see the gifts she had brought.

Titus rode alongside her.

"I'm glad you've come along," she told him.

"Are you expecting things to run afoul?"

"No, of course not." She smiled. "I'm excited for you to meet Calla and Cohen. More than anything, I want to take Calla to Mercia—her skill with a bow..." She smiled again. "And Cohen, he's an incredible swordsman, and at such a young age. I think it will be good for them to see Mercia and Kharav's greatest warriors: you, Bhastian, Kiran, the others."

"Do they not have anyone?"

"They have their grandparents. Their grandfather trained them. Their parents died in battle, fighting for Kharav."

"So, they're generational soldiers," he said with an approving nod. "Like me."

"Your father was in the army?"

Titus nodded again. "Yes, and his father, and his father, and on a long line before. Almost as long as the lord justice's family."

So much pride in family commitment. She could understand that. "Will you have any children of your own, Titus?" she asked him with a small smile. "To carry on the line?"

The seasoned guard grew quiet for a moment. "Regal High, I..." his voice fell low, keeping his words private. "This isn't where I would normally make such a request, but when I return to Mercia, it's my intention to find a wife. With your permission."

Norah gasped. "Of course you have my permission! I'm so happy for you!"

He smiled bashfully. She almost thought she saw some pink in his cheeks.

"Well, first let's see if a woman will have me," he said.

"You're a handsome man, Titus, and honorably stationed. I'm sure you'll have no trouble."

He gave an objecting snort, but she could tell he was happy.

The afternoon sun rose high with Norah's spirits.

"Why are you smiling?" Soren asked, bringing his horse beside hers.

"Oh. There you are. I'd almost forgotten you had come along to suck the joy out of me."

"You've been grinning ever since we left Ashan."

"Only you can make that sound like a bad thing," she said. Then she sighed. Was this how the entire journey would be with him? "I'm just looking forward to this visit," she explained in an attempt at civility. "These people are important to me. Let me be happy about it."

To her surprise, he didn't goad her further.

By late afternoon, the homestead appeared in the distance, and Norah felt a surge of excitement. She urged Sephir forward.

As they approached, Calla emerged from the house, with Cohen close behind her holding his sword. When she saw Norah, a grin came to the girl's face, and she bounded off the porch to meet them. "Salara!" she cried as Norah slid down from the mare.

"Calla." Norah smiled as she embraced the girl warmly. She looked over Calla's shoulder at the boy. *Hi*, she signed. Cohen smiled shyly and gave a bow, signing back to her.

"He said he's happy to see you, Salara. So am I!"

"I'm happy to see you both too! Where are Hamed and Marta?"

"In the garden, of course. I'll get them!" And the girl ran to fetch her grandparents.

Hamed and Marta came from around the side of the house, wiping their hands on their garden aprons.

"Salara!" Hamed said, bowing. "Quite unexpected, but we're most happy to see you again."

Norah clasped his hands with a broad smile. "And I'm happy to be here again." She looked at Marta, and the woman took her hands with a warm squeeze.

"Salara," Marta said in a heartfelt welcome.

Hamed stopped suddenly as his eyes found Soren. "Lord Commander," he said as he straightened as much as he could, then bowed.

Soren returned a reverent nod, something Norah hadn't expected. They didn't seem to know each other, but she didn't ask. Soren wouldn't want her to do so publicly.

"I've come on a proper visit this time," Norah told them, drawing the conversation back. "I wanted to thank you for all of your help. It meant the world to me."

"You've come all this way to thank us?" Marta asked.

"Yes, and I've brought a gift for you."

"Oh, Salara." Marta gasped. "You're too kind."

"It's the least I could do." Norah led them around the wagon and pulled back the cover. "Rice, grain, flour, dried meats. But perhaps most precious of all"—she pulled out a small, wrapped package from beside the bags of food and handed it to Marta—"clippings and roots for your garden."

The woman unwrapped it carefully and her eyes widened.

Norah pulled more wrapped packages, and Marta's eyes welled as she looked in each one. "Tresantha, oleiden, serium, and many more."

"Where did you get these?" Marta breathed. "They're only found in Japheth."

"They're clippings from the private garden and conservatory in the castle." Norah grinned. Mikael's grandfather had retrieved them for his Japheth bride, in efforts to give her a piece of home in Kharav.

Marta smiled, teary-eyed, as she looked at Hamed, and he put an arm around her.

Norah felt her own eyes brim with emotion. "I just worry that the winter probably won't allow them in the ground now."

"We'll start them inside. Then we'll move them out in the spring. Oh, Salara, thank you." Marta smiled through her tears. "Come inside. Surely the ride's been long. Let's get you in and fed."

The Crest made quick work of the supplies in the wagon and then set their attention on a small camp for the evening. Cohen was happy to help them while Calla made up a bed in the house for Norah. With the plant cuttings tended to, Marta busied herself with dinner. Norah found herself in the kitchen, looking for an opportunity to be useful. "What can I do to help?" she asked as Marta kneaded dough.

"Please make yourself comfortable. Dinner will take no time at all."

Norah smiled as she picked up the basket of vegetables and started washing them in the basin. "I'm not going to sit here while everyone else works."

"Isn't that what salaras do?" Calla joked as she joined them.

"Callamine! You'll show respect!" Marta scolded, but Norah laughed out loud.

"Amah, it was only a joke," Calla said quickly.

"And a very funny one." Norah laughed again.

Calla smiled, pulling out a cutting board and knife, and started to cut the vegetables as Norah washed them.

"Oh my," Marta shook her head. "I can't believe I have Salara cooking in my kitchen."

Soren and Hamed entered from the outside, followed by Cohen. They all froze, astonished, at the sight of Norah in the kitchen.

"Salara," Soren said slowly.

"Say a word and you'll be cutting potatoes," she warned.

Soren looked at Hamed and then Cohen, and the boy shrugged with a smile.

Cohen went quickly to fetch more water, while Hamed positioned the cast-iron pot over the fire. Calla scooped the chopped vegetables into the pot, gave a happy sigh, and sank down into a chair by the table as everything cooked.

"Calla, Cohen," Norah said, "might I have a private word with your grandparents before dinner?"

"Of course," Calla said, and Cohen followed her outside.

Norah glanced at Soren, then widened her eyes to silently urge him along.

"I'll check on the horses," he grumbled, before seeing himself out.

After the door closed, Norah turned back to Hamed and Marta. "There is something else," she started. "I wanted to invite you back to Ashan with me. Both of you, and Calla and Cohen. It would be an easy life, and the children could study and train. They could make a future for themselves."

Hamed looked at Marta and she smiled sadly.

The woman turned her eyes back to Norah. "I'm not from Kharav," she said. "A life in Ashan would not be an easy one for us, with me as an outsider. It's one of the reasons we live out here."

"I'm an outsider too," Norah told her. "But Ashan is beautiful. And I'll see you're taken care of."

"With all due respect, you're salara. Any other outsider in Kharav is a slave, and treated as such, even with a queen's support." She looked back at Hamed. "And we're happy here."

"What of the children?" Hamed asked his wife gently. "We can't keep them here forever. Augustan and Misa would have wanted a life for them, more than we can give them."

"They'd have challenges too," she said. "With their names. And Cohen being deaf."

Hamed shrugged. "The lord commander doesn't have a Kharavian name."

Marta scoffed. "He's the lord commander!"

Soren wasn't a Kharavian name? "Who are Augustan and Misa?" Norah asked instead.

Hamed smiled sadly. "Augustan was our son, and Misa, his wife." Marta's eyes welled as she stared at her hands clasped on the table.

Norah felt a pang of guilt. "I'm sorry," she said. "It wasn't my intention to bring back painful memories, or ask you to part with the children. Forgive me."

"We're extremely grateful for your kindness," Hamed said, "and for the offer. It's one"—he looked at Marta—"that we should most seriously consider."

Norah smiled apologetically. "I don't want to pressure you. Think about it. I'll be happy with whatever you decide."

Dinner was delicious, and Norah found herself accepting a second helping after Hamed offered. She looked around the table at the smiling eyes and the sound of laughter, and her heart was full. This little family felt like her own. She loved this place, and she loved these people.

After they ate, Calla and Cohen took hearty bowls of food outside to Soren and the soldiers. Norah smiled at Marta as she helped the woman clear the table.

"Could they visit us?" Marta asked suddenly. "If they went to Ashan."

Norah put down the plate she had just picked up and took Marta's hand. "Of course," she breathed. "Regularly. I would come myself at times, if that's all right."

Slowly, the old woman nodded. "All right. They should go. They should go with you. And they should return when you visit."

Norah smiled through her tears and hugged Marta.

The winter wind was cold, but Norah found warmth in the energy between Calla and Cohen as they excitedly journeyed back to Ashan. Calla's face held a wide grin, pulling a smile from her brother. Norah loved Cohen's smile. It was shy and sweet and full of heart. He wore his father's sword across his back, and Norah couldn't look at him for more than a moment without getting a little emotional. She wished their parents could see how beautiful their children had turned out to be.

She fell back, closer to Soren, and let Calla and Cohen ride ahead. The commander had been scowling at her all morning since finding out the siblings would be returning with them. Might as well get the argument over with.

His low voice cut through the beauty of the morning. "What are we going to do with children at the castle?"

She shrugged. "They'll study, and train. I promised their grandparents."

"You can't be serious. A mute and a farm girl?"

"He's not mute, he's deaf," Norah cut back. "And, yes, keen observation. Calla is a girl."

"They don't meet eligibility standards for the Kharavian army. Who will train them?"

She hadn't thought of that, but she refused his scorn. "Titus," she said. From the corner of her eye, she saw her Northman look at her.

Soren sighed through his teeth. "Surely they don't meet Northern standards either."

"We're not in Mercia."

Soren looked at Titus, who offered no support to Soren's objection.

"Did you know Hamed?" she asked him, changing the subject.

"No. Why?"

She shrugged. "When you saw him, you just seemed to respect him, that's all. It made me think you knew him."

"He is a man to be respected. His markings tell he was a great warrior. He's had many kills."

Norah shifted uncomfortably. "How could you tell? He wore a long-sleeved tunic." It was hard to imagine Hamed killing anyone.

The lines in the corners of his eyes deepened. He really didn't like explaining things to her, but it didn't intimidate her anymore. She found it rather amusing now.

"Kill markings are the only ones to reach the outside wrist," he shared finally. He extended his own arm out from underneath his cloak, showing her the patterns along his skin. "They start at the elbow, a lined triangle for every three kills—a solid for every ten. If one has markings to his wrist, he's a man to be respected."

Norah's eyes stayed on his skin. Geometric patterns formed larger images, deceivingly beautiful. Some swirled like currents of the sea, some were chained like mountains. She hadn't realized they were all made of triangles before. From his elbow to his wrist. So many triangles. So many deaths. And Hamed had them too.

"Mikael doesn't wear marks like that," she said. Surely it wasn't for lack of accomplishment. But she found herself happy for it—she didn't want to be reminded.

"Because he's salar." His eyes betrayed his snarky smirk underneath his wrap. "But if he did, he'd have more than I do."

She wasn't sure she believed him, but it was enough to drown the gratefulness she'd felt only moments prior. She pushed her disquiet down. This was what Soren liked to do to her. She wouldn't let him.

"Well, if Hamed was a great warrior, his grandchildren will be great warriors too." Preferably without scoring their arms with triangles.

Soren snorted his annoyance. Then his brow changed, and his eyes narrowed as he looked out across the hills. "You keep on with the Crest," he told her. "I'll catch up." And he urged his horse northwest, away from the group.

What had he seen that he was going to check out? She didn't really care. She was happy to be rid of him for a while. Norah continued with Titus beside her.

Titus urged his mount closer. "Will you really have me train them?" he asked her as he looked at Calla and Cohen up ahead.

"I'll have someone train them. It'll likely not be you, though." She smiled at the relief on his face. "Maybe Caspian, but don't tell him."

He chuckled.

They reached Ashan just before dark, and Norah saw Calla and Cohen to a temporary room in the castle until she could sort a permanent place for them. With them settled, she headed toward her own chamber.

Mikael was waiting for her. Norah had passed Soren in the hall on her way, so he'd have already informed the king of her new wards.

"Salara," Mikael greeted her with a kiss and pulled her close. "I almost rode out to find you."

She pulled back to look up at him and snaked her brow in mock disapproval. "I said I'd return today, and I did."

"Today. *Day*. It's night."

"I had to see Calla and Cohen taken care of. I've put them in the east quarters. I know they're for royal guests, but I'll have them out once I've found suitable accommodation for them tomorrow."

"Who?" he asked.

"Calla and Cohen, children from the family who helped me. I've brought them to study here in Ashan. Did the lord commander not tell you?"

He shook his head. "No, but no matter. Whatever you desire." He pulled her close again and kissed the top of her head.

Strange that Soren hadn't mentioned it. She had expected some kind of resistance, and smiled appreciatively in finding none.

They readied for bed. Norah climbed under the quilts and nestled against Mikael's warmth. He wrapped his arms around her, but his mind was elsewhere.

"Are you all right?" she asked.

"I am now that you're here." He tightened his arms around her. "I have to tend to something in the morning with the lord commander. I'll be gone before you wake, but I should return in time for breakfast."

"What are you going to do?" she asked.

He shifted and moved on top of her. "Right now, I'm going to make love to my wife."

Norah smiled as he lowered his lips to hers.

CHAPTER SIXTEEN

Norah woke with a chill. Her eyes fluttered open, and she reached across the empty bed beside her. She knew Mikael wasn't there. He had mentioned he'd be leaving early with Soren, but it wasn't his absence that disturbed her. Something unsettling hung in the air. She sat up. And gasped.

A strange man sat in the corner chair.

He wore fitted clothes, dark. Black. His head was covered with a formfitting cloth that showed only his eyes, similar to the Kharavian head wrap. But it wasn't a Kharavian wrap. And he wasn't Kharavian.

He waited quietly, watching her.

"Who are you?" she demanded. "And what are you doing here?"

He let out a low chuckle.

"Guards!" she cried. But the room was quiet. "Guards!"

"There is no one else," he said, then there was a sickening lull. "Only you and me."

Mikael stood with Soren around the remains of a small campfire in the hills, deeply bothered. They'd traveled out after Soren had spotted it on his return to Ashan. There were intruders in Kharav. He studied the campfire. It had aged a day or two, with very few clues around. Salara had just traveled through the area close by. The intruders had been near her, and the thought unsettled him.

"Large enough that it's more than one man," Soren said as he kicked over a charred limb in the ash. "And no sign of horses. They have to be on foot to leave no trace."

"They're bold to build a fire."

"They're bold to be in Kharav," Soren replied. "Do you think they're in the city by now?"

The thought seeded Mikael's anger. "Quite possibly."

There were only three ways to enter Kharav. One was through the labyrinth of one of the two canyon passes, under the watchful eyes of the Uru to the west and Kharavian forces to the east. Another was by sea, but cliffs lined Kharav's coasts and were violent with waves. A man could neither land a boat nor swim ashore. Kharav held only two ports safe for a ship's entry, and they were heavily guarded. The last option was crossing the river from the southwest kingdom of Osan, but since the incident with the Osan prince, where Soren had killed the group of trespassing young men, Mikael had increased forces along the border.

A man would have to be incredibly skilled to enter undetected. For several men, it was near impossible. Yet they were here. How?

"Find them. I want to know who these men are."

"What do you want?" Norah asked angrily, slowly sitting up more and getting her legs underneath her. She cursed her long nightgown. It would encumber her in a fight if there were to be one. And there would definitely be one.

Although his face was covered, she could see the wicked smile in his eyes. He stood slowly and then stepped toward the bed. He wasn't a large man, but the ease of his movement told her he was dangerous.

"Don't come any closer," she warned, backing toward the opposite edge. Almost quicker than she could react, he leaned forward to grab her. She narrowly escaped his reach, slipping off the bed and bolting for the door.

But he was fast and he caught her arm, twisting her back toward him. She fought against his hold, and the dagger at his hip brushed her stomach. Norah whipped it from its sheath and plunged it into his side, just under his armpit. A solid hit. She wasn't sure if it had reached his heart, but it would steal his breath.

The man grunted, releasing her, and stepped back in surprise. He looked down at the blade as the wound poured blood down his side, and he struggled to inhale. Then he fell to his knees and forward onto the stone floor as his strength left him. A hit to the heart. She'd been lucky.

But there was no time for relief. She threw open her chamber door and froze at the sight of the empty guard post. Blood streaked the wall and puddled on the floor. Whose blood was that? Who had been on guard? She fought back her panic and dashed out, but another man with a covered face stood in the middle of the hall.

"Impressive," he said. "You surprise me, Queen Norah." His accent wasn't entirely foreign.

Confusion hit her as she glanced back toward the bedchamber. Had he seen her stab the first man? But that would be impossible.

"Who are you?" she seethed.

"Let's say, a very old friend."

"Friends don't kill each other," she snapped.

"No, I suppose that's what family's for."

Again, his words confused her. "What do you want?"

"Is it not obvious?" he sneered, walking toward her. "You."

She bared her teeth. "Well, then, I'll have to disappoint."

He drew his sword as Norah stepped back, trying to devise a plan. She didn't have a weapon, but there was the downed man's dagger in her chamber. She spun and ran back toward the room, and he chased after her.

What had happened to her guard? She reached the chamber in only a few steps, but he was close behind. She tried to swing the door closed behind her, but he was already in the doorway. He bellowed as it caught his arm. Norah threw her weight behind it, but he surged forward, forcing her back. She lunged toward the dead man and pulled the dagger from him, then spun to face her attacker.

He swung his sword, and she jumped back. His blade caught the fabric of her gown and sliced it open. He swung again, high this time, and she ducked. It hit the post of the bed and lodged itself into the wood—a mistake. She jumped forward, slicing the dagger into his forearm. He released the hilt and staggered back, and she was ready. She jerked the sword free and advanced her attack. He wore no armor or leathers—cocky bastard—leaving his only defense to avoid her swings. She brought the sword down hard. He reached up to shield himself and the blade cut into his arm, partly severing it. He bellowed again as she whipped forward with the dagger in her other hand and plunged it into his gut. Then she arced the sword in a final blow, slicing open his neck. He fell back against the wall, spilling blood in fading pulses onto the stone floor.

Norah fled the chamber, trying to keep the fear from taking over. That had been close. Too close. It was by luck she had escaped them. They hadn't known her skill with a blade, and she'd caught them by surprise. The dagger and the sword were sticky in her hands, but she clutched them tightly. She passed a side hall. And froze.

Titus lay crumpled on the floor.

"Titus!" she screamed as she ran to him. She dropped the blades and pulled his face to look at her. But he didn't move. Norah let out a sob. "No! Titus!" she cried as she held his head.

She needed to find help. She stood shakily, grabbing her sword and dagger again, and using the wall for support as she staggered back into the main hall. She'd almost reached its end when two men turned the corner. *More attackers.* Where were they coming from? How were there so many? And where was her guard?

"You keep surprising me," one sniggered at her, as if continuing the conversation.

"Who are you?" she screamed in rage.

"As I said, an old friend. But not a friendly one."

Norah shook her head, trying to catch her breath through her tears and steady her mind. It was as if they were all the same man. And they were here to kill her.

The man to her left attacked first, cutting his sword upward. She jumped back and swung down, meeting it with her own. Then she turned and broke past, fleeing down the staircase. The men were fast, and one caught her at the bottom. She wrenched free but didn't run again. She couldn't escape them, and she clenched her blades as she faced them.

One of the men charged forward, and she turned just in time to escape his intent, but as he reeled past, it put her in between them. One chuckled, and they both backed up a couple of steps, giving space, taunting her.

Norah stood with her back toward the wall, looking left and right to keep her eyes on both. Panic threatened. Where was Bhastian? Sonal? Javed? Anyone? Was she all alone?

"*Salara,*" the man to her right taunted. "Not queen of Aleon. Even I didn't realize the vision of you on the Shadow throne meant a marriage to the Shadow King."

How did he know about the vision? And what did he care? "You're from Aleon?" she asked between her teeth. "You're here for revenge?"

"I'm most certainly here for revenge," said the man to her left. "But I'm not from Aleon."

She was confident now that only one man was speaking to her. "How are you doing that?"

"I have many talents," the assassin replied, now speaking again through the man on her right.

He was playing with her. Her skin burned in anger, and she attacked, driving him backward with her sudden onslaught. He wasn't quick enough, and she sliced her sword across his side. He fell to his knees, but it wasn't a fatal wound. She spun to meet the second man, and their swords clanged as she was forced back, toward the dining hall.

"I was disappointed initially," he said between strikes, "until I realized." His eyes smiled. "I can break both the Shadow King and Alexander with the same blow."

With *her.*

Norah paused. No one called Mikael the Shadow King in Kharav. And no one called the lord justice Alexander. These weren't men from Kharav. They weren't from Aleon. And whoever was talking to her knew Alexander well enough to call him by his name.

"Why?" she asked. "Why have you come?"

"They'll suffer, as I have suffered. Especially Alexander." His wrap couldn't hide the quaking breath of his anger. "Where is he? I want to see his pain. The pain he feels when he realizes he couldn't save his queen. Just before he dies."

Norah bared her teeth with an angry satisfaction. "You won't find him here. He's gone." She smiled when she saw the rage flash in his eyes.

"He's here!" the assassin barked back at her. "His blood touched your skin not even a fortnight ago."

From the lashing. How did he know that? She didn't have time to think about it. The second man was on his feet again and moved together with his partner assassin toward her. But Norah's fear was gone. Fury surged through her, and she lunged forward. She threw her dagger at the wounded man, hitting him squarely in the shoulder, and she swung her sword with full force at her other opponent. He met her with his own blade, and they twisted together in a dance of death.

He was larger than the other men, and their blades hit with a force that shot pain into her hands and up her arms. He was strong and quick, and she was tiring. She was desperate for help. He heaved another swing, and she dodged, knocking his shoulder and using his momentum to drive him sideways. She took her chance and bolted toward the dining hall.

Norah pushed through the doors and cried out to the servant who was carefully setting the table for breakfast. He spun around, knocking everything on the side of the table to the ground with a noisy clatter. The assassin laughed as he mercilessly cut him down.

She stumbled backward, turning to flee, but he caught her from behind again. She tried to swing her sword, but he was too close, and he tore it from her hands.

He flung her to the ground and straddled her, grasping her neck and squeezing the air from her. Norah clawed at his hands and beat at his arms, but his eyes smiled down at her. Darkness started closing in, and she struggled against it. She felt herself slipping away.

Then her fingers found something to grasp at her side—a fallen candle iron. She swung it up with as much force as she could muster, hitting her attacker on the side of the head and knocking him off her. She scrambled to her feet, gasping for breath, and fled from the dining hall, toward the throne room.

But the other assassin blocked her path. She backed up, her mind racing on where to run.

She heard a chuckle to her left as the attacker that had choked her walked slowly toward her from the dining hall. There was a split above his eye from the candle iron, with blood flowing freely. It hadn't been enough to take him down, though. A hopelessness washed over her. She had no fight left in her. She turned and darted down the side hall. Her last resort for help might kill her, but she was already a dead woman.

Mikael slid off his horse in the courtyard and stormed into the castle, followed by Soren. "I want increased guard around the castle," he said as he made his way toward the dining hall.

"And I'll bring in more men to sweep the hills," Soren said.

Mikael gave a nod, then he pushed open the dining hall door, where he expected to find Salara. They both stopped.

Before him lay an empty room with a dead servant surrounded by scattered table settings on the floor.

Mikeal's pulse picked up in his chest. He stood only a moment before he broke with a start and raced toward his chamber, with Soren close behind him. He bounded up the stairs two at a time, his sword ready. They reached the upper hall and wound around but paused at the side hall where the body of the large Northman lay.

His pulse raced faster. Had these intruders made it to Salara? He charged toward the bedchamber. As he rounded the corner, he stopped for half a heartbeat. Blood scored the wall at the end of the hall where the guards should be, and his heart hammered in his throat. The door to their chamber was partway open.

Mikael exploded into the room, flames of fury licking his skin, ready to rain his fire on any soul that dared to touch her.

But all was quiet.

The body of an assassin lay on the floor. He seethed with rage as he swept his eyes over the room and saw another assassin, dead on the floor as well. There had been a struggle, but there was no sign of Salara.

Soren brushed past the bodies to the bath chamber. "She's not here," he called back.

Mikael cursed under his breath, and they moved out quickly, down the stairs and back toward the dining hall.

Where would she have gone from there? And where were all the guards?

"Salar," Soren called, stopping him in his step. He motioned down the side hall.

Mikael looked down the hall toward the painting of his mother and late father, the painting before the hall to Soren's chamber. Just to the left of it—a smear of blood.

They darted forward and thundered down the hall. As they neared Soren's chamber, his heart pulsed battle fury through his body. The door was closed, but blood marked the frame. He let the rage take over.

Mikael burst through the door.

Cusco lay lazily in the center of the floor, and Norah sat beside him, stoically stroking the giant dog's back softly with her fingernails. A dead assassin lay on the floor. Nearer to the wall, Cavaatsa pulled entrails from another assassin's stomach with her razor-sharp teeth, eating eagerly as Norah watched her in a trance. She couldn't think, she couldn't speak. All she could do was sit with the dogs. And breathe. Breathe to keep the panic from taking over.

The door to the chamber crashed open, and it sent Cavaatsa backward with a threatening snarl. Cusco got his legs underneath him, prepared to attack.

"Cusco! Cavaatsa!" Soren's voice settled them. Norah didn't get up, but she let out a sobbing breath of relief as Mikael and Soren thundered into the room.

Mikael rushed to her side, pulling her up and wrapping his arms around her, almost suffocating her in his hold. He breathed heavily into the top of her hair, and just held her. She needed his arms as her tears came. Normally, she cursed her emotion, but now she let it come. Death had been close. She hadn't thought herself afraid of death before, when faced with it on her own terms, but this was different. Killing the first two assassins had been sheer luck, but the second two had played with her like a mouse—taunting her. What scared her more—while she might have been their target, they'd come to hurt Alexander and Mikael. And they could have.

Mikael pushed her back slightly, moving his hands around her face, cupping it, looking her over with fearful eyes. He asked her a question, but his words didn't register. His hands moved down her arms and body as he carefully looked over the bloodstained nightgown for any signs of injury.

"Are you hurt?" he asked her. Perhaps that was what he had asked her before.

Slowly, she shook her head, and he pulled her close to him again. They stood for a moment. Then Mikael pushed her back and made her meet his eyes. "You used the dogs?" he asked. "They could have killed you."

"Cusco and Cavaatsa would never harm Salara," Soren told him.

"I was already dead," she said as her voice came back to her. "They were all I had left." Her eyes welled again as a sob escaped her. "Titus," she said as the tears started again.

Mikael gave a sorrowful nod. "I saw."

"Sonal and Javed too," Soren said quietly. "They were on guard this morning. And likely a number of others, given that these halls are empty."

A wave of panic hit Norah. "Where's Vitalia? Serene? And Calla and Cohen?" If anything had happened to them...

"The girl and the mute were outside when we returned this morning," Soren told her. "They're fine."

A painful breath of relief escaped her. They were in her care, and her stomach roiled thinking of what could have happened. But she still didn't know how Vitalia and Serene fared. Had they been in the castle?

"We'll find your maids," Mikael promised. "First, let's get you to the sanctuary."

"No." She shook her head, letting her hand find Cusco by her side. "I want to stay here." She'd previously thought Soren's chamber was the darkest place in the castle, a place to be feared—the most dangerous place. Instead, she found it was dangerous for those against her. She couldn't leave. Not yet. "Please, just find them. Vitalia and Serene. Find them."

"I'll return with more of the Crest," Soren told Mikael. "Stay here with Salara until then."

Mikael brushed Norah's cheek. He paused, looking at the bodies. "Please. Salara, let me take you away from this."

But she shook her head again. "No. I want to stay here." She felt safe here. And she needed to feel safe.

Mikael nodded. He pulled Norah close once more and kissed the top of her head.

Cusco sat at her feet. The animal's shoulder was warm against her thigh. Norah dropped her hand back to his head, finding comfort in the fanged beasts—Soren's hunters of men.

CHAPTER SEVENTEEN

Despite Mikael's attempts to get her to go to her sanctuary and away from the bloody room, Norah didn't want to move. She'd found the place where she could let her mind come back to her, let herself settle, and she wanted to stay as long as she could.

Within moments, Soren had summoned an army to his chamber—the remainder of the Crest who had been on duty, and those off, as well as others. Norah was relieved to see Bhastian was all right.

With an army now by her side, surrounded by those she trusted, she felt her courage start to return. She managed to convince Mikael she was all right and that he should go see what Soren had found out. The Crest cleared the assassin's bodies from the room, but blood still smeared the floor. She didn't mind. She needed to see their blood.

They'd been here to kill her. No—not *they*.

He. One man.

He'd been here to kill her. But who was *he*? This man scared her. More than any other.

A woman's voice caught her ear. "Let me through!"

"Vitalia!" Norah cried, and she stumbled to her feet from where she sat in the side chair. Bhastian pulled the door open for her, and her maid ran to her, throwing her arms around her.

"I was so worried for you," Vitalia breathed. "Are you all right?"

Serene was right behind her, and Norah pulled her close too. "I'm so glad you're safe!"

"We were at the seamstress's this morning," Vitalia explained. "When we returned, the castle was in chaos. The lord commander found us, told us that you'd been attacked, but you were safe."

"We've taken Calla and Cohen back to their chamber, until things are settled," Serene added.

Norah clung to her maids' hands, thankful those she cared about were unharmed. Well, not all of them. Her eyes welled as she looked at Serene. "Titus" was all she could manage to say.

"He's alive!" Serene assured her.

Nora's heart faltered. "What?" He was *alive*?

"He's alive, and they've taken him to the soldiers' infirmary."

Norah reached out and clutched Bhastian's arm. "You have to take me to him!"

"You should stay here," he told her. "The Crest is here. I'll see how he is and bring you news."

"I want to see him," she demanded. "Right now."

Bhastian glanced at the other soldiers of the Crest in the room, then reluctantly nodded.

Serene ran to get a dress. Then she and Vitalia helped Norah hastily change from her torn and bloodstained nightgown in the side bath chamber.

After, Bhastian led Norah and her maids through the castle, outside, and toward the soldiers' infirmary, with the Crest close after. They entered from the side. The building was mostly empty, with all warriors actively sweeping the castle for any remaining threats.

They made their way through what appeared to be a large dormitory hall. Beds lined the walls. Some were empty, some held wounded men. At the end stood a small cluster of soldiers. She saw the concern in the men's eyes. Titus was a man of strength and had built respect from the Kharavian ranks, much like Caspian. The healer was at the foot of a bed, wiping his hands with a clean cloth. His face was solemn—not a face of good news.

Norah's heart raced as she drew closer. Titus's massive frame lay the length of the bed, and a clean blanket had been draped over him. His eyes were closed.

"He's still in grave danger, Salara," the healer told her. "He's lost a lot of blood. I've done all I can. Now we wait to see if he wakes."

If he wakes. He had to wake. Titus had been with her from the beginning, before even she could remember. She couldn't lose him now. This couldn't be his death—handed to him by some faceless bastard.

The healer left, and she stepped closer to the bed. His face looked so peaceful, not at all like he was on the brink of eternal sleep.

Norah sank onto the bed beside him. She laid her hand on his arm. "His family has served mine for generations," she said to the small cluster of warriors around her, not taking her eyes from him. She felt her emotion rising. "He deserves so much more than this."

The men all stood quietly. A deep sadness hung in the air.

"They found four more bodies of assassins in another hall," Bhastian said gently from behind her. "We think he killed them before he was overtaken."

"Mighty Titus," she whispered through her tears. "If there had been four more of them, I would have been dead for sure." She leaned forward and kissed his forehead. "Thank you."

Norah wiped her cheeks and stood. "Where did they take the bodies?"

"Salar wouldn't want you there," Bhastian told her.

She didn't care. "Take me."

Norah followed Bhastian with a small army of the Crest behind her. They wove down and underneath the castle, to the dungeon hall, and reached a large room where the bodies of the assassins had been taken and laid atop tables under the torchlight.

Mikael and Soren stood, their backs to her, looking at the dead men with a small group of warriors. Norah felt a pit in her stomach. "Who are they?" she asked as she came up behind them.

The men turned, surprised at her sudden appearance. Mikael's objection showed on his face, but he didn't voice it. "We don't know," he said.

Norah looked at the dead men, and a shudder ran through her. These were the men who had tried to kill her. But it wasn't these men she still feared, it was the one who sent them.

"I want to know who they are and what they want," Mikael said.

Norah knew what they wanted. "He seeks revenge," she said, her eyes on the dead man closest to her.

He followed her gaze. "This one?"

"All of them," she said. "They're him. One man."

"There is obviously more than one man," Soren said.

Anger stirred inside her. "It's one man that embodied them."

Soren raised a brow and glanced at Mikael. "She's in shock."

"I am not in shock!" she said angrily. "And don't speak about me like I can't hear you. I know how it sounds, and I don't understand it myself, but he spoke to me through each man, as if he possessed them. He sees through them, he speaks through them, but none of them are actually him."

"It's a trick," Soren told her.

Norah pushed out a frustrated breath. She didn't have the energy to deal with him, and instead turned her attention to the assassins. They didn't share a common skin color. Two were darker, like men from Kharav. Perhaps even darker. Several were white, like her. But they all wore their hair trimmed short. Then something caught her eye. On each of their foreheads was a small smear of rusty brown. She hadn't noticed it during the attack; it had been hidden under their face coverings.

"I've seen this before," she said, drawing closer. She reached and touched it, then pulled back, eyeing the substance closely as she rubbed it between her fingers. Blood, maybe? "On one of the drifters. Near the village that had been destroyed after we left Bahoul. The night..." her voice trailed off. The night she had been attacked by the Horsemen. Even after all this time, the memory still made her stomach turn.

"These men aren't drifters," Soren said gruffly.

Clearly not. But... "They're linked somehow," she insisted. "And the lord justice is his target. He attacked me to get to him." She looked up at Mikael. "He was angry when he discovered Alexander wasn't here."

Mikael's breath shook in anger. "Well, whatever he is, if he jumps to another body when you kill him, then he's still out there."

"Only if you believe this nonsense," Soren muttered.

"I do," Mikael said gruffly, and the commander's eyes darkened.

"Then the solution is easy," Soren said matter-of-factly. "We kill the Bear."

That was his solution to everything. "You won't touch him," she warned.

"If his only cause to come after you is to hurt the Bear, then we should eliminate the Bear to eliminate the cause," he argued.

"How convenient a solution for you," she seethed. "Will you kill your king as well?" She looked back at Mikael. The assassin had wanted to hurt both Alexander *and* Mikael. "This man wasn't a supporter of yours either."

Mikael stewed in anger. "I want to know who he is."

Norah sighed. "He wouldn't tell me his name, and his accent..." She paused. His accent was similar to her own, yet different. "Not Mercian, but close. And he called the lord justice *Alexander*, and you *the Shadow King*."

"Similar to the North, and now wanting revenge. Sounds like Aleon," Soren said, looking at her darkly.

"But he's not from Aleon," Norah cut in. "That much he said."

Soren tilted his head, as if mocking her. "And you believe him?"

She eyed him, irritated. "Yes."

Norah looked back at the bodies. Who were these men? And where were they from? This was personal, driven by a deep hatred. This was an enemy of Alexander, an enemy of Mikael, and they had no idea who it was.

The night was eerily quiet, and Norah woke in a cold sweat. She sat up abruptly, not able to shake the feeling of someone watching her. She and Mikael had moved to her sanctuary, out of their bed chamber that still made her jump at every turn.

Mikael sat up beside her and reached out, putting his hand on her arm.

"No one's here," he told her.

"He is."

Mikael called out in the Shadow tongue, and a guardsman quickly entered. "Have the Crest sweep the castle, every hall, every stair," he told him. "Recheck the perimeter."

"Yes, Salar." The guardsman bowed and left quickly, closing the door behind him.

Mikael rose from the bed and looked through the bath chamber, then checked the balcony to make sure the doors were latched. He sank into the quilts beside Norah and held his arm for her to come to him. She slowly lay back, pulling the quilts up and trying to calm her breath.

"Don't be afraid," he told her. "You've never been one to be afraid."

"But this... I don't understand. This man, whatever he is, he has unnatural powers. He's able to speak through other men, see through other men. He passed through what's supposed to be an impenetrable kingdom, into the city, into the castle. He knew you were away with the lord commander. He knew I was alone."

"He didn't know your justice had returned to the North."

She paused. No, he hadn't.

"And he underestimated you, like all other men," he said softly. He pulled her close. "It's he who should be afraid."

Norah drew in a long breath and let it out slowly, nestling against Mikael and soaking in his warmth. But the feeling of safety still escaped her.

Morning brought the sun, and Norah rose without having slept. Vitalia entered and dressed her as Mikael pulled on his leathers. Norah watched her reflection in the mirror as Vitalia tied her lacings. She looked unwell. Dark circles pooled under her eyes, stark against her skin that seemed paler than normal.

"Do you want me to stay with you today?" Mikael asked her softly.

She shook her head. "No. You've got things to tend, and I'm well looked after. Go."

He squeezed her hand and kissed her forehead.

Norah spent the day in the calm of her sanctuary, reading quietly with her maids and trying to settle herself. Kiran had taken Calla and Cohen to look after them and had started them on a training plan, easing at least one thing from her mind. Mikael checked in on her frequently, and she continued to remind him of the army that surrounded her. In the late afternoon, she tried to rest, but rest wouldn't come. She didn't feel like herself anymore—easily startled, anxious, uneasy.

She sat by the windowed doors to the balcony, drinking the tea that Vitalia had made, as the afternoon waned. A little brown bird landed on the railing, and she smiled. The bird looked at her, strangely interested, cocking its head back and forth.

Suddenly, her pulse quickened, and her smile fell.

On its head was a small smear of red. Blood. *The same that had been on the assassins.*

"Salara, are you all right?" Vitalia asked, seeming to notice a change.

"He's watching me," Norah breathed.

Vitalia looked out to the balcony and gave a small laugh. "He does seem to be fascinated by you. Cute little thing."

"No," Norah said, standing from her chair and stepping backward. "It's *him*. He's watching me!" She flung her cup against the window, shattering it and the pane of glass, and making the bird flutter off.

Hearing the commotion, Bhastian pushed open the door. "Salara, are you all right?"

"No!" she cried. "He's here!"

Bhastian and three other soldiers swept inside, pushing the doors to the balcony open and looking around.

"Where did you see him? The man?" he asked.

"It wasn't a man, it was a... a bird." She knew her words sounded like lunacy as she said them.

"A bird?" Bhastian asked.

She shook her head, her eyes welling. "I swear. It's him!"

Bhastian nodded. "Of course, Salara."

But she could see the disbelief in his eyes. She clutched her skirts in her fist. "Leave me."

Bhastian gave a reluctant bow. "We'll walk the perimeter again," he assured her, and then he and the other soldiers stepped out into the hall.

"Close the draperies," she ordered Vitalia, and her maid quickly pulled the heavy fabrics closed. She sank into the chair in the corner and drew up a quilt around her. What was happening? She bit at her nails until they hurt. Was she losing her mind? Was she imagining it? No, it was real. *He* was real.

There was a knock on the door, and Soren stepped into the room without waiting for an answer. Norah bit her lip as she turned away. Of course he'd come. No doubt he took joy in seeing her weak and afraid. That's what he relished.

Cusco and Cavaatsa trailed in after, following their master, but she didn't object. She found comfort in the dogs now.

He glared at Vitalia. "Get out."

Vitalia looked at Norah, and she nodded. The fewer people to see the commander poke at her, the better. Vitalia gave a wary glance at the commander and then slipped out of the room.

"You think you're being watched?" he asked after her maid had left. He pulled back the drapery from the window and looked outside.

Norah pursed her lips. "I am," she insisted.

"By a bird?"

Her cheeks grew hot. "Have you come to mock me, Lord Commander? You think I'm mad?"

He turned back to her. "No. I think your mind plays tricks on you because you're afraid." He stepped closer to her. "He's made you afraid." His voice held a scornful tone.

"Of course he's made me afraid!" she cried as she stood abruptly from her chair, spilling her quilt to the floor. "He almost killed me! And he's still out there. He's watching me!" She couldn't believe she had to defend her fear.

"But why are you afraid?" he snapped.

"Why do you care? And why are you so angry?"

"Because *I* bow to you!" he thundered. "You'll fear *no one!*" Rage seeped from his skin. He stepped closer to her, his voice dropping to a growling whisper. "He watches you? Let him. Open your windows. Beg him to come. You're salara, the Shadow Queen. You'll kill him again. And again. And again."

Norah swallowed and stepped back in surprise.

He reached out and gripped her arm tightly and pulled her forward. "Coward fuck doesn't even come himself. You will *not* be afraid of him, do you understand?"

She couldn't speak.

"Do you understand?" he snarled as he gripped her tighter.

She forced a nod.

He released her, but his eyes still blazed. "I'll put their heads on our gates. You'll send him a message—show him how the Shadow Queen welcomes him."

He turned to leave, but paused, snapping at Cusco and Cavaatsa in the Shadow tongue. The dogs jumped on Norah's bed, making themselves at home and consigning themselves to a new master.

The commander cast her another dark gaze before leaving her to her chamber.

173

CHAPTER EIGHTEEN

Weary and spent. The months of constant travel had left Caspian weary and spent. He had reached Mercia with Alexander, only to assemble a fresh unit of forces and start the journey back to Kharav and Queen Norah. But when the Northern army reached the Canyonlands, surprisingly Caspian felt like he was coming home.

The sun set, dipping into the earth, and the air grew colder around him. But a warmth stirred within when he saw the figures of the watchful Uru on top of the canyons, against the brilliant sky. It had been a long journey, made even longer by his eagerness to see Tahla again. He had always told himself he'd never be distracted by a woman. Duty first. But now it seemed he was constantly distracted, and by nothing of substance. He had merely promised a kiss—a promise that Tahla likely had already forgotten about, and surely would no longer care about. Still, he couldn't stop the pull inside him.

The Urun warriors rode down to meet them, circling around. As before, the Northern army set camp outside the sprawling village, but the Uru hosted Caspian in their company. He looked for Tahla as he entered the village and was shown accommodation, but she was nowhere in sight.

"Is Tahla here?" he asked his escort.

"She is in the hills, with the chief."

Caspian sighed quietly, and disappointment washed over him—he'd miss seeing her. But he knew it was best. He gave a polite nod and stepped into the small stone house.

He pulled off his shirt and washed his face and hands in the basin provided, appreciating the hospitality of the Uru. Cleanliness brought comfort, and despite his disappointment, he would sleep well.

He took a small cornmeal cake from the plate of food on the table. It was different from the staples of meat and rice of Mercia, which were coincidentally common in Kharav, with the addition of potatoes. He liked the cake. It was different in a good way. Like Tahla.

"Is it to your liking, Northman?" a voice called from behind him, and he turned to see Tahla in the door. She wore a fitted dress—more of a tunic—short, above the knee. Her hair hung loose, not braided now, falling past her elbows. He hadn't realized how long it truly was.

Caspian stared at her for a moment. She really was the most beautiful creature he'd ever seen. He couldn't help his smile. "It is now."

She smiled back.

"They told me you weren't here," he said.

"I had just returned and was cleaning up when I heard that Northmen had arrived. I knew it was you."

"I didn't think I would see you."

She pulled her bottom lip between her teeth as her smile widened. "Did that disappoint you?"

"It did," he answered honestly.

"I worry about you, Northman," she said with a sly smirk, moving inside and closing the door behind her.

He gave a jesting frown. "Do you?"

She raised her brows and nodded. "Kharav's not a place for a man like you."

"Well, I don't draw attention. I'm fortunate enough to be... insignificant."

Tahla stepped closer. "You're anything but insignificant." She lifted her chin and looked up at him. "And I believe you owe me a kiss."

Owe. He almost chuckled. One kiss from this woman would leave him forever in *her* debt. He reached up and brushed a lock of hair from her shoulder, something he had done before and had played over and over again in his head. He let his fingers linger on her shoulder. Never had he touched a woman with want, but everything about her seized him. He dropped his head lower; his lips were so close to hers. Tahla put her hand over his, and she smiled as she guided it to her breast.

Her nipple hardened through the cloth, and Caspian paused. He drew in a breath, calling back his senses, and dropped his hand as he took a step back. "Forgive me."

Her brows drew together in amusement. "What's there to forgive?"

He didn't respond, and her eyes widened.

"Have you never been with a woman before?" she asked.

The directness of her question caught him off guard, and his mind stumbled. Finally, he managed, "I've never been married."

"That's not what I asked."

He drew in a quick breath. This woman. "Where I'm from, intimacy comes only with marriage."

"Just because a kingdom claims values doesn't mean men follow them."

"I believe in Mercia's values."

Tahla looked at him curiously. "And if I don't share these values?"

Was she looking for his acceptance of the difference? Or was she testing if he would pass judgment? He wasn't sure, and he didn't answer.

Her eyes narrowed. She stepped closer again. "What if I've taken men to my bed?"

"I wouldn't like it," he admitted.

"Would you think me ruined?" she asked, her voice sharper.

The fire in her eyes could warm him in a winter storm. "Of course not," he said. A woman like Tahla could never be ruined. "But I don't like thinking of you taking pleasure with another man."

The hint of a smile came to her eyes. "Would you rather I take my pleasure with you?"

Caspian shifted, unable to hide his discomfort.

"Do you think about me?" she asked, seeming to enjoy his uneasiness. "My body?"

She had no restraint. It excited him and scared him at the same time. "Do you not know the answer?"

"I want to hear it," she whispered.

He reached up and gently touched her face. "I think about your eyes," he said as he brushed her temple. He drew his fingers down her cheek to her neck. "Your voice. Your laugh. Your hair, your lips."

She leaned even closer, bringing her face upward. "Is that all?"

He gave a slow shake of his head, letting his fingertips linger at the base of her neck. "I think about your skin against mine. How you would feel. How much I want you. I do want you, Tahla."

Her breath came shallower now.

"So don't speak again of being with another," he told her. "It's not for thought of ruin, but for the deep jealousy that eats me. The bitterness knowing that another man's possessed what I so desperately want to be mine."

She put her hand on his chest and ran it over the curve of the muscle. "I could be yours tonight," she whispered.

He smiled sadly. "But you wouldn't really be mine, would you?"

"I'm no one's." Tahla ran her hand up and over his shoulder. Her eyes followed her touch. She seemed to like his body, want it even, and it fueled the burn inside him hotter. She drew her fingers down his arm. The graze of her fingertips ignited a fire over his skin.

Tahla took his hand and pulled it down, turning his palm upward and slowly bringing his fingers between her thighs. She wore nothing underneath her dress, no barrier to her skin. He was dangerously close to losing himself. She guided his fingers between her folds and let out a small gasp under his touch. Then she lifted her chin to his. "I'll take that kiss now."

But a kiss would be his undoing. He pulled his hand from her, but gripped her arms and dropped his head to rest his forehead against hers. He breathed deeply and prayed for control.

"Do I not please you, Northman?" she asked.

"Quite the opposite," he panted. "Too much so."

"But you would deny yourself?" she asked.

Much more and he wouldn't be able to.

She let out a breath. "If you want me to go, I'll go." She pulled back from him, but he didn't release his hold.

"I don't want you to go," he said. "Please. Stay." He struggled through his words. "Not lost in our flesh, but just... stay with me."

The corners of her mouth turned up.

He sank down onto the bed and lay back, leaving a space for her. Tahla crept in beside him and lay on her side, facing him. He wrapped his arms around her and pulled her close. "Tell me what you dream about, Tahla."

"This is what you want to do in bed with me?"

He threaded his fingers through her hair. "I want to know you. Everything about you."

"You're a strange man, Northman," she whispered.

He lay with Tahla in his arms, soaking in the warmth of her body. They talked deep into the night. She told him about the Uru, their love and respect for the earth, about her childhood, and the Uru's friendship with Kharav. The story of her meeting Norah drew a chuckle from him. Then Tahla told him about her own failed marriage, which drew anger. The need to protect her overwhelmed him, but he knew she didn't need his protection. Or want it.

In turn, he told her of Mercia, the beauty of the capital city and the North. She asked questions of the people and their customs, of their gods, deeply curious. It made him happy to share it with her.

Morning came too soon. Tahla had drifted into slumber sometime in the dark hours of the morning. Caspian didn't sleep, but as the sun peeked over the horizon, he felt more rested than he had in a long time.

The time came to depart. He drew his fingertips over the skin of her shoulder to wake her. She opened her eyes with a smile.

"This isn't how I expected the night with you to go, Northman," she said softly.

He brushed her bottom lip with his thumb. "I'm sorry I didn't give you your kiss."

She pushed herself up on her elbow. "I think I'll keep the debt so that you have to return." She leaned in and brought her lips to his ear. "I do want you to return," she whispered.

"Then I'll have to," he answered.

Tahla let her lips graze his cheek as she pulled away, and she rose from the bed and straightened her clothing. "Goodbye, Northman," she said, and with one last smile, she disappeared into the morning.

CHAPTER NINETEEN

Norah stood on the wall, looking out across the city to the north. Despite the chill, the sun was warm on her face, and the wind lifted her hair like a flickering flame behind her. Spring was almost upon them. It had already arrived in the valley, and crops were abundant. Shipments of food had been sent to Mercia.

Caspian had returned weeks ago and, to her shock and complete joy, was appointed captain of the Crest. Of course the commander denied his hand in it, but Mikael had shifted Crest responsibilities underneath the commander after Artem's death. Kiran had rejoined the guard as well, after he was given proper exception papers. Titus, although still recovering, had taken over Calla and Cohen's training. Norah still needed to figure out something long term for them after Titus was able to rejoin the guard, but it was working well, and the sibling pair were making progress. Things almost felt complete. *Almost.*

She should be happy, but she wasn't. She didn't want to admit it, but she was still afraid. It had been over a month since the assassins had come, and still she was no nearer to understanding who wanted to kill her, or why. Her stomach twisted in thinking how close they'd come. How had men gotten through the Canyonlands and into the castle, especially so many of them? Caspian wanted to send for more Northmen, but that wasn't the answer.

Cusco sat beside her and nudged her leg for attention. She smiled and dropped a hand to the large dog's head. It hadn't been long since the commander had given her the animals, but she'd become quite attached to them. Cusco was always near, always seeking attention from her. Cavaatsa stayed to herself, just out of reach, avoiding touch, but she trailed Norah wherever she went and slept at the foot of the bed.

Norah looked across the horizon, to the north sky—her home sky. Alexander had gone back to Mercia, back to what felt like the other side of the world. But the emptiness hadn't stayed empty. The pain hadn't been quite as sharp as she'd once thought it would be without him. Yes, she loved Alexander, but in her heart there now stood another.

Mikael. This man, opposite of everything she thought she stood for, confounded her. Yet he brought a level of clarity she failed to find anywhere else. Her memories still eluded her, but with him, she felt... herself. Free to be herself, whoever she wanted that to be.

Still, she found her mind wandering back to Alexander. Especially on days with clear blue skies, like today, while she stood on the balcony looking northward, as she was now. As if her thoughts were playing tricks on her mind, she could almost see the Mercian army on the horizon—as if he were returning to her. She gave a sad smile. They were only tricks.

Then she stopped.

Her heart beat faster.

There *was* movement on the horizon. It wasn't real, she told herself.

The horn of arrival startled her, and she leaned forward, gripping the wall tightly. Her heart thrummed in her ears as she squinted against the light to see. It was an army unit, and against the sky, *the Mercian flag*.

She knew it was Alexander. Happiness mixed with dismay, and a cry rose in her throat.

Norah caught a sound behind her and turned to see Mikael. She sucked in a breath and looked back out at the approaching army. If Alexander had returned, how would Mikael react? Certainly not well.

The power of his body came behind her, and his arm curved around the front of her shoulders. He spread his hand wide over her chest, running it up to the base of her neck, and he pulled her firmly back against him. He saw them too. She struggled to calm her breath. Surely he could feel her heart racing. Norah closed her eyes as the possessiveness rippled through him.

He dropped his head beside hers, drew a deep inhale, and let it out slowly. She didn't move. The heat of his anger singed her ear, and she braced for the storm to come.

But he only whispered, "Go." She turned in surprise. Did he know Alexander would be with them? His eyes brimmed with darkness, and the muscle underneath his skin tremored with restraint. Of course he knew. "Go meet them," he said, and he nodded.

He knew. And he told her to go. She cupped his face in her hands, pulling him down, and kissed him. Deeply. Then she gave him a reassuring smile and gathered her skirts as she hurried down to the courtyard.

The size of the arriving Mercian army was a significant one. Soldiers parted the way for her, and she greeted them hurriedly as she sought out Alexander. But in the sea of men, she couldn't find him. Where was he? A weight pulled her heart to her stomach. Had he not come? She'd ordered him back to the North; perhaps he'd stayed.

As he should have.

It was better this way, she told herself, and she stowed her disappointment. She wanted him to have stayed; she needed him to have stayed and to not have her heart wishing him back at every turn. She loved Mikael. Things had changed. *She'd* changed.

Then she heard her name.

"Norah."

She spun to see him walking toward her, and her breath seized on her lips. Alexander pulled off his helm, and the sun caught the gold in his hair. And suddenly she was afraid that nothing had changed at all.

He stopped when he reached her, his blue eyes sparkling. The corners of his mouth turned up. "Hello, Norah."

She couldn't stop the rush of happiness to see him, and she threw her arms around him. To have him back, to have him near, to be able to see him and touch him. The return of something lost, of *someone* lost.

They stood in the center of the courtyard, surrounded by her arriving Northmen.

And then she remembered herself, remembered Mikael on the wall, and she pulled back. A sudden flash of anger twisted inside her as a pain needled into her heart. "You shouldn't have come back." She needed him to not have come back.

"I had to as soon as I heard of the attempt on your life." He stepped closer, and she couldn't breathe. "It's the second time, Norah. I couldn't not come."

She couldn't have this argument with him now. She stepped back to put some space between them. "You brought all of Mercia with you, I see." She struggled to get ahold of her mind as she swept her eyes around them. This was the most Northmen that had ever come to Kharav.

He nodded. "Caspian will need more men."

"He has plenty of men. All the Crest are at his call. Hundreds."

"Now he has thousands." He gave her a small smile, that smile that pulled at her heart. "I've missed you, Norah," he said softly. She didn't dare to speak her own heart. His eyes moved to someone behind her, and she followed his gaze to a familiar face.

"Adrian!" She grinned as he made his way to them. "I can't believe you've come!" He seemed to have grown even taller, and she stood on her toes as she pulled him into a hug.

"Yeah, well Alec's been trying to send me back since he found out I came along." He shot a smile back at his brother. "But he can't keep me away forever. I wanted to see the Shadowlands, now that they're our allies."

"Kharav," she corrected him gently. "It's called Kharav here."

His smile widened. "Kharav, then."

"It's a beautiful place." And she meant it.

"Is the Destroyer here?" he asked.

Alexander frowned. "What do you care about the Destroyer?"

"What do I care about seeing the most famed man of war?" Adrian asked cheekily. "Have you seen him?"

Alexander's eyes drew together in irritation. "He's just a man. You'll be sorely disappointed. And of course I've seen him."

"Is he here?"

"Don't mind the Destroyer. Your queen's here. You forget yourself."

Adrian grinned sheepishly and bowed his head. "Apologies, Queen Norah."

Norah smiled with a small laugh. "It's good to see you, Adrian." She nodded toward the castle. "Come on. I'll show you around."

As they left the courtyard, her eyes shifted up to the wall, where Mikael stood, watching her.

The door to the bedchamber stood slightly ajar, and Norah pushed it open curiously. She smiled. Mikael stood patiently while two tailors worked to correct the sleeve length on a jacket that looked quite uncomfortable for him. She glanced at the bed where Vitalia had laid a fresh gown for her. The joys of social gatherings. But she didn't want to think about the evening's activities at the moment.

"Leave us," she called. Mikael turned in surprise.

The tailors and Vitalia bowed and saw their way out of the room, closing the door behind them.

"I thought you wanted me to wear a proper jacket this evening," he said.

She couldn't help but smile again. She had asked him not to come to the welcome social in his battle attire. He'd taken it upon himself to select the jacket, no doubt feeling pressured in comparison to the elegant, more conservative style of Mercia. But she had other things on her mind.

"I don't really care about a jacket right now." She took his hand, carefully making sure the needles on the cuff wouldn't prick him. Then she pushed it off over his shoulders and laid it across the bench at the foot of the bed.

He stepped away from the mirror and sank into the chair by the window.

Norah sighed. She knew Alexander was on his mind. She stepped quietly over to him, climbing on top of him and straddling him in the

SHADOW QUEEN

chair. Running her fingers into his hair, she pulled his face up to look at her. "I know his return upsets you." She brought her lips close to his. "But, Mikael, I love you. You alone."

"Don't say things that aren't true."

She frowned. It hurt her heart for him to have insecurity. "You're my husband. I'm committed to you—*you alone*. I'm faithful to you. I love you." She brushed the backs of her fingers along his jaw.

The hard lines on his face softened. He needed reassurance, and she'd wholeheartedly give it to him. She might not have loved him when she'd chosen him, but she loved him now. And she chose him now, all over again.

She brought her lips to his and kissed him deeply. And he kissed her back. His body hardened underneath her. She loved how he responded to her touch—wanting, needing—and her body answered in kind.

Norah ruffled up her skirts and reached below, loosening his breeches and freeing his flesh. He was ready, and she was too.

And then the urgency came.

She struggled to hook her fingers on the hips of her underwear in the chaos of her skirts. She couldn't get them off fast enough. His hands found her flesh under her gown, and the silk of her undergarments tightened and bit against her skin as he tore it away. He moved his hips upward, grasping her tightly and pulling her down to join them together, and she gasped as he sheathed himself inside her. They stilled for a moment, their foreheads together, but only for a moment. The calm before the storm. Then she began to rock against him. His head fell back as her pace quickened. She felt his need growing. As she moved faster, he pitched forward and lifted her from the chair, and she wrapped her legs around him.

Mikael carried her to the bed and laid her down without breaking their union. He tore the top of her dress and chemise down below her breasts and kneaded the milky flesh with thick desire. She writhed underneath him. He buried himself in her, possessing every part of her, and she let him take her.

Mikael clasped her shoulder firmly, pinning her down, and a wave of heat rushed through her. She pulled him closer, urged him harder, and surrendered as he took what he needed. The fiend inside him tore at her—claiming her, consuming her—and her own need answered back. He brought his hand to her face, looping his thumb into her mouth, and she bared her teeth against his skin and bit him. His chest rumbled, and he thrust harder, gripping her tighter. Norah pulled him deeper—deeper into her body, and into her mind. She gave herself—she gave all of herself. She cried out as release came, and pleasure rippled through her. He followed. His body shook as he thundered to his finish, and he collapsed on top of her.

After, they lay in each other's arms, panting, sweat beading across their skin. Finally, Mikael pulled himself from her and rolled onto his back. Norah turned on her side in sweet exhaustion and reached out her hand to trail it down his chest.

He drew in a breath and turned to face her. "I'm sorry," he said as he brushed his fingertips across the marks he'd left on her shoulder and along her sides. "I should have been gentler."

She smiled and whispered, "Sometimes a woman likes a good ravaging."

A deep rumble came from him again, and he pulled her back to kiss him.

Music filled the halls. Mikael felt surprisingly settled going into the evening's social. Despite his loathing for the Northmen, they seemed allied with Kharav against this unknown threat to his queen, and he couldn't deny he appreciated the additional men. Anything to keep her safe, even if it meant tolerating the Bear.

He shifted his shoulders uncomfortably in his crimson jacket. Salara had been pressing him away from the usual battle dress, and his dark linen and leather. She was beautiful, in a gold gown with beaded patterns on the bodice. He walked with her on his arm and couldn't keep his eyes from her. As they reached the great hall, she paused.

"Salara-Mae has come," she said.

His mother rarely attended social events. "How did you manage that?"

She shook her head. "It's not my doing, but I'm going to go greet her."

"Of course," he said, and watched her make her way across the room. She really was beautiful.

Soren stepped in beside him, and his mind shifted.

"Where is he?" Mikael asked, and followed Soren's eyes to where the Bear stood with a small group of Northmen.

Mikael and Soren approached, and the surrounding men took their leave to give them space but kept a wary eye over their justice from a distance.

"Shadow King," the Bear greeted him coldly.

Mikael stood casually, watching Norah across the way. "I see you found your way back," he said, not taking his eyes from her.

"I needed to ensure the well-being of my queen, as is my duty."

189

"As you can see, she's quite well." Mikael cast him a sideways glance. "You can return to your place back in the North."

The Bear scoffed. "My place is by her side."

"I don't believe Salara shares your view. Has she not sent you back to the North twice already?"

The justice cut him a glance with a sharp brow. "She sends me away because our closeness disturbs you. But it's not what she wants, and I know you know that."

Mikael bristled at the Bear's boldness—at the audacity he would hint at Salara's affections for him so directly. His skin burned with the heat of war. Any other man he'd force to his knees and cut his tongue from his mouth. Any other man he'd split his neck with his bare fingers and pull out his throat. But this wasn't any other man, and Mikael attacked the only way he could. "Oh, I'm not disturbed," he said. "I find your visit a pleasant surprise."

The Bear gave an unbelieving chuckle.

Both men kept their eyes on Norah, but Mikael leaned in closer. "I enjoy what your visit brings. You see, when you're here, our lovemaking isn't how it normally is—gentle and passionate. It's raw. She comes to our bed with a wildness to her."

The justice inhaled sharply as the fake smile fell from his face.

Mikael's eyes burned cruelly. "I feel it when I'm inside her," he taunted. "Her body begs me to take it. And I do. Most violently."

The Bear's nostrils flared.

"Salar," Soren said as he stepped forward, putting himself between them.

Mikael broke from his attack, gathering himself and pulling back his shoulders. He stepped out onto the floor and looked back at the Bear with a smile. "So, Lord Justice, stay as long as you'd like." Then he turned toward Salara with the hunt in his veins. He clapped twice as the quartet finished their song to start a new one—the song of his choice.

Salara turned and saw him approaching, and her smile turned into a grin. She was the most beautiful woman on the earth. And she was his.

"I love this song," she said.

"I know." He moved behind her, slipping an arm around her waist, and bared his teeth against the smooth skin of her neck. She let her head fall back against his shoulder and closed her eyes as he led her through the dance.

CHAPTER TWENTY

It was late evening, and Norah found Soren in his study, sitting at his desk and looking closely at a map as he scribbled notes to the side. He sat without his wrap, his dark hair tied back, seeming almost... normal. He was a handsome man, more so than she cared to admit. He had a strong jaw, like Mikael, and a straight and proportionate nose, like Mikael. He could be desirable, like Mikael, if he weren't such an ass.

"Lord Commander," she greeted him, pulling his attention. "I have a favor to ask."

He glanced up and eyed her, annoyed. "Not to kill the Bear?"

Norah sighed. "All right, two favors," she said irritably. "There's a young man from Mercia, Adrian. He's very eager to meet you."

He took a drink from the chalice sitting to his right, and then set it down, suspicious. "Why would he be eager to meet me?"

"You would better understand the fascination with war idols," she replied, more elbowed than she'd intended. She inhaled deeply and gathered herself. "Please, I'm very fond of him, and it would mean a great deal."

"What's the favor you ask? You're salara. You don't need my permission to present him to me."

"No, but I want you to make it meaningful. And"—she paused—"he's the lord justice's brother."

He stilled. The commander's nostrils flared, and he sat back in his chair. "You want me to show a kindness to the brother of the Bear?"

Why did it sound so abhorrent when he said it? "Yes."

He snorted. "Then the Bear should ask me himself."

"Alexander will be looking to send Adrian back to Mercia at the first opportunity, preferably without seeing you."

The corner of his lip turned upward. "Then I would love to meet him."

"Yes, I suspected that would be the case with such context. But I'd also ask for your discretion. Alexander wouldn't be pleased."

The commander's lip twitched slightly. "Then what would I get from this if not the Bear's ire?"

"That's why it's called a favor," she said sweetly.

The lord commander leaned heavily into the arm of his chair. "Is this a favor I can call upon?"

Norah sighed. Of course he would be difficult. "Fine," she said stiffly. She was sure she'd regret it later.

He gave a small smile. "Then I suppose I can't refuse my salara," he said.

Despite her annoyance, she couldn't help a small smile. "I'll bring him to the stable tomorrow morning."

Morning came slowly with her excitement. Norah tried to chase the small wave of guilt back. Alexander would be upset if he found out what she had planned, but this wasn't about Alexander. Adrian was eager to see Kharav and to meet the commander. He embodied what she wanted of her kingdom and her men—genuine curiosity and appreciation for the other side. Men like Adrian could help her bring both sides together.

Norah found Adrian with several other Mercian soldiers near the barracks, already sparring. They all stopped and bowed when they saw her.

"Northmen," she greeted them. "Adrian, is the lord justice here?"

"No, but I'll fetch him."

"No," she said quickly, stopping him. "That's not necessary. I've actually come for you."

He lifted a brow. "For me?"

"Yes." She smiled. "I have something for you. Come with me."

He grinned and stepped promptly through the men.

She led him toward the stable, looking back at him. "How long are you staying?"

"As long as Alec allows, which probably isn't very long."

"No, I imagine it's not." Alexander, wanting to protect him, wouldn't be happy with him in Kharav.

He looked at her with a flash of hope. "Maybe you could talk to him?"

"I don't think I should cause any more aggravation with your brother."

He frowned. "What do you mean by *more*? Why would he ever be aggravated with you?"

They walked into the stable, and she waved her hand toward a shadow within. He followed her motion with his gaze, and his eyes grew wide. Soren stepped forward into view.

"The Destroyer," Adrian breathed.

"You'll address him as Lord Commander," she said. "His proper title."

"Yes, of course. Lord Commander." Adrian bowed. "I mean no disrespect, I'm honored."

The commander looked down at Adrian with a gaze that silenced him.

"What's your name, boy?" he rumbled.

"Adrian," he managed to get out.

"How old are you?

"Just turned twenty, my lord."

Norah hadn't realized he'd had a birthday. The time was passing quickly in Kharav.

"What's your hand?" Soren asked.

"Uh," Adrian stumbled, "a bow." He shook his head. "I mean, a sword."

The commander frowned. "Well, which is it? A bow or a sword?"

Norah scowled. She'd asked the commander to make it meaningful, not intimidating.

"I'm keen with a bow, my lord," Adrian answered. "But much better with a sword."

The commander's eyes narrowed. "Much?" He turned and pulled two swords from a side weapons wall.

Norah looked at him with uncertainty. She hadn't expected this exchange.

The commander handed him a sword and then walked out of the stable. Adrian followed excitedly. Out in the paddock, they squared off and circled each other. Adrian seemed timid at first and gripped the blade tightly.

The commander made the first move and swung, testing. Adrian jumped back, his nerves getting the better of him. Soren took a step back, swinging his sword wide and bringing it back to ready. Adrian moved forward. He settled his stance in preparation for the next move. Soren advanced again, but this time Adrian hit his blade away and spun, swinging a counter. The commander deflected it easily, striking the sword from Adrian's hand.

Norah stepped forward, but Soren put his hand up, stopping her. He nodded to Adrian, who picked up his sword and readied himself again. Her stomach twisted. The only thing worse than Alexander finding out about this was Alexander finding out with his brother in pieces. Perhaps this hadn't been the best idea.

The commander swung hard this time, and Adrian darted away. Adrian launched his own attack. The commander met it with a counter of his own, and Adrian danced away. Soren cut his sword upward, again pushing him back, but Adrian was quick and struck his blade to the side in its arc. He spun and brought his sword down, grazing the pauldron of the commander's shoulder.

Adrian gripped his sword tightly for the next attack, but the commander straightened. His eyes hinted a genuine smile, something Norah hadn't seen before.

"You're not bad," Soren said.

Adrian grinned and looked at Norah, and she smiled back in her own surprise.

"Keep practicing," the commander said.

"Yes, my lord," Adrian said breathlessly. "Thank you!" He looked back at Norah. She didn't think she'd ever seen anyone so happy.

"That's all," she told him. "You can go now."

He gave an excited bow of his head. If the lord commander hadn't been there, she knew he would have hugged her. "Thank you, Norah!"

he said. Then he turned to Soren. "Lord Commander." He bowed again, then turned and trotted back toward the barracks.

Norah smiled. "Thank you," she told Soren after Adrian left.

He gave a small grunt.

"If I didn't know better," she added, "I might think you enjoyed yourself."

"Well, it wasn't terrible," he said with mild irritation.

She pursed her lips to keep her smile from growing. "Again, thank you."

He shifted uncomfortably but gave a nod.

It was late afternoon as Norah made her way through the great hall and toward the conservatory, with the dogs at her side. She looked forward to spending some time in the gardens. Movement caught her eye, and she turned to see Alexander walking toward her.

"You took Adrian to meet the Destroyer," he said angrily as he drew near.

Cusco growled in warning, and she reached down to calm the animal. He had become quite protective of her, even growling at Mikael, which had given her a good laugh. "They were both out this morning," she said, "so I introduced them."

"How kind of you," he said shortly.

"Alexander," she pleaded. "Adrian was ecstatic."

"About meeting the man who's killed thousands of our people?"

"About meeting the greatest warrior of our time!"

Alexander took a step back, visibly insulted, and she instantly regretted her words. "I didn't mean it like that."

"That man is a monster," he said bitterly, "and I don't want Adrian near him. I don't even want you near him."

Anger rose in her cheeks. "Our fathers created that monster! Do you forget?"

Alexander gave a disgusted grimace. "You defend him?"

"He extended a kindness to the son of the man who led the forces that killed his own family! His father, his mother, his sister, his brother. Kharav has suffered at the hands of the North, and the lord commander has lost just as much as anyone else!"

Alexander's eyes burned in troubled astonishment.

Norah sighed. She didn't want to argue, especially not with Alexander over a man like the commander. She stepped closer to him. "Put aside your own bitterness. Allow your brother this small joy."

He snorted and looked away.

She reached out and took his hand. "Alexander."

He brought his gaze back to her.

She gave a small smile. "It *is* small. You know, if Adrian could choose to be like anyone, it would be you. He idolizes you."

Alexander looked down at their hands clasped together and sighed, conceding.

"And I wish you'd try to understand the commander." She glanced down at the dogs. "He's not always what you think."

But that, she knew, he'd never do.

CHAPTER TWENTY-ONE

Norah stood in the doorway of Mikael's study, watching him. He sat at his desk, his eyes on a letter but not reading it.

"What troubles you?" she asked.

He looked up at her in surprise, and she gave a reassuring smile.

Mikael drew in a breath as he sat back against his chair. He seemed reluctant to answer as he folded the letter back and set it on the desk. "Gregor," he said finally. "He arrives in two days' time."

"Japheth's king? Why is he coming?" Norah knew a little history from what her grandmother had shared with her.

Japheth had once been part of the greater Aleon Empire ruled by Phillip's father, but upon his death, the empire was split between his three sons. Feeling robbed of his birthright as the eldest, Gregor had killed his youngest brother, Aston, and absorbed Aston's kingdom of Hetahl under Japheth. When he rose against Phillip to take the remaining Aleon kingdoms, Mercia stood as Phillip's ally, prompting Gregor to seek an alliance with Kharav. Kharav, already motivated to go to war with Mercia, was quick to agree. This had been the start of the Great War.

Now that Norah and Mikael were wed, and Mercia and Kharav united, this no doubt left both their previous allies uneasy. She was surprised that Gregor would visit, especially with her presence at the castle.

Mikael gave a grumbled sigh, clearly annoyed by the news himself. "He comes to set new trade terms."

"Trade terms you're not pleased with?"

He cast her a hesitant eye. When it came to ruling Kharav, he still kept her at a distance. The ways of Kharav still bothered her—the harshness, the violence—and it was his way of sheltering her from them. But she didn't want to be sheltered. She wanted him to share his burdens with her. She drew closer and reached out, putting her hand on his cheek. "Will you not tell me?" she asked softly.

He looked at her for a moment. "I'm not pleased," he said finally. "I suspect he's allied himself with another." He stood. "His demands are outrageous. Something makes him bold."

"Who could he join who is greater than you? Greater than Mercia and Aleon?"

Mikael shook his head. "I don't know."

"Maybe it's a bluff."

Mikael snorted. "Gregor's a coward. He wouldn't take the risk."

"So, what are you going to do?"

He sighed. "I don't know. I can agree to his demands and appear weak."

"Or?"

"I can kill him."

Norah frowned. She wasn't sure why she'd expected anything different. "I'm glad to see we've covered options at both extreme ends of the spectrum." She pushed out a breath. "What about something in between?"

"There is nothing in between."

Her brow stitched down. "How about just refusing?"

"If Gregor leaves without an accord, it means he leaves as a potential enemy. And I can't have another enemy. Not with the North and Aleon both poised against me."

Her heart hardened. How could he say that? And to her... "Mercia is not against you."

He snorted. "Even your lord justice confirms your council won't stand with me. I need Japheth more than ever."

"Phillip waits for the moment to avenge his youngest brother and kill Gregor. Japheth needs *you*."

"He clearly doesn't!" he snapped. "And if he's not with me, he's against me, and then I have to remove him." She took a step back, and his shoulders fell. "I don't expect you to understand how any of this works," he said shortly.

Norah raised a brow, a flash of anger coming to her cheeks. "Fine. Since *you* know how this all works, I'll leave you to continue planning how you'll lose *all* of your allies and the support of your nobles. You have a good start. Don't let me stop you." And she turned and left in frustration.

The great hall was loud with celebration when she entered. Norah moved gracefully through the bowing nobleman to the table where Mikael sat. He stood when he saw her, and she took her place beside him. Unlike in the dining hall, the table sat longways, facing the festivities, with chairs lined on only one side and Mikael and Norah at the center. She was glad for it—to be beside him, to be able to touch him.

He cast her an unsettled look, seemingly wanting to break the icy wall between them, but the doors swung open before they had a chance to speak.

An overly extravagant procession swept through the great hall, and in its center—Gregor, king of Japheth.

"I thought he'd already presented himself to you," Norah said quietly, unamused. Gregor had arrived earlier that morning.

Mikael sighed. "He did."

"Then why the show?"

"To present himself to you, I'm sure. Appearances are not for friends."

Not for friends.

The Japheth king was not as Norah had imagined. He was tall and thin, gaunt almost, with a fragile walk, albeit a cocky one. His cheekbones sat high and sharp, stretching the skin taut, and the bronze of his hair was speckled with gray. He had a prominent brow that shadowed his eyes, hollowing them. Norah thought back to the portraiture of Phillip she had seen. The only thing he seemed to have in common with his brother was the mustache. And Gregor looked much more than fourteen years Phillip's senior.

"Salar," he greeted Mikael, with no nod and no bow. Kings did not bow to kings, although they generally gave a dip of their head in greeting—a sign of respect. But there was no respect here, and anger rippled through her. She tempered it, though. If she felt the flame of anger, Mikael certainly had, and while she didn't like this Japheth king, bloodshed was not the answer. Not yet.

Gregor's eyes fell on Norah. "North Queen," he said in a gravelly voice. He didn't hold the Japheth accent, being from Aleon.

"King Gregor," Norah said. "Welcome to Kharav."

He gave a forced smile, clearly not liking a welcome to Kharav from the Mercian queen.

"King Gregor." Mikael's voice echoed through the hall, stiff and forced as well. "Tonight we celebrate, to welcome Japheth, our friend and ally. Please," he said, motioning to the chair to his right at the long dining table.

They all took their seats, with Gregor on the opposite side of Mikael from Norah, and music picked up in the air.

"How long will you keep me waiting on my proposal?" Gregor asked Mikael as he eyed the food placed in front of him. Norah lifted her chalice to her lips but willed her breathing quiet to listen.

"As I said, tonight we celebrate," Mikael answered. "Tomorrow we'll speak of trade."

Gregor let out a small chuckle. "So, you don't like my proposal."

Brazen persistence.

Norah couldn't tell if the heat in the room was from her anger or Mikael's. She placed a hand on his thigh under the table, settling them both.

Gregor leaned forward and looked past Mikael at her. "Tell me, North Queen. Now that you're wed to Kharav, does Mercia consider herself friends of Japheth?"

The Japheth king *was* bold, and it bothered her even more. A few more moments and she might be asking for the sword to end Gregor herself. "I suppose we'll see," she said calmly, then took a bite of lamb from her plate.

"See what?" he pressed.

Norah took her time to chew and swallow her food before answering. He would wait for her. "If Japheth is worthy of our friendship."

Gregor snorted. "You insult Salar and I both."

"My husband's ego is not so fragile," she said sweetly. She met Gregor's eyes and smiled when she saw his offense. Under her hand, she felt the faint vibration of a near chuckle from Mikael, and he seemed to relax. These restrictions he forced himself to in the name of an alliance with Japheth—they didn't apply to her. "You should try the lamb," she told Gregor. "It's delicious."

With the festivities over, Norah and Mikael bid their goodnights and took to their chamber.

Norah let out a liberating breath as Vitalia pulled the heavily adorned gown from her and helped her into her nightgown. "That man is insufferable," she said to Mikael as she pulled down her hair.

He waved off Vimal as his servant moved to take off his attire. "Leave us."

Vitalia gave Norah a curtsy and followed Vimal from the room.

Norah looked at Mikael with a raised brow. "What's the matter?"

He shook his head.

"Tell me," she pressed.

He reached out and pulled her close. "The only thing the matter is the way I spoke to you before about Gregor."

A small smile came to her lips, and she let him wrap his arms around her. "I accept your apology, if that's what it was supposed to be."

"It was. It *is*. I'm sorry."

"I thought you might be angry with me for goading him."

He shook his head and held her tighter. "You say things I can't. And, I'll admit, it does allow me greater leverage when you hint the threat of the North against him, if I appear the advocate on his behalf."

"Well, I'm glad to be in service to my salar."

He smiled, and his eyes grew darker. "Say that again."

Her lips peeled back to reveal her own smile. "I'm glad to be in service to my salar."

And he picked her up and carried her to the bed.

Water puddled on the cobblestone streets. A billow of gray hung over the city. Alexander pulled his hood farther over his brow as he stepped out into the rain. He was appreciative of the weather for once, as a hooded man wouldn't draw attention. But as he made his way toward the castle, he was acutely aware he was being followed. He stepped into a side street, intending to cut through to another walkway, when a man stepped into the path in front of him. Alexander stopped and looked behind him, where the other man who had been following him cut off his retreat.

"The Mercian lord justice," the man in front of him called out. "I heard you were here." He had a chopped cadence to his accent—he was a man from Japheth.

"Good day, gentlemen," Alexander said, then he moved to continue walking.

But the man in front of him stepped into his path, and two more men appeared.

"What's your intention?" Alexander asked them. "I'm expected at the castle."

The man in front of him smiled. "Be a shame if you didn't make it there. An accident, perhaps?"

Alexander put his hand on his sword's hilt. "An unlikely accident."

He heard the draw of a sword behind him and looked back out of the corner of his eye. The men were closing in. In a singular motion, he pulled his sword from its scabbard and spun with a blow to the closest opponent behind him. The man fell backward, onto the cobblestone street. He followed with an upswing at the man on his right, who met his attack with his own blade. Alexander fought him back before turning his attention to the advancing man to his left. But a blow to the back of his head dropped him to his knees. He tried to stand but was met with a swift knee to the chin, sending him spiraling backward.

Alexander rolled to his side and staggered to his feet, but he had dropped his sword. A man rushed him with a short sword, and he ducked, pushing the man to the side and bracing for another attack. A sword swung wide, and he leapt back. It sliced through the fabric of his shirt but didn't reach his skin. But he couldn't escape the second swing that bit into his thigh.

He stumbled backward, losing his balance and again falling to his knees. There was no time to react to the blade that came for his head.

But a small battle-axe hit his attacker in the chest, killing him and dropping him to the ground. Alexander swayed on his knees as the Shadow commander walked by him, killing two more men with shots from his double crossbow. The commander turned back toward the fourth man, who was picking himself up off the ground.

"Are you mad?" the man yelled as he looked at his fallen companion with an axe in his chest. "That was King Gregor's nephew!"

The lord commander paused, and the man took the opportunity to run away. He turned back to Alexander. "Get back to the castle and don't leave," he snarled. Then he pulled his axe from the king's dead nephew and disappeared into the rain.

Norah found Mikael with Soren in Mikael's study. He stood, gripping the sides of his desk and leaning over it with a stoic look on his face. Soren stood across from him, his eyes dark.

"The lord justice told me what happened," she said breathlessly as she entered. Her pulse beat in her throat. Alexander's recount had her running to find Mikael before he'd even finished his words.

"Your justice is exactly the problem," Mikael snarled. "If he wasn't here, this wouldn't have happened."

"W-What?" Norah stammered, caught off guard by the direction of the conversation. "Those men attacked him! This isn't his fault!"

"No? It's not his fault that he works to align the North with Aleon? It's not his fault that he provokes hostility from my ally, and my lord commander is forced by duty to aid him?"

"*Mercia* is your ally!"

Mikael swept his books from the desk, and they scattered to the stone floor. "And will they join me when the Aleon king invades to build his new empire?"

"Gregor won't stand by and let his brother build his empire around him," she snapped back.

"Will the North stand with me against Aleon?" he pressed again.

Norah looked at him, speechless. They both knew the answer to that question.

"That's what I thought," he said. "And now you force me to break with my ally if I can't resolve this."

"Give me to him," Soren said to Mikael. "He'll punish me, but he won't kill me. You know he's wanted me for his army for some time now."

"I won't do that, brother," Mikael told him.

"If you lose the alliance with Japheth, you'll lose the support of the nobles," Soren said.

But Norah knew Mikael would never give up Soren, even in the face of losing everything. "You aren't going to lose your alliance with Japheth," she said, trying to reassure him. "We'll figure something out."

"*I* will figure something out," Mikael snapped at her. "You've done enough."

She stepped back in surprise, but Mikael didn't give her time to react. He turned and left the study. The commander gave her a cold eye before following after.

Gregor burst through the doors of the throne room, where they waited. Norah sat to Mikael's left, beside him on her own throne. Soren stood to his right, just off the dais.

She hadn't tried to talk to Mikael again before they'd gone to face Gregor. She'd wanted to, given the stress written over his face, and the challenge of how to fix this. Losing the alliance would bear severe consequences, some from which he might not recover. The question was—how far was he willing to go to mend things before severing the alliance—and Gregor's head with it?

"I want his head!" Gregor bellowed. This stupid man truly didn't know how much danger he was in.

Mikael rose, poised, calm, not showing any of the signs of worry he'd had just moments before. But Norah knew what lay below the surface.

The king of Japheth glared at Soren, who stood silently while he waited for the determination of his fate. "You'll give me his head!" he seethed at Mikael.

"You don't want his head," Mikael replied coolly.

Gregor trembled with all the rage a frail man could muster. "I want justice! Give him to me, and I'll take him to Japheth to decide reparation."

"And what would that be?" Mikael asked.

"I'll let the boy's mother choose."

Mikael's voice was calm and steady. "We both know that's not a solution. Let's come to an appropriate punishment and it will be done here. Today."

Punishment. A tremor rolled up Norah's spine. Would he really punish Soren? And how?

"We're speaking of my nephew! The son of my wife's sister."

She frowned. There was a woman who could stand to be married to this man?

"A mere lashing won't be sufficient," Gregor spat.

"There's nothing *mere* about a lashing," Mikael said, his voice getting edgier.

Norah's skin prickled. Soren would *not* be getting a lashing.

"You'll give him to me," Gregor demanded. *Demanded.* He had the nerve to demand.

"I can't do that," Mikael told him.

"What do you mean you *can't*?" Gregor spewed each word with venom. "You mean you *won't*?"

While Mikael stood calmly, he was on the verge of blood rage, which wouldn't end well for anyone. Norah stood. "He means the lord commander is no longer his to give," she cut in, a sharp edge to her tone. She shot a steely glance at Mikael. "*Or* to punish."

All heads turned toward her, and she heard several audible surprises. Even Soren's head snapped up. Mikael stood motionless. He said nothing, but his eyes were fixed on her.

"He's *mine*, sworn to *me*," she said firmly, stepping down the stairs toward Gregor. "And I most *certainly* won't be giving him to *you*."

"You seek war?" he challenged.

"Your nephew waged an attack against the highest command of the Mercian army, which in itself is the very act of war!" Norah spat back, letting her rage cut through the hall. "The lord commander, now the servant of Mercia, was compelled to act on this threat. *As am I.*"

The king of Japheth took a step back at the ferocity of her words.

Norah calmed, but still pressed toward him. "However," she continued, "my husband has tried to tell me that this was merely the foolishness of a young man, for which he's unfortunately paid with his life. And so Salar has asked for compassion, that I not take this as an intentional threat, and that I not rouse our combined forces and *allies* on such a misunderstanding."

Norah stepped directly in front of Gregor and stared at him with an icy fire. There was no question of her reference to allies. *Aleon.* And it hung heavy in the air. "So, I ask," she said, "is this a misunderstanding? Or does Japheth seek war against the queen of Mercia and salara of Kharav?"

Gregor stood, speechless. An eerie quiet hung in the hall as all eyes waited for the Japheth king's response. No single alliance could be stronger than the forces of Mercia, Kharav, and Aleon together. *If* they were together. Norah knew her threat, if believed, turned the tables. And it showed this pitiful excuse of a king that Mikael was the only thing that stood between him and a crushing war.

Finally, Gregor gave a slight nod, acquiescing. "Forgive me, Salara, for I neither knew the commander was sworn to you, nor the circumstance by which my poor nephew suffered his fate. I ask your pardon, and your understanding, as sometimes young men make poor choices without thought of consequence."

She gave a pursed smile and looked back at Mikael. "I'm just thankful to Salar, otherwise I may have acted in haste. But his friendship with Japheth is of importance to him." To *him*, not to *her*. She hoped she'd made that clear. And this king should grovel at Mikael's feet to keep him.

"It was wise counsel," Gregor replied, "and Kharav is of great importance to Japheth." He dipped his head low, toward Mikael.

As he should. *Grovel.*

"Then I'll let you both get on with your negotiations, keeping that importance in mind," she said with a warning smile.

Gregor gave a final nod and left them, his entourage following him out.

Norah swallowed back the bile that was building in her throat. Her knees shook, and she was thankful for her layered skirts.

Mikael stepped close behind her. "You risk another Great War," he said.

She turned to face him. "Japheth against three of the most powerful kingdoms in the world would not be a Great War."

Mikael cast his gaze to the side before bringing it back to her. "Is this to mean that you've negotiated Aleon as your ally?" he asked.

"Aleon doesn't have to be an ally to join me against Japheth in war. Phillip wants Gregor's head above all else. Everyone knows this."

She turned to leave, but Mikael caught her arm. "I'm beginning to think you know exactly how all of this works."

"I was waiting for you to figure it out."

The corners of his lips curved ever so slightly.

"Did you really intend to lash Soren?" she asked.

He frowned. "If it would get us an accord and save the alliance, yes. And he would have gladly accepted it."

"I wouldn't have," she said firmly.

He leaned back on his heel.

"I meant what I said." Her stare locked with his. "Soren's mine."

Clouds covered the sky. Winter had lost its power, giving way to the rains. The wind blew cold, but the ground was no longer frozen. Having left Mikael to work things through with Gregor, Norah wriggled her toes in her boots against the mud under her feet as she watched men in the corrals working the new herd of horses that had come in. They were beautiful beasts, giants. They looked like mounts of the gods. When they ran in unison, their hoofbeats shook the earth.

Another giant moved to stand beside her, and she didn't need to look to know it was Soren. They stood quietly, watching the horses.

Unexpectedly, Soren reached out, holding a dagger in front of her. Alexander's dagger—the dagger that had been taken from her when she was captured by Mikael as she traveled to Aleon. She hadn't expected to ever see it again, and she stared at it.

He held it by the blade, and, very slowly, she reached up and curled her fingers around its hilt. He released it, all without taking his eyes from the corral. His thanks.

Soren said nothing.

And Norah said nothing.

But the nothing felt like friendship. And that was nice.

CHAPTER TWENTY-TWO

Sun poured through the paneled crystalline windows of the great Kharavian library and spilled across the mosaic floor; it was quite heavenly for the kingdom of Shadows. Norah sat at the black ash-wood table, with books strewn about her.

King Gregor's entourage was in the courtyard, preparing to depart back to Japheth, but she didn't join Mikael to see them off. She'd done enough—to help or to hurt, she wasn't sure.

But despite the tension-riddled weeks, between Alexander's return to Kharav and Gregor's visit, Norah found herself grateful for the distractions. While she was still wary, her fear of the mysterious enemy who had tried to kill her had mostly dissipated. She wasn't continuously looking over her shoulder or jumping at sudden noises. Now she was able to think more clearly, more rationally, about who'd sent the assassins, and she set her thoughts to action.

They'd found no additional clues on the assassins' bodies, no threats had been received, no sign of more intruders. It was as if he'd given up.

She knew he hadn't given up. An effort such as the one he'd made was not taken on by a man who gave up easily. But still, the question hung over her—who wanted to kill her? Who wanted to hurt both Alexander and Mikael?

If only she had her memories—something else that still evaded her—surely she'd have a few more clues.

She leafed through the pages of yet another book. She didn't know what she was looking for in the aged archives—histories of tenuous or soured political relationships, forgotten rifts? Not that she really expected to find anything, but she might uncover a history she didn't know before. She frowned. At this point, any history would be something she didn't know before.

In front of her lay open a historical account of the Great War. It was written in a combination of Kharavian and Northern tongue and contained a number of drawings. As she flipped through, one image in particular caught her attention, and she looked at it for a long time. It was the battle between what appeared to be the senior Kharavian king and her father. The title was faded but she could still read it—"Clash of Kings."

She eyed the image of her father closely, but it was only a simple drawing. She ran her fingers over him, and over his horse. Was this the horse of the Wild? Would the witness to it be recorded in the words of this book? She wished she could read the rest of it. While she was becoming more familiar with Kharavian words in conversation, written words were still entirely foreign. She sat back in the chair with a sigh.

"I thought I'd find you here," a voice came from behind, and she turned to see Alexander. He wore a warm smile on his face, and she couldn't help but smile back.

"Am I that predictable?"

He chuckled. "Tell me one other thing predictable about your life. I'll wait."

Her smile widened. He was right. Predictable her life was *not*.

He took the chair beside her, and the air grew quiet between them. He cast his gaze down. "Are you angry with me?"

She rolled her bottom lip between her teeth, but then let out a long breath and shook her head. "No. I don't blame you for what happened with Gregor."

He sat back in his chair, and his lips thinned. "Perhaps you should."

Her brow dipped. "Why would you say that?"

"Norah, we both know I haven't made this easy for you."

"It's not been easy for anyone," she countered.

"But especially not for you, and I haven't helped that."

"You're doing the best you can."

His nostrils flared. "I went to Aleon against your will."

"It was a task from the council."

"Stop defending me!"

She quieted.

He turned to her and reached out, cupping his hands around hers. His eyes held the weight of a mountain. "You have so few you can trust, so few you can lean on. But you can trust me, Norah. I won't ever give you another reason to doubt me. Whatever you ask of me..." He shook his head and dropped his gaze again. "And if you tell me to go..." He pulled her hands to his lips but stopped short of kissing the backs of her fingers. "Please don't tell me to go." He clasped her hands tighter. "But if you do... I'll go."

He needed to go. She needed to tell him to go, for the complications that his presence brought, for his own safety and Mikael's. So why couldn't she tell him? The brilliant blues of his eyes glistened with emotion. They begged her.

Their fingers laced together. She knew he would do anything for her. And the world felt right with him by her side, right enough to face any challenge. And she *did* trust him. He said he wouldn't harm Mikael, and she believed him.

She would tell him to go. But not right now.

As if he could read her mind, the corners of his mouth drew up ever so slightly, although his eyes still reflected a sadness. And they settled.

As things eased more between them, Alexander sat back in his chair. He glanced at the books strewn around her on the table. "What are you doing in here?" he asked.

Her heart skipped a beat. She'd completely forgotten to tell him her discovery about her father and his horse from the Wild. "Hamed, Calla and Cohen's grandfather, fought in a battle against Mercia. When I first met him, he figured out who I was by my hair and because I rode a horse of the Wild—*like my father*."

Alexander shifted. His brow creased, and his lips parted.

She could tell from his expression this was news to him too.

"I never saw your father on a horse of the Wild," he said. "When was this?"

"I don't know. I should have asked. Calla and Cohen's parents were both killed, so it would have been a battle with heavy losses for Kharav."

"The first Battle of Bahoul, maybe." Alexander hadn't fought in the original Battle of Bahoul, the battle that had claimed her father's life. His eyes shifted back and forth in thought.

"What?" she asked.

"If your father rode a horse of the Wild, it's not a coincidence that you do too."

Her thoughts exactly.

"And the Wild protected you from the drifters," he added.

"I don't know about *protected*. It killed trespassing men."

"But not you."

These were all things that had swirled in her mind.

"Norah, the Wild is known to mess with the minds of men. Again, this can't be a coincidence. What if we can find answers there? What if you can get back your memories?"

She stilled. Was he proposing they go there? "But the Wild is a dangerous place."

"Not for you. And, Norah, if you could get back your memories..." He leaned forward, holding her hand tighter. "If you could remember."

If she could *remember*... she'd have her whole life back, everything that she was, everyone that she loved. Perhaps she'd be another step closer to finding out this unknown enemy.

"I could take you," he said. He reached across the table and pushed through the books to one that had a loose map parting the pages. He spread it wide and drew his finger from Kharav along a path north, stopping when he reached an unlabeled area just southwest of Mercia. "Here. I could take you back to where I found you."

She bit along her bottom lip. "Alexander, that's a long journey. And it's not that simple."

"Why not? If there are answers there—"

"No. I can't just leave."

His brow dipped. "But you would come back. I'd bring you back. You'd only be gone a few weeks."

"It's not that. I mean, it is a little, but it's not that I don't trust you to bring me back. It's..." It was complicated.

His face hardened. "The Shadow King."

A silence came between them.

"He wants you to forget," he said.

"No, he doesn't want me to forget."

"But he doesn't want you to remember."

She shook her head. "He's never said that. But Alexander..." Her stomach twisted, and her voice dropped to a near whisper. "What if it makes things harder?"

He stilled, and the muscle along his jaw tightened. "Do *you* not want your memories back?"

"Of course I do. How can you say that?"

He quickly drew in a breath and shook his head. "I'm sorry."

She leaned forward and took his hands again. "I think about getting them back all the time, about *needing* them back. But it's also a little scary, I guess. What if the person I was isn't the same as the person I am now? I know that sounds silly—"

"It's not silly." He sighed, looking down at his hands covering hers. "Norah, this is your decision. Not mine, not the Shadow King's. Whatever you choose, I will support you. But if you do want your memories back, I think there are answers in the Wild, and I would gladly take you. Just think about it." He moved to release her, but she held him, pulling his attention back.

"Alexander. Thank you."

He nodded, giving her fingers a gentle squeeze, then stood and left her to the quiet of the library.

Norah pushed out a breath, trying to keep her mind from tumbling into chaos. Of course she wanted her memories back; there was still a desperation to unlock them. So why was she hesitating about the Wild? Because it was a dangerous place, she reminded herself. And they were only drawing conclusions of her ties to it. What if the Wild hadn't been keeping her safe from the drifters? Maybe it just hadn't noticed her. It didn't mean she'd be welcomed back.

But hope sprouted along the cracks of doubt. What if there were answers for her in the Wild? If she wanted to go, would Mikael understand? He'd once said her memory loss might have helped them come together, that she might not have wed him otherwise. And if that was true, how would he feel about her getting them back now?

As if thoughts summoned him, the library doors opened, and she turned to see Mikael walking toward her. Had he seen Alexander departing? His demeanor suggested he hadn't. Yet his stride wasn't an easy one.

There was a strangeness between them, but she couldn't quite place it. They hadn't talked much since her handling of King Gregor the day before, and since her bold claim on Soren.

Mikael had come to their bed late into the night and left before she woke to continue his discussions with Gregor. Midmorning, she'd joined them both for a formal breakfast. While Gregor didn't look at her, Mikael's eyes never left her. He seemed settled, calm, but there was a hook to his gaze, and she couldn't shake it. And the look in his eyes... not anger, but... a challenge? *No*—not a challenge. But what?

She had forced herself to stay composed—unshaken—copying the mask Mikael wore so often, until she could deal with him later.

And that later time would be now, she told herself as he strode toward her to address this strangeness between them. She stood as he neared.

"Gregor's just departed," he told her.

"So, you've reached an accord?"

He tipped his head slightly. "For now."

The king of Japheth had been scheduled to stay another day, but she wasn't surprised by his earlier departure announcement. "I'm sure he was eager to be on his way."

"I'm sure," Mikael said, his voice low. "After seeing a side of the North Queen he wasn't expecting. A side I wasn't expecting either."

This was the root of what lay between them. She'd overstepped, she knew. Both on Soren and Gregor. "I know I've probably made things more difficult..."

He stepped nearer, quieting her. "Perhaps it's a side you'll let me see more often." His eyes burned down into hers, the same as they had at breakfast.

And it hit her. It wasn't the fire of challenge his eyes held.

He stepped closer but didn't touch her, and his voice came in a raspy whisper. "And perhaps I like difficult."

He had liked her control—more than *liked* it. A smile poked at her lips, but she didn't let herself show it. She only stared back at him with the same solid calm she'd given him that morning.

Mikael swallowed, and his eyes darkened until the outer ring was as black as the inside. Hunger pulsed off him. He wanted that control from her now, as if he'd been waiting, as if he couldn't wait any longer.

Her own pulse quickened. The thought of obliging him... It was all she could do to keep her breath from quivering.

Then the words came before she could stop them. "Get on your knees," she told him. But then her mind raced. What was she going to do with him? He wanted from her what she wasn't accustomed to doing—taking.

His nostrils flared as a tremor rolled over his skin, and he sank to his knees. But as he looked up at her—hungry, waiting—her own desire flared, and she knew exactly what she wanted from him.

She pulled the corner of her gown up, raising it slowly. "Kiss me."

A smile peeled across his lips, and his mouth opened slightly, flashing his teeth like he might bite her as well. Heat pooled in her stomach. She might like that.

He slipped a hand under her gown and pushed it up to her right knee, then he bent and brushed his lips across the skin of her upper calf. It was all she could do to keep from trembling under his touch, but there was no hiding the prickles that sprang across her skin.

And he worked his way up, slowly, savoring each spot, teasing her. He reached her thigh, letting her feel his teeth now, and she shuddered. He chuckled darkly—now who was in control? She ran her hands into his hair, mussing it from its tie and weaving her fingers through, then she clenched tight and stopped him. He raised his eyes to hers, his mouth still open, his bottom lip on the inside of her thigh. He would listen to her. She would make him. She clutched him tighter, then she pulled him farther upward, and he followed.

Mikael nipped the sensitive skin inside her upper thigh, too eager, and she clenched him tighter to hold him. She moved a hand from his hair to the side of his face, curving her fingers down underneath the line of his jaw, and tightened her grip—a warning—and he followed with soft kisses. She shifted her leg out to give him more access.

His breath warmed the joining between her thighs, and Norah let her head fall back as anticipation rippled through her. She didn't want to wait any longer—she couldn't—and she hooked her fingers in the silk that covered the most sensitive part of her and pulled it to the side.

And he kissed her.

He kissed her like he did when he took her mouth—his tongue tormenting, his lips worshiping, consuming her. Her spine arched back, and it was all she could do to keep on her feet.

He unleashed the darkness within him that she'd summoned, and she reveled in it. She wanted to drown in it, and she *was* drowning. But still, she needed more, and she'd have it.

Norah pushed him down to the floor, on his back. He reached down and tore at his breeches, but she grabbed his arm, gripping him tightly and stopping him.

"Do not," she hissed.

He would do what *she* wanted. *When* she wanted. The corners of his open mouth flicked upward slightly, and he panted as he yielded.

She didn't know this woman—this woman who moved herself up over him, who was on her knees, straddling his chest. She didn't know this woman who moved up farther, bringing her body back to his mouth. But she liked this woman. She liked the power inside her. The power he gave her—*no*—the power she took. And she liked the feeling of the Shadow King beneath her.

Still, she needed more. Norah moved quickly, impatiently, sliding back down and ripping his breeches open. She released his length and slid down onto him before he was completely free, still fighting to get their clothing out of the way. He was ready, more than ready. He hardened to near bursting inside her, but she gripped him under his jaw and held him. "You'll wait for me."

Everything within him surged under the force of restraint, the struggle of it, and it was enough to send her over. She broke.

As she shattered around him, he found his own release, growling as his body quaked. She clutched him with her thighs—holding him, taking him, absorbing him into the very essence of herself. And as the waves of complete abandon washed over her, she collapsed on top of his chest.

They lay in the silence, still as one, simply breathing. When her senses returned, when her body calmed, she raised her head and propped herself on her elbow, looking at him.

He brushed the tresses of her hair back over her shoulder, and a quiet chuckle rumbled through him. A sudden bashfulness came over her, and heat rose to her cheeks. "What?" she asked him, but she knew she'd gotten carried away.

His eyes moved back and forth between hers, and his lips held a satisfied smile. "If you ever look at me and I seem to get weak, know that I'm thinking of this moment, and how you made me get on my knees for you."

The bashfulness fell away, and his words made her want to do it all over again. She pulled her bottom lip in between her teeth and bit into the soft flesh to stop herself.

They didn't have time to play all day. Unfortunately.

Norah pushed herself off him and rose, re-situating her clothing. The silk of her underwear was slick against her skin—from them both—and it stirred a dip in her stomach again. He watched her as he tied his breeches. Could he see the lust still behind her eyes? Heat rushed to her face again, and she scolded herself. What was wrong with her? He'd done... quite enough. Yet she felt like she couldn't get enough of him.

And suddenly, it dawned on her—they were in the library. She'd been so caught up she hadn't even cared.

"What's wrong?" he asked.

She swallowed as heat rushed to her cheeks. "We just... in the *library*."

His smile widened as he reached out and pulled her close to him. "What's wrong with the library?"

"Someone could have seen us." *Alexander* could have seen them, and her stomach twisted.

He brushed the line along her jaw with the back of his fingers and pulled her attention back to him. "Then they'd see how their salar loves their salara." He bent to kiss her cheeks. "How he worships her." He trailed his mouth back to her lips. "How he sees to her every need."

This man. "You're going to get us on the floor again," she warned, and his eyes darkened with new intent. She put a hand on his chest to contain him.

He chuckled as his eyes drifted to the table and the books scattered around. "What are you even doing in here?" Then his eyes fell on the map, the map Alexander had been walking through with her not even an hour earlier... in the same place she'd told Mikael to get on his knees.

Guilt flooded her.

She shook her head, trying to push back the overwhelming shame filling her to the brim. "Nothing, Alexander was just—"

"He was here with you?"

Her breath seized in her chest. She hadn't meant to say that. Not that she was trying to hide it, but the timing... "Mikael, we were only talking—"

"I'm not upset."

She swallowed. "You're not?"

"Salara, I'm fairly confident that when you think of this library now, you won't be thinking of your justice."

A deep heat flushed across her cheeks, and he smiled. Then his eyes trailed to the table and the map spread wide on top of it. His smile faded.

"It appears one of us still thinks about my justice," she said.

His eyes met hers. A silence hung over them. He didn't ask her what she had talked about with Alexander. She knew he wouldn't, even though he clearly wanted to know.

She wouldn't make him wonder. "He thinks there may be answers for me in the Wild, possibly a way to get back my memories."

Mikael shifted. "Why would he think this?"

"My father was seen riding a horse of the Wild, as I can now."

"Yes, you've told me this, but it doesn't mean the Wild has answers for you. This one connection—"

"It's more than one connection—it's both me *and* my father. And don't forget, I was found in the Wild. Still, it's more than that. Before I was found, I was attacked by drifters."

Mikael stiffened.

"But when they tried to harm me, something intervened and made them kill themselves. It might be a stretch to think this something saved me, but now, with my being able to ride a horse of the Wild, the same as my father..." She shook her head, wiping her face as she pieced it all together for him. "Stories are told about the Wild taking over the minds of men, and my memory loss is a problem of the mind. It can't *all* be a coincidence. And I do wonder—what if there *are* answers there? What if I can get my memories back?"

He said nothing.

She frowned. "Do you not want me to get them back?"

He took her hand. "It's not that." His eyes were dark, but soft. Worried. "It's selfish, I know," he said quietly. "But I fear it. What if remembering everything changes who you are today?"

She slipped her arms around him and leaned against his warmth, breathing him in. They stood in the quiet. Then she said, "I feared that too. But one thing I know for sure—I love you. I know you, who you are." Her voice dropped to almost a whisper. "I just really want to know myself. I want to know my father, and my childhood. Memories are a place where the things you lost aren't fully lost. And maybe I'd discover things that could help us face today's challenges."

He pulled back from her, enough to look at her, and cupped her face in his hands. His eyes moved between hers. "Then you should go."

Her brow dipped, and she sucked in a breath. "Really?"

Mikael nodded. "I'll take you myself."

"Are you mad?" Soren's voice echoed out of Mikael's study and into the halls, making Norah jump.

Alexander stepped closer to her.

"Calm, brother," Mikael said.

"You want to go to the Wild?" The vein on the side of the commander's temple pulsed.

"That's what I said," Mikael said coolly.

"This isn't an enemy you can fight. And you're needed here in Kharav."

"I don't plan to fight. And the Circle will manage things until I return."

Norah had almost forgotten about his council—they could look after things for a short time.

Soren snorted in frustration. "It's too dangerous."

Norah glanced at Alexander, knowing all too well the dangers of the Wild, and she tried to swallow back her building worry. Ever since Mikael had agreed to go, she'd been second-guessing herself. What if they traveled all the way there and found nothing? Worse, what if she'd assumed wrong and there wasn't a connection? What if the same thing that happened to the drifters happened to them? What if someone was hurt? What if Mikael was hurt? "Maybe the lord commander is right," she interjected. "The Wild is a dangerous place. And I've already been there. If there's something or someone there that could help me, why wouldn't they have done so then?"

Mikael shifted his gaze to her. "Maybe because you weren't asking them to." He turned his head back to the commander. "We'll go."

Soren crossed his arms and let out a snarling sigh. "Then I'll take her. This is a suicidal journey."

"*I'll* take her," Alexander said, his eyes fixed on Mikael. "I can take her back to where I found her. It's the best place to start."

Mikael's face darkened. "Then you'll lead the way. But I'm going with you."

"As am I," Soren added, his glare at Alexander matching the daggers in his voice.

Alexander sighed. "Fine."

"Fine," Mikael echoed.

Soren grunted. "Fine."

A fog of quiet rolled in.

Norah swallowed. "Well, then," she said uneasily. "Looks like we're *all* going." She drew in a breath, trying to calm her nerves, then nodded slowly. "I'm sure it will be... *fine*. All of us. Together. Going to the Wild."

Just fine.

CHAPTER TWENTY-THREE

Norah breathed in the cold air of morning, but her excitement warmed her. Or maybe it was her fear. Fear of the Wild and—she looked at the men riding with her—fear that if tempers ran afoul, they might not even make it there.

They rode north. Their route would take them through the Canyonlands of the Uru, through more Horsemen tribes, and then northwest, to the Wild. She looked forward to seeing Tahla again. A smile came to her face as she thought of the Horseman chief's daughter.

Despite Soren's and Alexander's vehement objections—the first time she'd seen them agree on anything—they journeyed without an army or even the Crest. Mikael felt they'd travel more safely without attracting attention, although Norah suspected that Soren and Mikael drew as much attention as any army. Caspian came with them, and he and Alexander rode ahead. Mikael rode beside her, and Soren followed behind.

The journey was quiet. They reached the clefts of the canyons on the second day, with everyone still alive and somewhat civil. Now if only they could repeat that for ten more days or so.

As expected, the Uru swarmed in welcome.

"Salar," Tahla greeted Mikael as she reached them. She grinned at Norah. "Salara." She slid off her horse.

Norah did the same, and they embraced warmly. "Hello, Tahla."

"This is a happy surprise." The chief's daughter laughed. "What brings you?"

Norah looked back at Mikael.

"We travel to the Wild," he said.

"Sol!" Tahla exclaimed. She stared at Mikael for a moment before looking at Soren, then to Alexander, then back to Norah. "All of you?" she asked. "Together?"

Norah pursed her lips and nodded. "Yep," she said stiffly. She held back the jest of whether they'd even make it there.

"Why would you go there?" Tahla asked.

"We think it holds answers to questions I have," Norah told her. "Answers that I desperately need." Tahla didn't know about her memory loss, or the assassins, and neither were something Norah wanted to explain, at least not right now. Luckily, Tahla didn't push her for more.

Tahla's brow furrowed as she clutched Norah's hand and looked at Mikael and Soren with a concerned eye. "But the Wild isn't a welcoming place."

Soren grunted. "We don't like to be welcomed."

Tahla rolled her eyes. "Come," she told them. "Come get something to eat, and rest before you're off again."

They made their way to the settlement on the river that glowed against the evening's setting sun. Mikael broke off to give his respects to Chief Coca Otay, and Tahla showed Norah to her room.

"I can see you're worried," Norah said as they stepped inside, and she put her pack on a chair.

Tahla nodded. "The Wild is a dangerous place, Salara. You hold Savan's favor, but Salar and Soren don't. I fear even for your Northmen. Promise me you'll take care of them. That you won't let them be harmed."

"I promise," Norah whispered.

Tahla gave a warm smile. "It's good to see you, sister."

"And you. Maybe on our return, we can spend more time."

"I'd like that." The chief's daughter gave another smile with her hand on the door. "Salar should be along soon. I'll let you rest now."

Caspian smiled as he pulled off his jacket. He wasn't facing the door, but he knew she was there. He laid his jacket on the chair and turned. By the gods, she was beautiful. But she wasn't smiling.

Tahla stepped inside, closing the door behind her. "How did you do it?" she asked him. Her tone was almost angry.

His brows drew together. "Do what?"

"Make me think about you every day, every moment that you were gone? It's a cruel thing."

He almost smiled again, but he couldn't tell if she was truly angry. "I would never be cruel to you."

Tahla crossed the space between them, and his pulse quickened. Her nearness both freed his spirit and captured him at the same time. She reached up and grazed her fingertips against his chest before spreading her palm flat. Even through his shirt, her touch ignited a fire across his skin. His body came alive. As much as he tried to conceal it, he knew she felt his energy when the corners of her mouth turned up.

"Have you suffered this cruelty too?" she asked.

The cruelty of wanting—he knew it well. But he didn't answer.

"I'll be taking that kiss now," she said as she lifted herself onto her toes.

Instinctively, he dropped his head to hers so that their lips were almost touching, but his mind screamed restraint. He had known temptation would come with seeing her again, but he hadn't expected it so quickly. He'd almost forgotten the power she had over him, and how strong it was. It took every ounce of self-control.

"Tahla," he breathed.

She clutched his shirt in her fist and pulled him closer. "Kiss me, Northman."

It was enough to push him over. His body betrayed him and moved before his mind could stop him. He swept his arm around her and covered her mouth with his. Tahla kissed him back with a hunger that drove a frenzy within. Her body moved against him, demanding more than a kiss. She pulled up his shirt, and he broke from her lips long enough to let her take it from him. Then they collided again.

While he'd never touched a woman, he wasn't ignorant in ways of the flesh. Primal desire whispered in his ear, instinctively telling his body exactly what to do. He ran his hands over her hips, down the backs of her thighs, and lifted her against him. She wrapped her legs around his waist.

Caspian walked her to the bed as she peeled her dress off over the top of her head. She wore nothing underneath, and the feel of her skin against his drove an animalistic desperation to escape the rest of his clothing. He laid her back onto the bed, not knowing quite how he managed to shuck off his boots and breeches and find himself naked over her. Not that he cared for how. The warmth of her body was intoxicating, and he was rapt in it.

He moved between her thighs, but as she positioned him to slip inside her, he paused.

"What's the matter?" she panted.

He shook his head softly. "Nothing," he whispered, trying to temper his need. "I just want to look at you for a moment."

Her large brown eyes moved back and forth between his. How could any man not be swallowed into their depths? Everything about her was perfect, even her imperfections. Caspian had never thought he'd be pulled from the values he'd held all his life, but it didn't feel like he was acting against them. Something more than temptation called to him now.

Slowly, he brought his mouth back to hers. He slipped his hand behind the nape of her neck and—gently, tenderly—held her to him. He let his lips bare his heart. When he pulled back again, her eyes held a look he didn't understand.

"That's a lover's way to kiss a woman," she whispered.

"Then I've revealed myself."

She shook her head slowly. "Don't say things like that."

"I don't want to just madly take you like this, Tahla."

She raised a brow. "Is this where you deny yourself pleasures of the flesh again, and we spend the night drunk on each other's words?"

"No," he whispered, "this is where I decide I'm yours." He had been since the moment he first laid eyes on her. "But I want to give myself to you, not lose myself in you."

She reached up and brushed his cheek with the back of her fingers. "I told you not to say things like that. I can't love you, Northman. I cannot be yours." Her voice held a twinge of regret.

"I know," he said sadly, and bent his head to kiss her again. It didn't stop him from being hers.

She kissed him back, and he tightened his arms around her. Tahla reached down to guide him back to her, and he sank inside her. They both gasped and lay still in the silence. His body begged to move, to thrust, to fill his need, but he stayed. He wanted to feel her, to know every part of her.

Slowly, she started to rock her hips against him, and he matched her rhythm. They moved together as one. Never had he felt so close to someone. He pushed himself deeper. His need for her was beyond the want of the flesh, beyond desire. He loved this woman.

They alternated between love and desire—between moments of feverish build and the slow of relishing one another.

As they moved, he felt her hunger for him grow. She shifted and rolled them so she could take the top, and she straddled him with her hands spread wide against his chest. Her breaths came faster now, and the thrust of her hips more fervent. He worried he might not last until her peak, but as her body clenched and bucked around him, he let his own climax come.

He was no stranger to the pleasure of release, but with Tahla it came deeper, richer, etching her mark into his innermost self. The fall of a thousand rains stippled across his skin, and the hold of a thousand chains bound him to her.

She collapsed on top of him, and they both lay panting. Caspian wrapped his arms around her and mouthed gentle kisses along her shoulder. He could stay like this, with her, forever.

Tahla pushed herself up to sit but didn't pull free. Her warmth still surrounded him. She brushed a lock of hair from his brow.

So many things he wanted to tell her, but most were confessions of his heart—things he couldn't ask from her in return.

"I fear for you going to the Wild," she said.

She feared for him. He smiled. "Don't. I've lived a life to be envied, and I'm grateful. I accept my fate whenever it may come."

"I don't accept it," she told him. "Come back to me, Northman." And she leaned forward to kiss him again.

Chapter Twenty-Four

The journey to the Wild felt endless. It took longer than what it would have taken to reach Mercia. The flatlands of the Horsemen tribes gave way to rocky hills, slowing their pace. Norah found herself looking northeast, knowing Mercia wasn't far beyond the horizon. Her heart longed to change her course, ride to her grandmother, her kingdom, her home. But they journeyed on.

The Wild came into view as any other forest, ordinary and unremarkable. Norah knew it was anything but. They stopped at the edge of the tree line and dismounted. Sephir tossed her head, and Norah put a hand on the mare's neck to calm her.

"I forgot this is home for you," she told the animal, smiling sadly. She knew what she needed to do. She loosened the girth on the saddle and pulled it from the mare's back. Then she took off the pad underneath. Sephir tossed her head again, feeling her freedom, and bolted into the forest.

Norah stood, holding the saddle pad in surprise. She sheepishly looked back at the men. "That wasn't exactly how I had imagined it," she admitted. "I thought I'd at least get some kind of goodbye."

Alexander gave her a sympathetic smile.

The men dismounted and hobbled their horses. Norah raised a brow as they situated their weapons. Soren wore a crossbow on his back along with his short sword, and a dagger and axe at his waist. He held his massive battle-axe in his hand. It seemed excessive, but had she expected anything else?

They left their horses at the boundary and continued into the trees. Norah wasn't sure what she was expecting, but she found breaching the edge of the Wild to be somewhat anticlimactic. Everything about the forest seemed like a forest should be—filled with natural beauty. Serene. Peaceful.

They walked deeper into the Wild, but nothing was unusual about the needled trees, the wood-spiced air, or the mossy ground. Spring hadn't fully come to the northern lands, but the rage of winter had passed and given way to a sprouting of small greens.

Her eyes combed the trees. She didn't even know what she was looking for—a random animal? The fox friend she'd met when she first found herself lost in the Wild? Norah started to feel foolish. What if this was all for nothing? She chided herself for expecting a white fox to show up and lead her to a magical faerie that would restore her memory. What if they found nothing here?

"I'll scout ahead," Alexander said, and picked up his pace, splitting away from the small group.

"I'll go with him," Caspian added, and followed.

She didn't like the idea of them breaking off, but she didn't stop them. They were likely safer away from Mikael and Soren, anyway.

"We're wasting our time," Soren muttered as Alexander and Caspian disappeared into the trees.

"We keep going," Mikael pushed.

Deeper into the forest they went. Norah let her hands skim the trees as she walked by them. The rough bark against her skin was strangely comforting. There was a beauty to this place that felt like home.

"There's nothing here," Soren growled, thumping the head of his axe on the ground in agitation.

No sooner than he'd spoken, a strange feeling rippled through her, and the forest became suddenly silent. Too silent. Norah scoured the trees around them. They weren't alone. "Something *is* here," she breathed. Prickles rose across her skin.

"Salar," Soren called out. Norah looked back to see the commander stopped. He bared his teeth in pain.

Mikael paused and looked back. "What is it?"

"Run!" Soren shouted as he dropped his axe and pulled the crossbow from his back.

Mikael glanced around them, looking for the danger. Norah did the same, but she saw nothing.

"Run!" the commander begged.

Then Norah realized what was happening. Terror flooded her, but before she could react, the commander released a bolt from the crossbow at Mikael. The arrow hit him squarely in the shoulder with a force that twisted him back.

"No!" Norah screamed.

"Run!" Soren pleaded.

"He has no control!" Norah cried. "Mikael, run!"

But Mikael couldn't. He clasped onto a nearby tree for support, gripping his shoulder as blood poured between his fingers. "Soren!" he called back. "You're stronger than this!"

Soren shook his head, raging through his clenched jaw in the agony of helplessness. A second bolt still sat in the double crossbow, and he wept as he took aim again. "Run!" he pleaded.

"No!" Norah screamed again as she jumped in front of Mikael.

"Salara, get out of the way!" Mikael bellowed.

"Soren, stop!" she called to the possessed commander. "Look at me. You're not going to hurt me."

Just then, Alexander burst through the trees with his bow and took aim at the commander. Caspian was ready beside him with his sword drawn. "Drop the bow!" Alexander roared.

"End me!" Soren begged.

"Norah, get out of the way!" Alexander yelled.

"Don't shoot him!" she cried back.

"Bear!" Soren begged again. "Kill me!"

"Alexander! No!"

"Salara!" Mikael yelled from behind her.

Soren strained against the unseen force. "Bear—do it!"

"I said no!" Norah screamed back.

Alexander snarled through his teeth, but he held firm.

No arrow pierced the air. From either of them. A quiet came again.

Caspian put himself between Soren and Norah, and as Alexander moved closer to the lord commander, his bow still drawn, the force released him. The crossbow fell from Soren's hands, and he dropped to his knees. His head hung low as he gasped for breath.

Norah turned and ran to Mikael, helping support him as he sank to the floor of the forest. She gasped at all the blood. "Are you all right?"

He grabbed her arm and pulled her close. "Why would you do that?" he hissed through clenched teeth. He held her tightly, his eyes glistening in a raging fear. "You'll be the death of me before any arrow!" He released her arm and reached up to clasp her cheek. "You can't ever do that again. You can't risk your life for mine."

But she couldn't promise that. "Are you all right?" she asked again.

He groaned as he pulled the arrow from his flesh and held his shoulder tightly. "I think so," he panted. "How did you make it release him? How did you make it stop?"

"I don't know, but I think I'm safe here."

"Safe from what?"

"From you," a voice answered him, startling all of them.

A woman stepped out from behind a tree. She was small, but not a child. Her dark hair hung long, with a few tendrils braided with forest greens. She wore earth-toned fitted layers, delicately woven with beautiful but subtle embroidery. Norah had seen this before—on her dress when she woke in the Wild. But she didn't have time to reflect on it, for what she found most shocking were the small, elegantly curved horns that sat atop the woman's head.

"Princess Norah," the creature said.

Did she know her? "Who are you?"

"Why do you protect the Shadow King? And what power do you bring here?" There was a sharpness to her tone.

"Are you the Wild?" Norah asked her.

"All around you is the Wild." The woman tilted her head curiously. "This is unexpected, Princess."

"Queen," Norah corrected her. "Queen Norah."

The woman's eyes widened, and she pursed the slightest of smiles. "We knew you had made it home."

To Mercia? Norah didn't know how to respond to that. Surely, a longer conversation would follow. In the meantime, she looked back at the men. "They're with me," she told the creature.

"They're not welcome here!" a voice called from Norah's right, and she turned as another woman emerged from the forest. She was slightly taller than Norah and looked as if she had been formed from the earth, with a soft hue of green to her skin. More striking were the thin roots that grew from her head, weaving back into the mane of flowers and ferns that fell heavily around her shoulders. She was beautiful, and she moved with grace, making no noise as she drew closer. But there was a pain in her eyes and a rage in her tone.

She brought her hand up as if clutching the air. Roots sprung from the earth and seized Mikael.

"No!" Norah screamed.

Alexander released the arrow from his bow at the Wild women.

"Naavi!" the horned creature cried to the woman, and knocked the arrow from its path. Naavi stepped back in surprise, and a third Wild woman leapt from a tree to join her. She was similar to the green woman called Naavi, but her skin shone a shimmering bronze. Above her cheeks and around her temples grew wisps of branches twisted back into the hair woven high atop her head.

A wave of power surged through the air, but it seemed to only pass through them. Alexander released another arrow, unfazed, and this time it found its mark. Naavi cried out in pain, grasping the protruding shaft in her side. The Wild women stumbled backward, and Norah gasped.

Soren leapt forward to Mikael, axe in hand, bringing down the blade and freeing him from the clutches of the forest.

"I can't control them, sister," Naavi cried. "There's a shield!"

Norah's mind swirled, trying to understand what was happening. Then the realization hit her—the women couldn't get inside their minds.

Alexander pulled another arrow into his bow as he advanced closer. But Norah didn't come here for this. "Stop!" she cried, stilling everyone. Alexander paused but held his stance, his bow ready.

"Please," Norah called, "we mean no ill will."

Naavi pulled the arrow from her side, and Norah watched in astonishment as tiny threads of roots braided themselves over the wound, closing it. "Then why do you bring these monsters here?" the woman demanded. "Norah, how can you protect them?"

Norah's heart stopped in her chest. "You know me?" she breathed.

Naavi looked back at the other woman, the one she called her sister.

"Please," Norah begged. "I've come for your help."

"We'll never help the Shadowmen," Naavi said bitterly.

"I said *I* need your help."

"And what makes you think we'll help you?" the sister asked coldly. "You made your choice."

What did *that* mean?

Naavi straightened, recovering from the arrow's wound as if it had never pierced her. "What is it you seek?" she asked.

The bronze woman cut Naavi a sharp eye, and Naavi seemed to withdraw under her sister's gaze.

"My memories," Norah said.

The Wild women looked at one another again in surprise. "You cannot help her," the bronze woman hissed to Naavi. "Not now. But we can rid her of this wickedness that surrounds her."

The sisters looked at the Shadowmen with bitterness, seemingly contemplating their end. But Alexander pulled up his bow again and stepped in front of Mikael and Soren. "I can't let you do that."

"Sana," Naavi called back to her sister, "do you feel it? It's *him*." She stepped toward Alexander, and he fixed his aim on her again.

"I feel it," Sana said between her teeth. The bronze woman cast a daggered glare at Norah. "You say you want our help, but you come with the means to fight?" She looked at Alexander. "I feel your power, seer," she seethed. "But I don't need to take your mind to kill you."

What?

Alexander glanced at Norah and back to the Wild woman. "I'm no seer."

"Then what are you?" Naavi demanded.

"I'm the lord justice of Mercia."

"*What*, not who," Sana said icily.

Confusion flashed across his face, matching Norah's, and he shook his head. "I'm but a simple man."

"And a liar," Sana snapped. "You serve the Shadows?"

Alexander bristled, deeply insulted. "I'm not a liar, and I serve Mercia's queen."

"If you're not a seer, what are you?" she demanded.

Norah's mind spun. Alexander wasn't a seer. He had no powers. But what were the sisters sensing? He glanced back at her, and she could see he had no idea how to answer.

"If you truly come with no ill will, you'll let us look inside him," Sana said to Norah.

Alexander tightened his stance, his bow ready. But Norah hadn't come for violence. She'd come for answers. She needed their help, and she realized she needed to make the first move of trust.

"Alexander," Norah called to him. "Put down your bow."

He hesitated a moment, then reluctantly, he lowered it.

Sana nodded to Naavi, and the green-hued woman moved toward Alexander. She reached out to touch him, but he stepped back. The Wild woman looked at Norah.

Norah couldn't deny her own curiosity. What power did they think Alexander had? "Let her touch you," she told him.

Alexander stilled as Naavi reached out again. She put her palm against his chest. Norah glanced at Mikael and Soren, then at Caspian. They all watched with equal curiosity. The forest was silent as they stood, waiting.

Naavi's eyes widened, and she looked back at her sister. Something unspoken passed between them, but Norah wasn't sure what.

"What are you?" Sana asked Alexander again. "What is this power?"

"I told you, I'm but a man."

Naavi took a step back, giving some space between them. "You serve Mercia but ally yourself with the Shadow King?" she asked him.

"I serve Norah Andell, Queen of Mercia *and* the Shadowlands."

Both sisters jerked their heads toward Norah in surprise. "How is this possible?" Naavi breathed.

"The most obvious way," Mikael said shortly. "We're wed."

Naavi's face twisted. "Norah, this cannot be true."

"It's true," she confirmed. Although she didn't want to talk about her marriage, she wanted to understand what had happened with Alexander. But she didn't get a chance.

"We cannot help you," Sana said firmly.

Cannot or *will not*? "But I've been helped here before," Norah pressed. "It was you, wasn't it?" she asked Naavi, the green-hued sister she felt the most connection to. "You helped me escape the drifters."

Sana scowled at Naavi, who didn't answer, but Norah could see she was right.

"I came here riding a horse of the Wild," Norah continued, "and I've been told my father's ridden the same. Whatever this bond, whatever this connection, I beg you, can you help me? I have no memories, and I'm desperate to get them back."

But Naavi shook her head sadly. "No."

"Who can?" Norah pressed.

"No one," Sana said. "Once memories die, they're gone."

"No," Norah breathed, shaking her head. "That's not true! Pieces have come back. I just need to find out how to get the rest."

Naavi's eyes widened in surprise, and she looked back at Sana. "This cannot be. Perhaps I missed something."

Missed something?

"Naavi," Sana hissed to quiet her.

Norah gaped at her in horror. "You took them?"

The pain in Naavi's eyes answered for her.

Norah let out a quivering breath. "Why?"

The Wild woman shook her head. "That's not an easy question to answer."

"Try!" Norah pleaded, her eyes welling.

Sana glared at Mikael and the commander. "Enough of this foolishness," she told Naavi angrily. "Be done with them."

"Please!" Norah begged.

"Sister," Naavi said softly to Sana, "if this is possible—"

"It's not."

"We must make certain. And"—she looked at Alexander—"do you not want answers about him? We should take them to the pool. The water will show us."

Sana eyed Alexander, then Norah.

"Sana," Naavi pleaded.

Clearly, Sana held more power. Was Sana queen of the Wild? Was there such a thing? Why didn't she want to help?

Sana sighed, relenting. "Only for answers," she said sharply.

Naavi let out a breath and turned back to Norah. "Come. There is much to talk about."

Norah's relief brought a wave of emotion, but she swallowed it back.

"But not them," Naavi said, looking back to Mikael and Soren.

"Please," Norah asked softly. "They mean no harm, and they brought me all this way."

Naavi looked at Sana, and Sana looked at Mikael and Soren. Then Sana said, "I won't kill the Shadow King and his fiend so long as they don't remind me they're here."

The commander snorted, and Norah shot him a daggered look. Mikael grimaced as he stood upright.

The sisters turned and started along a small path.

Norah let out a breath. Whatever drove the hate for the Shadowmen ran deep here. She clutched Mikael as he started forward, and they followed the sisters farther into the forest, and deeper into the Wild.

CHAPTER TWENTY-FIVE

The Wild was hauntingly beautiful, with long tendrils of earthy binds falling from the trees and into the shadowy mist of the forest floor.

A movement to her right caught Norah's attention, and she looked to see a fox, a white fox. She smiled. "It's you," she called incredulously.

"He's missed you," the small, horned woman said.

Her comment confused Norah, but before she could ask more, they came to a large tree with reptilian roots wound thick at its base. A knotty cleft sat in its center, and Sana climbed gracefully upward and slipped through. Naavi followed. Norah stepped into the cleft of the tree and looked back at the men—they'd have trouble getting through. Alexander was already pulling off his breastplate. He gave her a nod, and she turned back to the tree and slipped through the gap.

As she stepped into the darkness, she caught her breath as it opened into a grand cathedral. Tall trees lined the sides like pillared walls, coming to an arched peak, with medallions of stained glass set deep into the woven branches, like windows. Lights hung like stars strung from above, filling the hall with an enchanted glow.

Norah looked back to see how the men were faring. Alexander and Caspian had made it through, but both were without their armor. And then Mikael showed, surprisingly.

"Where's the lord commander?" she asked.

"He's coming," Alexander said with a wry smile.

Soren finally emerged from the passage, stripped of his weapons strappings, his guard covers, and even his winter tunic to fit through. Blood smeared his chest from the scrapes of skin. But in his hand, he still managed to pull through his axe.

Of course.

They followed the sisters through the cathedral and down a hall leading to two ornately arched doors. The doors opened as they approached, and Norah saw they were as thick as the walls. As they walked through, she looked around the room in wonder. Moss and trailing ferns covered the stacked stone. In the center was a crystal-blue pool, lit with floating flowers and vining lights from above.

"It's beautiful," she breathed.

"It is a place of great power," Naavi said. She stepped into the pool and waded to its center. Sana followed.

"Come," Naavi said.

Norah stepped forward, but Sana stopped her.

"Him first," she said, pointing to Alexander.

But Alexander shook his head. "No. I'll give you whatever you ask, but only after you give Norah the help she came for."

Norah's heart swelled.

"We never said she would get her memories back," Sana said.

"You said you would look to see if it's possible," he pressed.

"We will," Naavi said.

"Then you will do that first," he insisted.

Sana pursed her lips, then nodded reluctantly.

Norah wondered what they wanted so badly from Alexander that they would comply.

He nodded to her, and she pulled off her boots and stepped slowly into the water. It was cool, but not uncomfortably so. She waded toward the Wild women, feeling the water move upward, past her thighs and through her clothing. When she reached Naavi, she stopped, waiting.

But Naavi looked at her apprehensively.

"Why do you hesitate, sister?" Sana asked.

Naavi was quiet for a moment. "What if they are back?"

"They are not."

"But what if they are?"

Sana softened. "Then you will see him."

"Who?" Norah asked.

The Wild women paused. Norah didn't understand the reluctance.

"Your father," Naavi answered finally.

Why would the Wild woman care about seeing her father? But Norah didn't have time to think about it before Naavi reached out and took her face in her hands.

Norah closed her eyes and felt herself fall into a glowing darkness, her memories swirling around her. Unlike with the traveler seers, there was no blood spell. She couldn't see Naavi beside her, only her memories being searched before her like the turning pages of a book. Most flew by quickly as Naavi sorted through, but Norah noticed the Wild woman lingering on memories with Alexander, seemingly looking for information. She found the memory of the kiss in Mercia under the tree and watched it slowly—from the initial spark of memory to the kiss.

Naavi drew it back and watched it once more. Norah flushed, but she noticed Naavi moving deeper to the memory from within. Then came the memory of Norah at the tree, waiting for Alexander. The vision expanded and shrank as Naavi looked through each detail.

The pages of her memories turned quickly again as Naavi sifted through her mind. Through Mercia, through her time there, through the castle itself. Naavi stopped in the hall to the throne room. On its wall was a painting of her father, King Aamon. Naavi looked at it for a long time.

The Wild woman finally let the image go and began looking once again through the memories. She shifted to Norah's capture, through the journey back to Kharav, her journey to Odepeth, her time with Mikael. She slowed for a moment on the vision of them lying together in her sanctuary, Mikael holding her close. Norah's cheeks flushed again. She could hide nothing.

Naavi pulled up from the memories and flipped back to the beginning—when Norah first woke in the Wild. She seemed already familiar with the drifters, spending little time on them. But suddenly Naavi slowed, seeing Norah come upon Alexander in the forest. She watched him with seemingly great interest.

Suddenly, her images blurred forward to the temple in Odepeth, quickly pulling the vision of Alexander shown by the traveler seer, comparing it with the image of Alexander in the Wild. Then everything went dark, but Norah still felt her moving, searching through time.

And then she was released. Norah opened her eyes to find herself back in the pool with Naavi.

"I have nothing for you," Naavi said sadly.

Norah's eyes welled. "There must be another who can try," she said.

The Wild woman shook her head. "It does not work that way. We sever them, and they die. You cannot bring them back."

"So, you didn't hide them?" Norah's voice broke. "You just destroyed them?"

Naavi sighed sadly and nodded.

"Why would you do that?"

"For your protection. We severed your link to the Aether. It was the only way we could hide you. As a result, your memories were lost."

Norah shook her head. "I know they're not gone. Something triggers their return!"

"No, it isn't possible to bring them back."

"No!" Norah cried. "If it's not possible, then I wouldn't have gotten any memories back. But I did!" She turned to Alexander. "When you kissed me in Mercia, I saw you, I saw your face. Us, together. We were lying in the fields under the sun, and you loved me. I remembered." A new thought struck her, and she looked at Alexander. "Maybe *you* can bring them back. Maybe you do have power, you just don't understand it."

Alexander shook his head, but Norah's breath shook as she thought aloud. "We were at the tree. Perhaps it's what gave you strength. This pool is a sacred place, a place of magic. Maybe you can use it?"

"Norah, I've spoken the truth," he said. "I'm only a man. I don't have this ability. I don't have any power."

"There's a great power within you," Naavi countered. She turned to her sister. "I saw it. He is the one who found her. But his shield hid him from us. It covered her too. It's why she disappeared from our sight." Naavi paused as she shook her head. "But I don't understand. The vision from the traveler clearly shows his face. How can the traveler see when we cannot?"

"How do you know there's a power?" Norah asked. "What is it you feel?"

Sana didn't answer, visibly reluctant to share, but Naavi explained, "It's not so much the feeling of his power, but rather the interruption of our power. Seers are protected from the sight of others by their shield. It creates a void. We've never seen a shield strong enough to cover others, but," she paused and nodded at Alexander, "his does. It's why you seemed to disappear from us when he first found you. And why we didn't sense you in the forest today until he distanced himself from you."

When Alexander had gone to scout ahead.

"I told you I'm not a seer," Alexander said, growing short of patience.

"Where there is a shield, then there must be sight," Naavi insisted. "And with a shield as strong as yours, then a very great sight."

"If he had sight that powerful, he would know," Norah said.

"Unless he's not telling the truth," Sana replied.

"I speak only the truth," Alexander said agitatedly. He turned to Norah. "I swear to you."

Naavi looked perplexed. "Then how does he have a shield? And how can the traveler see him when we cannot? None of this should be possible."

Soren snorted. "How long will you keep saying things are not possible when they are obviously so?"

Sana shot him a warning look. "You were not to remind us of your presence," she snapped.

"What must you do to try to help her?" Mikael asked Alexander directly.

"I don't have power," Alexander stressed.

"You will try!" Mikael snapped.

Alexander sighed in resignation and looked at the sisters. "Tell me what to do, and I'll do it."

But Sana shook her head. "You're talking about a power that we don't know. We only guess at this point."

"You said the memories came when you touched him?" Naavi asked Norah.

Norah nodded uncomfortably. "When I kissed him." Mikael's face darkened.

Naavi waved Alexander to the pool. "Come."

Slowly, he pulled off his boots and stepped into the water.

"Think of a memory that is important to you," Naavi told him. "One that you share with her, one that is strong within your being."

Alexander took Norah's hands and closed his eyes. His hands were warm around hers. Norah watched him as he drew in a deep breath and exhaled slowly. She wondered which memory he'd choose. Would she see it as hers? Or from his perspective? She closed her eyes too. And waited.

But nothing came.

Norah opened her eyes again. She glanced at Naavi, then back to Alexander, who still stood immersed in his mind.

"You must push against your shield, beyond it," Naavi told him. "Dig into your being. If you love her, use it."

Alexander broke from his memory, straightening. Norah bit her lip. He would never admit such a thing so openly.

Yet he didn't deny it. He glanced at Naavi, then back to Norah. He stepped closer.

Norah's heart raced in her chest.

He brought his hands to her face and brushed her cheeks with his thumbs. Then he pulled her even closer as he lowered his head to hers.

Her breaths came quicker now.

"If this doesn't work," he whispered, "forgive me."

Alexander and Norah stood in the pool of the Wild. A memory that was important to him, the Wild woman had told him. There was such a memory. There were many—ones he thought about often. But one in particular filled his mind. It wasn't a great event, or one that many would think was significant, but those weren't the memories that fueled his love. The memories most important to him were the smaller things—Norah's smile, the way her eyes gave away every emotion, the way she laughed.

Slowly, he brought his lips to hers and kissed her, deeply. He willed her mind to come back to her. And he focused.

Alexander walked through the kitchen of the castle, searching for something sweet to eat. He grinned as he spied a fig and pulled his knife from his belt, grabbing it and cutting it in half. Just then, Norah sprang through the door, laughing in surprise at seeing him.

"What are you doing?" he asked her with a grin as he slipped his knife back in its sheath.

"Hiding from Grandmother!" she smiled breathlessly. "Don't tell her you saw me."

He chuckled and shook his head. "I'll not lie to your grandmother."

"Alec!" she pleaded.

"She'll know."

They heard voices in the hall, and Norah looked at him wide-eyed, but he shook his head again.

"You're intolerable!" she exclaimed as she grabbed his arm and pulled him along with her. "You're coming with me, then." She ran down the back hall and into a small supply room, pulling him in and closing the door behind them. They stood together closely in the cramped space, facing each other.

"Why are you hiding?" he asked her.

"Quiet," she hushed him, and covered his mouth with her hand. "Seriously, Alec, you've no concept of whispering whatsoever."

He grinned under her palm. But they both froze as the voices echoed through the hall and drew nearer to the door.

"Where has that girl gone?" he heard Catherine say. "Victoria, check the stables."

Alexander's heart beat faster, and he knew Norah felt it. She drew her hand down to his chest and looked up at him with smiling eyes. Her nearness intoxicated him, and she seemed to like it. He still had half the fig in his right hand, and he brought it up toward her mouth.

"Fig?" he breathed.

She smiled and cupped his hand with hers, bringing it to her mouth and taking a bite. He let his fingertips graze her cheek, and his thumb line her lips. He dipped his head and brought his mouth to hers, drinking in the sweet taste of fig and the honey of her being. She pulled him closer and kissed him back.

She gently broke their kiss, looking into his eyes. "Do you love me, Alec?" she whispered.

"I've always loved you," he told her. "Surely you know this." Then he bent his head to kiss her again.

When he pulled away, they were standing in the pool again.

"Did you see?" Alexander asked her, still holding her face in his hands.

Norah stood with her eyes closed, her mind swirling. A tear fell down her cheek, but not from the memory.

From failure.

She had felt nothing. Seen nothing. Remembered nothing. They'd come all this way, braving the dangers of the Wild. And for nothing. She'd lost them, her memories. They were gone.

She shook her head, opening her eyes.

"I'm sorry," he said softly.

A trickle of blood ran from his nose, and she quickly forgot her sorrow. "Alexander," she said, alarmed.

He moved to step back, but his legs gave out and he sank to his knees, nearly falling forward. His eyes closed as his consciousness faded.

"Alexander!" she cried, and grabbed him, keeping his head above the water. "Help me!"

Naavi and Sana grasped his arms and pulled him to the edge of the pool. Caspian grabbed him, dragged him out, and rolled him onto his back.

Fear surged through her. "What's happening?" she cried.

Naavi pursed her lips together. "His shield is very strong. When he works against it, it's too much for his body."

"Why didn't you say something?"

"We told you we don't know what his power is!" Sana snapped. "We don't understand it. We don't know why he has a shield but not the sight.

We don't know how some of your memories came back, or how to bring back the rest. We certainly don't know the consequences if we try!"

"Sana," Naavi whispered, trying to calm her sister.

"Do you know if he'll be all right?" Norah asked through her tears.

A heaviness hung in the air. "He should regain his strength with rest," Naavi told her.

Norah knelt beside him, brushing the wet locks from his face.

"Try to look inside him now," Sana told her sister, "while his strength is gone."

"I don't know if I like that," Norah said.

"We've kept our part," Sana said. "He promised us."

She was right. Alexander had promised. And maybe they could learn more about this strange power Alexander had. Reluctantly, Norah nodded.

Naavi knelt over Alexander, putting her hands on his chest, and she closed her eyes. Shifting her shoulders, she bowed her head. A frown formed on her lips. She paused, opening her eyes briefly and looking at her sister, and then ran her hands to Alexander's head before trying again.

Finally, she stopped, shaking her head. "It's too strong, sister. It protects him even now. I can see nothing. Not his memories, not his dreams. I can't even feel his mind. I don't know what he is. But if I can't see him, others can't either."

"Well, you're wrong," Soren cut in. "We saw the visions of him with our own eyes."

"There is no power escaping this shield. Whatever creates those visions, it's not here."

"Or it is, and you can't see that either," he said gruffly.

SHADOW QUEEN

Sana's eyes burned. "I'll see you cut out your own tongue."

"Please," Norah begged for civility. She fought to hold back her tears of disappointment, the upset. She would never get her memories back, but if she focused on that right now, she'd fall apart. She turned her mind back to Alexander. "We'll stay until he wakes, and then we'll be on our way."

There was a darkness to Sana's eyes, but she said nothing.

"Bring him this way," Naavi told them, turning down a long corridor.

Caspian looped one of Alexander's arms over his shoulders, but Alexander was a larger man, and Caspian struggled to rise.

Norah looked pleadingly at Soren, and he clenched his jaw as he grudgingly pushed Caspian aside, picked up Alexander over his shoulder, and carried him after the woman.

Naavi led them to a chamber with a small bed and soft woven blankets. Soren dropped Alexander onto it less gently than Norah would have liked, and she glared at him.

Norah straightened his head on the pillows and brushed his hair from his face. With his eyes closed, he looked so peaceful.

"Rest now," she whispered to him as she clutched his hand.

CHAPTER TWENTY-SIX

Naavi offered Norah a cup of hot tea as she sat down in a side chair. "Sana's gone to the library to search the manuscripts, to see if there's anything that can be found."

Norah gave a nod as she took the tea. "All I keep thinking is that there was the tree in Mercia."

"There's no tree in this world with magic more powerful than the Wild, and the greatest of our powers is in the pool. If there was magic that could give you what you wanted, it would be the water."

"Then it has to be Alexander," Norah said.

"Or it's you," Soren interrupted.

Norah looked up with a start. "What?"

He shrugged. "Maybe it's not that you're bringing memories back to life. Maybe you just didn't let them die. Not all of them." He nodded to Alexander. "At least not of him. And then maybe you uncovered only the pieces still there."

"No," Naavi shook her head. "I broke the bond."

He grunted in annoyance. "Only a fool would believe they could."

The room fell silent. Mikael sank onto a bench by the wall, his face stoic. Even Caspian shifted uncomfortably in his place near the doors.

Her heart sank with the thought that maybe Soren was right. When she'd seen the traveler in Mercia, there was a door that wouldn't open to her. Then the kiss with Alexander brought back the memory of them at the tree. With Bhasim, the traveler in Odepeth, that same door had been opened, that memory inside, but nothing else. He'd told her there was nothing else, but she hadn't believed him. She believed him now.

"So that's it then," Norah said softly, breaking the quiet. "The rest of them are gone." She felt the tears on her face and wiped them away. Anger suddenly welled inside her, and the cup of tea shook in her hand. She looked up at Naavi. "What a cruel thing," she said. "Those memories were mine, and you took them!"

Naavi sighed. "It wasn't meant to be cruel. It was meant to save you."

Norah stood abruptly, dropping her cup to the floor. It shattered against the stone. "But you didn't save me, did you? I was still taken by the Shadow King, and as if that weren't enough, everything I loved was stripped from me. My home, my family—you took everything from me."

Sana stepped into the room and came quickly to the defense of her sister. "Your father saw the vision of the Shadow King taking you, your lifeless body carried away by a monster." She glared at Mikael with a bitterness in her eyes, then looked back at Norah. "He brought you here, begged Naavi to protect you. He knew what would happen, but he begged her anyway. And she did as he asked."

Naavi's eyes were filled with tears. "It was the hardest thing I've ever done," she said, recalling. "Your father didn't want this for you, but he was desperate." She looked at the unconscious justice. "To hide you from the Eye, I had to break the bond to the Aether. When you could no longer cry out for those you loved, I stopped. And you disappeared from the eyes of this world."

Those she loved...

Mikael stood. He didn't meet Norah's gaze as he stepped through the side door into an adjoining chamber.

Norah glanced at Soren, and he cut her a dark scowl. What did he want from her? She had nothing left to give.

"I'm sorry, Norah," Naavi said. "If there were more I could do for you, I would." Then she and Sana slipped out of the room, leaving Norah to her despair.

Norah put her head in her hands. Cruel, cruel fate. She let out a defeated breath. She had lost everything. Then she stopped.

Not everything.

She stepped through the side doorway, into what she had thought was an adjoining chamber, but it was a large outdoor hall with a small fountain in the center. Mikael stood beside it, gazing into its waters.

"Mikael," she said softly.

He stirred slightly, hearing her, but he didn't answer.

She came to his side, letting herself take in the calming sound of the fountain. "I said things I didn't mean," she said.

"You did mean them, but they're things I already knew to be true."

"I'm sorry," she whispered. "I know this is hard. But, Mikael, I love you."

He shook his head. "You wouldn't if you could remember." He looked blankly at the fountain. "So strong it was, your love for him, that even the Wild couldn't take it all from you. It's but a shell now, a fragment of what it once was, yet... I still not dare ask you to choose."

She brought her hand to his face. "Mikael," she breathed. "I—"

But he clasped her hand gently and pulled it down. "Please, Salara. Leave me for a while. Just a while."

She didn't want to leave him. She wanted to take back what she said. But it was too late for that. He thought she didn't love him, at least not as she loved Alexander, but he was wrong. She would make him see that. But for now, she squeezed his hand before leaving him to the quiet.

Norah returned to the room with Alexander and sat in the chair beside the bed, at a loss for what to do or what to say.

Soren watched her with his same menacing scowl.

"I know you're angry with me," she told him.

"We should never have come here."

"Do you really believe that?" she asked.

"So, you had one question answered. At what cost?" he said bitterly. "Salar almost died today. Your Bear lies unconscious. All so you can live in the past. What about your future? What about all of our futures? Is that not enough?" He turned and left, walking back toward the great cathedral, where they first entered.

Her gaze found Caspian's. His eyes weren't unkind.

"Was I selfish to come here?" she asked.

He shook his head. "No. I don't think so. It seemed... very possible before... that you could get your answers here. All of us wanted that for you. And we all knew the Wild was a dangerous place."

She nodded, but inside she felt herself about to fall apart, and she swallowed it back. Soren was right. They should have never come. She'd known the Wild was dangerous. Why had she let them?

She moved to sit beside Alexander on the bed. Caspian gave a small bow and excused himself from the room. Alone with Alexander now, she brushed her fingers through his golden locks just above his brow. What had he tried to show her in the pool? Perhaps it was best he couldn't. A tear fell down her cheek.

"These Northmen aren't easy on the heart, are they?" a voice called behind her, and she turned to see Naavi. The Wild woman had seen everything, knew everything, Norah remembered.

"You loved my father," Norah said.

Naavi nodded. "Very much."

"It's why you helped me before."

The woman took a deep breath in and let it out slowly. "It's why I've done everything that I have."

"How did you come to love him?"

Naavi sat down in the chair nearby, pausing a moment in silence. "It was perhaps a year or two after your mother died. Your father would ride out for days at a time, wandering, thinking, wanting to be alone. That's when he found himself lost in our wood. So many trespassing souls we've taken, death for all who enter. But something was different about him. A... sadness."

Naavi closed her eyes, seeming to remember. She continued, "I don't know what made me do it, but I allowed him to see me. He stopped, got off his horse, and came to me, as if he knew my power, as if begging for the mercy of an end to his pain. I asked him about this sadness inside him, but he couldn't talk about it. It was too great. So, I looked through his mind, and I saw your mother. I saw you. I asked him if he wanted me to take her away, take away the memories. But he didn't. He said, 'How will I tell my daughter of her beautiful mother if I can't remember her?'"

Norah's eyes welled.

"We sat for a long time," Naavi continued. "He told me about you, how you had hair like the brightest rays of the sun, and how you smiled." She paused. "That's when I fell in love with him. That's when I fell in love with you."

Naavi let out an emotional breath. "I sent him away, home, but he was all I could think of—his eyes, his sad smile. When he returned several weeks later, I knew he thought of me too. He came many times over the years, our love growing stronger each visit." Her face fell. "But when he came in the night, with you, with war on the horizon—I can't see visions of the future, but I knew it was the last time I would see him." She reached out and clasped Norah's hand. "I'm so sorry. But I did what I thought was right."

"I don't fault you," Norah said softly. "And I'm sorry for my words. I understand that without your protection, I would've been visible to the seers. Had I been found by the senior Shadow King, as opposed to his son, this would have been a very different story."

Naavi nodded, and they rose. Norah followed her to the window, and they stood quietly in the soft glow of the setting sun.

"Was I here all this time?" Norah asked.

"Yes," Naavi told her. "I loved you like my daughter."

"Is that how I was able to ride the mare? Did she know me?"

Naavi smiled. "All the Wild knows you."

"And you gave the horse to my father, the one he rode in battle?"

Naavi nodded. "My own stallion, Lethos. But Lethos returned to me, alone, after the battle with the Shadow King." The woman looked away, unable to hold her emotion.

That's why Naavi so hated the Shadowlands. Norah waited until her own emotion passed, then she asked, "Did I know my story when I lived here?"

"I told you pieces, enough that you decided you had to return. We rode to the edge of the Wild, where we said goodbye. Kiku was to lead you back to Mercia."

Kiku? Norah smiled. The fox.

"But you didn't follow him, not at first." Naavi pursed her lips. "I should have known that would happen. You've never been one for signs. I hope fate has learned to be very direct with you."

They both let out a small laugh.

But then Naavi grew serious. "I did intervene, to save you from those men. You were so scared. I wanted to come to you, comfort you, but you no longer knew me." She seemed wounded by the memory. Then she straightened. "You followed Kiku after, though, and I let you go. But then he returned before nightfall, much too soon. He said a man had found you, taken you away. But we couldn't see this man. We couldn't see what had happened to you. I... I almost left the Wild to find you." She took a breath. "But the wind brought us whispers that the Mercian princess had returned. And I knew you were safe."

"Why did you take the memory of this place from me too? The memory of you?" Norah asked her.

"You made the decision to leave and return to Mercia. We must protect the Wild, and the secrets here. That is why Sana wouldn't let you keep the memories."

"You let my father keep his."

"She shouldn't have," Sana's voice called from behind her. Norah turned with a start. Sana's eyes locked with Naavi's. "Knowledge of the Wild cannot be trusted with men, with their greed and their need to destroy things." Her gaze shifted to Norah. "And we cannot let you keep what you have seen here."

Norah's heart dropped. Not that she had uncovered many answers, but she had more than she had before, and the thought of losing them again crushed her.

"Do you understand?" Sana asked.

As devastating as it was, she nodded. She did understand.

"And it's why the seer can't return with you."

Norah sucked in a breath. "What?"

Naavi sighed, her eyes pleading Norah to understand. "We can't let Alexander go, Norah."

"He's not a seer!"

"Regardless, he knows too much, and we're unable to take it from him."

Norah shook her head. "No. I'm not leaving without him."

Sana's voice came cold as death. "Then none of you will leave."

CHAPTER TWENTY-SEVEN

Norah sat in the darkness in the room where Alexander lay, trying to quell the threatening panic. Her hands shook as she tried to think of what to do. She wouldn't leave Alexander. Mikael had returned, and he sat with her on a stone bench. Silence hung around them like a thick fog.

Alexander stirred, and Norah moved to his side. His eyes opened, and he stared at her for a moment. Then his brow creased. "Where am I?" he asked. "What happened?"

"We're still in the Wild," she told him. "You exerted yourself too much."

He lay still, his eyes hazed, but then she saw the memory flood back to him. Alexander tried to sit up, but he was still weak. He caught sight of the commander and Mikael, and then Caspian against the far wall, and he looked back at her. "What aren't you telling me? Are we being held here?"

"Not exactly," Soren spoke out. "We leave at dawn. Well, all except you. They're unable to erase your mind, protect their secret, so you stay."

Norah struggled to swallow through the tightness in her throat.

"Well, I suppose we were already down a horse," Alexander joked in rare form.

Soren let out a chuckle, but Norah wasn't amused.

"I'm not leaving without you," she said adamantly.

"You're not staying here," he told her.

"You can't make me go."

"I trust the Destroyer to do what needs to be done to get you away from this place," he said as he settled back and let his eyes close again.

Norah glanced at Soren with a flash of anger, daring him to respond. He refrained, but his look told her he would.

Just then, the chamber door opened, and Norah spun around.

Naavi stepped inside. "Hurry," she said in a hushed voice. "We don't have much time."

"What?" Norah asked, her eyes wide. "Where are we going?"

"Hurry! You're leaving. All of you." She eyed Alexander. "Even him. But you must come quickly."

"Help me!" Norah called to Soren as she tried to pull Alexander to stand. Soren's chest rumbled in objection, but he handed his axe to Caspian and stepped forward. He put a shoulder under Alexander's arm and supported his weight with his own frame.

Naavi led them through the doors and into a narrow hallway. "Stay close," the Wild woman said, setting a fast pace. "His shield covers us, but he's still weak. We have to stay together."

Naavi clasped Norah's hand and pulled her along faster. They wound through a series of halls before reaching a door and emerging into the forest. The cold wind hit Norah's face, and she shuddered.

"We couldn't have entered from this way?" Soren muttered.

"Quickly," Naavi said as she pulled Norah through the trees. Mikael and Caspian followed, with Soren behind them, supporting Alexander.

"We're almost to the tree line," Naavi told them. "Hurry!"

The flight out of the Wild seemed shorter than their journey in. Norah's mind reeled. The magic of this place confused her. They reached the edge of the trees where their horses were waiting for them. All but Sephir.

Soren pushed Alexander onto his destrier, but the justice wavered. He wouldn't be able to stay atop a horse by himself.

"Norah," Naavi said, pulling her to a pause. "I give you your Northman, but"—she looked at the commander and Mikael—"I can't let the Shadowmen go knowing all they've seen. They can't remember the pool, and how to find us. I have to take their memories."

"Take them," Mikael said, surprising Norah. "Take everything of this place." He looked at Norah with a pain that shook her. "And you'll be very cautious of what you tell me."

Norah's eyes welled.

"He must go," Naavi said of Alexander. "I need him to leave so I can use my power."

Norah looked to Caspian. "Take him. We'll catch up to you."

Caspian started to object, but Norah stopped him. "Go," she pressed.

He reluctantly mounted behind Alexander and urged the horse into the darkness.

Naavi looked at Mikael. "Step between the trees."

They could flee, Norah knew. The Wild woman held no power over them beyond the forest. But Mikael stepped between the trees, and Soren begrudgingly followed.

Naavi approached the commander first. "I'll leave you with one memory—just how close your king was to his end. And if you return, there will be no mercy." He grunted as an invisible force took hold of him. She reached up and brought her fingers to his temples, closing her

270

eyes. His body twisted, and he let out a growl as she worked into his mind. She dug deeper, and his growl grew to a roar. Every fiber of his body strained against her, but she held him still.

"What's happening?" Norah asked, her worry rising. "Stop! You're hurting him!"

"It's because he fights," Naavi told her. "It makes it painful."

A cry ripped from his throat as she took the last of the memories from him. Finally, his body grew limp, and his head fell forward.

Norah's breath faltered. She knew she would have fought for her memories. This was her past as well. The commander dropped to his knees, upright, his eyes closed.

"Careful when waking him," Naavi warned her. "There's still a fight inside."

Norah trembled as the Wild woman stepped in front of Mikael. She didn't think she could watch.

But Naavi paused. "I see you, Shadow King. And you're not what I thought you were." She reached out and spread her hand over his bloodied shoulder from where the arrow had struck him. He winced, but then stilled. When she pulled her hand away, the hole in his flesh was fused with thin forest threads.

He looked at her in surprise as he tested his arm.

She nodded. "It will be sore for a few days. This is the only grace I give you, enemy of Aamon. You're not to enter this forest again. And same as your Destroyer, you'll remember the consequences." Then she reached up and put her hands on either side of his face to take his memories.

"Please," Norah begged. "Please don't hurt him."

Naavi closed her eyes, but all was quiet. Mikael made no sound.

"Is it not working?" Norah asked.

"It's working," Naavi said softly, her eyes still closed, "he just doesn't resist."

Finally, Naavi stepped back from Mikael and lowered him to his knees. "Remember," she said, "take care in waking them." She paused. "I'm sorry, Norah," she said, with tears in her eyes. "I'm sorry for everything."

Norah shook her head and caught her in a warm embrace. "I'm alive because of you. Thank you for keeping me safe. Thank you for saving me from the drifters. And for tonight. But most of all, thank you for bringing my father happiness again."

Naavi hugged her tightly. "You'll always be in my heart, and any creature of the Wild will serve you as my daughter. I love you, Norah."

Norah wiped the tears from her cheeks as Naavi disappeared into the darkness of the wood. She turned back to Mikael, and kneeling in front of him, she pulled his face to hers and kissed his eyelids softly. They fluttered underneath her lips, and she trailed her kisses to his cheeks.

"Wake, husband," she whispered.

His hands came up to her arms, and he pushed her back slightly as he opened his eyes to look at her. Confusion flashed across his face in the moonlight, but his emotional pain was gone. Suddenly, he reached up and felt his shoulder. "What happened?" he asked, looking around.

"I thought I lost you," she whispered.

"I'm here," he said softly.

She smiled and kissed him again. But then the urgency returned. She wanted to get away before Sana found them missing. "We have to go. We have to leave now. Will you help me wake him?" she asked, looking at Soren.

His eyes found Soren, who was kneeling and slumped in an unnatural sleep. Mikael stood, shaky at first, but found his footing. He looked at her for a moment, then back to the commander, still trying to make sense of what had happened. She knew he still had the memory of being shot, but now wasn't the time to catch him up on the rest.

"We have to hurry," Norah pressed.

Mikael walked to the commander and put a hand on his shoulder. "Soren," he called.

The lord commander twitched, but he didn't wake.

Norah felt a deep unease in her stomach. "Careful," she warned.

"Soren," Mikael called again, leaning closer.

Suddenly, Soren's hand flew up, grabbing Mikael and pulling him to the ground. He clutched Mikael by the base of his throat, a fury pouring out of him.

"No, stop!" Norah cried.

Her voice made him pause, and he glanced around in confusion.

"Brother," Mikael grunted, and Soren released him, stumbling back from his attack as he recognized his victim. He gripped his head, and Norah suspected some lingering effects. "What happened?" he growled.

"Now's not the time," she said quickly. "We have to go."

"Where's the Bear?" Soren demanded. "And my axe? And my sword?"

"And my armor," Mikael added.

"The justice has ridden ahead. We'll meet up with him soon," she explained. She looked at Soren. "Your axe is by your horse. Forget about everything else. We have to go." Norah reached out and took Mikael's hand. "Please," she said softly. "Trust me." She could see his uncertainty.

Mikael let out a troubled breath, yielding. Then he mounted his horse as Norah climbed onto Caspian's, and they rode into the night.

They journeyed south with a thick silence between them. Mikael glanced at her as they rode, no doubt with questions heavy on his tongue.

But he asked none, and she didn't know where to start, or what to even begin to share.

They caught up with Caspian and Alexander, who had set a small camp. Alexander lay against a rock by the fire, still weak. Caspian cooked a small rabbit over the flame.

"Put out that fire," Soren said angrily. "You tell the world we're here."

"We need warmth, and food," Norah argued.

"Leave it," Mikael told the commander.

Soren grumbled under his breath. "What happened to him?" he said as he looked at Alexander.

Mikael slid off his horse and caught Norah by the hand. He pulled her close and spoke for only her to hear. "Why did you think you lost me?" he asked her. Then he glanced at Soren. "I was shot?"

She took a breath in and nodded.

"And I've been healed, yet I don't remember. Tell me what happened."

Where should she start? Naavi trusted her to keep the secrets of the Wild safe, and she would, but she wouldn't deny Mikael an explanation. A real one.

"Did you get them? Your memories?" he asked.

She shook her head. "No," she whispered. "They're gone. Forever."

His brows drew together. "But you weren't made to forget again?"

Like he was.

"No," she said again.

He looked at Alexander. "Was he?"

She didn't want this to be about Alexander. "It's complicated. My father had a deep friendship with the Wild. It's where he took me to protect me during the war. It's where I was all those years, and it's why

I don't remember. My memories were lost when I was hidden from the seers."

His eyes drifted back to Alexander. She kept silent about Alexander's power, whatever it may be. There was already enough mistrust for him.

"They blame Kharav for my father's death," she continued. "There's still a lot of animosity." She took his hand. "But they saw you differently than they had before and gave a small mercy and healed you."

He thumbed the mended injury to his shoulder.

"Although," she added, "if you return, they'll kill you. So I... wouldn't recommend that."

He smiled sadly as he cupped her cheek in his hand. "I'm sorry," he said softly.

"Thank you for bringing me. It was... a significant risk for all of you. And while I don't have what I came for, I do have *some* answers. And I'm incredibly grateful for that."

He kissed her. "It was worth it then." He turned and pulled a roll from his saddle and laid it near the fire. "Sleep," he told her. "We've a long journey back." Then he left to tend his horse.

Norah sat on the bedroll, but she didn't lie down. She couldn't sleep. Caspian offered her the rabbit, and she ate it slowly as she watched Mikael, who now stood off in the distance, almost blending into the darkness.

Soren came to the fire and dropped down on a large rock nearby. She still felt his scowl upon her. She'd tell him more when he wasn't so angry, which would be a while.

Mikael drifted back toward the fire, but as he moved to sit by Norah, they were interrupted by a sound in the night. They jumped to their feet, and Mikael and Caspian pulled their swords. Soren drew up his axe, and even Alexander staggered to his feet.

Norah looked around, but she couldn't see in the darkness. Her pulse quickened. They should have put out the fire. What else lurked about in the shadows, unseen? She was tired of the constant battle, the constant threat of danger. She wanted to be home. She wanted to feel safe.

A shadow stepped out of the darkness.

Norah let out a breath as she grinned.

Sephir.

The mare had returned. The horse tossed her head with a nicker, and Norah ran to her, throwing her arms around the animal's neck.

"I didn't think I'd see you again," she told her as she exhaled a sigh of relief. "And I also thought you might have been a monster."

Caspian chuckled, a little embarrassed as well. "That horse is not what I was expecting either."

Norah couldn't help but laugh herself. Even Soren gave an amused snort. For once, there was a good surprise.

CHAPTER TWENTY-EIGHT

The Uru welcomed them back in celebration, and Tahla's relief at their safety was palpable. Norah smiled, grateful for friends who cared so deeply.

Caspian followed Norah to the large central fire, where she sat on a large elongated rock. Tahla took a seat beside her.

"I'm so happy to have you back safely," Tahla said. "Tell me of it. Tell me of the Wild."

Of course she'd be curious about it—home of the spirits they had so much reverence for. But Norah had been trusted with its secrets, and she would keep them. Still, it was harmless to share some things. "It's a magical place," Norah told her, remembering its beauty. "But dangerous. And as you said—unwelcoming, even to Northmen. Once you step into the trees, you're at their mercy, and they have little of it."

Tahla leaned closer, captivated.

"The spirits within are powerful," Norah continued. "They embody not only the animals, but the earth, the trees, the wind."

"The wind?" Tahla breathed.

Norah nodded. "But it's not a place for men. And we shouldn't have gone there. We were lucky to leave, all of us."

Norah could see more questions on Tahla's lips, but the chief's daughter seemed to sense her hesitation, and she didn't ask them. She was a good friend. She only asked, "Did you find what you were seeking?"

Norah shook her head sadly.

Tahla reached out and clasped Norah's hand, squeezing it warmly. "Well, I'm grateful you've returned safely."

Norah smiled as she looked around the village. She noted there were quite a few Horsemen, and they looked different from the Uru.

"Who are these men?" she asked Tahla.

"They're Kartan, a neighboring tribe. They're friends."

An Urun woman came and held a bowl of broth out to Norah, and she took it appreciatively. It was delicious, and she tried not to gulp it down too quickly. Caspian accepted a bowl as well, taking a seat nearby.

Chief Coca Otay came and took a seat on a thick log beside Tahla. He said a few words to her that Norah didn't understand, and Tahla responded back—an argument of some sort.

"What's the matter?" Norah asked Tahla quietly as she warmed her hands against the large fire.

Tahla shook her head. "My father's been attempting to convince me I should wed again."

Norah raised a brow and looked at the chief.

"You must look to the future," the chief said. "This would be a good match. Boshtok would make a fine husband for a chieftess."

Tahla mouthed his name at Norah with an annoyed look, clearly disliking it, then she turned back to her father with a smile. "That he would. For some other chieftess."

"Who is this Boshtok?" Norah asked her.

Tahla nodded her head at a man a short distance away who was standing with a group of other Horsemen. "Son of Totekah, chief of the Kartan."

The man she had pointed out was tall. He was lean and muscular, with long, black hair braided back. Norah shrugged. "He's handsome, at least."

Tahla smiled. "That he is."

"And taken with you," the chief prompted further.

Caspian shifted uncomfortably, and Norah smiled. Marriage made some men so uneasy. But she supposed she couldn't blame them, thinking back to how she originally felt about her own.

"Let me prepare you, Father," Tahla said. "There will be no more wedding ceremonies for me."

The old man snorted and poked at the fire. "Foolish woman. An alliance with another tribe will bring strength."

Tahla wrinkled her nose. "I'm strong enough."

"What of an heir?" Coca Otay asked.

She shrugged. "If I want an heir, then I'll have a child."

"Without a husband?" Norah asked in surprise.

Tahla's eyebrows drew together. "Besides the means to make a child, what will a man bring that I don't already have?"

Norah dipped her head to one side, then the other. She couldn't argue with that. Caspian shifted again, to her amusement. Her Northmen would have to accept the more liberal ideals of other peoples, eventually. There were much worse things than a child out of wedlock.

Coca Otay pointed at the lord commander as he approached. "At least be wise enough to choose a powerful father for a child. Soren perhaps."

The commander stopped midstep, realizing he'd entered a conversation he had no interest taking part in. He backed away and slipped into the night. Norah couldn't help the laugh that escaped her.

Caspian rose abruptly, and Norah looked up at him. "I think I'll go check everything before you turn in for the evening," he said, giving her a small bow of his head.

"Of course. Thank you, Caspian." She watched him curiously as he disappeared into the darkness.

But her attention was pulled back to Tahla, who stood and took her father's hand. "I know that you mean well, Father, but these decisions are ones I must make for myself." Norah felt her words all too deeply.

Tahla leaned down and kissed him on the cheek. "Sleep well." She turned to Norah. "Goodnight, Salara."

"See you in the morning," she replied.

Coca Otay gave Norah a respectful nod goodnight and followed after his daughter.

Alexander took Tahla's place on the rock next to her. She was hoping she'd get the chance to talk to him.

"How do you feel?" she asked.

He nodded. "Better. Almost normal."

"But you're not normal, are you?" She watched him for a moment. "Are we going to talk about what happened in the Wild?"

He shook his head. "Norah, there's nothing to talk about. I don't have the gift of sight."

"Why couldn't Naavi control your mind?" she asked. "Why couldn't she see you?"

"I don't know. But I can be seen. You've seen the paintings. The seers *have* seen me."

Norah's stomach knotted as the vision of Mikael's end came to her mind.

Yes, they had.

Caspian sat at a small table in the one-room home he'd been given. He cursed himself. He couldn't think of Tahla as his. She'd been very clear with him, and he'd agreed. At least in his mind.

He cursed again. Of course there would be expectations of her. She was the daughter of the chief. What had he hoped for? That she would marry *him*? He was a simple captain of the Kharavian Crest and Mercian Royal Guard. He had no true wealth, nothing to offer her. In fact, their marriage would dishonor her. He hung his head; he had already dishonored her.

There was a knock on the door, and Tahla stepped inside. Caspian rose to his feet. He hadn't expected she would come to him. She hadn't so much as cast him a gaze since they had returned, and after the conversation around the fire...

They stood, their gazes locked on one another. Then she moved to him. Still, he waited. The silence between them ate at his strength.

Tahla reached up and clasped the side of his neck at the base of his jaw. Not hard, but not gently. "I worried for you, Northman." She pushed herself up on her toes as she pulled him to her. "More than I should have." And she kissed him.

It was a move he hadn't anticipated, like many things with Tahla.

Caspian's body responded, as only she could make it, and he caved to his need. He pushed her back against the wall with their mouths together, and cupped the bare skin of her buttocks underneath her leather sarong. Tahla pulled at the ties of his breeches and freed him, and he lifted her as she wrapped her legs around him. They both shuddered as he sank inside her.

They paused for a moment, and then she shifted to take him deeper. The warmth of her body called to him, and he pulsed with a growing fire, giving in to his want. He moved more fervently.

Suddenly, her thighs tightened around him, almost crushing him. He let out a painful growl as he stopped and strained against her hold.

Tahla smiled and drew her lip between her teeth. "Slow, Northman."

He stilled as he waited for his panting breaths to calm. She was right. He was losing himself.

Caspian carried her to the bed and laid her down on it, without breaking their bond. They peeled off their clothes, somewhat awkwardly, and she laughed as he twisted to shake off his breeches. Then they lay still, looking at one another. Gods, he loved this woman.

He pushed himself deeper, joining their bodies and their souls. He buried himself in the essence of her, but it wasn't enough. "I need you, Tahla," he breathed. "I need you to be mine like I am yours."

A line wrinkled over her brow, and her eyes dipped in sadness. He immediately regretted his words.

"Caspian," she started, "I—"

"Don't answer," he whispered as he cupped her face in his hand. He shook his head. "Don't answer." Then he covered her mouth with his to keep silent the words he most feared—that he would have to let her go.

CHAPTER TWENTY-NINE

It had been several weeks since Alec and Norah had returned from the Wild, and Adrian's mind still spun, wondering what had happened. Norah had shared only that she couldn't get her memories back, that they were gone for good, but no one would actually speak of what had transpired. Not Norah, not Caspian, and certainly not Alec.

He made his way along a cobbled road veining out from the castle. Perhaps he'd ask the lord commander. But that would make Alec furious, as would knowing Adrian had been outside the castle and exploring the city. Anger rose in his cheeks, and he snatched up a rock and flung it behind him, high into the air, toward the wall of the castle. Everyone treated him like a boy still, but he wasn't a boy. He was twenty now, and better than most men with a sword. He picked up another rock and flung it even farther.

Voices caught his attention, and he focused his gaze ahead of him, where a young woman walked with three men around her. She was perhaps his age, her dark hair pulled back and up, although he couldn't see her face from behind. One of the men put his arm around her shoulders, but she shoved it off. She spoke firmly in the Shadow tongue, her words sharp with objection. Laughter rang out from the men, but she wasn't laughing.

Adrian watched closely as he trailed behind, quickening his pace. Another man snaked his hand around her hips and pulled her to him. She tried to twist away, but he held a firm grip, taunting her. Adrian couldn't understand the words, but he knew the message. The man sneered something into her ear, and she twisted back, giving him a sharp slap to his cheek. She had spirit.

The man grabbed her wrist and pulled her closer, and she cried out.

"Leave her alone!" Adrian shouted.

The men paused their noxious play and turned in surprise. On seeing Adrian, one gave a low chuckle. "This doesn't concern you, Northman."

"Yet here I am, concerned," Adrian cut back as he caught up to them. He looked at the young woman. "Are you all right?"

She gave a small nod, but the fear in her umber eyes told him otherwise.

"You see?" the man nearest to him said. "She's perfectly all right with things. Be on your way."

Adrian gave a challenging smile. "But *you* see, *I'm* not perfectly all right with things." He looked at the young woman. "Can I accompany you to where you're headed?"

"How noble of you," the man that held her retorted. "But she's not going anywhere."

Adrian dropped the forced smile. "Release her."

The man pulled the girl closer to him. "If you want her, come get her."

Adrian cursed himself for not having his sword, but he was never one to refuse a fight, and this would certainly be a fight.

As if on cue, the man nearest to him charged with a balled fist for his stomach. Adrian curled forward with his elbows down and together, blocking the attack. He spun and delivered a sharp blow to the man's back as he passed, knocking him to the ground. The second man leapt forward, arcing his fist in the air and bringing it down. Adrian knocked it aside, countering with his own. The first man was back on his feet, and he delivered a steel punch to his ribs. Adrian doubled in pain as he stumbled to the side. The man advanced with a second attack, but Adrian blocked, saving himself from another hit to the side. He threw his elbow up, catching the man under the chin and sending him backward.

The second man grabbed him from behind, pulling him into a choke hold. His first attacker jumped forward, delivering a blow to the stomach that knocked the wind from him, followed by a hit to the side of his face. Adrian coughed and gasped for his breath as blood ran down his cheek. Another blow to his stomach made him drop to his knees.

Adrian fell forward, struggling to draw his breath. The man who held the girl pushed her to the side and drew a dagger from his belt. He grabbed a fistful of Adrian's hair and pulled his head back.

"Would you rather lose your tongue or an eye, hero?" he asked with a grin.

"Fuck you, coward!" Adrian spat.

The man's grin fell, and his breath quivered in anger. He brought the tip of the dagger to Adrian's eye. "I'll take them both, then."

But the tip of a sword touched the man's neck, stopping him.

"Release him," a familiar voice ordered.

The man let him go, and Adrian sank forward, coughing. When he looked up, he was surprised to see the lord commander.

The three men stood obediently at attention and bowed.

Adrian gritted his teeth through the pain as he rose and bowed as well. "My lord," he said, grimacing.

The lord commander looked at the young woman. "See her home," he said to Adrian.

Adrian felt a wave of appreciation—whether for being saved from losing an eye or for the opportunity to walk the woman home, he wasn't sure. "Yes, my lord."

The woman gave a small bow of her head. "Thank you, Lord Commander." She stepped forward, waiting for Adrian to reach her side, then started down the cobbled street.

Adrian looked back over his shoulder as they walked away, but the lord commander stood watching him, presumably waiting until they left to deal with the others. He wondered what the commander might do.

They reached a corner street, and the woman turned and started across the burial grounds.

"This is the way to your home?" he asked.

"It's shorter than going through the city. And generally safer."

He eyed the burial grounds. "You call this safe?"

She shrugged. "Dead people are safer than live ones."

Very true. But he paused at the ground's edge. He'd heard about how the Shadowmen buried their dead, chaining their spirits to this world. The grounds lay covered in marked stones—hundreds of bodies were buried here. Hundreds of souls. What would they think about being walked on? Did they haunt those who disturbed them?

Her brows drew together. "Are you scared?"

He snorted. "Of course I'm not." Still, he lingered.

Her eyes narrowed. "You'll provoke three men and almost get yourself killed, but you won't walk across burial grounds?"

"To be fair, I did see that going differently back there."

She frowned a smile. "How so?"

He didn't want to brag, but... "I'm actually pretty good, I just, uh... I didn't have my sword."

"Oh, I see." She nodded slowly. "Right."

"No, really, I am."

Her smile widened. "Okay."

He couldn't help but laugh. Blood trickled from his eye and down his cheek, and he wiped it away.

"Let me see," she said, and stepped to him.

He dropped his head lower as she examined him with a grimace.

"You've got a pretty nasty gash there." She pulled a handkerchief from her pocket and pressed it against his brow. He winced.

"Sorry," she said, her voice soft.

"What's your name?" he asked as they awkwardly stood and waited for the pressure to stop the bleeding.

"Sevina."

"Sevina," he repeated as he looked at her.

She had large, expressive eyes, but they weren't dark like the eyes of the Shadowmen. They shined of burnt umber, like Mercian summer fields, and light danced in them like each was its own world, with its own sun. She had dark, short-cut locks that fell over her forehead, and longer hair swept back and up, with a few strands loose on the sides. The round of her face curved down to the small point of her chin, and her full lips parted slightly as she held the handkerchief to his head.

"Yours?" she asked.

His brow creased in confusion. "Mine?"

She gave a small laugh. "Your name?"

"Oh, right. I, uh... Adrian," he stumbled over his words. "My name is Adrian."

She bit the bottom of her smile and folded the handkerchief over itself. "You should keep holding this, I think. The cut is deep."

"Right," he said, taking hold of the cloth against his brow.

She started across the burial grounds, and this time, he followed.

"You're from Mercia?" she asked as they walked.

He gave her a smile. "What gave it away?"

"Are you in the army?"

"Not exactly."

"Do you serve the queen?"

"Yes. Well, kind of. I mean, I'm not on the guard yet. I will be, though."

She glanced at him, questioning. "Why are you here in Kharav, then?"

"My brother's here. And I wanted to come see the notorious Shadowlands. Kharav, I mean," he corrected himself. "And meet the lord commander."

"Why?"

Adrian looked at her in surprise. "Because he's a great warrior. And your kingdom is famed."

"As is the North. And you have the Bear. He's supposed to be a great warrior too."

Adrian grinned. He hadn't liked that they called Alec *the Bear* initially, but he'd come to like it. It was a name said with awe, and sometimes a little fear. "He is," he said proudly. "The greatest."

They reached the end of the burial grounds and came to a cobbled road, then took it until it joined another. Rows of houses stood tall against the late-afternoon sky. The homes were quite grand, grander than what was typically found in Mercia, even for nobles.

Sevina stopped in front of a large house with iron gates at the walk. "I'm glad you're here, Adrian," she said. Then she stepped up on her toes and gave him a kiss on the cheek. "Thank you for walking me home."

He grinned. "You're welcome."

She unlocked the gate and stepped inside, then closed it behind her.

"Sevina," he said, making her pause. "Can I see you again?"

She looked back at the house hesitantly, then smiled. "I plan to go to my cousin's tomorrow at midday, if you'd like to walk me."

He'd walk across a hundred burial grounds to do that. "I'll be here."

"All right," she said in a half whisper.

Adrian watched her as she walked to the house and slipped inside. Then he made his way back toward the castle, smiling to himself. He'd seen many women since coming to Kharav, and none were as he had expected. The army had female warriors, powerful women. Sevina was different. Not that he would have minded if she were a warrior—she would have been able to fend for herself, certainly, which Adrian would have liked. But Sevina was delicate and soft, and he liked that too.

When he reached the gates of the castle, the lord commander was waiting. "Lord Commander," he said in surprise.

"Is she home?"

"Yes, my lord."

The commander reached out and clasped his chin, turning Adrian's head and judging the cut above his eye. "That'll need stitches. Come on."

It was worth it.

They walked across the courtyard, but Adrian slowed in seeing Alec striding toward them. His stomach knotted. He'd promised his brother he'd keep out of trouble, which was the opposite of what he'd been doing.

"What is this? What happened?" Alec asked when he reached them.

"It's nothing," Adrian said quickly.

Alec was calm, but his eyes blazed. He was angry. "Did you do this?" he asked the lord commander.

"No!" Adrian said quickly. "There were these men—"

"You got in a fight?"

"He'll need stitches," the lord commander said.

Alec's voice came low, composed—the voice that Adrian hated the most: the voice of disappointment. "You dishonor me, Adrian; you dishonor your queen."

The lord commander snorted. "Seems to me that honor is what he was brawling about."

"You know nothing of honor," Alec cut back.

The commander's eyes darkened.

"What's going on?" Norah interrupted from behind, and all three turned in surprise. "Adrian! Your face!" she exclaimed.

"It looks worse than it is," he assured her.

"How did this happen?"

"Foolishness not to be repeated," Alec promised.

"It was for a woman's fancy, so it probably will be repeated," the commander said with an amused smirk on his brow.

Adrian felt his brother's eyes on him, but he couldn't meet them.

"Are you all right?" Norah asked him.

"Yes, thanks to the lord commander."

The commander moved to leave, but not before pausing in front of Norah. "That's three favors now," he said to her. "Is this another I can call upon?"

Adrian wondered what he meant.

She sighed. "I almost had a positive sentiment about you. Must you ruin everything?"

He shrugged and left them to Alec's disappointment.

CHAPTER THIRTY

Norah lay awake in the blissful light of morning, staring out the window. Mikael was sprawled sideways across the bed, his head on her hip. It was a rare moment, relaxing together in the calm, not rushing to duties or responsibility.

Things had settled since they had returned from the Wild. Even the contempt between Mikael, Soren, and Alexander had seemed to die down somewhat. *Somewhat.* But she couldn't shake her guilt. She'd asked a lot from Mikael, and he gave her everything. What had she given him?

"Why haven't you asked me to return the mountains of Bahoul?" she said, breaking the silence.

Mikael drew in a long breath, clearly not expecting this subject. He rolled to his side, looking up at her.

"You want it, yes?" she asked.

He swallowed. "Surely you know the answer."

She bit her bottom lip. "I'm sorry I haven't thought to discuss it with you until now. But... why haven't you asked me for it?"

He turned his head and looked out the window. "I should have negotiated it with our marriage agreement, but the truth is I wasn't even thinking of it at the time." He paused. "Soren pressed me to discuss it with you after. But, as the days passed, the harder it became." He grew silent for a time before continuing. "I feared the answer, that you wouldn't give it to me. Not that I'm so desperate to get it back now, but... are you unable to deny me... the way I'm unable to deny you? I... don't think I want to know."

Norah reached down and ran her fingers through his hair before resting her hand on his cheek. "It's yours, husband."

His eyes grew thick with emotion, and he put his hand over hers, bringing it to his lips and kissing her palm.

They lay naked together in the beautiful quiet.

"There's something else I've been reluctant to press you for," he said. He ran his hand over the skin of her stomach, swirling his fingertips so that prickles rose on her skin, and then he widened his palm against her flesh again. "A child."

Norah's pulse quickened. They certainly hadn't been trying *not* to have a child, but they never spoke of it, never made it an intentional effort. And she wasn't sure how she felt. She wanted children, eventually, but was she ready? She still didn't feel in control of her own life enough to now be responsible for another. But with a husband who loved her, and whom she loved in return, she started to feel a stirring for something more. A child between them sounded less and less of an obligation, and more of a beautiful life.

Norah put her hand over Mikael's on her stomach.

He shifted and moved up, rising over her and covering her with his body. "It's now the most important thing, Salara. I need an heir to settle the nobles. Unrest will build as time goes on. And"—he paused—"it's what will keep you safe when I'm gone."

His words rippled through her. When he was dead, he meant. She shook her head. "Don't talk like that."

"We need to talk about these things. The nobles won't follow the North Queen alone. But an heir will keep you on the Kharavian throne, even after I'm dead. An heir will keep the peace, keep the alliance. It will keep you safe, even if the North turns against you."

"Mikael, stop," she said, her eyes welling.

"Kharav needs an heir. We need an heir." He bent to kiss her lips. "And I want a son, a child, with you." His eyes brightened. "I would be a good father, Salara. I would love him."

Norah had never imagined Mikael as a father. She had never tried. She wasn't sure why. There was no doubt that Mikael would be a good father. The thought made her smile. It made her happy. Then why was she hesitant?

She wasn't.

She threaded her fingers back into his hair and nodded.

Mikael grew serious. "Do you mean it?" he breathed. "We'll have a child then?"

The thought filled her with an unexpected joy. She caressed his cheek with her hand. "Well, it's not exactly like we haven't been trying." She raised a teasing brow. "Do you not know how children are made, husband?"

He smiled. "I meant, isn't there planning—a specific time?"

"Mmm..." she moaned as she pulled him closer. "How about all the time?"

"That's an excellent plan," he rumbled as he covered her mouth with his. He moved between her thighs and slipped his arm underneath her, running his hand down and lifting her hips to him.

Norah gasped as he sank inside her. She didn't think it was possible to need someone the way she needed Mikael, with a deep and desperate hunger. He consumed her—her body, her mind, her spirit. And still, she needed more.

They moved together, as one. Mikael wove his fingers into hers and pushed her hands above her head. She let him take what he needed, because their needs were one and the same.

Norah wrapped her legs around him, pulling him deeper, begging him with her body. The rush was sudden and fierce, and it took her breath. She bucked against him as she lost herself.

Mikael's body hardened as he neared, and Norah settled to just watch him. She pulled her hands from his grasp and ran them down his chest, feeling the muscle tighten under his skin. He was beautiful, every piece of him. She drew her hands up to his face and pulled him down into a kiss, but he was too taken to kiss her back. She smiled as she caught his bottom lip between her teeth. A rumble built in his chest, and it grew to a thunder. Mikael came with a growl as he buried himself inside her. He dropped his head beside hers, and she could feel his panting breath on her cheek, in her ear. His whole body shook, and she savored it.

He nuzzled her neck as his body calmed. "When I'm inside you, nothing else matters," he breathed. "Nothing." He stayed a moment longer. Then he pulled himself from her and shifted his weight to the side, resting his head on her breast.

"I want you again," he said, with his eyes closed and his breaths still heavy with fatigue.

Norah gave a small laugh. "You don't have the energy." She looked at him as she brushed her fingers through his hair. She loved this man. How could anyone not? If they didn't, it was because they didn't know him.

"Let's go to Mercia," she whispered.

His eyes opened. "This is what you think of right now?"

She drew his face back up for his eyes to meet hers. "Let's go to Mercia, Mikael. You're not who they think you are. They need to know you. Once they do, they'll love you like I do. I know they will."

The quiet answered for him.

"Please?" she asked.

His face creased with sadness. "I can't."

Norah blinked back emotion. "Will I never see my home again?"

Mikael pushed himself up and lay over her again, bringing his hand to her face. "Go," he said softly.

Norah's eyes widened. "What?"

"Go. See your grandmother. See your people. Then come back to me."

She let out a shaky breath, not sure if she was understanding. He was trusting her to do this? "Go to Mercia?"

He nodded. "I only ask that you take the lord commander, and that you leave your justice there."

She drew in a shocked breath, nodding.

He dropped his head down closer. "Now, as I said, I want you again." And he covered her mouth with his.

Adrian paid no attention to the morning cold seeping through his clothes as he sat on the stone wall of the courtyard. He was too focused on carefully crimping the small metal cuffs to the woven leather necklace in his hands. He smiled as he worked, seeing it come along better than he had imagined. It was soft and delicate, like Sevina.

"What are you working on?" a voice called.

He jerked his head up in surprise. "Queen Norah!" He curled the necklace in his hand and stashed it down, giving a small shake of his head. "It's nothing."

Her eyes narrowed. "Let me see."

Slowly, he pulled up his hand and opened his fingers, sheepishly showing her the necklace.

She let out a small breath as she picked it up. "Adrian, this is beautiful!" She inspected it closely. "How did you get the leather to sparkle like this?"

Her admiration brought a smile to his lips. "I crushed peoly shells and made a mix, soaked the strips in it."

She handed it back to him. "Is it for someone special? Perhaps a beautiful girl with large brown eyes?"

Adrian shrugged bashfully. Of course Norah had picked up on things, having seen him with Sevina a couple times now. "Uh," he started as he stared down at the necklace.

"She'll love it." Norah smiled, saving him from words.

Adrian had been wavering all morning on whether to give it to Sevina, wondering if she'd even like it or if she'd find it silly. But Norah's reaction fueled his confidence, and his excitement grew.

"Where's your brother?" she asked.

"In the sparring field, last I saw."

She nodded, but paused, lingering a moment. "I'm going back to Mercia, Adrian."

A grin spread across his face. "That's great news! Your grandmother will be so happy to see you." But then he felt a weight in his stomach as he looked down at the necklace in his hands. If Norah was going back to Mercia, that would mean he would be too. "When?" he asked.

"A few days, maybe?"

He nodded as he rolled the soft leather between his fingers. He looked up at her, and she gave him a sad smile. But he swallowed his emotion. Norah's return was exactly what Mercia needed right now. He smiled back at her. "I'll start to prepare."

She squeezed his arm and then went to find Alec.

Norah found Alexander in the sparring field, as Adrian had told her. She thought it mildly entertaining how the Kharavian soldiers and the Northmen would watch one another, each progressively growing more aggressive in their sparring to impress the other. But her presence on the field drew a pause, and Alexander handed his sword and shield to another soldier as she approached.

"Queen Norah," he greeted.

"Lord Justice," she said, trying to keep the bubbling joy from her face. "Will you walk with me?"

She waited until they cleared the field, and the ears of the men on it. "I'm returning to Mercia."

Alexander stopped. A smile came to his lips.

"I don't know for how long, probably *not* long," she added quickly. "But I need to see my grandmother and the council, and how everything is there."

"And the king?" he asked.

"Will stay here."

He nodded, unable to hide the relief on his face.

"Mikael's supportive, but he's asked me to take the lord commander. And I've agreed."

Alexander's smile fell. "What? You can't allow the Destroyer into Mercia."

She sighed. "Alexander, stop calling him that like he's a demon of destruction. He's a foul-tempered man with a questionable conscience."

"Questionable?" he scoffed. "Are you serious?"

Norah swept her eyes around them. "I didn't come here to talk about the lord commander. I only meant to share the news, the good news, that we'll be returning to Mercia. We'll leave in a few days, if you'll ready the men. I want to take them all home. I also want to bring the Crest. I think it would be good for them to see Mercia."

He eyed her skeptically.

"They're good men, Alexander."

He looked out toward the sparring field. "Caspian has said as much."

"Let's go home."

Excitement rippled through the ranks as they marched out of Ashan and toward the canyons to Mercia, home. But despite this excitement, tension hung in the air. The Mercian units marched with the Kharavian commander, who traveled in his signature style. Even though the Northmen had seen him as a man, and had grown somewhat accustomed to his presence, his weapon-laden battle dress and the scream of his armored destrier still unsettled them.

Caspian's heart beat heavily in his chest as they drew closer to the Canyonlands, his mind on Tahla. Never had he imagined himself with a woman, or hiding it from those closest to him, but Tahla made him feel ways he had never imagined, ways he never understood. She would break him, eventually, he was sure of it. But it didn't stop his need for her.

They arrived in the Urun camp, and his eyes combed the Horsemen warriors, but there was no sign of Tahla. Caspian worked to settle the army quickly. As was the normal Urun custom, they were welcomed to eat by the large center fire. Caspian took a seat on a rock, and Alexander sat on the log that lay beside it.

Caspian stared into the hypnotic flames of the fire. Through its dance, the eyes he so often dreamed about stared back at him. He straightened as he realized Tahla watched him from the opposite side.

"It feels strange to be going home with the Destroyer," Alexander said.

Caspian pulled himself from Tahla's gaze and tried his best to focus his attention on Alexander.

The justice took a drink from his bowl. "It feels strange to be going home with Norah. I... wasn't sure this day would come."

While Caspian understood, he didn't feel quite the same. Mainly, he didn't feel the queen had been lost, as Alexander did, merely by her being in Kharav. And Kharav had come to feel like home, too, now. But that was something he could never share with Alexander.

Caspian tried his best to stay attentive to Alexander's words, but his eyes and his mind found their way back to Tahla, who flashed him a mischievous smile, seeming to enjoy his suffering. Finally, when he could bear it no longer, he excused himself to his quarters. He lingered a moment, looking for Tahla, but she seemed to have disappeared. Caspian started back toward the houses, hoping she would come to him.

As he cut between the houses, a hand snaked out, bringing a blade to his neck. "Did you think you could just slip away from me, Northman?" came the voice, and the corners of his lips turned up into a wry smile.

"You shouldn't threaten a man with a knife unless you intend to use it," he said.

Tahla stepped out in front of him, still holding the blade to his neck. "Who says I don't?"

Blood coursed through his veins. This woman woke something inside him.

But Caspian hadn't become captain without merit. Before Tahla could react, he threw up his arm and knocked the blade away. Catching Tahla's wrist, he pulled her to him, forcing her along a sidewall and pushing her back up against it. She moved her body against his suggestively. This game was new. And it excited him.

She grinned. "Unexpected, Northman." Her body relaxed, but as soon as he loosened his hold, she snapped up a knee against his thigh, almost dropping him, and ducked to slip past him. But he caught her and spun her around, pressing her against the wall again. Her back was to him this time, and he leaned against her, his mouth to her ear.

"I am generally not a man who enjoys a fight, but—"

A hand grabbed him from behind and threw him back against the opposite wall. The commander snarled at him with a deep rage, swinging his axe in attack. Caspian dodged the blade, and it hit the stacked stone behind him.

"I thought I knew you better, Northman!" the lord commander seethed.

"Soren, no!" Tahla cried, but he was focused on Caspian. He swung again, just missing, but the axe gave a skin-prickling sound as its tip scraped Caspian's armor. Caspian scrambled back, but the walls of the joined houses gave him no escape. The commander coiled back for a final blow.

"Soren, stop! Stop!" Tahla cried. "I love him!"

The lord commander paused his assault, and both he and Caspian gaped at her in surprise.

"I love him!" she said again, breathless. "We're together."

The commander shifted his gaze from Tahla back to Caspian with an angry trench in his brow. He was quiet for a moment. "A *Northman*?" he asked Tahla, with a tinge of disgust in his voice.

She nodded.

His rage faded, but his anger remained. He glared at Caspian. "Who knows about this?"

"No one, my lord," Caspian admitted, looking at the ground in shame. "But I'll tell the queen."

"You won't," Soren growled.

Caspian's eyes widened, and he jerked his head up. "What?"

"You won't," the commander said again. "She has a weak heart, and she'll release you to be together."

Caspian looked at Tahla. While he would never choose to leave the queen's service, the thought of being with Tahla, together, always, was a pull he didn't expect.

The commander grabbed him by the breastplate and pushed him back against the wall. "Salara needs you," he said between his teeth. "If you leave her, I'll kill you."

Caspian knew he meant it, but he had no intention of leaving the queen's service.

"Soren," Tahla gasped.

"I'm sworn to Salara!" the commander snapped. "Don't make me choose."

His statement surprised Caspian.

"What do you mean you're sworn to her?" a voice called out behind them. *Alexander.* Caspian prayed he hadn't overheard the exchange about Tahla. He didn't want him to find out this way.

The commander let out a long breath, baring his teeth. "It's not your concern, Bear."

Alexander looked at Caspian. "It is my concern. I'm her lord justice. And that is my captain."

Soren chuckled. "And I'm her lord commander."

"That means nothing," Alexander said.

The beast of a Shadowman turned. "Does it not? I command the armies."

Alexander shook his head. "Not the Northmen."

Soren frowned with a shrug, as if allowing Alexander a small victory. "Not *all*, that's true."

"None," Alexander stressed.

"I lead the Crest. That makes Caspian my captain. And now I command Bahoul." His eyes smiled wickedly. "More will come. Give me time, Bear."

"Bahoul?" Alexander repeated.

This was the first Caspian had heard of this as well. The queen had given the mountains back to Kharav? To the Destroyer?

"Perhaps you should talk to Salara," the commander said, before casting a warning gaze at Caspian and leaving.

Alexander found Norah in a large stone house in the village's center. His skin burned in anger. "You gave Bahoul back to the Shadowlands?" he asked when he saw her.

Norah turned. He saw her anger in response to his own, but he didn't care.

"I gave Bahoul back to Kharav, where it rightfully belongs," she said with an edge in her voice.

Surely, she didn't know what she had done. "Your father died for those mountains."

"No, my father died for a war fueled by fear and hatred."

He stepped back in surprise. How could she say that? "The Destroyer says he is sworn to you."

She hesitated before replying. "He is."

Had she not wanted him to know?

"Norah, you can't accept his oath. He can't truly swear himself to you."

Her eyes narrowed defensively. "Why not?"

He couldn't believe he had to explain this. "He's the Destroyer. Oaths are for men who know loyalty!"

"There's no man more loyal than the lord commander," she snapped back.

Her words struck him. He couldn't reply.

She closed her eyes momentarily. "I didn't mean it like that. Of course I don't consider you in that statement. You know how I feel about you."

He wasn't so sure anymore. He took another step back, then turned and left her to the evening.

CHAPTER THIRTY-ONE

The glory of Mercia shone brightly on the horizon, and Norah felt a spring of joy in her heart. *Home.*

Adrian rode beside her, and he wore a lopsided smile. He was happy to be returning too. She'd wanted to bring Calla and Cohen, but she wasn't sure if Hamed and Marta would approve of their grandchildren traveling across the continent to a kingdom that used to be their enemy—to the kingdom that had claimed the siblings' parents. So she'd had them stay. Soren had just put them into a training regimen and assigned tutors for their studies, without Norah even asking. He'd likely cite it as another favor to call upon, but for the moment, she was grateful. They'd be looked after until she returned to Kharav.

Norah turned her attention back to Mercia. She shot Adrian a grin. "How fast is your horse?"

"Faster than Sephir," he challenged.

"Salara," Soren called out in warning behind her.

She glanced back over her shoulder, knowing that his large destrier didn't have the speed. "Am I hearing you want to race too, Lord Commander?"

"Don't break away from the army," he gruffed.

Don't break away from him, he meant. "Then they need to keep up," she said with a smirk, and urged the Wild mare into a gallop toward Mercia.

The gates of Mercia opened wide as the bells rang out. Norah and Adrian rode through the city, across the bridge, and into the courtyard, followed closely by Alexander and Caspian. Norah brought her mare to a stop in front of the grand entry to the castle.

At the top of the stair stood Catherine. Norah didn't take her eyes from her as she slid off Sephir to the ground. She hadn't exchanged words with Catherine since receiving her letter in Kharav, urging Norah to return home.

Now she *was* home.

Catherine stepped down the stairs slowly. Cautiously even. Norah's heart hurt. Did her grandmother think of her as the enemy now?

When they reached each other, they stopped. Catherine's face was difficult to read, but then her eyes welled. She reached out and pulled Norah to her, holding her tightly. "My dear child," she breathed. "I wasn't sure I would ever see you again."

Norah tried to blink back the tears in her own eyes. "I wasn't sure if I would see you either."

Catherine pulled back and gave an emotional smile. "I'm so glad you're home." Then she stiffened. A cold fell over her face as she looked past Norah to the arriving company. Norah followed her gaze to see the lord commander with the Crest. All eyes were on him.

His destrier let out a ghostly scream. Soren slid from his mount like thunder to the ground and strode toward them.

Mercian soldiers parted warily.

"Grandmother, may I present—"

"How dare you bring this monster here!" Catherine spat bitterly. "Do you not think of your people, Norah? How many Northmen has he killed, and you waltz him in as our guest?"

Norah took a step back, surprised. "I know that this is difficult," she started, "but—"

"Take him!" Catherine commanded the guards. The Northmen pulled their bows, and the sound of steel rang out as Soren drew his sword.

"Stand down!" Norah shouted, backing up to him with her arms raised.

"I didn't believe it when it was said to me," Catherine said, her voice shaking. "You side with the Destroyer?"

"I'm queen of Mercia *and* Kharav, and the lord commander serves me, under my protection. Anyone who defies this will answer to me," she stressed, loud enough for everyone to hear.

Her Northmen lowered their bows, and she looked back at the commander, who sheathed his sword.

"Then put him in the tower," Catherine seethed. "If he must be here, then I want him out of my sight."

"No, he'll stay in a royal guest chamber, as is right for his position," Norah said firmly.

"Are you mad?"

"I'm getting close," Norah said shortly.

Catherine's face darkened as she stepped back. "He's here to guard his king's interest, isn't he? The Shadow King has made you a prisoner, even in your own castle."

Norah glanced back at Soren. It was an easy assumption to make, but it wasn't true. Not now. Mikael trusted Soren. She trusted Soren. And she was glad he'd come.

Catherine puffed a breath of disgust, then turned and strode into the castle, but the Northmen were still on high alert.

Norah turned to Soren. "Caspian will show you the stables, and you can see to your horse. Then he'll take you around the castle."

Caspian stepped forward. "Of course, Regal High." He nodded to the commander. "Lord Commander."

But Soren didn't move, clearly disliking the thought of leaving her.

She spoke low, pleading. "You'll see me again after Caspian has shown you around." But his face told her he wasn't interested. "You are quite literally moments from starting a battle in this very courtyard." She dropped her voice to a whisper. "Please."

Reluctantly, he gave a nod, deciding to cooperate, and then turned and let Caspian lead him to the stables.

Norah watched them go, praying no further drama would follow. She knew it was wishful thinking. Soren was the symbol of the Shadowlands, and to Mercia he was the symbol of evil, everything they'd warred against for the past ten years. Mending these perceptions would take time.

She turned toward the castle and made her way to the drawing room, where she knew she'd find her grandmother. As she reached the alcove of the door, she paused and took a deep breath before entering. She needed her grandmother's support, especially if Norah hoped to win over the council. She pushed open the door and stepped inside.

Catherine stood by the window on the far wall, looking across the courtyard below. "This wasn't the return I was expecting. Or hoping for."

A pang of hurt needled her heart. "Would you rather I not have returned at all?"

Catherine puffed a breath. "Don't be ridiculous."

"Why didn't you come to the wedding?" It still crushed her.

Her grandmother's brow dropped. "You know why."

Norah's eyes welled. "I needed you!"

Catherine's eyes cut back with an icy stare. "You didn't need me when you made this decision, all on your own."

Norah scoffed as she shook her head. "I don't expect this to be easy, nor do I claim it a perfect solution, but I'm queen, and I've made my decision. I didn't ask for this responsibility, but I have done—and will always do—what I think is best and right."

They stood for a moment in the silence.

Slowly, Catherine softened. "I know," she said finally. "I know you do what you believe is right."

Norah crossed the distance between them and reached out and took her hand. "I still need you," she whispered.

Catherine looked at her with emotion in her eyes. "And you have me, my dear girl."

Norah let out a long breath, giving her a warm smile. She pulled her grandmother to a side table that held a hot pot of tea, and they both sat. Norah poured them both a cup.

"So other than my marrying the king of all things evil and breaking the prophecy to unite Mercia and Aleon, ending the world, how has everything been?"

"Oh, Norah, for gods' sakes."

Norah wrinkled her nose. Too soon for humor, she supposed. "Fine. But really, how are things?"

Catherine sighed. "It both pleases me and pains me to say, somewhat better. Our people are fed, only a couple more months are expected of the winter, and we don't have a war looming on the horizon."

Norah wanted to smile, but she knew better.

"But"—Catherine took a sip of her tea and then set the cup back down on the saucer—"Mercian villages are still under attack. Drifters seem to grow in number, and now that our ships are sailing with trade again, they're being targeted by pirates."

Norah's brow creased with worry. "Still?" Alexander had told her about the pirates. Pirates had always been a challenge, but in times of desperation, such as the lingering winter, their attacks became increasingly bolder. But she'd thought their ships had been faring better.

Catherine nodded. "We just lost another twenty-eight men and a quarter haul of steel. The council will want to hold a state session, and soon, to hear from you on the matter."

Norah bit her lip. She didn't even have a fully formed thought around these challenges, let alone a solution.

Catherine squeezed her hand. "Don't worry, my dear, we'll figure it out. I'm just glad you're home."

Norah made her way toward the great hall, not quite with a destination in mind, but simply trying to sort her thoughts. She ran her hand through her hair, pushing the wayward strands out of her eyes. She hadn't expected things to be easy in returning to Mercia, and she couldn't shake the sinking feeling that her grandmother's sour welcome was only the beginning.

The sun had started to set. She glanced out of the window-lined hall toward the purple sky and spotted Caspian in the courtyard, still with Soren. He was explaining something with his hands and motioning westward.

She followed the hall to the side door and took it outside. "Do you have a plan of attack scoped out yet?" she asked as she came up behind them.

Caspian turned. "Queen Norah."

Soren raised a questioning brow through the eye opening of his head wrap.

"That's what people will wonder," she told the commander. "Do you know how you'll attack?"

Caspian gave an uncomfortable chuckle at her joke.

Soren frowned. "We've been trying to assess the North for years. I doubt I'll have a plan after only an afternoon."

Norah eyed Caspian in amusement, realizing Soren hadn't understood she'd asked him in jest.

"But," the commander said, "I'd start with your mainland city. They lack defenses. You should be building houses of stone. You certainly have enough of it. Stone doesn't burn."

"You would burn the city?" Caspian asked.

"To draw the army out."

"They wouldn't come," Caspian said. "They'd stay on the isle to protect the queen."

Soren shook his head. "No. One Northman at a time—their screams in the air as I peel the flesh from their body. One after another. Then the army would come." Soren nodded at Norah with a dark eye. "*She* would send them."

Norah swallowed the bile building in her throat. He was a master at his craft. "Thank you, Captain," she said, turning to Caspian and breaking the unease. "I can show the lord commander to his chamber."

Caspian stood for a moment, disturbed. "Regal High," he finally bowed. "Lord Commander."

Soren watched him leave.

She scowled at him. "Was that necessary?"

"It was what you were really asking, yes? My perception of your weakness?"

"I congratulate you for finding it—my compassion for human life," she said irritably.

"And there's your other," he said, and she followed his gaze to Alexander, who was leaving the stables with Adrian. She saw Adrian smiling, and Alexander gripped his shoulder warmly. It made her happy to see them as brothers, and she lingered a moment before turning back to Soren.

"I'll show you to your chamber," she said with a sigh, resigned.

He followed her through several hallways, to a room looking out at the temple. "You'll sleep here," she told him.

"By the temple?"

"You need prayers," she said shortly. "Many prayers."

"It's too far from your quarters."

Composure, she reminded herself. "Do you not see my struggle? I'm in my own home. You don't have to sit outside my door or make it more difficult than it already is."

So much for composure, she thought to herself.

There was a deep rumble in his chest, but he gave a small nod in acceptance. "Fine."

She moved to leave but paused. "Oh, for the rest of today, I would ask that you stay here. Out of sight."

"Be confined to my chamber?"

"I just want things to settle, to let tensions calm."

"Should I wear chains? Would that make your men feel better?"

She looked at him with a sigh, absent of any energy, and turned wearily from the doorway.

"I'll stay," he called after her. She paused and looked back, surprised by his compliance.

"Thank you," she said.

Norah made her way toward the dining hall, and a wave of guilt rippled through her. Despite how she loathed him sometimes, Soren was a good commander and not a completely reprehensible man.

A servant passed her in the hall, stopping first to bow.

"Will you take something to eat to the lord commander?" she asked.

"Yes, Regal High."

She paused and thought for a moment. "Add a plate for me as well. And tell my grandmother that I'm tired and will be taking dinner privately this evening."

"Yes, Regal High."

The servant hurried to the kitchen, and Norah made her way back to the commander's chamber.

His face flashed with surprise when he opened the door and saw her.

"I thought I would join you in confinement," she said. "At least for dinner."

"I don't need your pity. I'm well suited alone." His voice was edged with annoyance.

"Well, maybe I'm not yet suited to face the continued judgments of my grandmother and my council." Or Alexander, who was no doubt still stewing over Bahoul and her decision to bring Soren to Mercia. "So, will you bear my company?"

He relented and opened the door wider, and she stepped inside.

A servant whisked in behind her with a tray of food and set it on the table. The maid set down two goblets and a carafe of wine and gave Norah a bow before slipping out of the chamber and closing the door behind her.

Soren motioned her to the table. Norah pursed a smile and sat, and he took the chair across from her. He pulled off his wrap, and she let her eyes travel over him. She saw his face often; he didn't cover himself inside the castle in Kharav, but somehow, he looked different here. Sharper. Unsettling.

"No blood bowl?" he asked as he looked at the food.

Norah filled her wineglass and handed him the carafe. "I thought it might be a little too much. At least in the beginning, until everyone's acquainted with you." She wrinkled her nose. "Because asking for blood is... weird... and creepy."

He let out a small snort as he filled his own cup. "I wasn't serious. I'll manage."

She couldn't help a smile. He was always serious. Her curiosity couldn't be contained. "Why do you drink it? Blood."

"It makes me strong."

She raised a brow. "So does food and water."

"I like it," he answered shortly.

Norah brought her cup to her lips to fill the tensioned silence.

Soren leaned back in his chair. "When Salar and I escaped Bahoul after the North overran us, we traveled for days. I protected him. I hunted. We ate the food raw because we couldn't build a fire." He picked up his chalice and took a drink. "I remember the blood on my tongue. And when I drink it now, it reminds me of who I am."

Norah had never imagined herself feeling emotional over a story about drinking blood, but she felt that way now. Soren drank from a blood bowl because it reminded him of when he had been strong. It made him feel strong. And she could understand that.

"I'll hunt," he told her.

"Hunting sounds perfect. I'm sure Adrian would love to take you."

He paused, then said, "I would like that."

Norah took a bite of the dauo root and rice on her plate. She watched him as he made an effort of the karo fish. He grimaced, and she realized he likely had never eaten fish from the North Sea. Its taste wasn't for everyone. She couldn't help a smile. They sat quietly for a moment.

"There's something I would ask your help with," she started again. "Something I need a fresh perspective to resolve."

He didn't answer, but his eyes met hers and his face grew even more serious.

"Pirates," she told him.

"Pirates?"

"Mercia and other seafaring kingdoms have always been plagued by the threat of pirates. One of our ships was attacked last week, and we lost twenty-eight men. Alexander is increasing forces and weapons to defend our shipments, but that spreads our ranks thin and takes up valuable trade space."

"I know nothing of the sea."

"But you know war. You know how to deal with threats. The *Evanya* sails in a week's time, and she'll have our largest trade of steel this year. I have to find a solution."

"The *Evanya*?"

Norah gave a smile. "The ship named for my mother. They're all named after Mercian queens."

"Do you have one?" he asked.

She nodded. "The *Norah*." She sighed, thinking. "I have to find a way to keep my men safe. I can't tolerate it anymore." She paused. "I don't need a lord justice. I need the Destroyer."

He seemed surprised but nodded. "Let me look into it. I'll see what there is to be done."

"Thank you."

They ate quietly, and Norah's heart was light. He was dropping his guard with her. "There is something else I've been wanting to ask you," she said.

Soren looked up from his plate in curiosity. She waited, and he gave an urging nod.

"What did the seer show you? In Odepeth?"

His face grew dark, and he sat back in his chair. He looked away, his mind obviously drawn back to the memory.

"Tell me," she pleaded. "Is it Mikael? Is it you? What did you see?"

"Put it out of your mind," he said in a low voice.

"I can't. Why didn't you tell Mikael?"

He set his fork on his plate. "I think it's best if you leave now."

Norah stood, leaning over the table. "Have you not told me the worst I might imagine about Alexander? About Mikael? What else is there?"

"Leave me," he growled, rising from his own chair. He moved toward her and used his size to push her back toward the door.

"Whatever it is, you can tell me—"

"I kill you!" he thundered.

Norah's breath caught in her throat as she stumbled back against the wall.

"You want to know what the seer showed me? It's your death." He boxed her in against the doorframe with his arms, bringing his face inches from hers. "I kill you," he said in a fierce whisper, "willingly." His eyes were cruel, and they hurt her. Surprisingly, they hurt her.

He reached and opened the chamber door, and she stumbled backward, out of the room. Their eyes locked again as she stood, trying to get her breath, and he closed the door between them.

Chapter Thirty-Two

Norah stared at herself in the mirror while Serene laced the back of her dress. All the while in Kharav, she had dreamed of returning to Mercia, but now that she was here, it didn't feel as she'd expected. It didn't feel right, just as Soren's words the night before hadn't felt right. She wasn't sure she believed him.

She wondered how he felt, finally in the kingdom he had worked so hard to invade—the kingdom he had tried so hard to destroy.

"Has the lord commander risen?" she asked.

Serene nodded. "He already left, Regal High."

She met her maid's eyes in the reflection. "What?"

"Early this morning. Lord Adrian went with him."

Norah shifted uneasily. They must have gone hunting. She *had* proposed that he take Adrian hunting, but she'd thought she'd have more time to warm Alexander up to the idea.

"Is everything all right?" Serene asked.

"Um, yes, of course. Just let me know when they return." Until then, she'd try her best to avoid Alexander.

Norah chewed her sausage slowly. It had been too big of a bite.

Her grandmother watched her between her own bites. "You've barely said a word all morning."

She swallowed and wished she had more sausage. It was better than talking. "Oh, um... I'm just thinking about the upcoming state session with the council, and other things..." She let her voice trail off. She didn't mention Soren's threat, or her current worry of Adrian's whereabouts, or that he was with the lord commander. She suspected Catherine would be beside herself, and Alexander would send a full army to recover him. That wasn't the situation she cared to deal with at the moment.

"The lord justice was looking for you earlier. Did you speak to him?"

Norah quickly put a large bite of bread in her mouth and shook her head. It was shocking that he hadn't been able to find her while she so actively avoided him.

"What will you do about the demon?" Catherine asked. "Is he to wander Mercia as he pleases, assessing our weaknesses, devising his plans?"

Norah swallowed the piece of bread she had over-chewed. "You *do* know he's not a demon, right?"

"Flesh and blood or no, there's evil in him."

Norah took a drink of her tea and tilted her head. "Yes, everyone seems to have that impression. Is it the eyes, you think?"

"The gods' mercy." Catherine sighed. "Norah, this is not a joke."

"It almost is!" she said with a slight smile that garnered her grandmother's scowl. "He's a grudging, resentful, angry man, rather large, slightly scary-looking, who's managed to frighten entire kingdoms." Norah shook her head. "I think he just doesn't like people." Then, a little quieter, she added, "You should understand that."

Catherine let out a breath of offense. "Are you really comparing me to the Destroyer?"

"No, of course not. I just think you'd get along. Well." She shrugged, looking at the cat lounging on a pillowed bed against the wall. "He's an animal lover, you know."

Catherine's face was dark for one so pale. She dropped her napkin on her plate and rose from the table, leaving without a word.

Norah sighed. She hadn't meant to upset her grandmother or be disrespectful, but she was frustrated. It seemed there was no reasoning, no logic, only hate and intolerance. She knew she wasn't dealing with it well, but she didn't know how to, and in these moments, her emotions seemed to choose her words for her.

Alexander's voice behind her made her cringe, but Norah turned with a forced smile.

"Queen Norah, I've been looking for you everywhere."

"Oh. Really?"

He raised a brow, and she cursed herself quietly. Why was she so obvious?

"I don't mean to disturb you at breakfast, but have you seen Adrian?" he asked.

"I haven't," she said. *Not this morning.*

His eyes narrowed, and her pulse quickened.

"I wanted to go over what will likely be discussed in the state session tomorrow," she said, changing the topic. "Grandmother has let me know there are a few challenges. With the pirates."

"I'll handle them," he assured her.

"Alexander, you can't take this all on yourself. It's a challenge for more than one person."

"I said I'll handle it."

Norah wanted to suggest help from the lord commander, but for once her mind controlled her tongue, and she was quiet.

Evening came, and Norah was relieved to be back in her chamber, away from the eyes of judgment. She'd left Vitalia back in Kharav, and she missed her desperately. She could use a bit of sarcasm and support right now. Her Mercian maid Serene was happy to be back, Norah could tell. The girl dashed around the castle in high spirits. Norah felt a pang of guilt. The Shadowlands were too harsh a place for her. She would leave her here in Mercia when she returned to Kharav.

"Did you hear about Titus?" Serene asked as she pulled down the coverlet on the bed.

"What about him?"

"He's found himself a wife. Well, not a wife yet, but they're to be married."

Norah's eyes widened. "Already? He hasn't even been back long enough to put his horse away from the journey."

Serene laughed. "He's a high-ranked soldier of the queen's guard, of good lineage. And handsome. He had his pick as soon as word was out that he was looking."

Yes, she supposed that was how marriages worked around here. "Well, good for him." If Titus was happy, and his bride was happy, then she was happy for them.

"Any word of the lord commander?" Norah asked as the maid busied herself drawing a bath.

"No, Regal High."

Norah felt an anxiousness creeping in. Hunting wouldn't be as it was in Kharav. She knew they'd have to ride far, but not a whole day, and it was unlike the commander to be away from her for so long.

"The lord justice still looks for Lord Adrian as well," Serene added. "He's getting worried."

Norah's stomach knotted. "You... didn't mention anything, did you?"

"No, Regal High," Serene assured her.

She nodded as she let out an uneasy breath and prayed they'd return soon. She stripped off her dress, but as she stepped out of her undergarments, her eye caught the spotting of blood on the fabric. Her stomach dropped. Not that she was expecting to be with child, but it occupied her mind occasionally, and she found herself hoping. Daydreaming, even.

"Are you all right, Regal High?" Serene asked.

She nodded, pushing out a breath. "Of course, I just started my bleed and don't feel very well."

Serene scooped up her clothes. "Why don't you get into the bath? I'll go fetch you some tea. That will make you feel better." The girl gave her a warm smile and swept out of the room.

Norah stepped into the steaming water and sank down to the bottom of the tub. At that moment, everything flooded her at once: Mercia being home but not home, challenges for which she had no solutions, the fact that her memories were gone forever, the continued tension between Mercia and Kharav, the weight of her kingdom's disappointment at her every decision... and now there was no child.

And she missed Mikael.

She covered her face in her hands and let the tears come.

CHAPTER THIRTY-THREE

A knock on the door pulled Norah from her thoughts. She had skipped breakfast with her grandmother. Her stomach knotted enough at the thought of meeting with the council; she wasn't sure she could bear another conversation with Catherine prior to it.

She groaned as she rose from the settee—this was probably Catherine coming to chastise her now.

But Caspian was at the door when she opened it. "Queen Norah." He bowed. "The lord commander has returned. He asks you to come."

Thank the gods, he was back, but... "Now? I'm about to go meet the council."

Caspian's lips formed a thin line. "You should come."

She'd thought it wasn't possible to feel any more anxious. She'd been wrong.

Norah quickly followed Caspian to the stables with a looming sense of dread. When she saw Soren and Adrian, she let out a breath of relief. But her relief quickly turned to anger. "Where have you been?" she demanded before she even reached them. She looked at Adrian. "I've been avoiding your brother like the Cold Death." Turning her attention to the commander, she said, "When I mentioned that you should go hunting, I didn't mean immediately. And what took you so long in returning?"

"We didn't go hunting," Adrian said.

She paused, her eyes bouncing between the two of them. "Then where have you been?"

"Doing as you requested," Soren answered. "Finding a solution."

Norah felt a weight in her stomach. "For what?"

"Your pirates," he said, and motioned to a group of boys in one of the horse stalls awaiting their fates.

She raised a brow. "Those aren't pirates."

"No," Soren said, "they're the sons of pirate captains. And while in our care, the North's ships will no longer be attacked."

Norah looked at him, bewildered. Her bewilderment turned to a sickness rising up in her throat. "Where did you get these children?"

"The inlet port city," he said matter-of-factly.

Norah shook her head, a horror swelling inside her. "They're hostages?" she stammered.

He shrugged. "Wards," he suggested.

She brought a hand to her head, trying to calm her breath and think. "Wait, there are many more pirates than just those out of the port city."

"All you need is a few," he told her. "They'll keep the others away."

She shook her head again. "What happens if a Mercian ship is attacked?"

The commander frowned. "Salara, you knew my methods wouldn't be favored, yet you asked me regardless."

She huffed a small breath. "I didn't mean—"

"You said you needed the Destroyer. I've provided you a near guaranteed solution with no lives lost."

"Unless a ship is attacked!"

He shrugged. "I doubt that will happen. But if it does, then yes, and only one will be required to send a message."

"We won't harm a child!" she snapped.

"Then how many men are you willing to lose? Is one pirate boy worth the lives of twenty-eight soldiers? Is he worth all the men you lost before, or those you've yet to lose?"

"I can't answer a question like that," she whispered.

"You need to do what's necessary. That's the worst case. It's most likely these boys will be kept safely as wards of the crown, as their fathers won't seek to put their lives in danger, and then they'll be exchanged in a few years."

Norah looked at the boys with a heavy weight in her chest. "I can't do that."

"Is that not why I'm here?" he growled. "Consider this situation resolved."

Norah forced out a breath. "You will not, under any circumstances, harm a child. *Ever*. Pirate or no." She turned to Caspian. "Have the men see them fed and placed somewhere safe, *not* a horse stall, until I can figure out what to do with them." Then to Adrian, "I would advise you not to announce your part in this to your brother."

Adrian nodded. "I kind of figured."

Norah pushed down the sickness in her throat as she turned and made her way toward the judisaept. Soren followed behind her. She almost told him to return to his chamber, but if she was completely honest with herself, she needed someone with her who was on her side. Despite what Soren said and did, and despite his threats, he was on her side. And if his position were recognized properly, he should be part of the council, as

Alexander was. Of course, the council themselves wouldn't agree. Well, she told herself, if there was to be a battle over her decisions, might as well make it a war.

"What is he doing here?" Edward called as she entered, without so much as a greeting.

As expected. "He's attending our state," she replied. "Good morning, Councilman Edward," she added as she took her seat at the head of the table.

All eyes were on Soren.

"He cannot be here," Alastair argued.

Norah looked at James to find his gaze upon her, dark and disappointed. But he said nothing.

"Where's the lord justice?" Catherine asked.

"On his way, I'm sure," Norah answered.

"This is a private meeting," Henricus voiced, "not one that should be privy to our enemies. He must go."

"He won't," she snapped. "He'll attend what's appropriate for his station. He's lord commander of my army in Kharav, and he commands the forces in Bahoul."

There was an audible gasp from the council and her grandmother.

"You've given Bahoul to the Shadowmen?" Edward asked, astonished.

"I've given my husband what is rightfully his," she cut back. "It will continue to be a base for soldiers of both Kharav and Mercia."

"The army won't have this," Edward said angrily. "They'll rebel."

Norah looked at him with a cool calm. "I've found the army will support that which their leaders support, and rebel when inspired to do so. Are you saying you'd inspire them to rebel, Councilman?"

Soren stepped closer to the table, and Norah realized he still carried his battle-axe.

"Of course not," Edward stammered.

For once, she appreciated the commander's intimidation. "We agree, then," she said. "On the next topic—"

Alexander thundered into the room, making them all rise. All except Norah.

"So, we're taking hostages and slaughtering children now?" he started angrily. Just then, he caught sight of Soren. "This is your doing," he seethed.

"What are you talking about?" Catherine asked, alarmed.

"Word through the docks." Alexander glared at Soren. "Apparently, the Destroyer seeks to solve our pirate problem by taking their children and threatening to kill them."

The council gasped again in horror. Norah had a feeling she'd be hearing them gasp a lot.

"Take your brutality back to the Shadowlands," Alexander snarled at Soren. "No one asked you—"

"I asked him," Norah said.

All eyes shifted to her. Alexander paused, and the color drained from his face. "You asked him? You would kill these children?"

"It won't come to that," she said. She wouldn't let it.

"And what if it does?" James asked. "Is this what we've become?"

Norah stood. "We lost twenty-eight soldiers on the *Celeste*, eleven on the *Anne*, and sixteen on the *Mary*. I'll not lose another man."

"But you can stand to lose your soul," Alexander cut back.

"Lord Justice," she warned him, "enough."

"And who will do the deed?" he said, throwing his hands up as his eyes burned into the commander. To Soren, he said, "Ah, the Destroyer. Or better, my brother? You seem to have quite the appetite for pulling him into your vices." He turned back to Norah in his rage. "Will you watch as they die?"

The commander stepped forward. "Caution, Bear, you speak to your queen." His defense of her caught everyone by surprise.

But Alexander ignored him and looked at Norah. "Yes, I appreciate the reminder, for I barely recognize who's in front of me." He sighed, dropping his voice and taking a softer approach. "You can't seriously be thinking of this as a solution. I told you I'd handle it."

"I've been letting you handle it, and our ships are still being attacked, our trade stolen. Mercians are dying!"

Alexander's nostrils flared, and he looked at Catherine, exasperated.

Edward shook his head in disgust. "So, is the *Evanya* to sail on the blood of children? Your mother would be heartbroken to see her ship leave harbor under this circumstance."

"Then send the *Norah*," she replied.

Waves crashed high on the bow of the *Norah* as the Mercian ship cut through the water. The worst of winter had passed, but large chunks of ice still floated atop the icy blue of the sea, thundering into the hull as she sailed. But her captain, Theander, wasn't worried. This is what their ships were built for; they were strong with Mercian steel, able to withstand the best the sea could throw. No ship of the North had ever been sunk. But this strength came at a cost. The fleet was slow, which made them easy targets for pirate attacks.

The *Norah* was smaller and faster than the other Mercian ships, fitting of her namesake. But she still couldn't outrun a pirate's ketch, and Theander had the largest trade of Mercian steel this year. The queen had felt confident in fewer arms and men to make room for more trade. He felt a little less so.

On the horizon, another ship came into view. Theander looked through his scope and felt his pulse quicken.

His first mate stood beside him. "Pirates?" Austus asked.

Theander nodded.

CHAPTER THIRTY-FOUR

The table was quiet as Norah and Catherine ate their breakfast in the chill of the morning. Her grandmother had hardly spoken to her since the state meeting, and Norah didn't blame her. She knew she was disappointing them—Alexander, her grandmother, the council. But she wouldn't have made decisions differently. Perhaps that's why she couldn't shake the guilt.

The doors opened, and Alexander strode in with a letter in his hand. He looked pale and uneasy.

"What is it?" she asked him.

"News," he said, holding it for her. "From the *Norah*."

News from the ship. Her stomach knotted, and she swallowed back the bile building in her throat. Her hands shook as she broke the seal and opened it. She covered her mouth with her hand.

"What is it?" Catherine asked.

"They've reached port," she breathed. "They encountered a pirate ship but were left alone."

Catherine let out a breath and leaned back against her chair.

Alexander's eyes were cold and calm. "Congratulations on your victory."

Norah forced herself to draw air into her lungs. Her racing heart slowed to a heavy pulse.

"But don't mistake this for a bluff well played," he added. "The only reason they believe the Destroyer will kill their children is because he will. And he has. Killed children, that is."

Norah knocked on Soren's chamber door and waited restlessly for him to answer. He opened it and, seeing her, swung the door wider, inviting her in. She held out the letter with the news of the *Norah* for him, and he took it, unfolding it and reading it calmly as he stepped back into the room. He looked back up at her and gave a small nod, handing the letter back.

"Alexander called it a victory, but he didn't mean it," she said quietly. "And if I'm honest, it doesn't feel like a victory."

He shrugged. "Your trade made it to market. Your men are safe. That's a victory."

She nodded reluctantly as he buckled his weapons strap across his chest.

"What are you doing?" she asked.

"I'm going out to look at more of the city," he said as he pulled the strap tight.

"You're not going to battle. It's perfectly safe."

"It's safe for you—but I'm the enemy."

Norah paused, realizing that he was alone in a strange land and surrounded by longtime adversaries, just as she had been in Kharav. She knew this loneliness. It was hard, surely even for the Destroyer.

He pushed the end of the final strap through its buckle and picked up his head wrap. She sighed. Not seeing his face added to her men's suspicion, but she wouldn't be able to talk him out of it. The only time he didn't wear the wrap out was when he was in the castle in Kharav.

He reached for his axe, and she shook her head, drawing the line. "No. Not the axe. I don't want you scaring people." His eyes showed his objection, but she stood firm. "No."

He gave a deep protesting rumble in his chest but left the axe leaning against the wall.

"Come on, I'll walk with you," she said.

The morning air was chilly.

"These are your people, too, now," she told him.

He snorted. "The North will never see me as one of their own."

As they reached the stables, a boy came careening around the corner, colliding with Soren's legs and falling backward into the dirt. He wasn't more than seven or eight years old.

"Oh!" Norah exclaimed, rushing forward. "Are you all right?"

The boy scrambled to his feet, shaken. He stared at Soren with wide eyes. In the dirt lay a makeshift axe that had been refashioned from a wooden toy sword.

Norah looked at the lord commander. His eyes showed no emotion. She turned back to the boy. "Hello there," she said. "What's your name?"

The boy didn't answer.

"Do you not have a name?" she asked.

The boy looked at her, then back at Soren. "Thomas," he said finally.

"Do you know who I am?"

He nodded. "You're Queen Norah."

She smiled. "Do you know who this is?" she asked, waving a hand at the commander.

"The Destroyer," the boy said, his eyes still on the lord commander.

Norah looked back at Soren and scowled at his formidable posture. He shifted, reaching down and picking up the wooden axe from the ground.

"You have an axe?" Soren asked him.

"I made it myself," the boy said, a boldness coming to him.

"Why not a sword, or a bow?"

"Everyone has a sword," the boy said. "And I don't want to stand and shoot arrows. I want to fight!"

Norah thought she saw a hint of a smile in Soren's eyes. He held the wooden axe back out to the boy.

"I'm going to make a bigger one, like yours," Thomas said.

"There's no skill in a big axe," Soren told him. "And it's not an easy battle weapon. Smaller is better for quick work."

"Why do you have a big one?"

He shrugged. "More blood when I kill someone."

"Lord Commander," Norah scolded, but the boy grinned.

Soren reached behind and pulled a smaller battle-axe from a sheath belted around his waist and flung it at a nearby railing, burying the head into the wood. Thomas let out a small laugh in amazement.

Soren walked to the railing column and pulled the axe free, then returned to the boy. "Try it," he said, holding out the weapon.

Thomas's eyes grew even larger, and he took the axe, positioning himself toward the column. He moved his arm to swing.

"Arm up, boy, not out. You want it to fly straight and not arc sideways."

Thomas raised his arm upward and flung the axe toward the column. It fell short, clanging on the cobbled walk. The boy looked back at Soren, waiting for his reaction.

"Don't expect a hit on your first try," the commander nodded. "Go fetch it."

Thomas ran and grabbed the axe off the ground and brought it back, holding it out.

"Do it again."

The boy flung it harder this time, and it hit the column but bounced back, onto the ground. Soren nodded again, and the boy ran to fetch it. When he came back, he held the axe out to Soren.

The commander paused. "Keep it," he said. "Practice."

"Yes, Lord Destroyer," Thomas exclaimed, grinning and holding the axe tightly. Surely it was now his most prized possession.

"Soren," Norah said softly, "I hardly think this is an appropriate gift for a child."

He looked at her for a moment, seemingly surprised. Then he shrugged, turning back to Thomas. "Don't go throwing it at your friends. It's a weapon. You'll kill someone."

"I won't kill anyone," the boy grinned. "At least not my friends."

Norah raised an eyebrow.

"One more thing," Soren said. He pulled off the belt with the axe sheath, holding it wide and eyeing its size. "It's big, but..." he stopped. "Hang on," he said as he drew his dagger and used the tip to cut notches down the length of the belt. Then he looped it around Thomas's waist and fastened it. "A little thick, but you'll grow into it."

Thomas beamed.

"Run along now," Soren told him.

"Thank you, Lord Destroyer!" the boy said with a clumsy bow, then darted away, into the sun.

The commander chuckled, a genuine chuckle, a sound she hadn't heard from him before. "He forgot about you," he told Norah.

She let out a laugh. "He forgot about the world, I think. That was very kind. You made for a very happy little boy, but... let's not give any more weapons to children."

Soren shrugged with a smirk, and for a moment, it was hard for Norah to believe he could hurt anyone. Especially a child.

CHAPTER THIRTY-FIVE

Norah stepped carefully as she made her way through the darkness of the cave. It had been a long time since Alexander had shown her the hidden hot springs. She realized now that perhaps it wasn't the best idea to be traipsing into the darkness and down a path she vaguely remembered, and also having not told anyone where she was going. But the wine she had finished off just a short while ago had been very convincing of the adventure, and away from the bustle of the castle and the weight of the crown, she already felt her energy returning. She just needed to escape for a while.

The wet walls seeped cold into her fingers as she felt her way deeper into the darkness. She stayed to the left, following her touch. The cave was longer than she remembered, and for a moment, she feared she might find herself lost. But she calmed. She'd followed a singular wall, and she could merely turn around and feel her way back out at any time. She continued.

Her persistence paid off as the darkness started to fade. She could make out the walls of the cave now—she was almost there. Just as she remembered, she turned a small corner, and the tunnel opened into a massive cavern. It had been day when she had last come with Alexander, with the large opening at the top spilling in the sun. She had thought it was the most beautiful place she had ever seen. Now, moonlight lit the cavern, and it was even more magical than before. She smiled as she saw the pools of water. In the sun, they'd shimmered a beautiful turquoise. Not tonight. In the night, they were pools of darkness. But she liked the darkness now.

Her teeth chattered as she pulled off her shoes and wriggled out of her gown. She paused at her undergarments, but then chided herself for being silly. She was alone, and she stripped everything off. She rolled her clothes and put them beside a large rock, then walked to the edge of the pool and dipped her toes in the water. Its warmth made her grin, and she stepped out farther, letting herself sink down into its abyss. The rush of heat surrounded her body, and she breathed out her worry as it enveloped her.

Norah swam out farther, past the rock formation in the center and around to where the cave opened to the starry heavens. Rolling onto her back, she floated in peaceful bliss under the light of the night sky. She closed her eyes and breathed in a new energy.

How wonderful it would be to stay in this magical place, away from everything and everyone. She smiled, remembering Alexander telling her that no one came to the cave for fear of monsters lurking in the deep. She rolled and let her body sink down so only her eyes and nose rested above the surface. The edge of the water softly lapped against her lips, caressing them like a lover's kiss. Perhaps the pool wanted her to stay. She could be its monster.

She glided quietly through the night like a serpent of the sea. Each stroke through the water brought her strength. Its power flowed through her—her power now—queen of the dark and the deep.

A disturbance in the air pulled her from her peace. Norah stilled, listening.

There it was again.

It had only been a stir, but she was one with this cavern now, and she felt it like thunder.

Someone was here.

She swam silently back to the center rock formation to investigate.

A man stood waist deep in the water, his back to her, and a wave of intrusion washed over her. If she were a monster, he'd be her first victim. She imagined it—slipping through the darkness under the still of the surface, coming up behind him, then reaching up and taking hold. She'd pull him down into her depths, and into the clutches of death. That's how she'd welcome those who disturbed her.

She pulled her mind back from its murderous thoughts and scolded herself. She was spending too much time with Soren.

Norah watched this intruder from the shadows. But as she looked closer, her pulse quickened. She knew this man, and a smile came to her lips. *Alexander.* What was he doing here? Did he come often? He obviously hadn't seen her clothing rolled up by the large rock to the side.

She slipped closer. The warm water rolled over her skin as she moved, and she felt every bit a prowling monster of the deep. It made her bolder.

Norah bit her lip, feeling mischievous. "Who disturbs my waters?" she called in a low voice.

He looked around with a start. Her voice had echoed through the chamber, not revealing her position. She watched him comb the cavern for her, but he couldn't see her from her place among the shadows.

"Only another seeking the calm," he called back. He turned, still searching, his back to her again.

She held her voice deeper, husky; her best serpent voice. "These are my waters."

"I've not seen you here before," he answered.

She grinned. He hadn't recognized her voice. She moved from behind the rock formation, silently drawing closer. "Are you sure about that?" she called.

He spun to face her. She hung deep in the water, showing only her head. It took him a moment, but his eyes softened, and she flashed him a smile.

"Queen Norah?"

"No," she said. "There's no queen here." Only a serpent of the deep. She came closer as he stepped farther into the water.

His eyes locked with hers. "Are you a phantom, then?" he asked. His voice was smooth and warm, like the water.

She rolled her lips together to hold her smile. "Perhaps I'm only in your mind."

"You're always in my mind," he confessed, and a quiet settled around them. His admission sobered her.

This wasn't a game.

"Are you still angry with me?" she asked, now more serious. They hadn't spoken much in the past couple weeks. She'd felt a distance between them, a distance that grew with her every decision, her every action. And now, after the meeting with the council, and her employment of Soren to help solve the situation with the pirates, it felt like they were further than they'd ever been before.

He stepped farther into the water, not taking his eyes from her. Norah circled him. Was he wearing only his skin, like her? The thought stirred a heat in her stomach, but she pushed it down. She needed to leave.

"I could never stay angry with you. Surely you know this."

She thought she did, but lately she wasn't so certain.

He drifted closer, close enough for her to touch him. His nearness called to her, and before she could stop herself, she reached out and brushed his chest with her fingertips. Quickly realizing her mistake, she moved to pull back, but he caught her, covering her hand over his chest with his own.

Norah's breath faltered.

Alexander reached up and clasped the nape of her neck, pulling her to him. He dropped his head and caught her mouth with his. His kiss was deep and possessive as he pushed her back against the rock and snaked his arm around her. The smoothness of his skin against hers stole her resistance, if she even had any.

Norah tasted the sweetness of berry on his lips, with the faint scent of wine on his breath. She realized the wine had gotten the better of them both, and she pulled back. "You're not yourself," she whispered. Neither was she.

He paused, seeming to call back his senses, and his face sobered. "Forgive me."

But he didn't release her, nor did she pull herself from him. But they couldn't be here, not like this.

Norah pulled him down and brought her lips to his ear. "You need to leave. Now." Any longer and she wouldn't let him go. Then she slipped from his arms and drew back into the depths of the darkness.

Alexander stayed for a moment, lingering in the silence. Then he waded slowly to the edge of the pool. Norah watched him, the smooth round of his buttocks, the curve of his thighs, as he rose from the water. She couldn't take her eyes from him.

She moved slowly, stalking him from the darkness. She felt every bit a monster lurking in the shadows, wanting to call him back to her. And he would come. She knew he would come.

Alexander picked up his clothes and disappeared into the darkness of the cave, and Norah let out a long, shaking breath, begging her senses to come back to her.

Norah stood in the library by a towering shelf that stretched to the ceiling. She focused her eyes on the pages of an open book in her hands, but found herself unable to read it, or even see it. Every time her mind wandered, it took her back to the cave, back to Alexander.

She cursed herself, angry at what she had done, for what she had almost done. He still held a piece of her, and she loathed herself for it.

The doors opened, and she turned to see Catherine sweeping toward her, clearly upset about something. *Perfect.* Norah needed a good berating to take her mind away. She wondered what she had done—or maybe what Soren had done—to warrant the deep scowl her grandmother wore, although she didn't really care. She'd appreciate a scolding for just about anything right now—anything to keep her thoughts from the cave.

"What did you say to him?" Catherine demanded when she reached her.

What? "To who?"

"To Alexander."

Norah's blood ran cold, and she swallowed as her stomach knotted. She had been hoping to be chastised for something different, something very different. Surely there was a myriad of other things for Catherine to be angry about. "Why?" she asked, with a crack in her voice that made her cringe inside.

"Weeks ago, he finally accepted a marriage with Ismene, but this morning, he came to advise me he'd changed his mind."

Norah's chest tightened. *Ismene?* The young woman Catherine had worked to match him with so long ago? Were they courting? For how long? Why hadn't he told her?

"What did you say to him?" Catherine demanded again. "I can only assume you've had an influence on his decision."

"I didn't even know he was betrothed!" Norah looked around. She needed to sit down, but there was no chair. Alexander had agreed to marry Ismene? The heat of jealousy flooded her, but she knew it was a jealousy she had no right to feel.

"He'd already asked her father's permission, and Lord Dartan has given it. Rescinding his marriage offer now would be a disgrace."

Was her grandmother really blaming her? "Then you shouldn't have forced it on him!" Catherine *had* forced him. He hadn't wanted to. *Right?*

"This is what is best for him," her grandmother said angrily.

"How?"

"That girl loves him!" Catherine snapped back. "Selfish child! Look what you do to him. When you were captured, a madness took him. He marched to war without listening to reason. When he returned with the news of your marriage, all he could think about was getting back to you. And when he did, you sent him home beaten and broken. And still, wherever you go, he longs to follow. Is this what you want for him? You have to let him go!"

Her emotion spoke for her. "If he wants to be free, then I free him."

"He would never want to be free from you." Her grandmother's eyes burned into her. "But you let him love you, Norah. You're responsible for his pain, and his disgrace."

Norah's lip trembled, and her eyes welled. Deep in her heart, she knew this was best for him, and she couldn't push down the rising guilt—perhaps she'd just ruined it.

Catherine turned and left, and Norah leaned back against the wall of the library as the wave of emotion washed over her.

The sun rose slowly, eating back the frost on the ground. She sat on a bench in the garden in the chilled air of morning, but she didn't feel the cold. Norah hadn't slept, and she wouldn't. She didn't deserve rest—the peace it brought, the renewal.

Heavy footfalls came behind her, and she turned to see Soren approaching. She quickly wiped the tears from her cheeks.

"Your maid told me you were here," he said when he reached her. "That you wanted to be alone."

"Which apparently means nothing to you," she said shortly.

He snorted in amusement and took his post by the bench, standing with his axe between his feet and his hands resting on the wood of the handle.

"And where have you been?" she snapped angrily. She needed to be angry, to hold her other emotions at bay. "I looked everywhere for you yesterday."

He stiffened and dropped a shoulder as he leaned back on his heel. "I took the boy hunting," he said. Adrian, he meant. "Why? Did something happen? Did you need me?"

She folded her arms and rocked gently as she stifled a sob, but there was no holding back the emotion now. "I'm messing everything up. I shouldn't have come back." She buried her face in her hands.

Soren shifted again. "What happened?"

She drew in an uneven breath. "I ruined his marriage."

He stepped around closer to her. "Whose?"

"Alexander's!"

His brows drew together. "The Bear would never wed."

"It was arranged by my grandmother. He'd agreed." Her voice shook. "But I ruined it."

The bench shifted as he sat down beside her.

"You're the Destroyer," she cried. "You're supposed to be the corruption, the darkness. But it isn't you, is it? It's me." She sucked in another sob. "What have I done?"

Soren turned and grasped her arm. "Salara," he said in a low voice—a steely voice rich with warning. His eyes were dark and intense. "Did you lay with him?"

She paused through her tears, but then shook her head.

He dropped his head as a small breath escaped him.

"But I kissed him," she said. "I swam naked in a pool with him. Is that not practically the same thing?"

"No, it's not." But a deep, angry line folded between his brows. "Not exactly."

"What will I tell Mikael?" she breathed.

The shadow under his brow darkened, and he tightened his hold. "You'll consider this your confession, and never speak of it again. Ever."

His eyes demanded an answer, and shakily, she nodded. He let go of her arm, and they sat on the bench until the sun rose enough for its rays to reach them.

"I want to go back," she whispered.

"Then we'll go."

"To Kharav."

"I knew what you meant," he said.

CHAPTER THIRTY-SIX

Norah chewed her dinner slowly as she watched her grandmother stir her tea. Her eyes wandered to Alexander, only to find him looking back at her. Her stomach turned. It would only get worse the longer she waited, she knew.

"I'm returning to Kharav," she said before taking another bite of potato and looking back at her grandmother.

Catherine's head snapped up.

Norah clenched her dress in her fist underneath the table and avoided Alexander's eyes. She chewed her potato methodically, trying to appear calm.

"You've only just gotten here," Catherine said.

"I've been here a month," she replied. "And the lord commander is needed back in Kharav."

"Well, he's free to go," Alexander said with an edge to his voice.

Norah still couldn't look at him. She took a drink of wine and shifted in her chair. "I need to go with him. He's the only one the king trusts to see me safe in my travels." Norah felt guilty about using Soren as an excuse to leave, but what other reason could she give? That she couldn't let Alexander go so long as he was near? That she couldn't bear the shame? That she needed to leave? Perhaps what would be the most offensive to them—she wanted to go back to Kharav. She wanted to go back to Mikael.

She pulled a small piece of bread from the loaf by her plate, but she worried that she might not be able to swallow it if she put it in her mouth.

"What has he to worry?" Alexander asked. "The Shadowmen are the only ones who would attack the queen of Mercia as she travels."

"And the drifters?" Norah shot back at him.

"I'll see your return to the Shadowlands," he said. "The drifters are pockets of rogues, and they can be managed by any capable army."

"Mercia needs you here," she told him.

"Mercia needs her queen."

Norah banged down her goblet with a force that splashed wine onto the table. "I won't argue this. I'm returning to Kharav. Tomorrow."

She stood abruptly and left the dining hall. As she reached the stair, she heard Alexander's voice behind her.

"Norah," he called, following her.

She kept walking.

"Norah! Please!"

She paused, then turned, forcing herself to look at him. Pain etched across his brow, and she thought she might come undone.

"Why? Tell me why," he begged. His voice dropped to a whisper. "Is it because of me? Because of us? Because of what's between us?"

"There is no us! There's nothing between us." Her words shook as she cried them, and his breath shook as he heard them. "And I don't belong here," she whispered. "I shouldn't be here." And it completely broke her.

Footfalls sounded behind him, but Alexander didn't need to turn to see who it was. He knew.

Adrian.

It was only a matter of time before his brother heard about him calling off the marriage to Ismene, a marriage Adrian had tried so hard to talk him out of accepting to begin with. Why had he accepted it? He had no interest in marrying, he had no interest in Ismene.

But Adrian didn't say anything about the marriage. They sat in the quiet.

"She's leaving," Alexander said finally. "Norah's returning to the Shadowlands."

"Grandmother told me."

Of course she had. Had Catherine also told Adrian to come talk to him? To get Alexander to convince Norah to stay? As if he could. Or perhaps... to make sure Alexander stayed. If only she knew how little choice he had. Norah would go back to the Shadowlands alone.

She would continue to struggle against the world, alone.

Alexander stilled. She didn't have to be completely alone... "You'll go with her."

Adrian's eyes widened. "Me?"

"I can't go." He gripped Adrian's shoulder. "Please. Brother. If things go poorly in the Shadowlands, I need you to get her out. I need you to protect her."

Adrian's mouth opened slightly, with words that wouldn't come, then he said finally, "Of course. Of course, I'll go. But she'll also have Caspian."

Alexander gripped him tighter. "She needs you too. *I* need you with her." Caspian couldn't protect her alone. Adrian was still young, but his skill with a sword rivaled the best of Mercia, and Adrian knew what Norah meant beyond her role as queen. Adrian knew what she meant to Alexander. He would keep her safe.

Norah made her way to the courtyard where the lord commander waited. The Crest sat ready on their mounts, with a new unit of Northern soldiers prepared to march as well. Soren had even arranged for the pirate wards to come with them, not trusting Mercia to retain them.

Alexander walked with Adrian to his horse. She'd been most surprised that Alexander had allowed him to come. She wondered how Adrian had talked him into it.

Alexander clasped arms with his brother, saying words she couldn't hear, then he pulled him into a tight embrace. Norah's heart hurt. She felt like she was taking everything from him.

She stood quietly as he approached her. The blue of his eyes was dull and somber. For a moment, she didn't think she could leave. She wasn't sure when she would see him again, or even if she would see him again. She had no intentions of returning to Mercia, and...

"You can't return to Kharav again," she whispered. Her throat wouldn't give her the voice.

He nodded.

She wanted to hug him one last time, to put her arms around him, but she didn't. "Goodbye, Alexander." She thought she might choke on the words.

"Goodbye, Norah." So cold, with finality.

She mounted Sephir, then looked at her grandmother, who stood at the top of the stair. Catherine had embraced her stiffly inside. It was everything Norah could do to not break. Did everyone she loved hate her now?

The remnants of her heart barely beat in her chest, and she urged Sephir on and away.

Outside the city, Norah stopped and gave one last look to Mercia as Soren pulled his horse up beside her.

"Can it be now?" she whispered.

"Can what be now?"

She turned to him with tears in her eyes. "The vision the seer showed you. If it's to be, let it be now."

The army moved relatively quickly, and Norah was glad for it. She was desperate to get back to Kharav. She traveled with a new unit of Northmen, absent Titus, who she'd left back in Mercia with his new wife.

Norah rode in silent sorrow. It was hard to imagine a life without Alexander. And her guilt ate her. She hadn't let him love someone else, and she'd ruined his hope for happiness. Norah added the weight of the council's disappointment, her grandmother's disappointment, and the hidden enemies she was no closer to finding and no closer to stopping. And now returning to Mikael with no happiness in her heart and no child, she couldn't hold the tears that ran down her cheeks.

Soren moved his mount beside her, drawing close, but still looking ahead. "You bring the young bear back with you. It's unexpected."

Adrian.

She nodded. "I know. I'm surprised Alexander let him come. But I'm glad."

He held out a small cloth, still not looking at her. "And you have your captain. And the mute and the girl are waiting for you back in Kharav. Salar waits for you."

She took the cloth. She knew what he was doing, this destroyer of men. He was trying to make her feel better. And he did. She watched him, sitting on his destrier like a foul-tempered seraph, and she felt the smallest of smiles through her tears.

He eyed her irritably. "Wipe your face. Tahla can't see you like this."

The cool air chilled the beaded sweat on his skin. His panting slowed, and Caspian's body came back to him again. He brushed his fingers along the length of Tahla's bare back as she lay nestled against him on a blanket by the river. They'd slipped away from the village as the sun set, away from the music and the ears and eyes of others.

He'd last left her after she'd confessed her love for him—something he'd never expected to hear. Every day, her words ran through his mind again and brought a smile to his face. And now he was back in her arms, his heart was full.

She propped herself on her elbow and swirled a finger over the curve of his chest. "I've missed you, Northman."

And he'd missed her, more than anything.

She rolled back down, laying her head on his shoulder, and looked up to the sky. "Sometimes I feel like we're Hakah and Umai."

"Who are they?"

She turned her head slightly toward the horizon and pointed to where the sun had already set. Only the fading twilight remained. "See how Hakah stretches his light, even after he's been pulled under the earth? He's trying to catch a glimpse of Umai." Her gaze moved to the eastern sky, searching. She found the faintest outline of the moon starting to appear. "There," she said, pointing. "There's Umai."

She smiled sadly.

"Their paths don't allow them to be together," she continued. "Saddened that he couldn't be with Umai, Hakah's heart broke into thousands of pieces. He scattered them across the sky to create the stars so that when Umai wakes, she can see how much he loves her."

Caspian watched as the sky grew darker and the moon fully emerged with the stars all around.

Tahla nestled against his shoulder again. "But then I remember that Hakah can never hold Umai in his arms. He can't kiss her or touch her. They can't be one." She tipped her face up to his. "Hakah and Umai wish they could be Caspian and Tahla." She stretched her neck to bring her lips closer. "Kiss me, Northman."

And he did.

CHAPTER THIRTY-SEVEN

Kharav welcomed her return. The breeze kissed her cheeks and lovingly brushed through her hair. The sweet scent of the gardens embraced her. Norah was finally home.

When she reached the courtyard, Mikael was waiting for her. She stopped when she saw him. Nearly two months had passed since she left—two months they'd been apart. Too long. She slid off Sephir, her body stiff and aching. It had been a long journey, a seemingly endless one. But she was finally back where she belonged.

Norah knew how this was supposed to go: she would bow her head in greeting, he would bow in return, then he would offer his arm and she would accept, and he'd lead her into the castle. This was the general way of royal things, not unlike Mercia.

But unlike Mercia, none of that mattered too much to Mikael, and when she reached him, she threw her arms around his neck. He picked her up and held her tightly, and she clung to him.

He pulled back to look at her and cupped her face in his hand. "Are you well, Salara?"

She wasn't well, but he was making it better. All she could do was nod.

"Let's get you inside." With his arm around her, he practically carried her into the castle. She didn't mind. She was almost too tired to carry herself.

Mikael waved everyone off as they reached the great hall. When they were alone, he stopped and turned her to him. "Let me look at you," he said softly. His eyes moved over her face. "You've been gone too long but returned sooner than I'd expected. I"—he brushed her cheek as he paused—"I worried you might not return at all."

"I had to."

His face changed, and he brought his hand to her stomach with asking eyes.

Norah swallowed, then shook her head. The hope on his face gave way to disappointment. Disappointment that there was no child. A deeper sadness seeped into her. "I had to return because Kharav is my home," she told him. "And you're here."

A small smile came to his lips.

Her words weren't just to lift his spirits. They were true.

"And the Bear remains in Mercia?" he asked.

"He won't return."

His smile grew. "Let's get you settled."

Mikael followed her up to their chamber, where Vitalia met her with an unconventional squeal and hug and then went to draw her a much-needed bath. Norah pulled off her overcoat and draped it over the bench at the foot of the bed.

"I've missed you, Salara," he told her as he sat down in the side chair and watched her loosen the lacing on the back of her dress.

Norah stepped in front of him and took his face in her hands. She had missed him too. His skin was warm, and she liked the way his short-cropped beard tickled under her nails.

"I'm hungry," he said, gazing up at her.

She reached up and pulled her hair free from its tie and unraveled the braid with her fingers. "You should call for some food," she said as she stepped toward the bath chamber. "Eat something. I'll just get cleaned up and join you after."

He caught her wrist and pulled her back to him. "It's not food I'm hungry for," he said in a low voice.

Norah couldn't help her smile. She loved his want for her and that he didn't hide it. "You should let me bathe. I'm terribly dirty."

"I like a dirty woman," he argued.

She laughed. "I'll make better love if I'm a clean woman."

His jaw tightened, and a protest rumbled in his chest, but he released her. "Go on then. I'll wait. But not long."

When the water was ready, Vitalia helped her peel off her dress, and she climbed into the tub, relishing its warmth. Vitalia soaped up her hair and poured pitchers of water to rinse it. Years seemed to wash away, and their heaviness with it.

After her hair was clean, she leaned her head back against the tub and closed her eyes. She was tired, but she knew sleep wouldn't come.

"You can go," Mikael's voice came, directed at Vitalia. "I'll take care of my wife tonight."

The door shut behind her.

Norah kept her eyes closed, but a smile crept across her lips. Finally, she opened them to see him leaning against the wall of the bath chamber and watching her.

"So, you missed me, husband?" she asked.

"I did," he replied as he kicked off his boots. He pulled his shirt over his head, and her smile grew.

"What are you doing?" she asked him.

"I'm getting ready."

She raised a brow. "Getting ready for what?"

"For when you say you're clean."

Norah laughed. She'd certainly missed him.

Mikael shucked off his breeches and braies and leaned back against the wall, naked. She turned in the tub so she could lay against the side and see him. The lines of his body stirred something inside her, and suddenly she didn't seem quite as tired.

"Are you clean now?" he asked.

She shook her head with a smile. "No, not yet."

He snorted impatiently. "Hurry up or I'm going to drag you from that tub."

Norah bit her lip to keep from grinning. She'd love to be dragged from the bathtub. She stifled her smile as she pulled a small round of corian root from the dish on the small table beside the tub. She dipped it into the water and worked it into a lather. Rolling her head back, she rubbed it over her neck and her shoulders, taking her time and working it deep, as if soothing her muscles.

A rumble vibrated from him again. She liked this game. How long would he wait? Slowly, she rubbed the soap down her breasts and swirled the sweet-scented lather around her nipples. Then she paused to look back at him.

Mikael was visibly roused for her now, but he kept his place against the wall, patient—too patient for her taste. Norah ran her hands down over her stomach and raised a leg from the water, lathering one, then the other.

Still, he waited.

Her eyes narrowed. She brought her hand down between her thighs, under the water, and gave a small moan. She rolled her head to look at him again, and finally, he surged forward with a growl.

Norah screamed a laugh as he clambered into the tub with her, spilling water over the sides.

"I still have soap on me!" she protested as he moved to carry her out.

"It's a root. I'll eat it off."

"Mikael!" she screamed.

Relenting, he hurriedly splashed her in a quick rinse as she laughed, and then he settled for a moment. "Are you done now, Salara?" he asked her.

She bit her lip and nodded.

His face was serious now. The game was over. Mikael lifted her up and stepped out of the tub. He carried her to the bed and dropped her onto the silken sheets of darkness before prowling over her. Her skin prickled—from the air against her wet skin or his hunting gaze, she wasn't sure.

His body held a different hunger now. No more playfulness in his eyes or sweetness on his lips. He stretched his hand across her chest and held her firmly as he moved between her thighs. She realized this wasn't a taking of passion or of lust, but a taking of need. He claimed her. She was his.

Norah understood this need. She angled her hips to meet him, yielding, and he buried himself inside her. He drove hard, and deep.

She let his madness consume her, knowing it wouldn't last long. Mikael rolled his body as he bared his teeth, pushing himself even deeper. She didn't reach up to touch him, she didn't try to tame him. She let him fill his need, and he did, shuddering to an end.

Mikael held his weight on his elbows as he recovered, panting into her ear. Only then did she dare to touch him. She ran her fingers up his arms and over his shoulders, to the nape of his neck and into his hair. He pulsed inside her, but his body calmed.

He pushed himself up and looked into her eyes.

"Are you back now?" she asked him.

He nodded. Concern marred his brow. "Did I hurt you?"

She shook her head but tightened her grip in his hair. "No," she whispered. "But I'll hurt you if you think you're finished."

A smile came to his lips, and he lowered himself to kiss her.

CHAPTER THIRTY-EIGHT

Weeks fell to months. Norah wanted to believe she'd settled into a new normal, but the hole in her heart still lingered. She wondered how her grandmother was faring, and Alexander. She'd received two letters with reports of the kingdom, but that's all they'd contained—reports.

She passed the sparring fields on her morning walk and smiled when she saw Cohen. The boy was coming along nicely in his training. He'd been doing well ever since coming to the capital with his sister, Calla.

Cohen was matched with a young Kharavian soldier, and their blades sang through the afternoon sky as they practiced their skill. She stopped and leaned against the fence to watch them.

"He's unbeaten, out of all the earlies. Even second years," Calla said proudly as she came up beside Norah, beaming at her brother.

Norah's eyes widened. "That's impressive."

Earlies were men in the army who showed special promise. They were pulled from the normal regimen and put on an accelerated training plan with the hope they might make the Crest. Even so, less than half of all earlies made it to the Crest. Norah knew all this since Soren regularly told her Calla and Cohen didn't deserve to train with them. Yet, he still had them train with the earlies, the same as he had done with Adrian.

"He'll be a soldier of the Crest one day," Calla said. "The best swordsman in Kharav."

Norah smiled at the girl. Calla was a strong spirit, who loved with the same fervor as she fought, and her loyalty to her brother made Norah emotional sometimes. "I'm sure he'll be amazing."

"He'll never be in the Crest," Soren's voice called behind them.

Norah sighed as she rolled her eyes. *Destroyer of hopes and dreams.* "Way to inspire, Lord Commander," she said.

"False hopes will see you starved in the winter," he said dryly.

Calla scoffed. "But he's the best swordsman on the field!"

Soren cut the girl a daggered look. No one questioned him among the soldiers, and Calla brought a new test he wasn't accustomed to.

He leaned close, using his size. "He can't hear, so he can't control his sound. He's deaf, but he doesn't know what silence is. He can't talk, so he can't command. And at any moment, I could come behind him and slit his throat."

Calla's eyes blazed, and her hand clenched the dagger at her waist.

"Calla," Norah said, breaking the girl from a rash reaction. "Get your brother and go on to your studies."

The girl fumed for a moment before she slipped out from under the commander's force and went to fetch Cohen from his match.

Norah looked at Soren and shook her head.

"What?" he growled. "I'm just being truthful."

"No," she said, shaking her head again. "Sometimes you're just mean."

Norah and Adrian walked through the courtyard as the afternoon waned. They were spending more and more time together, and Norah had started to think of him as her own brother. His playful candor, his cheeky teases, his easy laugh—he made the distance of family seem not so far.

"Anything new from your brother?" she asked him.

"I got a letter from him yesterday, but nothing new. He mainly just asks about me, and if I'm seeing to all my duties." He chuckled.

Norah smiled sadly. "I hope you write him regularly. I'm sure he misses you. You're the only family he's ever had, other than your parents, and now you're gone."

Adrian glanced at her. His mouth opened slightly, but he hesitated before saying, "We had another brother. Did you not know?"

Norah stopped, stunned. She shook her head. How had she not known this?

"He died."

"Oh, Adrian," she breathed. "I'm so sorry. I had no idea. No one's ever talked about him."

"No, I know. And it's all right. It was a long time ago, before I was born. I never knew him. But he and Alexander were close." He started forward again, and they continued walking. "Lucien was his name."

So many questions flooded her mind, but all seemed prying and intrusive. What does one say in times like these, other than *Sorry*?

"And I did send a letter," he said, turning the conversation back to Alexander. "I let him know you were well."

Norah smiled appreciatively. She didn't think it appropriate for her to write him just to tell him how she fared, but he would worry for her, and she did want him to know she was doing all right. "How's Sevina?" she asked.

A bashful grin came to his face, and he looked down at his feet. "She's well. I, uh... I've been meaning to talk to you... about her."

She smiled at his nervousness.

"I, um... I plan to ask for her hand."

Norah's eyes widened as she searched for words. "Adrian, that's exciting and... unexpected!" She paused. "Are you sure?"

"Of course I'm sure. I know I'm young, but I can still know what I want."

She didn't disagree, but it was such a big decision. "Have you thought about asking Alexander's advice?"

Adrian quieted, then he said, "No, he wouldn't approve of a Kharavian wife."

Norah's heart hurt that Adrian would keep something from Alexander, and something so significant. "But he's going to find out eventually," she said. "And that would make things very hard between the two of you."

He bit his bottom lip but didn't answer.

"I'm not saying to ask his permission," she said. "Of course you can make your own decisions. But you should still talk to him. Just think about it, okay?"

He nodded.

As they drew nearer to the castle, Nora slowed. Two wagons sat by the fountain, with Mikael beside them reading a letter in his hand. His face was dark and fixed, and Norah knew him well enough to know something bothered him.

"I'll catch up with you later," she told Adrian.

"Of course," he said, and headed back toward the sparring field.

"Is something wrong?" she called to Mikael as she approached.

He looked up from the letter and folded it before slipping it inside his jacket. "Nothing you need trouble yourself with," he said.

She raised a brow. "That wasn't condescending at all."

He sighed. "I'm sorry." Then he offered her his arm, and they walked toward the castle. "Gregor only sends a quarter of his due trade," he told her. "He says he's suffered a failed crop, and it's all he can part with."

Norah pursed her lips as a weight sunk in her stomach. "Do you believe him?"

Mikael shook his head. "No. Our own crops have fared well. Japheth has some of the most fertile lands in the world, and I've not heard of any news of pests or disease. And the herbs he doesn't send—they're medicinal ones, those that can be found only in the Colored Valley. They're the most valuable to us."

"So you think he does this intentionally?"

Mikael stopped. "I don't know what to think. If it's intentional, it confirms what I feared. He's built an alliance with another." The line of his jaw rippled as he looked back at the wagons. "We have shipments of rice and grain to be sent within a few weeks' time. If I send them, it's a statement that I accept his excuse. If I don't, I essentially call him a liar and force his next move."

"What will you do?"

He shook his head. "I haven't decided."

Quiet filled the room as they ate their evening meal. Since returning from Mercia, Soren had resumed eating with them, and even Salara-Mae had taken to joining. But the king's mother still made no attempt to hide her disdain for the lord commander.

Cusco and Cavaatsa lay at Norah's feet, and she shuffled her toes under Cusco's warm belly. She watched Mikael as he sat without eating, only drinking from his chalice. Japheth and the trade dilemma were still heavy on his mind.

Salara-Mae dropped a small chunk of meat to the ground for Cusco, and the large dog swallowed it without chewing. Soren looked at her in surprise, but she avoided his eyes. "The beasts have become quite tolerable," she said to Norah, "now that you've been seeing to them."

Norah smiled but swallowed it back when Soren turned his offended eyes to her. She'd done nothing different with the dogs, other than allow them some additional poor behaviors. She shrugged at Soren apologetically. He set his attention back on his meal, and Norah's lips curved upward again. But her amusement was short-lived. Mikael smoothed his short-cut beard on his chin, gazing out the side windows, and it drew her thoughts back to his worry.

"You haven't gone hunting in a while," Norah said, pulling his attention back to the present.

He drew in a long breath and let it out as he set his chalice on the table. Then he nodded. "That's a good idea. I think I'll go tomorrow."

"Will you take Adrian?" she asked. Not surprisingly, neither Mikael nor the commander balked at the idea. Adrian was doing well in Kharav. He was smart, learned quickly, and could handle his own on the field. He was already growing on them, and—she smiled—they didn't even realize it.

"Have you decided what you'll do about King Gregor?" she asked, and Soren sat back in his chair, also curious.

Mikael's eyes met hers, but he didn't answer.

"Send me to collect the rest of the trade," Soren told him.

Send him to intimidate him was more like it. "That's the opposite of what you should do," Norah said, drawing an annoyed look from the commander. "You should talk to him."

"You would have me call him out as a liar?" Mikael said.

"I'd have you talk to him like a rational human being—I think it's okay if he knows that you're unhappy with this situation, that it raises suspicion. But I wouldn't so boldly threaten him."

Soren snorted, "Like *you* did when he was here last?"

She pursed her lips at him. "Let me remind you that was to save *your* skin, which I assumed was more important than a partial shipment of herbs." Her eyes narrowed. "I do wonder if it was the right decision sometimes." She looked back to Mikael. "Either talk to him or send your shipment due."

"He tests me," Mikael said.

"You should be sure that Gregor's leaning away from his alliance with you before you act. Buy yourself some time to discover more, or time to prepare if there *is* to be a confrontation."

"He'll think me weak."

"Which is why you should send me," Soren insisted.

Norah disagreed. "You should respond in a way that shows less paranoia and more confidence. Just send your shipment. It gives you time, it makes it easier if you ever come to your senses and actually decide to talk to him, and it shows you aren't worried. Act as though: Who of any intelligence would dare break an agreement with Salar of Kharav?"

Mikael sat, mulling. He took a drink from his chalice as she and Soren watched him. Then he turned to Soren. "Send the shipment."

The commander glared at Norah with anger thick across his brow, but he gave a forced nod to his king. Still, she knew this situation was anything but resolved.

"Did you know Alexander had another brother?"

Caspian's head snapped up. "Where did you hear this?"

They stood in the library, and Norah pushed the book in her hand back onto its place on the shelf. "Did you know?" she asked again.

He nodded with a long exhale. "I did." His eyes grew somber. "Lucien."

"Why has no one talked about him? No one told me."

He gave an apologetic tilt of his head. "It was a long time ago."

"Still, it seems important."

"It was," he admitted. "*Is*."

"Will you tell me about him? What happened?"

Caspian glanced down uncomfortably. She knew he didn't like speaking about others, especially their private lives, and especially Alexander's.

"If I were in Mercia, I'd ask Alexander himself," she added. "But I can't, and it's not something I'd write him about."

He still seemed to mull over her ask.

"Would he not tell me?" she asked.

"Of course he would." He glanced around them to ensure their conversation stayed private, before giving a relenting sigh. "They were very young when Lucien died. Seven, eight. They were very close."

Norah waited for him to continue, but he didn't say anything else. It was as if he thought that were enough. "How did he die?" she pressed.

"A sickness took him."

And? Caspian was the worst storyteller. "Is that when Alexander came to stay at the castle?" she prompted. "When did Adrian come? And what happened to their mother?"

Caspian sighed again, not pleased at all with her questions. "After Lucien died, their mother went mad with grief. She would have nightmares and couldn't sleep. She would hear him." He paused again, but continued before Norah asked another question. "She became confused and would lock everyone out of the house. Massey would find Alexander forced outside almost every time she stopped by."

Norah's heart hurt. "Who's Massey?"

"She ran the kitchen in the castle. Still does. Lady Catherine had Massey take meals to Alexander's mother because her mind was too far gone to look after herself. One day, Massey came back and said Alexander was forced outside again—it was the dead of winter—and Lady Catherine went and got him and brought him back to the castle."

"My grandmother?"

He nodded. "She does have a heart, Regal High."

"What happened to his mother?"

"She went through a period where she seemed to get better. But it wasn't long after Adrian was born that she started to deteriorate again. Things were rough for a long time, and she ended up taking her own life. That's when Adrian came to the castle."

"Oh," Norah breathed. That was so much more terrible than she'd thought. She was actually relieved she hadn't asked Alexander about his mother. She'd come close several times. Surely it would have been hard for him to have told her this story. Her mind turned to Caspian. He'd been close with Alexander growing up. He obviously knew everything about him, even the most private of details.

"Did you live in the castle?" she asked him.

He shook his head. "No, but I was always there, it seemed. My father was a field captain, gone a lot, and my mother taught the nobles' children there. She even helped tutor you."

Norah smiled. "Were you and I close as children?"

Caspian shook his head again. "No. We didn't know each other, really. Alexander and I studied and practiced together, but you had private schooling." He chuckled. "But I know Alexander taught you the sword. I used to ask him all the time if he wanted to spar, and he would tell me he wasn't up to it. Then I'd see you both in the field behind the stables with your swords. That's how he got so good, you know. He wasn't sparring with other boys; he was sparring with you."

They both let out a laugh. An easy quiet returned between them.

"Thank you for sharing all of this with me, Caspian," she said softly.

CHAPTER THIRTY-NINE

Norah sat on the edge of the bathtub, holding her wadded nightgown in her hands. Inside it were the few spots of blood that told her there was still no child. The months had fallen away, and still there was nothing. She had consulted with fertility wisewomen, charting her cycles and meticulously planning. She had talked to the healer, and even Salara-Mae, who had put her on a regimented diet of disgustingly healthy food. And yet, nothing.

Mikael still wrestled with the foretelling of his own end, and with the nobles growing more restless without an heir, she could feel his increasing desperation with each passing month. They needed a child. As each month came and went, she felt like she was failing him.

Norah put her hand on her stomach, wondering what it would be like to have a child. *A baby.* How strange it would feel to have something inside—living, growing, kicking.

She spread her fingers against her skin. What if she couldn't bear a child? No, she couldn't think like that. She breathed deeply and tried to channel positive thoughts. She imagined herself already pregnant. But her mind drifted to other worries. Would Kharav love him? A half Northman. Would Mercia accept him?

She still needed something more positive, she told herself. What would she name him? What would she lovingly call him? She wondered if he would look like Mikael, or like her. Surely he would look like his father, and she smiled.

"Salara," Mikael's voice called softly, and she looked up to see him in the doorway. His breaths came short and uneven in seeing her, his eyes hopeful.

Her smile fell. He had misread her. Emotion swept through her. All she could do was shake her head.

Mikael let out a long exhale but came to her, pulling her up and holding her close. This was their monthly ritual, their monthly curse.

He kissed the top of her head. "Don't worry yourself," he whispered.

"The summer is beautiful," Salara-Mae said as she cut a lemon in half and squeezed it into her cup of tea. "It will be gone too soon."

"It will," Norah said quietly. It was late summer in Kharav and more stunning than she had ever imagined. The earth was green with life, flowers of every color covered the ground, glowing brilliantly against the black of the mortite rock.

They finished their breakfast and walked through the doors and into the sun. Since learning about Norah's efforts to become pregnant, Salara-Mae insisted that she get regular exercise. Norah didn't mind. It felt good to be out and stretch her legs. They'd made a habit of walking the castle grounds after eating, soaking in the light and clipping colors from the gardens. Norah had come to care for Salara-Mae. She reminded her of her grandmother—cheekily foul and unintentionally amusing.

As they walked, Salara-Mae pulled out a small sachet and held it out for her.

Norah looked at her curiously and then took it. "What's this?"

"For the child," she said. "Torith root, from Lorys. My cousin has written to tell me how effective it's proven with women trying to conceive."

"Your cousin's in Lorys?"

"No, no. Of course not. She's in Etreus, but after I wrote to her, she wrote her sister-in-law in Pryam, who said that her own wisewoman, who is from Lorys, recommended it. Eat it directly. But she warns, it's bitter."

Norah pursed her lips. Salara-Mae meant well, but at this rate, the entire world would know her plight. She could see it now: her grandmother receiving a message from a port merchant that she was trying to get pregnant with the Shadow King. And failing.

"Don't worry, I didn't mention your condition," Salara-Mae said, seeming to read her mind. "I merely asked."

This woman was as inconspicuous as Catherine. "And who will they think you're asking for?" Norah scoffed back. "Not yourself."

"Regardless, it's already obvious. You've been married quite some time now, and anyone can count the months and know there's a challenge."

A wave of emotion took her by surprise. Perhaps it was the pressure, the constant disappointment, or maybe the desperation. She bit the inside of her cheek to hold it back. She shoved the sachet in her pocket and noticed Caspian approaching.

His face told her he brought news—bad news, likely. Whatever it was, it couldn't be as bad as the conversation now.

"Queen Norah," he greeted as he drew near. "I need to speak with you. Urgently."

She was relieved to slip away from the conversation with Salara-Mae, but a weight grew in her stomach at what Caspian brought. She nodded to Salara-Mae, who gave a small bow of her head in return, and she followed Caspian back toward the castle.

"News just arrived," he told her as they walked. "Aleon has taken Tarsus."

"What?" That *was* news. "King Phillip has taken Tarsus?"

He nodded.

The island kingdom of Tarsus was small but extremely wealthy. It was a premier trading port, where merchants paid high royalties for inclusion, but collected wealth in the sale of their goods many times over. Only goods of exceptional quality were sold in Tarsus, and it was common for luxury merchants to deal only in trade that had been exchanged there, as demanded by their buyers. Mercia sold most of her steel goods there.

Few had ever dared to attack the trading nation. The island was known for their fierce warriors, who savagely protected their harbors.

Norah's brows drew together. "Why would he take Tarsus?"

Caspian shrugged. "To accomplish what his grandfather couldn't, perhaps? But Queen Norah, this will surely make Salar nervous. If Phillip is trying to succeed where his grandfather failed, he could set his sights on Kharav."

Aleon had once tried to take Kharav.

Norah shook her head. "No. That doesn't make sense. Phillip doesn't have the power to war against Kharav and Mercia and Japheth."

"But does Mercia really stand with Kharav? The council's already been in contact with Phillip. You know this. You have a standing offer of marriage. And it's rumored that Kharav and Japheth's alliance is failing."

"Where did you hear that?"

He frowned. "Most everywhere."

Norah's stomach twisted. This would put Mikael on edge.

Caspian held out a letter. "And this arrived for you."

Norah's breath caught in her throat. The letter bore Alexander's seal. She nodded to her captain, excusing him. "Thank you, Caspian."

She paused for a moment and sat down on a bench at the edge of the garden, holding the letter in her hands, desperate to open it but afraid. They hadn't written to each other since she left Mercia. She imagined what its words held.

Norah ran her fingers over the seal, a steely blue wax that shimmered in the sunlight—the seal Alexander had poured and stamped with his own hand. Gathering her courage, she pulled the paper apart, careful not to crack the wax bear embossment.

But as she read the words, her heart sank. Then she rose, turning to the castle to find Mikael.

The king stood with the lord commander in his study, his face stoic and overly calm—the face that worried her.

"You've heard the news then?" he asked when he saw her enter.

She nodded. "Caspian's just informed me."

He frowned. "The Aleon Empire grows."

"Why would he want Tarsus?" she asked.

"Who doesn't want Tarsus?" Soren rumbled.

"It just doesn't make sense that he would do it now."

"Of course it makes sense," Soren said. "This Aleon king is just like his grandfather."

"But while he's on the brink of war with Japheth?"

"It boosts Gregor's confidence, I'm sure," Mikael said. "To know his brother is occupied."

He wasn't seeing her point. Norah sighed. She didn't come to debate Aleon. She held up the parchment from Alexander. "A letter's come from Mercia."

"From the Bear?" Soren asked.

She nodded. "The outlying villages of Mercia are still being attacked. The lord justice has stretched our forces across the kingdom, and it's still not enough. He asks for men."

Soren's brow dipped in irritation. "We can't send men to Mercia. Not while Aleon advances, and Japheth plays games."

"Aleon does not *advance*," Norah argued. "Tarsus is in the opposite direction of Kharav."

"You know his plans?" Soren asked.

"No, but it just doesn't make sense that Phillip would march on Kharav, not right now."

"Whether it makes sense to Salara, the threat is still there," Soren argued to Mikael. "We need all men in Kharav."

Mikael moved to Norah and eyed the letter. She offered it to him, and he took it and read it quietly. "It's so formal," he said.

Norah swallowed. It was. He hadn't even asked how she was. She guiltily pushed down the emotion. She shouldn't want him to. She should want him to not think of her, as she tried not to think about him.

Mikael refolded it, and looked at the seal for a moment before handing it back to her and glancing at Soren. "Send two thousand men."

Norah's eyes met his in surprise. He was giving her men?

Soren pushed out a breath between his teeth in anger, but he didn't speak his objection.

She nodded. "Thank you."

Mikael reached up and brushed her cheek with his fingers. "Of course."

CHAPTER FORTY

Alexander sat back in the chair at his desk and let out a weary sigh. He stacked the army's status reports and shuffled them into a leather cover before standing and sliding it into the cabinet behind him. It was late morning, and he'd worked all night—preparing updates for the council, issuing directives, reviewing grievances, approving payments—anything to keep his mind occupied.

To keep his mind from her.

Norah.

He'd written her out of desperation, to the horror of the council. They didn't want help from the Shadowlands, but they were out of options. Alexander had put it off as long as he could—partly at the council's urging, partly because he couldn't form the words that he knew Norah would be reading from his pen. He'd started his letter a hundred times, and the fireplace in his study had burned bright with his discarded pages. He wanted to know how she was, if she was well, if she was happy. Did he really want to know if she was happy?

Happy with *the Shadow King.*

He could still feel her kiss on his lips, see her smile when he closed his eyes, hear her voice in his mind. But he wrote none of this, at least not in the letter he sent.

Did she think of him? *No.* She cared for him deeply, he knew, but he didn't have her heart. Not anymore. Not in the way he used to.

But he did want her to be happy. Even if it wasn't with him. Even if it was with... he put the thought from his mind. He settled with the hope that she was simply happy.

He wondered how Adrian fared. He surprised even himself when he had sent his brother to Kharav. But Norah needed loyal men, trusted men, good men, and his brother was as good as they came. Adrian would hold the Mercian values and remind her who she was. He wouldn't let her drown in the darkness of the shadows. Alexander needed him, but Norah needed him more.

The bells rang out, and he headed to the courtyard. His eyes widened at the army of Shadowmen approaching. It was larger than he'd expected, a pleasant surprise, and he strode out to meet them.

James and Edward stood at the top of the castle stair. Edward shook with disgust, and Alexander followed his eyes to the Shadowman leading the army.

Not Shadow*man*.

Shadow *woman*.

A wrap covered her face, as with all Shadowmen, but she wore a fitted breastplate molded to her shape. Her *every* shape. He peeled his eyes from the steel breasts and swallowed back his discomfort as she slid from her horse.

She cast a cold eye around the courtyard. "I'm here for the Bear," she called.

"Have you come to serve?" Alexander asked.

She stepped in front of him. "Call him."

"He doesn't come to your call."

In a flash, she ripped her short sword from the sheath on her back and had it at his throat. Around him, his Northmen pulled their swords, and the whole of the Kharavian unit followed suit.

"I'm not here to play games, Northman," she seethed. "I've been sent by the lord commander to aid your failing Bear."

That certainly sounded like the lord commander. "Then perhaps you might lower your blade from his neck."

Her eyes narrowed. "You're the Bear?"

He gave an ever so slight nod of his head.

"You don't look like a bear."

"So I've been told."

She eyed him suspiciously as she needled the tip of her blade into his skin.

"Do you mean to draw blood?" he asked her.

Her eyes smiled. "Consider it a proper Kharavian greeting." Slowly, she withdrew the blade and took a step back, still eyeing him as if deciding whether to obey her orders or kill him.

"I knew this was a mistake," Edward called from behind them. "We don't need the help of heathens! Send them back."

They did need the help, heathens or no, but were the Shadowmen really here to help them? Alexander supposed he'd find out.

Alexander stood in his bath chamber. He leaned forward and tilted his head in the mirror, eyeing the mark still on his skin from the Shadow woman's blade. She'd cut him. It was a small break in the skin, but she'd actually cut him—in the middle of his own courtyard, surrounded by his own men. He pulled on a shirt over his head and tucked it into his breeches, but then he couldn't help but be drawn back to the mirror and the mark on his neck. She'd *actually* cut him.

Of course the lord commander would send her—a woman like that. No doubt she'd give him more than a small cut if he wasn't careful. Perhaps he might want to sleep with one eye open. He pushed out a breath and finished dressing. The best he could do was resolve whoever was attacking the Mercian villages, and send her and the Shadow army back to the Shadowlands.

He walked out to the barracks and a tented station beyond where the Shadow soldiers were settling. Two thousand men were a lot to house, but it was only for the evening, until he dispersed them out to their assignments. Now to find this woman...

It didn't prove difficult. As he reached the Shadow army, she stepped out to meet him. Her eyes were large and dark and steeped in distrust. "Have you come with your orders, Bear?" she asked with daggers in her voice. She didn't want to be here any more than he wanted her here. Good—she'd be motivated to help him find out who was attacking the villages, end it, and leave.

"What's your name?" he asked her.

"Captain Katya Sator."

Captain? Interesting. "Can I call you Katya?"

"No."

This was going to be challenging. "Very well, *Captain*." His gaze traveled down until it met the molded full breasts on her breastplate, and he glanced away.

"You can look," she taunted. "I worked hard to make it exactly the same." She stepped closer to him, enjoying his unease.

He met her stare but didn't let his gaze wander again.

Her eyes smiled. "You don't like it?"

He didn't answer.

"I hear Northmen don't allow themselves pleasures of the flesh if they're not married. Is this true?" She was purely seeking his discomfort now, trying to get a rise out of him.

And it was working.

She stepped closer. "What's wrong, Bear? Worried I might corrupt you?"

As if she could. "I'm worried you might like it here and decide to stay," he quipped back.

She snorted, and her eyes laughed. "If you Northmen are as bad in bed as you are with a sword, you needn't worry about that."

He drew in a breath as he leaned back on his heel, and she gave him a cruel wink and stepped around him.

CHAPTER FORTY-ONE

Norah breathed in the crisp autumn air, trying to appreciate it while she could. She urged Sephir back to the stables and slid to the ground. It felt good to be outside, to feel the wind on her face and to spend time with the mare. She held some carrot pieces in the palm of her hand and gave a small laugh as the horse lipped them up.

She waved at the stable boy, who took Sephir for a brush down, and she set her thoughts on the rest of the day. But she turned when she heard Adrian's voice.

"Queen Norah," he greeted her, and she smiled.

"Adrian."

"Uh, I was hoping, uh..." He shifted with troubled eyes. "Can I speak to you?"

Her brows drew together. "Of course. Is everything all right?"

Adrian wrung his hands nervously as he took a breath. "Sevina's with child," he blurted.

Her breath caught in her throat. "What?" she breathed.

He opened his mouth, but no words came. He only nodded.

"Oh, Adrian. I... I don't know what to say." She paused. "How is she?"

He shook his head. "I, uh..." He shuffled as he drew a breath. "I, uh, asked her father for her hand."

"Oh!" she said, nodding. This was good then.

"He said no."

"Oh," she breathed again. This was bad.

"He doesn't know, though, about the baby, but"—Adrian licked his lips—"she's scared now." He paused again. "I am too. I... I don't know what to do."

Norah nodded, taking it all in. "Why did her father say no?"

He shrugged, and she could see his frustration. "Because it's customary for nobles to make a Provision Promise, a large payment that can be put aside to sustain a woman—well, their children—if her husband dies."

"Oh, Adrian," she said, letting out a breath of relief with a small smile. "I can help you with money, if that's all you need."

He shook his head. "Alec would kill me. It would dishonor him for the crown to pay for what's my responsibility. And it's more than just the money. I'm a Northman and brother to the Mercian lord justice, who does *not* hold favor here. Understandably."

Norah sighed sadly. "You should write to Alexander."

"And tell him I got a woman from the Shadowlands pregnant out of wedlock?" He shook his head. "I'd rather face her father." He swallowed, shifting nervously again. He was worried, and her heart hurt for him. This should be the best of news, not the worst of news.

"I have to go," he said. "The lord commander's expecting me."

She nodded. "Hey," she said, making him pause. "We'll figure this out. There are options, just let me think on it. Let's talk later, okay?"

He nodded somberly.

Norah needed air. Adrian's news brought complex emotions. She tried to put on a brave face, but she had no idea what they would do about Sevina. Returning to the castle wouldn't bring answers, and she decided to follow Adrian to the sparring fields. She leaned against the fence and watched the earlies—those soldiers hopeful of one day being on the Crest—testing their skills.

Adrian fought with them, although he wasn't one of them. The lord commander had explicitly told him he wasn't considered an early, yet he insisted Adrian be at every training. The same with Calla and Cohen. At first, Norah had thought he was purposefully making it as difficult as he could for them, hoping they would fail, trying to *make* them fail. But then she caught him occasionally offering genuine guidance—correcting their stance, adjusting their hold on the weapons, and even nodding approvingly when they did something right.

Adrian squared off on the field, sparring with a young man quite a bit larger than he was. Not that Adrian was a small man, by any means. He was a full head's height taller than Norah, like Alexander. Adrian's opponent attacked with powerful swings of his sword, but Adrian was fast and maneuvered around him easily.

"Shield up!" a voice boomed.

She turned to see Soren walking toward the men.

Adrian quickly brought his shield up as he continued to spar, but just as quickly forgot and dropped it back down as he darted around his rival.

"Shield up!" Soren bellowed again.

Adrian jerked it back up, continuing to work his opponent, but as he cut behind the early, he dropped it low again for more range of his sword arm.

Soren stalked out to the field and grabbed the early by his practice armor, shoving him back and pulling his own sword. He launched a swinging blow at Adrian. Adrian darted to the side, but Soren pivoted with a surprising grace. The commander sliced through the air and poured down blows on Adrian with a fury. The attack threw the Northman back, and he shouldered his shield as he crouched low behind it. Wood splintered from the shield as Adrian stumbled farther back. Each blow from Soren had the power of death behind it. Norah's breath caught in her throat. Soren drove Adrian against the railing, cornering him and raining a storm down over him.

"Soren!" Norah cried.

The lord commander paused and drew back.

Adrian straightened slowly, holding his shield high, breathless with the exertion of defense.

The commander grabbed Adrian's shield and pulled it down, using it to slam him up against the railing. "*That* is what battle's like," he snarled. "The enemy doesn't dance around. He attacks with everything he has because it's you or him. Your speed will help you, but your shield will save your life. *Keep. It. Up!*" Soren shoved him back and then walked to where Norah was standing. "Again!" he called back over his shoulder, and the men came together for another round.

Norah tried to steady her breath. "Was that really necessary?" she hissed. "You could have seriously hurt him!"

"He has to learn," he rumbled as he watched the sparring.

Or lose a limb, Norah thought to herself. More likely lose a limb. "You don't have to be that hard on him."

He pulled his eyes from the men and glared at her. "I do." Then he looked back out to the field. "I can't be soft with him. He's going to be a commander one day. A great one."

Norah stared at him. This man confounded her. He obviously cared, in his own strange Soren-like way, but she wasn't sure if it was a blessing or a curse. She hoped it a blessing because she needed his help now.

"Regarding Adrian," she said, "there's something I want to talk to you about."

"You're not sending him back," he said firmly.

"No, um," she paused, puzzled by his concern with that. "I'm not. No. Something else. Um..." Why was this so hard? "What if Adrian had his eye on someone, a woman, that he wanted to wed?"

"The doe?" he asked without looking at her, his eyes still on the men in the field.

Soren's description of the girl felt... strangely accurate. Any other time Norah would have been amused. "Sevina, yes. What if he wanted to marry her?"

"Her family's one of the oldest noble families in Kharav. Getting her hand won't be an easy task. The Bear needs to speak to her father. He's the head of the family, yes?"

"Yes, but... Well, obviously he isn't here, and even if he were, your entire army thinks he's the enemy of Kharav, so I don't imagine that would go well."

He chuckled darkly. "Probably not," he said, still not taking his eyes from the earlies.

Not helpful at all. "Then what should Adrian do?" she pressed.

He looked at her, his annoyance etched on his face. "He should find another woman," he said shortly. "Or better yet, no woman at all. I want him focused on his study." Then he turned his eyes back to the field.

Norah huffed a frustrated breath as she shook her head. This man was impossible. But she needed his help. Adrian needed his help.

"Sevina's with child," she said abruptly. She pursed her lips together and pulled them in between her teeth. Her stomach twisted as she waited for a reaction.

He didn't look at her, but neither did he look at the field. His brows came together, but he didn't speak. Concern? Anger?

"He told you this?" he asked finally.

"Yes. He asked for her hand, and Sevina's father denied it. Something about a Provision Promise and how he's a Northman and brother to the lord justice."

Soren was silent for a moment, then he said, "He needs to tell his brother. It will be the Bear's responsibility."

She shook her head. "I don't think I can get him to do that. He fears Alexander's disappointment too much."

Soren gave her an irritated scowl and then pushed himself off the railing with a rumble in his chest. "Spears!" he bellowed out over the field and left to rejoin his earlies.

Norah sighed in frustration. She didn't know what she had expected—certainly not compassion—but she'd hoped he might offer some options, a recommendation, even a sliver of advice. But he gave nothing, perhaps because there was nothing. She wasn't willing to accept that yet. She had to figure something out, and she turned and headed back to the castle.

Chapter Forty-Two

Norah sat on the bed, clutching her knees to her chest. Her blood cycle had come again. Still, there was no child. She tried to shake her growing obsession, but it was all she could think about. While Mikael showed kindness with each month's disappointment, she knew the burden weighed heavily on him. And it killed her. She couldn't bear telling him again. She sent her maids away and waited in the dim candlelight.

Norah heard Mikael's voice outside the chamber, and she quickly wiped the tears from her face. The chamber door opened.

"... send word to Lord..." His voice quieted. There was a pause, then he said, "We'll discuss it tomorrow." The chamber door closed. His footsteps were slow to bring him around the hanging panels.

He saw her and sighed, unfastening his sword belt and leaning it against the wall.

She stood as she searched for the words she'd said so many times before. "Mikael. I—"

"You needn't say it."

He stepped close and pulled her in, as he always did, holding her tight and kissing the top of her head, as he always did.

"Nineteen," she whispered.

"What?"

"Nineteen months we've been together. Nineteen months with no child." She couldn't stop the tears now. "Mikael, we need to come to terms with the fact that I may not be able to give you one." She pulled away from him and sat on the bed and covered her face with her hands.

"Stop," he said as he sat beside her, running his hands nervously over his thighs.

"No," she said through her tears. "We have to be honest about this." She shook her head through her tears. "I'm failing you."

His face twisted. He reached out and caught her hands and pulled them to his lips. He kissed her palms, breathing in deeply. "Or maybe it's me," he said finally.

Her brows drew together in confusion. "What?"

He stood and ran his hand across his face. "By the time my father was my age, he had four daughters between his other wives and concubines, and my mother became pregnant with me within the first few months of their marriage. I had three wives, and... others... but I haven't borne a single child—with anyone."

Norah swallowed, trying to make sense of his words. She shook her head. Mikael's inability to produce an heir was just as haunting. What would they do? What would the nobles do? And they didn't need an heir just for Kharav. She wanted a child. She wanted to be a mother.

Her heart beat with the weight of defeat. "That's it, then? We can't have a child?"

His eyes glistened with sadness.

She looked down as she gathered her gown in her fists. After everything she'd been through, the gods still cursed her.

Mikael ran his hands through his hair. "But we need an heir, Salara. You need a child." He pulled her chin to look at him. "You need to take another," he said softly.

"What?" she gasped as she stumbled up from the bed and backed away from him.

His voice came hoarsely. "You have to take another. It's the only way."

She pulled back farther, and her face wrinkled in disgust. He couldn't possibly be considering such a revolting idea.

"You think I suggest this lightly?" he asked.

"We can keep trying!" she cried.

He stood, moving toward her as she retreated. "And keep doing this? Month after month, year after year? Until I'm dead?" He grasped her arm to stop her retreat. "I *am* going to die, Salara. We've both seen my fall."

A sob ripped from her throat, but he didn't relent.

"And then you'll be overthrown," he said. "Whether by the Kharavian nobles or the North, you won't keep the throne without a child."

"Soren won't let that happen!"

"Soren is one man! And he'll die too. He won't tell me, but I know he's seen his death. I know that's what the seer showed him."

Her lip trembled. She knew what the seer had shown Soren, and it wasn't his own death. It was hers, by his hand. That's why he hadn't told Mikael, and she wouldn't tell him either.

Norah shook her head. "I can't..." She felt sick, and she ripped her arm free from him and took another step back. "I'll go to war first." Her emotion came thicker now; a deep hurt spiked her heart. "And that you would even think..." She couldn't finish through her tears.

"Salara—"

"No," she said as she took another step back. Her hurt turned to anger. "How can you even ask that of me? To whore myself?"

He stopped, and pain snaked across his brow. "That's not... Salara, I didn't mean..." He reached out and pulled her back to him, wrapping his arms around her. "I'm sorry," he whispered. "Forgive me. I should have never said it. I should have never thought it." He squeezed her tightly. "I'm sorry."

Sun poured through the windowed halls giving the impression of warmth, deceivingly so. Outside, the air was frigid. Norah walked deep in thought. When her emotion had subsided, her anger toward Mikael faded. She had spoken harshly to him. When he had suggested... she'd felt so betrayed. But his words weren't an act of betrayal; they came out of desperation—desperation for her.

They needed a child. She wanted a child. But a child would require a pregnancy and a pregnancy would require... another. An overwhelming shame came with the thought—the shame of sharing something so private, the shame of defeat. And there was no one she trusted with that shame. Even if she could, who could be trusted with a secret that could break a kingdom?

Norah turned the corner and almost collided with another, breaking her abruptly from her thoughts.

Soren reached out and caught her. "Salara."

"Lord Commander," she said, shaken. He always seemed to catch her off guard at the worst times.

"Where's the boy?" he asked.

She shook her head, trying to get her wits about her. "What?"

"Where is the boy?"

"Um, Adrian? I don't know," she said, looking around. "The field, or the stables, maybe?"

"He's not on the field. Come on." He turned on his heel and headed toward the stables.

Norah let out a breath of confusion. She wasn't sure what was going on, but she followed. She almost had to run to keep up. "What's going on?"

"How quickly can you manage a wedding?"

"What? What do you mean?"

"How quickly can you manage a wedding?" he asked again.

She rolled her eyes. "When I ask you for more, you can't use the same words." She grabbed him, pulling him to a stop. "Soren! What wedding?"

"Where is the boy?"

She pursed her lips in frustration. "Stop answering a question with a question—" She stopped. Her eyes widened. "Did you get Sevina's father's blessing? Is Adrian to marry her?"

The lord commander pushed out a breath. He wasn't wearing his wrap, and his annoyance was written all over his face. "What other wedding would I be referring to?"

Norah drew her brows together. "You're a terrible communicator."

His jaw tightened and his nostrils flared.

"There!" she pointed to the end of the stable. "There he is."

"Boy!" the commander thundered.

Adrian came quickly to the commander's call. "Yes, my lord," he said when he reached them.

"Go get your doe, get ready."

"What?" Adrian asked.

The commander snorted his frustration at all the questions. "You're getting married."

Adrian looked at Norah with the same shocked expression that she was sure she'd had only moments before. Then he looked back at Soren. "I don't understand. What about her father? He denied me—"

"I've managed it," the commander told him.

"How?" Adrian breathed.

"You needn't worry about that. Go see to your preparations."

Adrian grinned, almost in tears. He rushed forward and hugged Soren, catching the commander by surprise. Soren stood stiffly, his wince giving away his distaste for affection. Norah bit her lip to hold back her own emotion. Then Adrian hugged Norah and ran off to find Sevina.

She looked at Soren incredulously. "What did you say to her father to make him change his mind?"

Irritation rippled over his brow. "Am I not a persuasive man?"

Norah smiled.

The wedding was relatively small, but beautifully arranged, given that it was done in two days' time. A surprising number of soldiers attended. Norah hadn't realized all the friendships Adrian had formed, especially among the Kharavian army.

Serene and Vitalia had hung strings of flowers from a private hall in the castle, and Calla braided winter blossoms into Sevina's hair. The girl was beautiful, and she beamed at Adrian as he ceremoniously looped the silk ribbon around her waist and tied it.

Norah remembered her own wedding as she watched. She slipped her hand into Mikael's, squeezing it tightly. Was he feeling nostalgic too?

He put his arm around her and pulled her close. "Do you remember when you pulled out your own ribbon at our wedding?" he whispered. "Of course I already knew I wanted to marry you, obviously, since I was in the middle of doing so. But that is when I doubly knew."

She smiled.

After the ceremony, they hosted a dinner in the dining hall, and laughter rippled through the air. Norah's heart was full. Everything was perfect.

She walked around the mingling guests, and found Aman Arvedi, Sevina's father.

He bowed his head as she approached. "Salara," he greeted.

"Lord Aman," she greeted back. "This marriage has made Adrian extremely happy. He's going to be a wonderful husband. He loves your daughter. Very much."

Aman nodded, obligingly.

"May I ask, what made you change your mind? I know Adrian asked for her hand prior."

"A Provision Promise by the lord commander is not one to be refused," he said.

What? Norah's mouth fell open. "The lord commander made the Provision Promise for Adrian?"

He nodded. "Not just the payment, but he endorsed the Northman under his own seal, in his own name. It's an honorable marriage now."

Norah gaped across the hall at Soren, who stood near the wall begrudgingly watching the evening's festivities, with a chalice of wine in his hand and a slight scowl on his face.

"Congratulations, and I hope you enjoy the rest of the evening," Norah said as she gave Aman a parting nod.

He bowed. "Thank you, Salara."

Norah made her way to the commander. He didn't look at her as she stepped beside him.

"You made Lord Aman a Provision Promise for Adrian?" she asked. "And endorsed the marriage with your own seal?" She had planned to ramp up to the question, but it just poured from her lips.

Soren shifted in surprise, but he didn't answer.

"Why would you do that?" she asked. "That's a big obligation."

"It's what was required," Soren said absently.

She frowned. "This will upset Alexander. He'll see this as his responsibility. Incentive for you, I'm sure."

"It *is* his responsibility," he growled back. "But the Bear doesn't need to know. Even the boy doesn't know."

Her eyes widened. "You should have told him."

"No," he said firmly.

"Why not?"

His nostrils flared as he glowered at her. "Because no matter how much he loves that girl, no matter how much trouble he's facing, he'll put his brother's feelings first."

Norah sighed, and her stomach knotted. "If Alexander finds out—"

"He won't," he snapped. "But if he does, then you'll say you didn't know."

Norah sat quietly as Vitalia brushed the braids out of her hair. She looked at herself in the vanity mirror, at her tired eyes and her worry-worn face. "I think I should like to be alone for a while," she whispered.

"Yes, Salara," Vitalia said, giving her a small smile and setting the hairbrush on the vanity. Then she bowed her head and left the chamber.

Norah gathered her hair to the side and gently pulled the brush through it. It fell in winding ripples from the press of the braids. Her eyes moved over her reflection. How pale she was in comparison to the people of Kharav. Perhaps even more pale with what weighed on her mind.

The chamber door opened and then closed. She waited.

Mikael stepped around the linen panels, coming up behind her. He traced his fingers over the bareness of her neck, prickling her skin.

She put the brush down. "There's only one," she said faintly.

His puzzled gaze caught hers in the mirror. "Only one of what?"

"Only one who can be trusted with a secret that could break a kingdom."

He paused a moment, then spread his hand across her skin and gripped her shoulder. "What are you saying?"

"You know what I'm saying. Only one can be trusted. And would a son of Soren not pass for your own? Are you not like brothers—large build and black hair, the shape of your face?"

"Salara," Mikael whispered. "No."

She felt the breath leave her lungs, and she struggled to draw it in again. She hadn't yet said it aloud, and it struck her like a blow to the stomach.

Mikael turned her in the chair toward him and dropped to his knees, bringing them eye to eye. He clasped her hands and brought them to his lips. "It was wrong of me to ask this of you," he said.

She cupped his face in her hand. "You need an heir. *We* need an heir." She looked into his eyes. "We need a child."

Emotion etched across his face. He bared his teeth against her hands, silent. He shook his head again. "It doesn't have to be Soren." He paused, then his voice came hoarse as he grimaced. "The Bear?"

She saw the pain in his eyes as he looked up to her, and she caressed his face with her hand. "No. A child between us, as your son, it would destroy him. And you. Let alone a fair-haired child would raise questions. It has to be Soren."

"And that would destroy you," he said softly.

"No." She shook her head. "I'm not the one he desires, and he wouldn't take pleasure in our desperation."

He leaned back slightly. "What do you know of his desire?"

Norah's eyes darted back and forth between his, and she cursed her carelessness. She shook her head again. "Nothing, I only meant he wouldn't take advantage."

"What do you know of Soren's desire?" he said again, his voice quiet but forceful.

Norah swallowed.

She couldn't answer.

She couldn't say Soren's secret out loud.

His brows creased. "You know. You know it's me. He told you?"

Her heart raced. He *knew*.

"Not willingly," she whispered. "He thinks you don't know."

"Of course I do." His voice held a deep sadness. "It makes it all the harder for me to ask this of him. But I'll speak to him tomorrow."

She nodded as a weight crushed her heart.

CHAPTER FORTY-THREE

Mikael knocked on Soren's chamber at first light. It was quiet, and his resolve threatened to leave him. He almost turned away, but then a shuffle came from inside, and the door opened.

"Salar," Soren greeted him.

He wasn't sure he had the strength for this conversation. "I have a taste for archery this morning," he said. "Let's go."

Soren flashed a rare smile and collected his bow.

Mikael clenched his own bow tightly as they made their way through the castle, outside, past the stables, and to the archery field. The walk was the longest he'd ever known. He was thankful his friendship with Soren consisted of few words, and the silence brought no awkwardness between them. But he would have to speak, eventually.

Just not yet.

When they reached the field, Mikael breathed in the cold morning air, trying to inhale courage as well. With his exhale, the fog of his breath came unevenly, and he worried it might give him away. Soren could sense fear. Surely he sensed it from him now. But if his commander did, he gave no indication.

A light dust of snow covered the ground. It was beautiful, but he couldn't appreciate beauty now. The barrels had been stocked with a fresh batch of arrows, and he pulled one for his bow.

"There's something on your mind, brother?" Soren started.

There it was. Soren knew something was wrong. Still, his prompt for conversation took him by surprise. Mikael wasn't ready.

"There's a lot on my mind," he said as he nocked the arrow onto the string. Mikael pulled up his bow, exhaling completely as he aimed, and released. The arrow whispered down the field and buried itself in the outer ring of the target.

"Must be serious if your aim's that off," Soren joked as he released an arrow of his own, finding the bullseye.

He had no idea how serious.

Mikael let loose another arrow, hitting the target only slightly better than the first. "Very serious," he said.

Soren's smile fell, and he handed Mikael another arrow instead of taking his own turn again.

The air seemed to turn colder. Still, Mikael could feel the sweat on his back. He nocked another arrow but didn't draw it back. "We've failed again for a child," he said. Then he raised the bow and released, and the arrow missed the target completely.

Soren stared at the target, with his face fixed. "You need more time," he said.

Time wasn't what he needed. Even if it was, he didn't have time.

Soren pulled another arrow from the barrel and held it for him, silent. But he didn't take it. "I need you."

Soren's head snapped toward him. "Me?" His brows came together.

Mikael lowered the end of his bow to the ground and leaned on it like a staff. He needed its support. "I can't give her a child." He paused—an agonizing, gutting pause. "I need you to give her your seed." Then he waited—an agonizing, gutting wait—giving Soren a moment to think about what he was asking.

Perhaps it was only a moment, but it felt like eternity. Then Soren shook his head, stepping backward. "No," he said. "No, I can't. She'll not have me."

"She will. We've discussed it. You're the only one I trust... with this, with my kingdom..." Mikael's voice cracked, and his eyes filled with emotion. "With my wife." He sank to his knees. "I know what I ask of you, but I beg you."

Soren lunged forward, grabbing him and pulling him back up. "No, get up. Get up!" Mikael got to his feet, and Soren let him go before leaning his own frame up against the arrow barrels.

They stood in silence for a long time. Too long. Worry sprouted in the pit of Mikael's stomach. He had been confident Soren would agree, but this was the most personal thing he'd ever asked from him. Had he reached Soren's limit?

Soren rubbed his face roughly with his hand. "She agrees to this?"

Relief flooded him, but it was short-lived. Nothing about this situation brought relief. Mikael couldn't speak, but he nodded.

Soren forced out a breath. He gritted his teeth as he broke an arrow. "I'll do whatever you ask of me," he said finally.

Mikael sighed heavily. He had been certain of it, but the words still brought a wave of emotion. He gave it a moment to pass. "I haven't thought through all the—"

"I don't want to talk about it," Soren cut him off. "Just tell me where to be, and when."

Mikael was grateful. He didn't want to talk about it either. He nodded.

They looked over the field as an icy breeze blew through. Soren held out another arrow.

Norah shoved a slice of marinated meat into her mouth, overly fixating on her food. Salara-Mae sat to her left, closer to her than Mikael, and across the table from Soren, who positioned himself more in the center. At the opposite end of the long table sat Mikael. This was their normal way of things, but dinner was anything except normal now.

Mikael had told her Soren had agreed. She cursed herself for not thinking of waiting to ask until the time of need. Now came the agonizing awkwardness of having to look at him, having to speak to him, knowing he knew what was to come.

Soren sat quietly, as he normally did, but it was a different kind of quiet—a troubled quiet. And he avoided looking at her, as he normally did, but it was a different kind of avoidance. He drained his blood bowl in large swallows. She almost wanted to offer him more if it would make him feel better. Would it make him feel better? Perhaps she might try it. Then the retching and upheaving would take her mind off things for a while.

She focused her attention on the plate in front of her, trying not to think about any of it. She wasn't sure how many dinners like this she could endure. And surely after, it would only be worse. She wouldn't be able to face him. Her cheeks burned at the thought of *after*—the shame threatened to melt her in her chair.

A servant stepped into the dining hall and quickly moved to Mikael, holding a letter in his hand. "This just arrived, Salar."

A small breath escaped her. Thank the gods there was something else to occupy her attention.

Mikael took it from him, and the servant departed. He glanced at Norah before he broke the seal and opened it. She didn't recognize the seal—bright yellow with a symbol she couldn't make out from the opposite side of the long table.

The line on his brow deepened as he read it. "From Surat in Kolkar," he said.

Norah had no idea who or where that was.

"He sends news that the kingdom of Rael has overthrown Serra." He tossed the letter to Soren.

Serra, Norah knew—that was the slavers' kingdom. Good riddance. But Rael... where had she heard of Rael? She searched her mind. It had been quite some time... "Wait, the usurper?" she asked. Her council had been upset the king of Rael had been usurped, if she remembered correctly.

The faintest hint of amusement came to Mikael's face. "Where did you hear that?"

She shrugged. "Mercia, some time ago, I think. Is it correct?"

Soren grunted but didn't say anything.

"It doesn't surprise me that the North looks at the Raelean king as a usurper," Mikael replied. "Rael's old king converted to the religion of the North, converted most of his kingdom, actually."

"So, of course, the North loved him," Soren added.

"But he was a cruel king," Mikael said. "He had men slay each other for entertainment, among other things you don't want to know about. I suppose you could call the new king a usurper, but he put an end to a lot of their savagery."

She supposed there could be good usurpers. "Who is this new king?"

Mikael frowned as he shook his head. "They call him Cyrus. Other than that, I don't know."

"So, this man usurped the Raelean throne, and now he's overthrown the kingdom of Serra? The slavers' kingdom?" she asked.

Mikael nodded. "And apparently, he's set all the slaves free."

Salara-Mae's eyes widened. "All of them? The entire kingdom?" She looked at Norah with a raised brow. "He should like Kharav, then, given that Salara has freed all our slaves," she added sarcastically.

Norah had freed *some* slaves, primarily those around the castle who stayed now as paid servants, much to Salara-Mae's horror and protest. But she hadn't freed as many as she would have liked, certainly not all across the kingdom. Kharav had thousands of slaves. It would require a significant change in Kharavian culture to do away with slavery all together, one that she didn't have the power to drive. Not yet, anyway. Mikael was already pressed with unhappy nobles. He wouldn't risk giving them yet another grievance, and one that would affect their economies on top of that.

But perhaps this usurper might bring a conversation on the idea. And action started with conversation. "Sounds like a rather decent man," Norah said, then popped a small potato into her mouth and smiled innocently at Salara-Mae.

Soren snorted. "Depends on what you consider decent. Impaling all the slavers on their ships and anchoring them in the harbors for all to see? Flaying them alive? Then yes, he sounds decent."

Ah, there was the Soren she knew—the Soren she kind of missed. "Is that what it says in the letter?"

"And other things," he answered.

"Don't read it," Mikael said to her, purely intending to shield her from its contents.

"What does all this mean?" she asked. "Should we be worried about anything?"

"Why would we be?" Mikael said, and took another drink from his chalice.

That didn't comfort her.

CHAPTER FORTY-FOUR

Mikael sucked in the cool morning air. He normally savored this time of day. Early mornings brought a peace with them. But not today. A weight sat heavy in his stomach, and a pain daggered his chest. Nothing could bring peace to him now for what lay ahead.

He found Soren in the stable, as he suspected he might. The commander's destrier stood in the mainway with leads fastened from its halter to the wall on either side, keeping the animal still as Soren replaced its shoes.

"We've farriers for that," Mikael said, even though he knew Soren preferred doing it himself. He needed something to say, words to speak, something to fill the suffocating air.

"I prefer to do it myself," his commander replied, not looking up.

Mikael waited for him to drive the last nail and release the hoof—an agonizing wait, but a wait that wasn't long enough.

Soren stood when he finished and patted the beast on the shoulder. When their eyes met, he stopped. He shifted back slightly as his face sobered. He knew.

"It's time, brother," Mikael said quietly. "She's at the safe house, on the hillside." He couldn't manage anything else.

Soren stood, silent and unmoving, and for a moment Mikael thought he might refuse—now that he'd had time to think, and now that the time was upon him. But he only nodded solemnly and then pulled off the leather apron and stalled the horse before heading toward the castle.

Soren arrived at the hillside house, his chest tight, his throat dry. Salara's mare stood out front. Alone. There were no guards. They couldn't risk suspicion. Mikael had personally brought her, then departed, but Soren knew he wouldn't have gone far.

His heart pulsed heavily in his ears. He felt calmer in battle, he mused. But then, he wasn't afraid of battle.

Tension gripped his shoulders. He hoped she would find him... tolerable. He'd washed and trimmed his beard short like Mikael's. He swore under his breath—he should have worn a shirt. He knew she didn't like his markings, and everything they stood for. It was too late now. He wished he would have thought of it sooner.

Soren let himself into the house, looking for Salara. All was quiet. He ventured into the sitting room and saw her at the window. She was looking out across the cliffs. She wore a simple riding dress—a gray split-front gown with breeches underneath. The creak of the floor under his weight made her jump, and she turned to face him. He hadn't meant to startle her.

They stared at each other in silence. Soren moved slowly, not sure how to engage her. He noted the knife sheathed at her waist, the one he had returned to her.

"In case you need to fend me off?" he asked.

Her brow tensed as her eyes grew wider, and her lips parted with silent dismay.

His attempt at humor had failed. "The knife," he tried to explain.

"Oh." She looked down and stared at it for a moment, then looked back at him, seeming to wait for what he would do next.

But he didn't know what to do next, or what to say. "Are you sure you want to do this?" he asked. Then he cursed himself. Why would he ask her that? She obviously didn't want to do this.

"Need we undress fully?" she asked, avoiding his question.

He shook his head. "No. Of course not." He hadn't expected it. He didn't know what he expected. He had tried not to think of it. "If you want to go to the bedchamber, I'll give you a few moments."

She stood frozen, as if contemplating fleeing or fighting. He felt like fleeing himself, if he was honest. But she nodded stiffly and turned down the hall to the back room.

Soren pulled off his cloak, and his fingers struggled with the buckles of his weapon's strap and spaulder. He wasn't sure why he had even worn them. He wasn't going to battle. Habit, perhaps, or comfort. But comfort still escaped him.

He wasn't sure how much time to give her, or how much time he should spend with her. He didn't want to draw it out, but he didn't want to be callously swift. The tension in his shoulders grew. He rubbed his hand over his face, trying to calm his own nerves. Soren had been with women before, but this was different. Mikael loved her and entrusted him with her care.

Soren walked down the hall and gave a small knock on the door before opening it slowly. Salara stood, still in her dress, but the small pile of clothes on the chair suggested she had removed her undergarments.

The knife lay on top of them, and he was appreciative of that. He still suspected he might not leave without another battle scar. He almost wanted one—this would wound her, and it only seemed fair he suffered the same.

She waited by the bed, and he stepped inside and closed the door behind him. Every sound rang loud in his ears—the latch of the door, his footfalls, even his own heartbeat. So loud. And she watched him warily.

Soren supposed he should initiate; she certainly wasn't going to take what she needed from him. He moved toward her, slowly unfastening his belt and untying his breeches. She backed toward the bed, and he followed. But as he reached for her, she shrank back, bumping up against the carved corner post.

"I don't want to do this," she blurted. She sucked in a breath and shook her head. "I don't want to do this."

He stopped. Did she mean for him to stop? It sounded like he should stop. Should he try to reassure her? Talk her into continuing? That didn't feel right. But not wanting to do something and not *actually* doing something were two different things. He didn't want to be here, yet here he was. That argument didn't sound right either. He looked around the room, searching for what to do next, but there was nothing *to* do.

So he just nodded. "All right."

She let out a shaky breath. "I'm sorry. I thought I could, but I can't."

"All right," he said again. He looked around the room again. Clearly, she didn't find him tolerable. He cursed himself. He should have covered his markings. Should he go?

"I'll... I'll go," he said.

He moved back toward the door, but as she sank onto the bed and buried her face in her hands, he stopped. Crying had never bothered Soren before. He found it annoying more than anything else.

But he didn't like Salara crying.

Worry sat heavy in his chest. He had never wanted to be gentle. Kind. Safe. Not until now. Curse this wretched woman for making him feel things.

"Are... are you all right?" he asked her.

She pulled her face from her hands and gaped at him, as if surprised he was speaking to her kindly. As she should be, he supposed. When had he ever been kind to her?

He moved to the bed and sat down beside her. He didn't look at her, but he knew her eyes were still on him.

And they sat.

"I'm sorry," he said finally, breaking the silence. "If you could have chosen, this might have been easier for you."

She looked down at her hands clasped in her lap. "I did choose. And I chose you."

His eyes darted to her as he turned. That couldn't be true. "Why would you do that?"

"Because you love Mikael, you'll protect him and Kharav, protect this secret." She swallowed and sucked in an uneven breath. "And you won't guilt me with the shame of our sin." She put her face back in her hands. "I can't believe I even considered this, though."

He sighed. "Desperation makes men do things they wouldn't otherwise dream of. And there are many sins of men, but wanting for a child isn't one of them." He looked up at the ceiling. He hadn't made it easy for her. Guilt had never afflicted him, but he felt it now—guilt for his harshness and his cruelty, and despite that cruelty, she chose him still. For Mikael, and for Kharav.

"Am I a terrible person that I'd rather fight for the throne?" she whispered.

He shook his head. "It appears I'm the terrible person, that you'd rather go to war than take me to bed."

She laughed through her tears and looked at him, and he was glad his jest lightened the air. Things settled between them. Thoughts and words came easier now.

"It's not just that," she said. "I imagine it wouldn't be... too terrible to lie with you. Now that I know you."

Not too terrible. He certainly hadn't expected her lusting after him, but he had hoped himself a little more than not too terrible. But he deserved that, he supposed.

"And you look"—she tilted her head slightly as she eyed him—"quite nice. Now. Different from how you usually do."

There was a compliment in there somewhere, he was sure.

"Anyway," she continued, "there are many women who would readily take you to bed... or"—her brows drew together—"many not women, I mean, people other than women... if that's what you wanted... you know what I'm trying to say, maybe. And it's not that I couldn't be with you. I trust you. You probably know that. I think. Maybe I told you"—she looked down at her hands again—"or maybe I didn't, because you're mean sometimes."

As much as rambling annoyed him, he didn't mind Salara's rambling. He found this rambling amusing, with her under the same strain of awkwardness that had plagued him only moments ago.

Her face sobered again as she paused, and she drew her gaze back to his. "But I don't just want any child. I want Mikael's child. I love him."

He grew serious again, too, and nodded. "I know." There was no doubt in him.

She rose, and he did as well. He turned to go.

"Soren," she said, stopping him. "Thank you. For not making me feel wrong, or humiliated."

"I would never humiliate you, Salara," he said. "And I'll tell you when you're wrong."

She smiled as she wiped her cheeks again. "Would it be weird to hug you?" she asked.

"Yes—"

"I'm going to anyway," she said as she stepped forward and snaked her arms around him.

He stiffened. This was the second embrace he'd endured lately, but surprisingly it was... nice. Not natural, or something that he'd want again, but warm and real and right. This vile creature—worming her way into his heart. He rumbled his protest, but slowly brought his arm around her and hugged her back.

They broke, and he straightened. She smiled up at him.

He hesitated before asking, "Should I wait here with you?" Why she would want that, he didn't know, but it seemed to be what he should say.

She shook her head. She just wanted him gone, and he understood. So he nodded and left her to the quiet.

Norah lay under the bed coverlet in the hillside house, winding strands of hair around her finger. She had come here filled with shame and guilt, but Soren didn't make her feel either of those things. He made her feel strong. And right again.

The door of the chamber opened and closed.

Mikael climbed into bed beside her and slipped his arm underneath her, sidling up and pulling her close. "Are you all right?" he asked softly.

She nodded. "Yes." She was all right. More than all right.

He let out an uneasy breath. "Soren told me..." His words dropped off.

She turned to face him. "I'm so sorry," she whispered. "I couldn't, I—"

"Don't. You've nothing to be sorry about. Never have I been so relieved." His fingers curled around the nape of her neck, and he pulled her closer. "I should have never..."

A silence sat between them, then he asked, "Was he... unkind?"

She shook her head. "No, not at all." *Not at all.* "In fact, he makes me feel safe where I struggle to manage my own morality. But Mikael, I couldn't. I just couldn't."

"And I'm grateful for it," he breathed as he wrapped his arms around her.

But what would they do now?

CHAPTER FORTY-FIVE

The small group of soldiers made their way through the foothills of Moray, a Mercian township in the outer reach of the kingdom. Word had come that it had been attacked, and they traveled to investigate. Alexander looked back at the men following behind him—about fifty. How strange to lead a group of Shadowmen through Mercia. He'd been sent two thousand Shadow warriors, much more than he had expected, yet still not enough to keep the North protected. But he couldn't ask for more.

The Shadow captain rode ahead of him, and he watched her. Two months she'd been in Mercia. She hadn't tried to kill him yet—at least, not that he knew of. But her eyes occasionally threatened it. Her words had lost some of their harshness, though, he noticed. Perhaps her hate had cooled a bit.

She'd shown herself to be smart, quick, strong, and decisive—a good captain. A good captain for the lord commander, he reminded himself, which would make her a bad captain for Mercia. Still, perhaps his own hate had cooled a bit too.

"Another one," the Shadow captain called to him, and he shifted his attention back. He followed her motion to the ground, where he saw a downed winterhawk. They'd found one of them shot already, and two more the day before.

"Someone doesn't like hawks," she said as she gazed at the dead animal on the ground. The Shadow woman slid off her mount and kicked over the carcass of the bird, then she bent down and pulled an arrow from its chest. She looked at it closely and shook her head. "I don't recognize it," she said, holding out the arrow for Alexander.

Alexander took it, eying the tip. It was smooth, sharp, well fashioned, and barbed on the edges for maximum damage. Wings at the base prevented it from being easily pulled from flesh. These were dangerous arrows, and they came from dangerous men.

"Inventive, though," she said, her eyes smiling. "I think I'd like to meet these men."

Alexander wondered what she looked like under her head wrap, what all the Shadowmen looked like. It felt strange not to know the faces of those whose company he kept so often lately. But he knew the captain's eyes—large and dark. Powerful.

He shifted his focus back to the arrow.

"Smoke," a soldier called out, and they looked to see a dark plume rising just south over the hills.

They reached the village of Moray, and it stood as the others did—in smoldering ruins. Bodies hung from bars above the gates, the victims' faces swollen and blue. The dead littered the streets. The captain called out in the Shadow tongue, and the men set to work, pulling the bodies down and dragging them to a pyre. Mercian bodies needed to be burned to pass to the next world—all except kings and queens, whose spirits were bound to watch over their realm. The Shadowmen buried their dead, but they respected Mercian customs and lent their help. Alexander was grateful.

He slid off his mount and surveyed the damage. He felt a deep fury building inside. The attacks were worsening, and he had no idea who was responsible.

Moray still had a few buildings standing, and he waved the men to look around. As he walked through the ruins, he noticed there had already been looting. *Drifters.* They always seemed to appear and fill their pockets before his soldiers arrived. He checked the bodies as he went, looking for anyone still alive. But there were none. Everyone was dead. This enemy was savage.

"Anything?" Alexander asked as the men came back together. They shook their heads. He looked at the captain.

"We can send half the men here to the two villages we passed along the way, and the other half to the lower hills," she suggested. "I can pull more men back from the west as well."

"We haven't enough men to cover them all," Alexander said.

"Will you write for more?" she asked.

He let out a long breath. "I can't. Two thousand men is more than generous. And I've already drawn the council's concern with the number of Shadowmen in our ranks." He paused. "I mean no offense."

Her eyes smiled. She looked around once more. "What do you want to do?"

"Send out your men. You and I will return to Mercia. I'll pull more from the castle, and from Bahoul."

Then they turned their mounts north and spurred them back toward the castle.

The judisaept felt colder than usual. Perhaps it was the winter, perhaps it was the disapproval that hung in the air from Alexander's acceptance and deployment of the Shadowmen—of the Shadow *woman*. But that weighed little on his mind now.

A letter had come from Eilor, the most southern kingdom of the Aleon Empire. Alexander handed the letter to James as he addressed the council. "News from Eilor. The usurper of Rael has met with Japheth's king."

Edward grunted. "Perhaps he intends to join Japheth and the Shadowlands against us?"

"The Shadowlands are our ally," Alexander said, as much as it pained him to do so. Edward scoffed, and Alexander shot him a warning gaze. "I advise you use caution," he added, and Edward quieted.

"And it's rumored the usurper holds no favor for the Shadowlands," James said. "The Shadow King supported the slavers' kingdom, which the usurper has recently taken."

Councilman Alastair gave an amused frown. "So perhaps this usurper has a redeeming quality after all."

A few of the councilmen chuckled. Alexander didn't. An enemy of the Shadow King was an enemy of Norah. And an enemy of Norah was an enemy of Mercia—an enemy of Alexander.

"For some time we have suspected the Shadow King might be at risk of losing his alliance," Councilman Henricus said. "Especially after the attack on the lord justice and Queen Norah's intervention."

Alexander frowned at the memory of the attack that resulted in the Destroyer coming to his aid, and Norah's subsequent confrontation with the king of Japheth.

"But it wouldn't make sense for Japheth to abandon an ally, *any* ally," James said, "given that Aleon waits for an opportunity to strike."

Henricus frowned. "Perhaps this usurper is a more powerful ally than the Shadowlands."

"Ridiculous," Edward said. "Even with the combined armies of both Rael and Serra, this usurper's power is mediocre at best."

Alexander's worry grew. Neither an additional ally joining Japheth and the Shadowlands nor the alliance between Japheth and the Shadowlands crumbling boded well for Norah.

"Have you heard anything from the Shadowmen on this, Lord Justice?" James asked him.

Alexander shook his head. "No. They haven't heard."

"Or they have and they're not saying," Edward said.

Alexander didn't believe that.

"When will we send them back?" Edward asked.

"I've no intention of sending them back," Alexander replied. "At least not yet. I need them to protect the villages in the outer reaches."

Edward snorted. "Can we not pull more men from Bahoul? Perhaps two thousand?"

"There was barely two thousand before, and I called the majority back just yesterday, leaving only a hundred there now."

"Only a hundred men hold the mountains?" Alastair asked in surprise.

"No, three thousand men hold Bahoul, but only a hundred are Northmen."

"Might as well bring the rest of them home," Edward said angrily. "We lost Bahoul when Queen Norah gave it back to the Shadowlands."

Just what he needed—men who knew nothing of war telling him where to place his army. "I can't pull them all. I need to keep men on the inside, to give our forces access should we need it."

An ache ran through Alexander's temples, and he realized he had been clenching his jaw. The gods were truly testing him.

The Shadow captain was waiting for Alexander as he stormed from the judisaept. "It didn't go well, I take it," she said, with a hint of amusement in her voice. "Do they want more men from Salar?"

"No, they want to send you and the rest of your men back to the Shadowlands."

"Ah, so the strategy of abandoning logic."

He couldn't help a small smile. Sometimes he almost liked this woman.

They reached his study, and he shut the door behind him. "Do you know anything about the usurper meeting with the king of Japheth?" he asked directly.

She straightened, her eyes narrowing. "Cyrus has met with Gregor?"

Katya was good at evading him when she didn't want to answer him, when she had something to hide. She wasn't hiding anything now, as he'd expected. Despite the tension between the Shadowlands and Mercia, he didn't believe the Shadowlands plotted against them. He couldn't say the same for Mercia.

He sighed as he sat down at his desk and pulled out a blank parchment. He wrote quickly, keeping his message short, pointed. Then he wrote a second, less short, less sharp. Katya waited patiently as he folded them and affixed his seal to both. He held them for her. "See the first gets to your Destroyer. The second, to the queen."

"You freely give the lord commander this information?"

"I give him what he needs to know to protect my queen."

She paused, studying him. "He will, you know. He will protect her."

He did know.

Now how to protect Mercia—Alexander stood and pulled the army records from his cabinet. Where to draw more forces...

"The council wants me to pull the last of the Northmen from Bahoul to help defend the villages," he said, freer with information than he would normally be.

"I won't argue with that," she said. "But then you'd be stupid. To Kharav's benefit, though, so by all means, listen to your old men."

He tightened his lips to keep from smiling. He could use a captain like Katya, especially with Caspian gone. He ran his eyes down the records and through the soldier counts and placements. "This is a cunning foe, whoever he is, is he not?" he said as he leafed through the pages of numbers. "Mercia has a large army, but he forces me to spread them across the kingdom, so in effect, I have nothing."

"He's a clever opponent," she said, nodding. "But then, Bear, so are you."

He lifted his gaze from the records to find her looking back at him. Her eyes smiled. Dark, but bright.

Captivating.

No. He caught himself. Just dark.

CHAPTER FORTY-SIX

The sun hung high in the cloudless hues of blue. Soren leaned against the rail of the sparring field, watching the earlies as they practiced. He was pleased with this group. Their movements were fluid, their weapons' work accurate and deadly. Several of them would make the Crest. He needed more of them, but he wouldn't take those who didn't meet his standard. He couldn't sacrifice quality, not when it came to Salara's safety.

Adrian caught his eye, and he watched him. The boy had skill, and he was clever—sometimes too clever. Soren had wanted to loathe him, this brother of the Bear, but there was nothing to loathe about him, aside from having to admit the Bear had trained him well. He was born of natural talent, he worked hard, his loyalty was absolute, and his spirit unbreakable. He was an excellent soldier.

And Soren could make him even better.

The Bear would call for his return eventually, and Soren would send him back the greatest warrior of both kingdoms.

"Boy!" he called.

Adrian turned mid-practice; he knew when Soren called him. He pulled off his helm and trotted up to him, breathlessly giving a quick bow of his head. "Yes, Lord Commander."

Soren eyed him for a moment. "Have you written to your brother?"

Adrian looked to the ground. "Uh, not yet," he answered. "But I will."

Soren shot him a steely gaze. It was one of the boy's rare faults—the fear of disappointing his brother. He still hadn't shared the news of his marriage. No doubt, the news would upset the Bear, but not telling him would cause a greater conflict between them. Soren didn't want that for him.

"You're a man now. You make your own decisions, but you must also own them."

Adrian nodded. "I'll do it tonight."

"You'll do it now."

The boy looked back out to the field. "But what about practice?"

"I said you'll do it now," Soren growled.

Adrian swallowed and then gave another bow. "Yes, my lord." Then he trotted off to do as he was bid.

Soren sighed. He hoped this wouldn't cause the Bear to call the boy back. There was so much potential in him, but he still needed a lot of work. He needed more experience—experience only Soren could provide. He needed at least two years. Soren would have to accelerate his training.

He turned back to the sparring field and caught sight of Salara beside the far railing. She must be out for a walk; she liked to occasionally take the route by the sparring field to see how Adrian and the sibling pair were doing.

Soren waited for her to see him and give him her usual stupid smirk, but when her eyes found him, she quickly looked back to the earlies, then abruptly turned and headed back toward the castle.

Why didn't she smirk at him? Or smile, or something?

A voice sounded beside him, but he paid it no mind.

Had she not seen him?

No—she'd seen him.

"Lord Commander," came the voice again, and he looked over to find his training captain, Vasil.

"What?" he rasped.

"Should I start the spear circuits?"

Spear circuits? Soren glanced across the earlies, who were finishing their sword rounds. *Spear circuits.* "Fine."

Vasil bellowed out to the earlies, and Soren looked back to find Salara. But she was gone.

"Gods, that's hot!" Norah exclaimed, and tried to soothe her scorched tongue against the roof of her mouth.

"I'm so sorry, Salara," Vitalia said quickly, rushing over. "I made it too hot."

Norah set the cup of tea back on its saucer. "No, it's my fault. I wasn't paying attention." Her mind had been... far away.

"Are you all right?"

"I'm perfectly fine." And she was fine... physically.

Mikael hadn't come to their bed last night. He'd said he had work to tend, but he always had work to tend, and he'd always slept in their bed.

And now three nights in a row she had slept alone—the three nights since she had returned from the hillside house. Was he disappointed with her? He'd said he was relieved she hadn't taken Soren, but perhaps now the gravity of her decision sat with him, as it did her. There would be no child.

Or perhaps now that they'd reached acceptance and were beyond desperations, he found himself regretting they'd even taken the option into consideration, like she did. She closed her eyes and gritted her teeth against the shame. Although brief, she *had* been willing. She'd chosen Soren, and Soren knew she'd chosen him. Now she couldn't even look at him.

And Mikael couldn't look at her.

"Here, I'll get you some wine to temper it," Vitalia said as she reached for the decanter.

Norah snapped back to the present. "No, it's all right. I should actually get out and start the day." She had let too much of the morning pass.

Vitalia smiled warmly. "Of course, Salara. I'll just set to tidying up, then."

Norah forced a smile back and rose from the small table by the windows. She slipped on her silk shoes and moved to the chamber door, but when she opened it, she jumped.

Soren stared back at her.

"Hammel's hell, you scared me," she said as her pulse slowed.

"Are you avoiding me?"

"No," she replied defensively. She was just trying to not talk to him. Or see him. She glanced back at Vitalia. "Leave us, please."

Her maid bobbed her head and left them to privacy.

His eyes narrowed between the slit in his wrap as he stepped inside the chamber. "You saw me in the field yesterday and didn't smirk at me."

"I thought you didn't like when I smirked at you."

"I don't."

"Then why are you angry that I didn't?"

"I'm not angry," he said, with angry eyes.

"Well, I'm not avoiding you," she lied.

He shifted back on his heel. "At dinner you didn't speak."

"*You* never speak at dinner."

"But you do," he said. "And you usually say at least one cheeky comment to me. But you didn't."

She stopped. She'd thought he never paid her any mind at all.

His voice came softer now. "I thought when we parted... at the hillside house... we were well."

"We are well. It's not that. I mean, it *is* that, but..." Why was this so hard to talk about?

"Then why do you avoid me?" he asked.

"Because I'm ashamed!"

He quieted and stood awkwardly. Or maybe it was she who was awkward. This whole situation was awkward.

"Why are you ashamed?" he asked. "You've done nothing. We did nothing."

"No, but I had decided to. Mikael had resigned to leave it alone, and it was *I* who brought it up again. *I* chose you." She rubbed her forehead with stiff fingers. "I obviously thought about everything, thought about being with you. So, to have thought about it, to have those intentions, and now to walk around trying to pretend like nothing ever happened..." She shook her head as she gave a self-scoffing laugh to keep herself from growing emotional. "But now you know. And Mikael knows. And he's barely looked at me these past few days. He doesn't come to our bed. So what's left to feel but shame?"

Soren sighed and pulled down his wrap as he looked around the room. He moved slowly to the windows and looked out over the courtyard.

Norah waited. But he said nothing. Was he just going to stand there?

"You asked me what the seer showed me," he said finally. "In Odepeth. You asked me what I kept hidden. It wasn't your death." His breath came uneasy now. "It was... of me... with a lover."

Oh. She tried to form words with her mouth, but none would come. Her heart raced faster, and she swallowed. "Who?"

He shook his head. "I don't know. I've never seen him before."

"Hammel's hell," she breathed, and let out a laugh.

He looked back at her with his brows drawn together. "Why do you laugh?"

"Because I thought you were going to say *me.*"

His face twisted. "Why would you think it was *you*?"

She laughed again. "You don't have to act so disgusted."

"*You* were the one who wouldn't bed *me.*"

Fair, but... "Well, you told me the vision was of you killing me, and if it wasn't killing me, then my mind just thought it was something else having to do with me. And we just, almost, you know..." She stopped and narrowed her eyes. "Wait, this entire time you were okay with letting me think you were going to kill me?"

He let out a long breath but didn't answer.

"That was an asshole thing to do, you know."

Soren glanced down. "I know. But it was the only thing that came to mind in the moment."

"Really?" she asked angrily.

"You kept pressing me. What else could I say?"

"You could have said 'nothing'! Or just 'mind your business'?"

"I know you," he argued back. "When have you ever minded your business?"

She rolled her eyes. "I didn't believe you, anyway."

"You didn't believe I'd kill you?"

She pursed her lips as she looked back at him. "I know you too."

They quieted again.

"Why are you telling me this now?" she asked.

He looked out the window again. "Because you tell me you feel shame, for your thoughts, your intentions. I know shame too."

"Why are you ashamed?"

"Because I think about him. Often."

"Oh, Soren. You can't be ashamed of that."

"Neither can you, of wanting a child. At least your thoughts were driven with purpose. Mine are only for my own... selfishness."

She stepped closer to him. "I don't think you're selfish at all."

They stood, and their eyes quietly locked. She gave a small smile.

He stiffened. "Don't hug me again."

"I wasn't going to," she lied.

He snorted, obviously knowing her better, then he pulled up his wrap and covered his face again. "Now are we well?"

She couldn't help another smile, and she nodded. "If I can just fix things with Mikael."

"If he can't look at you, it's not you. It's because he feels his own shame. You have to help him past it."

She nodded again. "Thank you."

Mikael sat alone in his study. Parchments covered the table: maps, letters, updates from his scouts and his army. And a letter from Japheth, again telling him Gregor wasn't satisfied with the terms of their trade and sought to renegotiate. The king of Japheth puzzled him. He had resumed his normal trade shipments, to Mikael's surprise. Now, Gregor invited him to Japheth, to resume negotiations of their contract.

Mikael had been to Japheth many times; it wasn't an unusual invitation. And no doubt Gregor wanted to avoid returning to Kharav, to the North Queen who had served him his manhood on a platter. But the words on the parchment held a different air, and Mikael wondered if Gregor's intention was truly to negotiate.

His eyes moved to the letter that had brought news of Aleon taking Tarsus—the island kingdom in the southern waters of the Atolean Sea. The ports of Tarsus hosted premier trading, where it never wintered, never stormed, and where only merchants of great merit were permitted. Tarsus was a wealthy kingdom, perhaps one of the wealthiest in the world. It was also fierce. Tarsen soldiers were renowned fighters, and they defended their island ruthlessly, drawing even Mikael's respect. As large an empire as Aleon had become, it still surprised him they were able to take the island. And it worried him. Phillip's grandfather had tried to claim Tarsus before and failed, but Phillip was forging ahead. Surely it was only a matter of time before he turned his eyes to Kharav, another kingdom that had eluded the empire's grasp.

And a continued worry still plagued him—he and Salara remained without a child. He couldn't deny the relief that came with Salara refusing Soren. He'd never been more grateful for anything in his life. He wouldn't have been able to look at Soren after, tolerate his presence, although his commander wouldn't have done anything wrong. Soren would have done what had been asked of him, and *only* what had been asked of him. Guilt riddled him at the jealousy that reared itself with just the thought, and at his relief it hadn't happened. It was a selfish relief. They needed a child. Without one, the nobles wouldn't support Salara on the throne alone—not a queen of the North. Soren would protect her, but he was one man. He wouldn't be able to keep her safe. Not completely. Of all Mikael's burdens, this one was the heaviest. He gripped his forehead in his hand, leaning heavily on his elbow over his ash-wood desk. The candlelight flickered beside him.

"It's late," Salara's voice said. He hadn't heard her come in. He looked up to see her leaning against the doorframe. "Are you coming to bed soon?" she asked.

Bed. He longed for it and avoided it all the same. Why, he didn't know. Perhaps because he felt like he was failing her. He wasn't worthy of her. "I still have some things to do yet," he said, turning his attention back to the work in front of him.

Norah reached up and loosened the ties of her nightgown, pulling it over her shoulders and letting it fall to the floor. She stood naked and let his eyes run over her body. She was beautiful.

She stepped around the desk and stopped in front of him as he gazed up at her. She took his face in her hands. "I won't wait any longer," she whispered.

And he wouldn't make her. "I'll come to bed then," he said softly. He moved to pile his parchments together.

But she stopped him, pulling his face back to her. "You don't hear me. I won't wait any longer." She pushed him back and climbed on top of him in the chair, her knees on either side.

Mikael watched her as she reached down and unbuckled his belt and breeches and pulled him free. She brought her lips to his, seeking, searching, wanting. She teased him with her fingers, asking him with her touch, and his body responded.

Salara shifted forward, positioning them, and slowly took him inside her. They sat a moment in the quiet of the candlelit night, their bodies and breaths together. She leaned forward and kissed his forehead, then drew her lips over his brow and down to each eye, kissing one and then the other. She moved down his cheek to his mouth. He kissed her back.

She moved slowly at first, containing the fire he felt inside her. He let her fill his senses: the taste of her tongue, the sound of her breath, the scent of her need. She rocked her hips, bringing them into a rhythm and making him rise to meet her. She ran her hand around the back of his neck and twisted her fingers into his hair, pulling his head back and biting his bottom lip. He growled and snaked his arm around her waist. But she caught his hands in hers and pushed them against the arms of his chair, holding him down.

She quickened her pace. He bent his head and bared his teeth against her shoulder, and she began to fall apart. She rocked forward, panting. Her body twisted against him, but he held her, not letting her free.

With a final cry, she collapsed on top of him, burying her face in his neck.

Mikael lifted her up, still keeping them joined together. He swept his hand across his desk, pushing everything to the floor—his letters, his parchments, his maps. They didn't matter anymore. He laid her down and felt her skin prickle against the polished wood of the desk.

Mikael pushed himself deeper. There was no control in him now. He gripped her shoulder and pulled her against him, letting his own desire take over. She raised a hunger in him that would never be satiated. It was more than the wants of the flesh.

She knew him.

She loved him.

She needed him.

He growled as he shuddered to a finish, clutching her tightly and holding her close. He filled her with everything of himself—his love, his worries, his insecurities—and she took him. All of him. Under the weight of the crown, he was cracking, but she bonded those cracks with gold, and made him whole.

CHAPTER FORTY-SEVEN

A knock on the door interrupted Norah from her letter, and Vitalia moved to answer it. Norah smiled when she saw the girl enter. "Calla."

But the girl didn't smile back. "Salara, you need to come to the sparring field. It's Adrian." Her tone told Norah not to delay.

She rose quickly and followed Calla through the castle halls and out through the courtyard, toward the fields. "What's going on?" she asked.

"Three of the earlies earned their sword entitlements today. Adrian was denied because he's not actually an early. He challenged the lord commander on it, saying he was just as good as every man there." She looked at Norah as they walked quickly. "He is, Salara! He's better!"

Norah's pulse quickened as she picked up her pace. "And what did the lord commander do?"

"He said Adrian could have his entitlement, if he defeated them. *All.*"

"All?" she repeated with her eyes wide. "That's ridiculous."

"I know." Calla shrugged breathlessly. "But when has being ridiculous ever stopped any of them?"

Norah frowned. That was true.

They reached the sparring field, where Adrian was engaged against an early. He moved with the grace of the Shadowmen, every strike calculated yet natural. He wore the black army breeches and boots, with no shirt, only a weapon's strapping. His hair was longer now, and he tied it back like the Kharavian men, sporting a close-cut beard to match. Aside from the stark difference of his fair complexion and no markings on his body, he looked very much like one of them.

The men exchanged brutal blows, each looking to overwhelm the other. Norah's heart pulsed in her throat. This wasn't a practice sparring; this wasn't a friendly match. Adrian was fighting for honor—a purpose the North took as serious as life.

The early launched another attack, driving toward Adrian and swinging his sword high. But Adrian met him with a counter, turtling under his shield and hurling his weight forward. He hit the man's legs with a force that knocked the early off balance, making him fall forward, onto Adrian's shield. Adrian used his momentum to lift the man over and slam him to the ground. He pivoted, his sword ready, bringing his blade to the felled early's neck, and taking the match. The man raised his arm, yielding.

But it wasn't yet a victory. Adrian spun to find his next opponent. The man was a little more cautious in his approach than the first, testing, looking for weakness. He moved with elegance and poise, despite his size. In practices before, Norah would marvel at the grace of the men as they sparred, appreciating their skill and strength. But today she only worried. She worried this early had too much skill, too much strength.

Adrian made the first strike. He beat the man back with both his sword and his shield, using them fluidly as though they were parts of his own body. But the early moved with the same agility, and on a strike where Adrian's shield came down, the man caught him with an elbow to the face. Adrian stumbled backward, and Norah gasped.

A low, rumbling chuckle to her right startled her, and she glanced to see the lord commander. She hadn't realized he was there. "Why are you doing this?" she hissed. "This is how someone gets hurt!"

"This is how a man makes his rise," he said without taking his eyes from the bout.

Adrian suffered another hit to his face. Blood came from both his nose and his brow now.

Soren let out another chuckle. "If he remembers to keep that shield up."

"He's not even wearing a helm," she said through her teeth.

"All the more thrilling."

"This is a game to you?" she snapped.

He shot her a gaze of icy fire, serious now. "This is most certainly not a game."

They watched as the men fought on. The early beat Adrian back with a brutal attack. But on a downward swing, he opened his shield arm. Adrian twisted and caught it with his own shield, knocking the man's arm out and exposing his front. Adrian was ready. He barreled forward with his shoulder, sending the man sprawling to the ground. Adrian leapt atop him, pressing him down against the earth with the edge of his shield and sweeping the tip of the blade to the early's neck. The man held his hands open, conceding.

But Norah didn't have time to feel happiness for him. Another swordsman stepped forward, and her anxiousness rose. Adrian was tired. These weren't general soldiers that one might find in everyday battle. These opponents were earlies. Many would be men of the Crest, and besting them took an immense amount of skill and energy. She questioned if he'd be able to withstand another bout.

The early charged forward in a fresh attack, and Adrian defended, but he was slowing. Their swords rang through the air and fell upon each other's shields in fatal blows. Adrian moved in a side swing, but his rebalance was slow, and his opponent delivered a hit with the edge of his shield, knocking Adrian to the ground.

"Soren," she breathed, her alarm growing. "Please."

The opponent sprang forward in a subsequent attack, but Adrian rolled away, stumbling back to his feet. The early saw Adrian's strength waning, and he attacked again. Their shields clashed together, and Adrian fell back with the man on top of him. But Adrian used the force in the fall, kicking the early up and over his head. With both men now on the ground, Adrian rolled to his stomach and reached forward. In a single motion, he grabbed a fistful of the early's hair, pulling his head back toward him and bringing his blade to his throat. They held until, reluctantly, the man yielded. Both men lay on the ground, taking a moment to regain their breath.

Then Adrian rolled and staggered to his feet, and a wry smile came to his lips with his triumph.

"I said all," Soren growled, and the men around the field looked at one another in surprise.

"You can't be serious!" Norah exclaimed. "He just beat three earlies! That's what you asked of him."

He looked at her with a scowl. "I said *all*," he repeated.

Another soldier stepped forward. Adrian's right eye had swelled shut, and blood trickled into his left. He wiped it away with the back of his hand. The early charged forward. Adrian moved to meet him, but he was slow, and the man spun with a blow, knocking him to the ground with his shield. He rained lethal strikes at the downed Northman, but Adrian rolled away and stumbled back to his feet. The early charged again.

"There's got to be a hundred men here," Norah said angrily. "You ask the impossible!"

The lord commander didn't respond. He only watched as Adrian suffered blow after blow, fall after fall. But Adrian didn't stop. He rose again and again. Beaten and bloody, he still welcomed the battle.

The early charged him again. Adrian sidestepped, but he caught the man's arm as he passed, pulling him back. With a sheer force of will and strength, he swept his blade to the early's armpit, threatening a thrust to the heart. The man stopped, his wrist in Adrian's grip, and he nodded his submission. Adrian swayed on his feet, but he stayed upright, waiting for his next opponent.

The next soldier stepped forward, and he looked at the lord commander hesitantly.

"Soren," Norah pleaded again, but the commander nodded, prompting the man to continue.

The soldier stepped forward, first to attack. Adrian deflected his first blow with his shield, but the early knocked it to the side with his own and delivered a kick that sent Adrian sprawling backward, to the ground. Before Adrian could fully recover, the early swung his shield again, catching Adrian in the chest and knocking him down again.

But the man didn't spring on his advantage.

Adrian struggled to his feet once more, but he could barely lift his shield. The early advanced again, throwing an elbow and catching him in the chin. Miraculously, Adrian stayed on his feet, but he didn't have the strength to defend against another blow.

Norah couldn't stand it any longer and stepped forward, but Soren caught her arm. "Don't dishonor him," he warned, his voice low.

She was about to argue when a soldier within the ranks of the watching earlies started to beat his shield with his sword—a slow and persistent drumming. Another soldier joined him, then another. And another. The circle of men all around them joined the rhythm.

Even the soldier facing Adrian beat his shield.

Norah looked at Soren in utter confusion. The commander stood for a moment, then he turned to the training captain, who handed him a sword. Her heart raced as Soren stepped out onto the field. Even as the shadow of the lord commander loomed over him, Adrian stood, bloody and bold, determined to fight on.

But Soren didn't attack. He only faced the Northman in silence. Then he gripped the sword by the blade and held it for Adrian to take. Adrian dropped his own sword to the ground and reached for the one offered to him. The beating of shields grew to a deafening thunder.

Norah glanced at Calla by her side, still not fully understanding.

The girl grinned. "He got it. He earned the entitlement. He's an early now."

Norah looked back out to the field as Soren returned to where she stood.

His eyes blazed a dark fire, ardent and fierce. "You just saw the best warriors of the Kharavian army call for a Northman to receive a position of status and a most coveted entitlement." He paused, almost seeming proud. "He rises."

Norah sat in the throne room, nearly suffocating from the tension of the air. Mikael sat beside her, facing his nobles who filled the room in front of them.

This was her doing.

At her insistence, Mikael had declined Gregor's invitation to visit Japheth. Surely it had been a trap. His words were too kind, too flattering, very unlike what he had shown in Kharav. He was wooing Mikael to come. And she didn't trust him. In response to the offense, Gregor stopped all trade—to wait until they discussed it in person, he said. Of course, this reached the nobles, who demanded an audience.

The relationship between the royals and nobles was different in Kharav than in Mercia. They held more power here; and the nobles weren't happy with Mikael. They didn't approve of his marriage to her, especially after he annulled his marriages to several of their daughters and executed a member of a noble family. And they most certainly didn't approve of his jeopardizing the alliance with Japheth.

They blamed her. Of course a marriage between Kharav and Mercia would offend Japheth. Mikael had told her Gregor had been upset that they hadn't attacked the Mercian army right after her capture. It was a prime opportunity—perhaps the only opportunity—to defeat her army and leave Phillip without an ally by his side. Alexander had driven her army across the Tribelands, and they were weak and vulnerable. She remembered the army of Japheth had been ready to unite with Mikael and attack, only for Mikael to send Mercia home to safety.

Then came the incident that killed King Gregor's nephew, which they blamed the North for, followed by Norah's confrontation with Gregor in protecting Soren. In their eyes, Norah was threatening the alliance between Japheth and Kharav, and Mikael was letting her.

"Your actions weaken us," one of the nobles said to Mikael sharply. Narsing was his name, and Mikael's previous wife Heta was his daughter. Norah had seen him only a few times before, but she knew him enough to know she didn't like him, and enough to fear him. He was one of the more powerful lords, and his lands stretched a good portion of the border between Kharav and Japheth.

"We give the North provisions, men, horses," he said. Then he looked at Norah. "And what does she give in return? Nothing, no steel goods—although they readily sell them in Tarsus. They don't even allow us the ability to forge what we need if we were to buy it ourselves. It doesn't feel like an alliance. The North Queen doesn't even give an heir."

Mikael rose abruptly, and Soren moved forward from where he stood beside the king. Fear flashed through her. They had enough to face from outside threats. They didn't need a battle within as well.

Norah rose from her throne, and all eyes turned to her. "I understand your frustrations, Lord Narsing. But I assure you, Mercia is Kharav's ally."

"You don't act as one," he challenged.

Anger heated her blood. "I've returned Bahoul."

"So you gave us what was already ours," he countered. "Is this all the strength Salar has?"

Narsing was faulting Mikael—judging him—for what they saw as her shortcomings, and giving ever so subtly the threat of what his failure could bring. Regardless of how subtle, that threat brought her blood to a boil.

"I gave you what Mercia took from you, and what I can take again," she snapped back. She was not a weak queen to be bullied, and Mercia wasn't a weak kingdom. They would do well to remember that. But she didn't care for what they thought of her, more that they supported Mikael. They needed to believe in their king.

"Salar has also spoken to me of shipments of steel trade," she said, "to which I have agreed."

Murmurs rippled across the nobles in approval. Mercian steel would be of great importance to them. Mikael hadn't discussed this with her, but she knew it was on his mind and that he wanted it. He needed it now, and he would have it.

"That's a start," Narsing said as he looked back at Mikael. "When can we expect the first shipment?"

"I only await word from my council on mining status." Her stomach twisted as she thought of her council. They would never agree.

She needed to make them.

Chapter Forty-Eight

Alexander stood over his desk, resting his weight on his palms on the corners. He stretched his neck to one side, then the other; he'd been sitting all day.

"You've not moved since I saw you this morning," came a voice, and he looked up to see the Kharavian captain in the doorway.

"I'm standing this time."

Her eyes smiled. "Barely." She tossed an apple at him, and he caught it. "So many papers. Now I see why you Northmen can't fight. You spend all your time doing this kind of work."

He chuckled. "I don't know about that—we've done a pretty good job fighting back you lot over the past ten years."

"Luck."

He chuckled again. But if he was honest with himself, he'd certainly had luck on his side. The Shadowlands were the fiercest of kingdoms, and it had taken everything he'd had to hold the mountains. In truth, he wasn't sure how much longer he could have sustained.

The Shadowmen. For so long, he'd known them as enemies. But he didn't truly know them. He looked at Katya, and he couldn't deny the questions needling him. He wanted to know them more. He wanted to know her more.

"Why do Shadowmen not show their faces?" he asked.

"Because we're to be recognized by our achievements only." She extended her arms, showing her markings. They ran from her shoulders to her wrists.

He set the book down on the desk and slowly stepped around it, closer to her. Unabashedly, he traveled his gaze down her arms. Geometric patterns formed larger images across her skin—they were really quite beautiful. But they held a darker meaning, he knew. Accomplishments for the Shadowmen meant death.

His eyes drifted up to hers. "Are you not allowed to show your face?"

"I'm allowed to do anything I want." Her eyes taunted him.

Alexander felt the pulse of his heart against his chest. "Would you *want* to show me your face?" he asked quietly. "Because I would very much like to see it."

Her eyes narrowed. "Come look then, if you're bold enough," she challenged.

Alexander stepped closer. Slowly, he reached up and brought his fingers to her cheek, where the cloth met her skin. Ever so carefully, he pulled it down, revealing her smile underneath. Her nose, straight and masterfully sculpted, sat just above the full arches of her lips. The line of her jaw ran as sharp as her wit to the elegant curve of her chin.

The warmth of her skin against his fingers sparked a heat through him. He dropped his hand, remembering himself.

"Am I not a match for Northern beauty?" she asked with a wry smile.

He hesitated a moment before saying softly, "You're beyond."

His admission quieted them both. Then she smiled again. Not a challenging, smirking smile that her eyes so often showed, but a smile of one unsure. A curious smile. She stepped nearer to him.

"Do you want to kiss me, Bear?" she asked.

He did want to kiss her, but he made no move, and no comment. Not when he loved another—another, he reminded himself, that couldn't love him back. Another that he could never be with. Norah was a dream, but Katya... Katya was real, and everything he told himself he'd never find in a woman. And Katya made him want to forget about dreams, if that was possible. Was it possible? Was *this* possible?

Katya pushed herself up on her toes and raised her chin, but she stopped just short of his lips. The sweet scent of her nearness dared him to come the rest of the way.

And he did.

He dropped his head and met her lips with his. The heat of her mouth stirred a burn inside him, and he pulled her closer, drinking her in. She tasted like the dew of summer, and he wanted more. But his mind caught up with him and pulled him back, and he broke their kiss.

They both stood breathless.

"I'm sorry," he said.

Her brows knitted together. "For what? Do you think you've offended me?"

He couldn't help an uneasy chuckle as he shifted his gaze down. "Have I offended you?"

She waited for his eyes to meet hers again, then she shook her head. "Not at all."

Words sat jumbled on his tongue. "Good," he said finally. *Good*? He cursed himself silently. A stupid thing to say.

She smiled again, this time a mocking one, and his cheeks grew hot. She stepped closer. "I like you pale Northmen," she teased him.

"Why is that?"

She stepped even closer. "Because your skin betrays you. Do I make you uncomfortable, Bear?"

"I think you know exactly how you make me feel."

Her smile widened, and she rocked onto her toes, lifting her lips. He dropped his head to meet her again, but before their lips touched, she pulled away. And smiled.

"Yes, I do," she said smartly, and left him in his study.

Ashan was a beautiful city. Norah stood on the wall of the castle, looking out. This was her city. Her kingdom. She was salara.

A noise behind her made her turn, and she smiled when she saw Adrian. It had been several days since his entitlement challenge, and his face had finally started to heal.

"I can almost recognize you again," she teased him. He grinned, and Norah noticed there was an air of excitement around him. Her eyes narrowed. "Why are you grinning like a derpy hound?"

He laughed. Then he pulled up his sleeve with a breathless smile, revealing the inked marking of a Kharavian warrior. Overlapping patterns circled his arm just below his elbow, and on the inside of his forearm he bore the image of a sword. "I got a sword marking," he said proudly.

It was beautiful, but a weight grew in her stomach. Mercian customs and beliefs kept the Northmen from marking their skin, and her mind turned to Alexander. "I'm so proud of you, Adrian," she told him. "You've done what no Northman has. You've gained the respect of Kharav." She paused, searching for how to handle her worry delicately. It wasn't as though he could change his mind now. "Have you shared any of this with Alexander? The sword entitlement, your plan to get the marking?"

The smile fell from his face, and she could tell he hadn't even thought about it. His brow creased with the beginnings of worry. "Do you think he'll be upset?"

She hesitated. "I think he might not understand. He won't know what it means, its importance."

Adrian gazed down at his arm solemnly, realizing what she was saying. "He's going to be angry. He's going to think I turned my back on Mercia."

"No, he won't," she said quickly as she shook her head. "You just need to talk to him. I think he'll be very proud of you and what you've accomplished here."

He nodded, but she could see she had given him little assurance. It saddened her. Adrian had so much to be proud of. Alexander had so much to be proud of.

"Have you told him about Sevina?" she asked.

"Uh, I wrote him about the marriage."

"And of the child?" she pressed.

He sucked in a breath and let it out slowly. "Not yet. I'm going to. Today, I suppose. I just wanted to give it some time... since my last letter."

She understood. He didn't want Alexander to connect that he had gotten Sevina pregnant out of wedlock. Not that she blamed him. "You might want to wait on the marking," she suggested. "I mean, it's not urgent. Maybe let him come to terms with the child first."

He nodded. "I'll do that."

Norah forced a smile. She wished Adrian weren't the only one with the announcement of a child. She'd give anything for the anxiousness of sharing such news. But that wasn't her future, and she'd come to terms with it. Instead, she'd be content with the blessing she'd been given as she looked out across her beautiful city.

The days felt like eternity, but the months passed quickly. Months—seven of them. It had been seven months since Norah had left and taken Adrian with her. Alexander sat at his desk, clutching the parchment in his hand.

"News?" Katya said from the doorway. "From the looks of you, not good."

He pulled open the side drawer and dropped the letter into it, then pushed it closed. This wasn't something he could speak about. Not right now.

He still felt her eyes on him, but he didn't look up.

"Are you really not going to tell me?" she asked.

He said nothing.

"Bear—"

"I don't owe you an explanation," he said sharply, cutting her off.

She rocked back on her heel. She said nothing, but her eyes betrayed her surprise.

He sighed. "I'm sorry. I'm upset. I don't mean to take it out on you."

Katya only stood. Waiting.

"My brother's wed," he said finally.

She stepped into the room and made her way around the wing chair in front of his desk and sat down in it. She waited until he looked at her, then raised a brow. "This isn't good news?"

"No, it's not."

"I thought that's what you Northmen liked, to be married off so you're not breaking your vows, or whatever keeps you from being normal men."

She had a playful tone, but he wasn't in the mood for play. "I didn't send him to the Shadowlands to be distracted by a woman," he said angrily.

"You make it sound as if that's a woman's intention. You mean you didn't send him to go distract a woman?"

He sat back in his chair and paused before nodding. "The fault's with him, not this woman."

"Why must there be fault at all?"

"He has his duties," he argued.

"He still has them. Can a woman and a man not find happiness in one another and still be loyal to their duties?"

Her words caught him, and they sat quietly.

"Can I see?" she asked, holding her hand out.

He sighed, relenting, and pulled the letter back out of the drawer before handing it to her.

Her eyes widened as she read it. "Sevina Arvedi?" She chuckled. "How did he manage to win *her* hand?"

Alexander drew his brows together. "Adrian's a high noble of Mercia, son of the previous lord justice, brother of the current."

"The Arvedi family is one of the wealthiest noble families in Kharav."
She shook her head. "Status in the North wouldn't have won him her
hand, even if he's as beautiful as you."

He snorted.

"He must be doing well in Kharav. He'd need the lord commander's
support. This means he represents you well and brings honor to your
family. You should be proud."

Proud. He looked down at the letter. He hadn't felt proud before,
but an honorable marriage was something to be proud of, especially
if it meant Adrian was proving himself and had won favor in the
Shadowlands. Alexander could certainly be proud of that.

She stood to go and stepped toward the door.

"Katya," he called, and she stopped. "Thank you."

CHAPTER FORTY-NINE

Mikael folded his letter and poured the wax before affixing his seal. He stamped it hastily, leaving only half his mark, but he didn't care. It was still recognizable. No one else used a black seal.

Soren stepped inside. "Salar," he greeted.

Things were normal between them now, and he was thankful for it. The nonsensical jealousy he'd felt before had passed. He knew what he had always known—Soren loved him and would give everything for him. Even himself.

"News from the Bear," Soren said. "Gregor has met with the Raelean king."

Mikael straightened. "Cyrus?" he said in surprise. He leaned back as he crossed his arms and brought his fist to his lips, pondering. "What business would Gregor have with Cyrus?"

"The Bear warns that Cyrus holds ill will against Kharav, for our part in supporting Serra and their slave trade."

Mikael snorted. "I wouldn't call giving our defeated enemies to Serra and trading provisions *support*." He hadn't liked Serra's previous king, King Milar. In fact, he'd almost returned his envoy's head when he attempted to renegotiate their contract. Salara had intervened, and he smiled slightly, remembering. But this new king Cyrus was beginning to irritate him as well.

"Let them talk, and let him come," Mikael said, annoyed. "If he seeks to make enemies of those involved with slave trade, it'll be a long list." His chest rumbled as he stood. "How much of a threat could they be? Even with the forces of Serra and Rael combined, Cyrus's army is but a mound of fleas."

"It's rumored that all the slaves who were freed from Serra have joined his army. If that's true, he'll have strength in numbers. And he has hundreds of blood sport fighters from Rael, if not thousands. No telling how many were kept in the arenas."

Mikael leaned against his desk. "So, Gregor meets with a known usurper who holds ill will toward Kharav. You think Gregor plots against me?" He frowned. That didn't make sense. Gregor needed all the help he could get against his brother, Phillip.

"Your marriage to the North Queen threatens him. If he took Kharav, he would take revenge on those who humiliated him. Not to mention, if he does align himself with Cyrus and the kingdoms of Serra and Rael, Kharav would be a valuable stronghold to move their armies north, closer to Aleon."

Mikael sighed. "We're making assumptions on rumor alone, none of which may be true. Gregor might still be an ally, with merely a disagreement on trade between us."

Soren's face told him he didn't believe that. Mikael wasn't sure if he did either.

"There's too much we don't know," Soren said. "Aleon may see us as a target as well, for Kharav would be a powerful stronghold in a position against Japheth, helping Phillip surround his brother. We need to pull back our forces. We need all men in Kharav, including the unit in the North."

Mikael shook his head. "Salara's using those men to protect her villages. And"—he rubbed his temples with stiff fingers—"did the Bear not send us this warning? In thanks, I turn and pull our forces when he still needs them?"

"Kharav needs them more," Soren pressed. "And you have no choice. You can't give Narsing and the nobles another reason to doubt you."

Mikael gripped his temple. This wouldn't sit well with Salara, but Soren was right. The threats were too great, and even if he could spare men to the North, he was already on the cusp of losing his nobles' support. He sighed, then nodded. "Call them back."

Soren gave a single nod. "I'll also send a message to the Uru, for them to draw back into the canyons and send half their warriors to the western pass."

"Call back our men from Bahoul as well," Mikael said.

His commander shifted his weight back. "What?"

Mikael knew Soren wouldn't agree, but the Bear could keep Bahoul for now. Some solace for the North, surely. "How many men do we have there?" he asked. "Three thousand? Bring them back."

"That will only leave Northern forces in Bahoul," Soren argued.

"How many?"

"Two thousand Northmen."

Two thousand men was enough to protect the stronghold, even it they *were* Northmen. "Do it."

Soren scoffed in anger. "We're giving it back to them?"

Mikael couldn't fight all threats at the same time. He'd have to worry about the risk with the North later. "I need your attention focused on Kharav."

Soren's face darkened, but he nodded stiffly and left to see to his orders.

Mikael sank back into his chair and rubbed his face again in his hands. Not only did this news weigh on his shoulders, but Mercia still hadn't sent their steel goods, and the nobles were growing restless. He knew Salara's intentions were true, but the North's council wasn't cooperating.

How quickly everything could fall apart.

Norah found Mikael and the lord commander in the army's planning office with several of their generals. She'd received Alexander's letter at the same time she'd learned of Mikael's decision to pull his warriors in Mercia back to Kharav. Heat of anger pulsed off her skin.

"You pull back your men from Mercia?" she asked as she stormed in.

Mikael nodded to his soldiers, who bowed and left. "I have no choice," he said when they were gone. "Aleon dreams of war, and Japheth is an unknown threat. Kharav would be a prize for either one of them. I've pulled my forces back from Bahoul as well. This should please the Bear."

Norah gaped at him. "Why would you do that, and why would it please Alexander?" Her voice betrayed her worry. "It means he can't pull men from Bahoul if he needs them, which, if you recall the Kharavian units back from Mercia, he will." She looked at Soren, desperate. "Surely you see this."

But the commander said nothing.

"He needs your help!" she said angrily.

"I need the North's help," he snapped back. "It's only a matter of time before Aleon has his eyes on Kharav, if he doesn't already, and Japheth schemes with a new ally who holds ill will against me. The North does *nothing* to show they stand with me."

She could feel the anger radiating off him, but her own anger stripped her of her patience for it. "Aleon is not planning an attack on Kharav," she argued. "It doesn't even make sense that Phillip's attention would be on you. The only thing he cares about is Gregor."

"I don't believe that," he said, his voice rising with his anger. "If all he cares about is his brother, why did he take Tarsus? And if he were to take Kharav, he would further surround his brother. I need to show him we're not an easy target."

"So you'll make Mercia one?" she cut back.

"I need to show my strength with the North behind me!" he boomed with fury. "I've not asked you for men, but I need them. And where's the steel? Your council still refuses to send it."

"I'll write them again."

"We're supposed to be allies," he bellowed, his anger now raging. "This is why I wed you. This is what an alliance is!"

Norah stopped. Even though his words were true, they still hurt her. "So, what would you have me do?" she asked coldly. "Will you have me let Mercia fall, to give you more forces in Kharav?"

"Your kingdom won't fall to drifters. You don't face a real enemy."

Her own fury grew with his words. "I don't face a real enemy? You know the attacks on our villages aren't from drifters. I have an enemy not only at my door, but in my home as well. Have you forgotten the attempt on my life? Do you forget someone wants me dead, wants my lord justice dead?"

"I want your justice dead!" he thundered.

Silence fell between them.

Norah couldn't think through her anger. "I'm sorry our alliance is failing you. I'm sorry our *marriage* is failing you." She turned and headed toward her sanctuary.

"Salara," he called.

But she didn't turn back.

Alexander walked down the main hall of the Mercian castle toward his study, lost in his mind. He didn't see the servant until the man appeared abruptly in front of him.

"A letter, my lord," the servant said with a small bow.

Alexander took it and turned it over, and his own seal looked back at him. The image of the bear had been his father's seal. Now it was synonymous with the seal of the lord justice—the seal Beurnat the Bear had used when he was justice, the seal Alexander now used. But really, the seal meant family. *Adrian.* He smiled.

He waited until the servant disappeared around a corner before opening it. And when the words found him, he stopped. He read them again to be sure and leaned against the wall.

A child.

Adrian was expecting a child.

A sudden wave of emotion hit him, and he wiped his face. He'd never thought about children in the family. He'd always pictured himself and

Adrian as the only two of their name. But now... now there would be a child. He'd be an uncle. His eyes welled, and he smiled.

He was going to be an uncle.

His lip trembled through his smile.

He was going to be an uncle.

He gave himself the moment of joy, then turned back the way he'd come. As he stepped into the courtyard, he spotted Katya walking toward him. He couldn't help the grin that came to his lips before he reached her.

Her brows drew together. "This can't be good. What are you grinning about?"

He handed her the letter but couldn't wait for her to read the words. "I'm going to be an uncle."

He couldn't see her face, but he knew her mouth dropped open underneath her wrap, and her eyes smiled back at him. "Congratulations, that's beautiful news. So much to be happy about."

He nodded, still smiling as she handed the letter back to him. But there was something in her eyes—something not right. "Are you all right?" he asked.

She nodded. "Of course."

They stood for a moment, a long pause between them. Katya reached up and pulled down her wrap, and she held out her own letter. "I'm to return to Kharav."

What? She was being called back? But she couldn't be called back. "You can't return, I still need the Shadowmen. I still need..."

He needed her. To stay.

"Kharav needs me. We depart tomorrow." Her words were firm, and he understood. Where duty called, one went. There was no other decision to be considered, despite racking his mind for one. Her eyes were on him, and he swallowed. Did she see how much it bothered him?

She smiled sadly. "I think your fears have proven true."

He shook his head. "What fears?"

"That I've decided I like it here, and I want to stay." She smiled again to hide the glistening in her eyes. "I hope I haven't corrupted you too much."

He looked at the ground. *Corrupted.* The truth was, he'd never felt so right.

"This won't be the last we see of each other," she said.

"No, it won't," he promised.

The weeks passed, slow and full of tension. Mikael tried to right his words, and Norah appreciated that, but things still felt unsettled between them. She knew she was also to blame. The council still denied her the trade she sought for Kharav, though not directly, the cowards they were. They undermined her efforts through *misunderstandings* and delays. They gave mining times that sounded too long, but she didn't know enough to question it. She wished Alexander were with her. Perhaps she needed to go to Mercia herself to resolve it.

No additional news came of Japheth, or of this usurper, or of Aleon looking to invade Kharav. Yet Alexander's letters came with increasing concerns. He didn't have enough men to stretch across the kingdom, and the attacks were continuing. He had to leave the outer reaches undefended. The council didn't understand why Kharav had recalled their men. Strange, Norah mused, because they had been actively working to send them back. But of course, Mikael pulling his forces from Mercia signaled to them he was preparing for something, and she was sure they would assume it was something dark and ill-intentioned.

She searched for ways to help Alexander. He could only encourage villagers in the outer realm to fall back to the central lands for safety. Norah resorted to sending all the Northmen in Kharav back to Mercia. Only Adrian and Caspian stayed with her.

Norah sat at the dining table. The meal was quiet, as they had become lately, strained under the pressures of the crown. She watched Mikael as he ate. He looked up to see her gaze, and he gave a small smile, but it was forced, she knew.

The doors opened and Caspian entered, followed by another Northman. "Queen Norah," he said, bowing, "there's news from Bahoul."

Norah's pulse quickened. The Northman that had entered with Caspian bowed to her. "Queen Norah, I come with an urgent message. Aleon now occupies Bahoul."

Mikael and Soren stood abruptly, and Norah rose as well.

"What?" she breathed.

"When did they attack?" Soren asked.

The Northman eyed the lord commander warily, but he answered. "They didn't attack. They came in peace, but with a vast army. We had no choice."

Soren's face shook with a growing fury. "So, you just let them in? You let them take Bahoul?"

"What were we to do with a hundred men? King Phillip came with tens of thousands."

"What do you mean a hundred men?" Soren asked. "There are two thousand Northmen at the stronghold."

The soldier shook his head. "No. The lord justice had to call them back to Mercia. They left about a week before your Shadowmen did."

Soren jerked his gaze to Mikael, who leaned his weight on his fisted knuckles against the edge of the table.

Norah's stomach twisted as the realization set in on her too—both Alexander and Mikael had withdrawn forces from Bahoul, not knowing the other was doing the same.

"The Aleon king is there?" Mikael growled. "At Bahoul?"

The Northman nodded. "He sends a letter," he said, pulling it from inside his jacket.

Mikael held out his hand. "Bring it."

"For Queen Norah," the Northman said, and presented it to her. "I am to see this directly to your hand," he told her.

She took the letter, her heart racing. It bore the blue seal of Aleon, the seal of Phillip. She nodded to the messenger. "Thank you. You may go for now."

He bowed and left.

Norah shakily broke the wax and read the letter's contents. "He says he bids us tidings of friendship," she started.

Soren snorted. Mikael drew closer as she skimmed her eyes over the parchment.

"He asks if he might set a stronghold in Bahoul, to better surround Japheth," she said.

"To be closer to Kharav, he means," Soren interjected.

"He offers whatever we ask in exchange." Norah handed the letter to Mikael to let him read it.

457

Soren fumed in anger. "Is he accustomed to doing as he pleases before asking?"

"Is that not what you all do?" Norah cut back. "At least Phillip has the courtesy to send a civilized letter."

"Not *we*," Mikael said, his eyes still on the letter.

"What?" she asked.

"He doesn't offer whatever *we* ask. He offers whatever *you* ask."

Norah pursed her lips. "You read too much into it. Plus, I can ask for the both of us."

Mikael's brow creased. "You aren't seriously considering this."

She knew he wouldn't like it. "Of course I am. How can I not? How am I to remove him? And I can't hold Bahoul on my own and defend Mercia. I need more men. Mercia needs more men. If Phillip will give them in exchange for a stronghold against his brother, I'll give it to him."

"Bahoul is mine," Mikael snarled.

"And you left it!" she snapped. Soren's eyes blazed with anger, but she couldn't let him sway her. She couldn't see another way. "Mikael," she said, softer now. "We can ask for help for Kharav as well."

"Are you mad?" he scoffed. "We would welcome an enemy inside our walls to move against our ally? We would allow him to divide us and take us one by one."

"Aleon's eyes aren't on Kharav. And you and I both know Japheth is not an ally." She stood firmly, her patience gone. "Those are my men in Bahoul, no matter how few. It is my kingdom that is *actually* under attack, and Phillip's letter is addressed to *me*. I will consider it."

Finding the lord commander had been more difficult than she thought. Norah had checked the sparring fields, the stables, his study, Mikael's study. Nothing. She bit the inside of her cheek in frustration. He had always seemed to be everywhere—perhaps that was only when he wasn't wanted. Finally, she knocked on his chamber door. She was just about to turn away when he opened it. In seeing her, he shifted back in surprise.

"Um," she started, wringing her hands. She'd had plenty of time to assemble her thoughts before, yet here she stood without the words. "Can I come in?" she asked.

He stepped back into the room, leaving the door ajar.

Not exactly inviting, she mused as she stepped inside.

"I know you're angry about Bahoul, and with me," she said. "But I don't know what to do, about Mikael, or about Aleon and Mercia. I need your help."

The stiffness in his shoulders eased ever so slightly. She wasn't placating him for amends. She had never faced the challenges she did now. Mikael leaned on Soren to help him make decisions for the good of Kharav. She needed that same help.

"I can't tell Phillip no," she continued. "I have no way of forcing him out of Bahoul. I have to make the most of it."

He said nothing, which was fine. Just to talk through her thoughts aloud with him was enough—he'd tell her if she was erring. This she knew for certain.

"I know Phillip's first priority will be Japheth," she said, "and his brother's head. A stronghold in Bahoul puts him in position to strike. Of course he would want to be there. And I could get more men for Mercia, which I desperately need."

Soren folded his arms. He spoke sooner than she had expected him to. "You assume Gregor intends to move against us. If he does *not* have this intention, then we would be helping to destroy our ally, against a foe who will turn on us next."

Norah shook her head. She'd seen the look in Gregor's eyes when she'd threatened him. She'd seen the hate that brewed inside. She'd read the words of his letter to Mikael, sickeningly complimentary in welcoming him to Japheth. Lies. Japheth was no ally.

"Who do you think is most likely to attack Kharav—Aleon or Japheth?" she asked pointedly.

Soren's eyes held a dark intensity, and his reluctance to respond answered for him. He finally broke the lock of their gaze, turning away from her. "It would be a bold move," he said, "to support Aleon in attacking Japheth—striking first before Gregor moves against us."

She noticed that the conversation had shifted from *if* to *when*. He believed Japheth was against them. "So, you agree?" she asked.

He looked back at her. "I don't disagree."

It wasn't the same, but she didn't have time on her side to appreciate the difference. "It's what I need to do, then."

"But, Salara," he warned, "don't be naive to think Aleon won't try to take Kharav. If we support Japheth's fall, you need to ensure we can stand against Aleon after."

"The council would never support a war against Aleon," she admitted. "Especially as we fight an unknown foe on our own soil."

"The Bear would. If you asked him. Your army follows him, not your council, and he comes to your call."

No. Norah shook her head. "Alexander's loyal to Mercia."

"He's loyal to his *queen*," he countered.

Silence hung between them.

Soren stepped nearer to her. "If you accept the Aleon king's proposal, you must be willing to protect Kharav. You must be willing to bring the Bear."

How quickly things had turned—from Soren feverishly working to get Alexander out of Kharav to now calling for him back. But he was right. She would need Alexander to bring her army if Aleon turned against them. Norah swallowed. That would mean she would defy her own council and ask Alexander to do the same—to turn his back on Mercia. But she didn't think it would come to that.

"Will you do that, Salara? Will you bring the Bear?"

Norah drew her bottom lip between her teeth. She would. "If Aleon tries to take Kharav, I'll call Alexander."

He nodded. "Then ask Aleon for men to help you."

Norah thought about her plan for a long time. Despite it sounding the best option, and even after her conversation with Soren, it still twisted her stomach. It was a gamble, for sure.

Now to do what twisted her stomach even more—tell Mikael.

She found him in his study with Soren, poring over maps and plans. He stopped and looked up when she entered. She wondered if Soren might have already told him.

"I've decided to accept King Phillip's request to base his forces in Bahoul," she announced. "In exchange, I'll ask him to send men to Mercia to help me with the attacks on my villages."

461

Mikael's face hardened. Soren hadn't told him. "So you'll allow him to position himself to march against our ally?" he asked. There was already an edge of anger in his voice. She'd known he wouldn't be happy about her decision.

"Is that really what you think Gregor is?" she asked.

"I don't know what he is," he said sharply. She could see his anger growing. He nodded, but it wasn't a nod of acceptance. "So you've decided, on your own, that you will divide Kharav and Japheth. This is a move I won't be able to recover with him. You would do this to me?"

"Mikael, he's not an ally," she insisted.

"You don't know that!" He leaned over his desk, gripping its sides. "Then what?" he asked. "I'm to stand alone against Aleon?"

"Of course not," she replied, forcing a calm back to her voice. "You'll have my lord justice, and the Mercian army."

He scoffed in disbelief. "You would call him back? He would fight against me, not for me."

"He'll fight for me," she insisted.

"Do you not see what you do? You set in motion the war in the vision. The four kingdoms on the battlefield! And you call back the man who will end me."

"We're not fighting! We're letting Aleon wage a war that benefits us both."

"You're a fool if you believe that. You know nothing about war."

"Soren does," she cut back.

Mikael shook his head in bewilderment and turned to Soren. "You agree with this?"

"I'm not in disagreement," he said. "If Salara can influence Aleon to remove a threat against Kharav, she should."

The king's brows dipped as if the words had hurt him. "And after, when Aleon rises against us? You put your faith in the Bear?"

Soren looked at Norah with eyes of shackled storms. "I put my faith in Salara."

CHAPTER FIFTY

The air of Ashan hung thick with apprehension. Aleon's forces in Bahoul, so close to Kharav, made the Kharavian legions uneasy, even with the Canyonlands between them. Messages traveled quickly now, with Phillip so near, and Norah had already received a response to the letter she had sent eight days prior. She had written accepting his request to occupy Bahoul, provided Mercian and Kharavian armies could use it as a shared base. Of course, she knew Mikael wouldn't station Kharavian forces there, wary of an easy escalation to war.

She had asked Phillip to lend his men in return, to help identify Mercia's enemies and stop them. And she had asked if Aleon still truly considered themselves friends of Mercia. It was a painful question to ask, after refusing Phillip's hand for marriage in favor of an ally of his enemy.

Norah held his response in her hand, unopened. She brushed her fingertips over the seal, her heart racing at what the words inside might say. She wondered if she should wait for Mikael before she read it. He hadn't yet returned from the Canyonlands, where he'd gone to ensure the Uru and their border forces were prepared. He could have sent Soren—it was the commander's job after all—but he'd gone himself. Alone. He was upset with them. Both of them. But they didn't have a choice. He just needed some time to calm, and he'd see things more clearly, she was sure. He'd see.

She broke the seal and opened the letter.

Dearest Norah.

Phillip's words had a personal feel. Too personal.

I found no sleep after I sent my last letter, unsure of how you'd respond, or if you'd respond at all. How different these circumstances are from what was planned so long ago. The hand of fate is cruel, isn't it? Twisting and surprising even the most assured of men. That was my lesson. I was too proud, too confident, and the gods sought to humble me.

And they have.

When I received your reply, I knew it was a sign of their returned favor.

In response to your first question, of course Aleon still looks to Mercia with deep affection and friendship. Were our fathers and grandfathers not bonded in the blood of battle? Were they not fused together in the kiln fires of war? These ties aren't easily broken. And your acceptance of my request to remain in Bahoul shows me these intentions still remain.

Your request for my help in protecting Mercia shouldn't even be a question. As I write these words, I've already ordered ten thousand men to flush out this unknown enemy of both Mercia and Aleon.

Norah paused, forcing herself to breathe. He was sending men—ten thousand of them. Why would he be so generous? She turned her eyes back to the words.

I've thought many times on the circumstance by which we'll meet again. I look forward to seeing you, Norah. We have much to discuss.

Most sincerely, I am,

Phillip

Norah refolded the letter with shaking hands. It felt as though he had whispered the words into her ear, like he knew her. Catherine had told her they'd met several times before she'd disappeared. Perhaps they'd been friends. But things had changed now. Why and when did he expect to see her again? It sounded soon. Why did it sound so soon?

She pulled a small wooden letter box from her vanity to place it inside, but when she opened the lid, she stopped. A small handheld portraiture sat between the stack of folded parchments, and she pulled it out. It was the small portraiture of Phillip that had been sent to Mercia, with the talks of marriage that felt so long ago. She looked at his face and his tousled hair of bronze, his smiling lips and kind eyes. He looked the way his letter sounded.

A knock on her door made her jump, and she turned to see Soren enter.

"Hammel's hell," she breathed, scowling at him. He never waited for a response to his knock. It merely served as a warning. Soren's peculiar friendship came with the dearth of privacy, a product of his absent self-awareness, or perhaps his absence of care.

"They said a letter's come," he said impatiently.

She nodded, clutching it in her hand, her stomach knotting. Then she held it out for him.

He took it, reading the words quickly, and then folded it back. But his face didn't reveal the anger she'd expected. "He sends the men you requested, and more than I expected," he said with a nod. "Much more. Good."

"Good?" she asked, raising a brow. "Did you not read the rest of the letter?"

His forehead creased. "What of it?" he asked.

466

She gave a small breath of disbelief laced with amusement at his lack of awareness. "He speaks as though our kingdoms are still united, Mercia and Aleon. Perhaps as though *we'll* still be united."

"Good." He nodded.

"Wait, no, it's not good," she argued.

His brow creased. "I do take you for smarter sometimes."

She pursed her lips as a flash of anger brought heat to her cheeks.

"Salara, you're trying to influence a kingdom that's not your ally to fight your war."

"It's *his* war," she argued.

"No," he said, shaking his head. "He only thinks it's his war. And he'll attack Japheth on his own time, unless you make it your time. You can't force him, as he's shown you with Bahoul. You must incent him. And if he is incented by the thought of the North and Aleon together, you'll use it."

"Soren, manipulation isn't the answer to everything. I actually do want a good relationship with Aleon. I want trust between us. We could be strong friends, allies."

Soren stepped closer, his eyes dark. "You can't be allies. If you ride beside the Aleon king, you bring Salar's end."

The thought of the vision hit her like a blow to the stomach, like it always did. She felt sick.

The horns sounded.

"Salar's returned," he said. He held the letter over a candle, lighting it afire.

"No!" she cried, reaching for it.

But he pulled it back. "Why would you keep it?"

"I keep all my letters."

He shook his head. "That's a stupid mistake. You'll not keep this one," he said as he tossed it into the fireplace, letting the flames consume the rest. "Now go meet your husband."

Norah walked quickly to the courtyard to meet Mikael, overwhelmed by the vision that she tried so hard to push from her mind. Would a pact with Aleon really put them on the path toward his death?

When she saw him ride in, she smiled. He had only been gone a few days, but she missed him. She had missed him before he'd even left. There was a distance between them now, one that left a crushing weight on her heart, one she didn't know how to fix. He felt alone. She needed to show him she was by his side.

His eyes searched for her, and when he saw her, he moved toward her. She waited until he reached her and dismounted before she stepped to greet him.

"Husband," she said softly.

"Are you well?" he asked.

She nodded with a small smile, but he didn't smile back. Worry still etched his brow. "I'm glad you're home," she said. Norah stood on her toes and kissed his cheek. "Come inside." She curled her arm around his, and they started up the stairs.

"Did you get your men?" he asked as they stepped inside, and the large doors closed behind them.

Norah didn't want to speak of Aleon, not now. She only nodded.

"How many?" he asked.

"Let's talk about this later. I just want—"

"How many?" he asked again.

Norah swallowed back the unease rising in her throat. She had hoped to ease things between them before venturing into this topic again. But not answering him would only fuel his anxiousness about it, she knew. "Ten thousand," she said finally.

His face held no expression, hiding the emotion behind it. "I should have given you the men."

She hated that he faulted himself. "You need them for Kharav," she tried to assure him.

"And I shouldn't have pulled them from Bahoul. Soren told me not to."

"You didn't know the Mercian forces had been stripped back as well. Mikael, you can't blame yourself."

"I'm salar," he snapped. "There's no one to blame but me." He rubbed his hand over his face, and his calm returned. "Forgive me. I'm tired. I'm going to clean up."

She squeezed his arm lovingly. "I'll send for some food, and I'll be right there."

He nodded and turned toward their chamber.

Soren came up beside her as the king took the stairs. "Don't speak to him of an alliance with Aleon," he said with a warning gaze. "And have an answer ready on why your council still hasn't sent the steel."

She nodded.

"Go to him," he told her. "I'll send Vimal with a meal."

Norah nodded again appreciatively and followed after Mikael. Now that he was back, she needed to show him she was with him, beside him. She understood his fears, the pressures closing in around him. They were pressures she felt too. They needed each other.

She reached the chamber and stepped inside, but stopped when she saw him. He stood by her vanity, oddly still and not yet stripped of his armor, his back to her.

"What are you doing?" she asked, giving him a curious smile. But her smile fell as he turned, and she saw the portraiture of Phillip in his hand. She cursed herself. Her earlier conversation with Soren had distracted her, and she'd forgotten to put it away.

"Why do you have this?" he said softly, but she could hear the upset inside him.

Norah forced a casual tone. "I was going through some old letters today. I was interrupted, and I forgot to put them away." She silently praised Soren for having the good sense to burn Phillip's latest letter. She felt like such a fool.

"Why do you have this?" he asked again. His words were slow, enunciated.

"I have everything. Every letter that's ever been written to me, by anyone." She nodded to the small wooden box. "It's all there. You're welcome to read them." She paused—not all would please him, but that wasn't the point. "I suppose I just feel like I have so little of my life. I try to hold on to everything. I don't want to forget."

"You want to hold on to *this*?" he asked as he clutched the portraiture in his hand.

"It's not like that."

His nostrils flared. "Does he have a portrait of you?"

"My grandmother sent one," she replied with a calm nod, "as is customary in conversations of marriage. I doubt he still has it, for I'm sure he's quite moved on."

"And you haven't?"

"That's not what I meant."

A coldness seemed to settle over him, and it frightened her a little. "He still remains unwed," he said.

"I haven't followed his marriage prospects. Nor do I think about them."

"Has the Bear not kept you apprised?" he asked. "It wasn't so long ago he brought the news of the Aleon's standing offer. And I doubt your council's diligence in solidifying an alliance has waned. Have you thought about that?"

"Don't be ridiculous," she breathed. She could see his anger reaching dangerous levels, but she didn't know how to pull him back.

Mikael shook as he crumpled the portrait in his fist and hurled it into the fireplace. Then he stopped—something caught his eye. He stepped closer to the hearth and knelt down to scratch at the melted wax that had hardened on the stone.

Norah's heart pounded in her chest. The royal blue wax of Aleon.

"You burned a letter from Aleon?"

Well, Soren had burned a letter from Aleon, but she wouldn't implicate him in this madness. "It was nothing," she insisted. Her pulse thrummed in her ears. "I've told you everything he's offered, and everything I've accepted."

"Yet you don't keep his letter, as you do with all your other letters. What do you hide from me?"

She shook her head. "Your mind's running away with you. Listen to yourself. I'm your wife."

"Then act like it!" he thundered.

Norah stepped back, speechless, and he brushed by her as he stormed from the room. She let herself sink down onto the side chair, out of breath and out of ideas about what to do. How could she get through to him? How was she going to fix this?

CHAPTER FIFTY-ONE

Soren walked briskly toward the stables, where he found Mikael leading out his horse. His pulse quickened. He'd heard Salar was preparing to ride out, and it surprised him he'd leave without saying anything, and after he'd just returned.

"Where are you going?" he demanded.

"Odepeth," Mikael said coldly.

Soren sighed. The seer. What did he expect to see? "I'll go with you," he said, starting toward the stable to get his own horse.

"You'll stay here," Mikael said sharply as he mounted his destrier.

Soren stopped in surprise. Perhaps it shouldn't have been a surprise; Soren had felt the distance between them growing. But they'd always gone to the seer together, faced the future together. Not now. "Are you angry with me, brother?"

"I don't know what I am," Mikael spat back, looking down from his horse. "You ask for the return of the Bear. The man who's to take my head. You would so quickly call him back?"

Soren shook his head. "Of course not, but I would have him bring the North forces if Aleon turned against you, to help keep your throne."

"They would join Aleon against me!" the king snarled back. "And what about keeping my queen? You encourage her treaty with Aleon?"

"She has no choice!"

"You do!" Mikael raged. He pulled up his reins and turned his destrier east. "I'll return in three days. If you're truly my brother, you'll help me stop this."

Tension cramped her shoulders, and anxiousness turned her stomach. Norah paced the length of her chamber, then back. She wasn't angry with Mikael. He had the weight of the world on his shoulders—crumbling alliances, mounting enemies and ambiguous threats, displeased nobles, no heir to solidify the hold of the throne, and uncertainty in his marriage. She'd hoped to alleviate at least one of those for him. He loved her, wholly, and she needed to assure him that he also held her heart. Only she struggled with how to show him. And something had to give—she couldn't take one more setback, one more worry.

The door to her chamber swung open. "Salara!" Vitalia called.

Norah jerked her head up at the urgency in her maid's voice.

"The child—it's coming!"

The child? Adrian and Sevina's child? *No*—it wasn't due for another month, *more* than a month. It was too early.

"The midwife is with them, and the healer," Vitalia said breathlessly. "But I thought you'd want to come too."

She most certainly did. Norah grabbed her cloak and followed her maid quickly down the halls and out of the castle. The Crest fell in step behind her, but she paid them no mind, she only went faster. If this baby was lost...

It was a long walk from the castle to the stately Arvedi home and was made even longer by her worry. She should have taken a horse. By the time she arrived, she was breathless. A servant opened the door to her, and she quickly stepped inside, ignoring the burn of the muscles in her legs.

Aman, Sevina's father, met her promptly in the foyer. "Salara," he said in surprise, and gave her a bow.

"Lord Aman. I'm so sorry for the disruption, but I had to come. How is the child?"

"Norah," came Adrian's voice, and she looked to the top of the stairs, where he stood by the overlook railing.

He moved quickly down them.

"Adrian," she said, "I don't mean to impose, but I had to come see if the baby is okay, if you and Sevina are okay."

He reached the bottom of the stairs and moved to her in three additional steps, catching her in a warm embrace. "You're here," he said. Then he stepped back to look at her. His lips formed a smile, but the crease along his forehead was deep with worry. "Thank you for being here. I'm sorry I didn't send word. He came so quickly."

He. The child had already been delivered.

"No, it's perfectly fine. How is he?"

He gave a jerky nod. "All right, for now."

"How is Sevina?"

He swallowed and nodded again. "She's well. It wasn't a difficult birth, but it's too early. The midwife and healer are both with them. They said we'll know over the next couple days"—he paused and swallowed again—"if the child will make it."

If the child will make it. His words hit her like a blow to the stomach. "Is there anything I can do? Anything you need?"

He shook his head. "Only prayers. His fate is with the gods now."

Norah clutched his hands tightly.

"Do you want to see him?" he asked.

More than anything. "I don't want to impose, I only—"

"You're not imposing. I would..." He paused when his voice cracked. "I would love for you to meet my son."

A tear escaped the corner of her eye, and she nodded. She let Adrian lead her up the stairs, down a wide hall, and to a large chamber in the back of the house. Inside, Sevina sat in the center of the bed, propped up with a small, wrapped bundle in her arms. A woman Norah assumed to be Sevina's mother stood to the side and curtsied as Norah entered. The midwife was cleaning up, while the healer had set to packing away his tools. Norah looked over her shoulder at Adrian, who smiled encouragingly.

She drew nearer to the bed. Sevina was beautiful. Aside from the sweat across her brow, she looked far from having just delivered a child. She smiled at Norah.

"Salara, you honor us by coming."

"I had to. How is he?"

Sevina looked down at the bundle in her arms. "He's well, only sleeping." She pushed back the blanket from the child's face, and Norah could see his black hair peeking out from underneath. She smiled.

"We've named him Theisen," Adrian said from behind her.

Norah glanced back at him in surprise. "A Mercian name?"

"As soon as I heard it, I knew it was the one," Sevina said. "Theisen Arvedi Rhemus. It's a strong name, for a strong boy."

"That he is," Norah agreed, "if he's anything like his father."

Sevina's smile widened.

Norah glanced around at the small family. Aman stood in the door. They were welcoming, but she knew she should give them space. "I should go," she said. "I only meant to see how you were. Please keep me updated."

"Of course, we will." Sevina still wore her smile, but Norah could see her worry underneath—the worry of a mother as she waited to see if her child would live.

The ride to Odepeth was long. It was warmer in the valley, and it brought a sweat to Mikael's brow. He coveted the cool walls of the seer's temple that channeled the breeze like funneled lips of the earth's breath. But the fear of what he might discover there sat heavy in his chest, and it suffocated him.

Still, he reached Odepeth too soon. He slid from his wearied destrier and walked the steps of the temple with a growing anxiousness. He thought about the gift of the seer often, a blessing and a curse. He questioned himself—if he had the ability to go back and not see his fate, would he? For the agony that came with knowing how little time he had left was maddening, and it made a man maniacal and obsessive. Visions fueled wars; they grew anger like crops in fields of suspicion and haunted even the best of intention. Yet, knowing this, he couldn't keep himself from returning. He supposed that answered his question.

The guards bowed their heads as he passed. They were keepers of the seer. Some kingdoms had several seers; Kharav had one. One was enough in Mikael's opinion. He knew that seers didn't all see the same visions, and he had no desire to have another purveyor of obsession.

As usual, the seer greeted him in the center of the temple, surrounded by the intricately carved columns of stacked stone. "Salar." The old man bowed his head respectfully.

Mikael paused under the gravity of the moment. He would know today—he would see if there was a different future for him now. "I've come to see my fate," he said.

The seer gave a long breath of regret. "But I have shown you your fate."

The seer's words cut into his chest like a blade of battle, stopping his heart, taking his breath, and draining his life force.

"So, I've not changed my future?" he asked.

"You do not change fate, Salar."

"You don't know that," Mikael snapped. "Perhaps you don't see. I wed the North Queen! I broke her marriage to Aleon, yet when I last came, you told me nothing had changed." He shifted his tone to be softer, hoping, pleading. "Perhaps you don't see?"

"Nothing has changed, Salar."

Mikael let out a shaking breath. This was the strongest seer in the four kingdoms. As much as he hated to admit it, if there was a change to his fate, he was sure the old man would have seen it.

"There are other visions, though," the seer told him.

Other visions. These he had to see. "Show me."

The seer led him down the narrow hall to the back room that Mikael knew well, and the king took his place on a floor pillow in the center. Mikael waited as the old man gathered his things and sat on the floor across from him. The seer poured wine into a small bowl and pricked his finger with a gemmed dagger, letting the droplets of blood mix with the sweet juice of fermented fruit. Then he breathed the words of the blood spell and held the bowl out to the king. Mikael accepted it and drank.

As he swallowed the last of the wine, he waited for the seer to enter his mind. As all the times before, they sat in the temple of draperied shadows.

Mikael rose, standing in the temple of his mind, with visions all around him. The seer waved him to follow, and he did. They walked in the darkness, with no light on their path, and then stopped at a room hidden by a thick drapery. The seer pulled back the curtain, revealing a room so bright that Mikael squinted against the light.

They stepped into it, outside and into the center of a sprawling city. He didn't recognize it, with its large buildings of marble and glass and patina copper domes. But his eyes caught the flags that lined the center mainway, leading to a large, opulent citadel.

Blue flags with a golden lion. The flags of Aleon.

His heart beat faster as he looked down the mainway to figures approaching on horseback.

Salara. Smiling. Crowds gathered on either side of the mainway, throwing rose petals. His blood chilled. Beside her rode Soren. Why would she go to Aleon? Why would Soren? So willingly, like Aleon was a friend. He felt the delirium of suspicion returning, but he forced it down. There had to be a reason—a completely rational reason, he told himself—for them to travel so freely to his enemy and to be received so warmly.

"Is this all you've seen?" he asked.

The seer hesitated, but answered. "It is all you want to see."

Mikael knew this moment well—the moment where he could choose the path of peaceful ignorance or the path of haunting knowledge. But then he asked himself, had it ever been a choice?

"Show me," he told the seer. "Show me all of it."

Mikael turned and stalked the dark hallways, not waiting for the seer to lead him, but searching on his own. He wandered through the visions he had already seen, those that were already etched into his mind. He wasn't interested in those, but one caught his eye—the image of Salara's capture. It seemed like yesterday, yet so long ago. He paused at the room, remembering. He watched himself as he carried her, her unconscious body draped across his thighs as he rode his destrier through the night. He remembered how she'd felt—small and fragile, warm and soft. She'd smelled like fresh-hewn adda trees, intoxicatingly sweet. It had lingered on him even after she was no longer in his arms. The pull she'd had, even when he'd hated her...

And now, now that he didn't hate her, now that he loved her...

Mikael let out a long breath. He ached for her now. He cursed himself. He had so little time left with her, and instead of spending it near her, with her, inside her, he had ridden to the ends of the earth, away from her. He needed to go back. He needed to leave this madness and get back to her. Ignorance—he chose it now. He didn't want to see. He turned to leave. And then stopped.

Norah sat on her knees at the edge of a bed in her nightgown. She looked at him, but not *at* him. He wanted to reach out, to touch her, to pull her to him, but he knew she was only a vision.

Her hair glowed bright in the moonlight, like she was the moon herself. He looked around her. Mikael didn't know this place. Another castle, perhaps, but not one he'd seen before. A cloaked man stepped past him from behind. Mikael's pulse quickened as he watched Norah slip off the bed. She spoke words he couldn't hear.

"What is she saying?" he asked, but he already knew the seer couldn't tell him. There was no sound in a vision.

She didn't seem to fear him as she stepped closer. Too close. Mikael gripped the hilt of his sword, but there was nothing he could do.

Faster than he thought human, she snatched her dagger to the man's neck. Mikael panted a breath as pride rippled through him. His salara.

But the man didn't counter. He only reached up slowly, showing his empty hands, and pulled back the cloak of his hood. Mikael felt his breath leave his body, and the heat of rage hit him like a battle charge.

The Bear.

Kill him. But Mikael knew she would never.

She dropped her dagger to the floor. Her mouth formed unheard words as she hitched a step back. He'd give anything to know what she said.

Norah reached out and put her hand on the Bear's chest but made no move to push him away. Instead, she spread her fingers wide. Emotion filled her eyes as she looked up at him. Her gaze moved to his face, his lips. She trembled. Again, her mouth moved in silent words. The Bear stepped closer and brought his hand to her face.

Mikael gripped his sword tighter. If only he could strike that hand from its arm. But he could do nothing.

She leaned into his touch, only for a moment... before she surged forward and threw her arms around him. Mikael had seen her embrace the Bear before, but the way she clung to him—like she'd missed him, like she needed him. She held him like she couldn't let him go.

Mikael shook with fury. He couldn't stand to watch but he couldn't look away. At last they broke, and Salara stepped back.

Then the Bear brought his hand up to her cheek again. That hand—he would lose that hand. And just when Mikael thought that was the end, the Bear pulled her closer and dropped his head to kiss her.

And what was most gutting—she let him. He backed her toward the bed, their mouths still together, and he laid her onto the mattress.

Mikael pushed out a breath through his teeth. There was no containing his rage. In the room where she slept, in the night, the Bear would come to her. And she would take him.

The vision faded to dark, a small mercy, and they stood in the emptiness once again.

"When?" Mikael breathed to the seer, who stood behind him. "When does this happen?"

"When she is still young and beautiful."

Mikael was quiet for a moment, taking in all the seer had shown him. "Are there any more?" he asked.

"Not new."

Mikael opened his eyes, and he was in the daylit temple of Odepeth once more. He stood, forcing his breath to calm and trying to harden his heart. "The other visions of the Bear... of my fate?" he asked.

The seer drew his brows together in regret. "As it always is, and always will be. Unchanged."

So that was it. The Bear would take his head.

Still.

And his wife.

"Salar," the seer said. "Salara has asked that I send word if I receive another vision."

"You won't," he said, and the seer bowed his head. Then he left the way he had come.

Norah came down the stairs just as Mikael stepped inside the double doors of the castle. It was late, and she hadn't heard his arrival. Soren had told her he'd gone to the seer, and she was desperate for news.

"Husband," she said as she crossed the floor to him. She wanted to tell him about Adrian's son and that she'd received the good news that they expected the boy to survive. But she could see torment on his face, silencing any news. The weight in her stomach grew. "Are you well?" He didn't look well.

He didn't answer.

"What did the seer show you?" she asked.

He still didn't answer, and that scared her. It hadn't been good news. She forced out an even breath. He would need her. He would need her reassurance. They walked toward their chamber in silence. She tried to stretch the tension out of her neck as she walked, but she knew nothing could take that away.

Suddenly, he stopped, turning and looming over her. "Has the Bear come to you in the night?" he asked.

His question came unexpectedly. "What?"

"Have you taken him to your bed?"

Where was this coming from? "Of course not!"

"Then it's still to come."

She shook her head. "I wouldn't do that."

"I saw you," he seethed.

"Mikael," she breathed, "this is madness."

He grimaced as he reached up and ran his fingers along her cheek. Then in a startling move, he clasped the base of her jaw and forced her still to look at him. Not painfully, but with an unnecessary strength. "Have you kissed him since we've been wed?"

Norah's heart raced. She'd kissed Alexander in the Wild, but the memory had been taken from Mikael. He wouldn't understand the circumstance now. But the greater weight on her heart—she'd kissed Alexander in Mercia in the cave. Guilt riddled her, but she couldn't tell him. It would only add to his mania.

"No," she whispered.

Tears filled his eyes. "You lie to me," he breathed.

A sob rose in her throat. She couldn't speak.

His face twisted. "If he had been here, would you really not have chosen him for a child? He's who you want, yes?"

"Mikael, stop," she cried.

"And you'll go to Aleon. I saw it. Freely you'll go, under a marriage alliance, I'm sure. A rose petal welcome. Will the Aleon king be as tolerant a husband as I am, I wonder?" he seethed. "Will he protect your lover? Will he be patient, as I have been? Not make you choose?"

"Mikael, stop it!"

He pushed her back against the wall. "No longer. Now you must choose." He bared his teeth with a trembling fury, pulsing fear through her. "You want me to send men to the North? I'll send them." His eyes were dark and full of hate. "And they'll bring me back his head."

No. Norah clawed at his hand to release her, but he held her firm.

"I'm going to kill him, Salara. I'm going to kill the Bear."

CHAPTER FIFTY-TWO

Soren sat in his study with his arms crossed, leaning forward onto his desk. He stared at the parchments in front of him, unseeing. He should have been present for Mikael's return from the seer. He wanted to know what Salar had seen. But it was better, he figured, that he hadn't been there. Better to let Salara calm him, reassure him. Soren might be able to better mend Mikael's anger against him after.

Just then, Bhastian tore into his study, and Soren jerked his head.

"Lord Commander!" the guardsman called urgently. "Salara's gone!"

"What?" he said, rising.

"She took her mare directly from the field. By the time the men got to the stables for horses to follow, she was gone."

What had happened with Salar? But more concerning, Salara was gone. "She's alone?"

"We think Cohen followed her."

Rage rippled through him. "So a mute can follow after her, but not the Crest?"

"It's a failure, my lord," Bhastian admitted.

Soren forced out an exhale. "Where did she go?"

Bhastian shook his head. "We don't know, but the men said she was upset."

Soren cursed himself. He knew Mikael was troubled. Why had he let her meet him alone?

"Should I ready the horses?" Bhastian asked. "We could catch up to her before she even reaches the Canyonlands."

The Canyonlands? No. She wouldn't flee to the North. It would unravel everything she had fought so hard to keep together. Soren forced himself to think. Where would she go? Somewhere safe, somewhere she could get her mind back, figure things out—he knew a place. "Tell them to prepare my horse. I'll go alone, after I tell Salar."

Bhastian bowed and left to his charge.

Soren walked quickly to the royal chamber, where he found Mikael stripping off his armor. "What did you do to Salara?" he asked without greeting. "What did you say to her?"

Mikael glanced at him. "She stays in the sanctuary. That should answer your question enough."

"She's not in her sanctuary," he snapped angrily. "She's gone. Left the castle."

Mikael took a step back. The thought seemed to strike something deep within him—a fear, a sadness. "Then she goes to warn him," he said quietly.

"Who?" Soren asked.

"The Bear."

Soren's chest tightened. The last thing Kharav needed was the threat of war against yet another kingdom, especially the North. Why would he think she'd ride to warn the Bear? "What did you say to her?" he asked again.

Mikael didn't answer. He stripped off his breastplate. "She's chosen. And now she rides for the North."

"They would respond to their queen fleeing Kharav with certain war. They're waiting for a reason. She wouldn't do that."

"She would for him."

Soren didn't recognize this man before him—was he giving up? "I'm going after her," he said.

"You won't find her if she's on Savantahla."

"Cohen's with her."

"The mute?"

"He's not mute, he's deaf," Soren snapped.

Mikael's nostrils flared at the small defiance, and his anger shifted to Soren. "I didn't think that when I made you swear to her, you'd so easily turn on me." His words cut like knives.

"You question my loyalty to you?"

Mikael bared his teeth. "You stand with Salara while she accepts a treaty with Aleon."

"I don't stand against you," Soren argued. "She doesn't oppose you!"

"She opposes me now!" Mikael bellowed. "And she must choose! Me or the Bear, and that's how I know she rides for the North." His eyes blazed. "And now you must choose, brother. Perhaps I should be especially grateful you didn't seed her with your child. Then I might have none of your loyalty left."

Soren grabbed Mikael by the throat and shoved him against the wall. "If you speak those words again, I'll cut them from your mouth," he snarled. He glanced over his shoulder to make sure the door to the chamber was closed and Mikael hadn't been overheard. Then he tightened his grip and leaned close so that their foreheads were almost touching. "That's how you lose your salara and your kingdom. It's how you lose everything. Do you understand?"

Mikael's body slackened under Soren's grip. Soren had never seen him this way. He pulled Mikael to him in a tight embrace, as the king shuddered under the weight of his burdens.

"She rides for the North," Mikael said hoarsely. "I know it."

"She wouldn't betray you. Not even for the Bear. I'll find her, brother," Soren assured him, "and show you this is madness."

A heavy thunder of hooves rang through the night as Soren drove his destrier east. Salara had fled the castle on her mare of the Wild faster than her guard could follow, but he knew where he might find her. She wouldn't be headed to the North. She wouldn't betray Mikael. Not even in his madness. Not even for the Bear.

When he reached the hillside house, he wasn't surprised to see a second horse standing with Salara's mare in the night. Both were without saddles, having been taken in haste. Cohen *had* been able to follow her. He wasn't surprised. Cohen's abilities didn't surprise him anymore. He had put the boy and his sister to train with the Crest. If they were going to be around Salara, they would have the best training of the Kharavian army. He hadn't expected them to perform so well.

While they hadn't picked up all the skills of a well-rounded soldier of the Crest, they both excelled in their specialty—the girl with her bow and the boy with his sword. Cohen was perhaps even better than Adrian, who Soren considered one of the best. He only cursed the boy being deaf. His disability created too much risk—too much weakness—to put him in the ranks of the Crest. But it was moments like this Soren questioned that decision.

He pushed the door of the hillside house open and stepped inside, where he was quickly greeted by the tip of a sword to his neck. He couldn't help a wry smile as he turned his head to find the raven-haired boy with his arm outstretched, the blade like an extension of his hand. What pleased Soren most was that he had no doubt the boy could kill him.

He pulled down the wrap from his face so Cohen could read his words. "Salara can shake the Crest, but not you?" he said. "I'm impressed, boy, as usual. Where is she?"

"What do you want?" she answered as she stepped into the foyer in front of him. She nodded to the boy, and he lowered his sword. "He sent you?" she asked, looking back to Soren.

He shook his head. "No. But he knows I've come."

Her face hardened. She looked ready for a fight. "So, you've come to drag me back?" she asked, her voice sharp and challenging.

Soren eyed her for a moment. He wouldn't dare. "You forget I serve *you*."

That seemed to pacify her, and she turned and stepped into the side sitting room. He followed. She took a seat in the chair by the fire, where it appeared she'd been sitting before he'd arrived, and she picked up a mug of steaming tea from the small side table.

"Salar thinks you've ridden for the North," he told her.

She took a drink of her tea.

He let out a breath as he sank into the chair on the opposite side of the fireplace. "This isn't him, Salara. This man isn't him."

"I can't live like this, Soren."

A pit seeded itself in his stomach. "Are you thinking of leaving?"

She took another drink of tea from her cup. Her silence worried him.

"Have you ever wondered what it would be like to live a life in a place where no one knew your name?" she asked finally. "Where no one wanted anything from you. No expectations, no burdens. Where you could simply love and be loved."

"No," he said. He had never wanted any other life than the one he had now.

She smiled sadly. "I envy you," she whispered.

"Are you going back to the North?" he pressed.

She stared into the flames of the fire.

The pit in his stomach grew. She couldn't leave. She couldn't go back to the North. It would destroy Mikael.

But she shook her head. "No, but I think I'll stay here awhile."

He let out a long breath. That, perhaps, was a wise idea. The hillside house was quiet, and safe. And it was not the North.

"Will you tell Mikael?" she asked.

He nodded.

"And have my maids come tomorrow? I'd like some company." She bit her bottom lip, thinking. "No guards."

"Salara," he objected. "I can't leave you in a house alone in the countryside, even if it is a safe house."

"I have Cohen."

That was true, and the boy was as good as two or three soldiers. But that still wasn't enough. "Let me send Adrian and the girl."

She pursed her lips together. "Fine."

"And Bhastian," he added.

"No one else."

"Kiran?"

"I don't need a whole army," she argued.

He snorted. "They're hardly the whole army."

"I'll think about it," she said as she stood and turned toward the hall. "But for now, I'll get some rest." She looked back at him. "Are you staying through the night?"

He shook his head. He didn't like the idea of leaving her alone, but he had to return to Mikael as soon as possible, and Cohen would keep her safe until he sent others. "No, I have to return to Salar tonight."

"By the time you get back, it will be morning."

"Already too long."

She pursed her lips. "Don't send an army."

"No army," he assured her. An army was thousands of men. He wouldn't send thousands.

CHAPTER FIFTY-THREE

Mikael stood, leaning his weight over the desk in his study. He gripped the edges until he could no longer feel his fingers. Spread in front of him were the letters from his scouts, warning him Cyrus was moving his forces across Japheth. Gregor had found his new ally, and war was on the horizon.

His eyes were fixed forward, but unfocused. Sleep had escaped him through the night. He felt the darkness of madness taking him, closing in over his head. He could smell it as it filled his lungs, taste it in his throat as it drowned him. But he couldn't stop it.

He was losing everything—his alliance, his power, his mind. It was only a matter of time before he lost his kingdom.

And he was losing *her*. Salara. It was his own doing. He felt himself pushing her away. He could hear it as he raged, but he couldn't stop.

And then there was the Bear. Mikael knew he wouldn't kill him. He wanted to, more than anything. Not because the Bear would bring his end, but because the justice held a piece of Salara's heart—enough of it to pull her back to the North to save him. And now Mikael would know what he feared the most—she loved the Bear more.

Soren had said she wouldn't go to the North. He believed that once, but not anymore. She'd have to still love him to stay, and he'd destroyed that love, he was certain. Perhaps it was best. She'd be safe in the North. With Gregor and Cyrus now more than just a threat, he didn't want her in Kharav.

The door opened, and he turned to see Soren enter, alone. He swallowed. That was his answer, then. Slowly, he looked back at his desk.

"You were wrong, brother," Soren said.

Mikael snapped his head back to him. Wrong? He couldn't mean...

"She didn't ride for the North."

His chest seized. She had stayed? "Where is she?" His voice broke as he spoke.

"The hillside house. She just needed some time."

The hillside house. So near, yet so far. He needed to see her. "Should I go to her?"

"I've only committed that I wouldn't send the army."

Mikael let out a breath of relief. Would she see him, though?

"You can get her to come back," Soren told him, as if reading his mind, "but you can't be as you were—thinking crazed things, spewing madness."

"I know. The seer—"

"I'm going to kill that fucking seer. Go to her. She loves you."

He nodded.

Soren bobbed his head toward the door. "Go," he pressed angrily.

Mikael reached out, clasped the nape of Soren's neck, and brought their foreheads together. He didn't deserve this man.

Then he turned and stepped into the sunlit hall to go get his salara.

The afternoon sun waned, fading under gray skies of rain before it dipped below the horizon. Norah looked out the windows over the mountains. She expected Soren to return soon with a full legion, completely ignoring her insistence for no army. It was unfortunate, as they wouldn't all fit in the house and they'd be unable to make a camp to keep them from the rain. Perhaps she should just go back. It would be selfish to keep them all here, just so she could be away from the castle—away from Mikael and his delusions. She had her sanctuary, and if she was honest with herself, it was a bit dramatic that she'd insisted on being completely away.

She'd go back.

Norah pulled her cloak from the hook on the wall and stepped toward the door. She should be able to make it back before nightfall, although she'd have to travel in the rain. She didn't mind. Water never bothered her. She had to find Cohen; he wouldn't be far. He'd spent his time constantly scouting the area around the house. But when she opened the door, it wasn't Cohen looking back at her.

Her breath caught as Mikael's dark eyes stared into hers. He stood, wet, in front of her. She glanced around him; he was alone. Not even Soren had come with him. Her heart beat heavier in her chest. Had he come to drag her back himself? Was he still angry?

He didn't look angry.

"Salara," he said softly, finally breaking the silence. He didn't sound angry.

She couldn't leave him standing there. Norah stepped backward and opened the door wider, inviting him in, and he followed. He shut the door behind him, then stood silently.

"I didn't expect you," she said.

"Are you upset I've come?"

She shook her head slowly. She'd never be upset about him coming to her.

He breathed out, as if relieved. "Would you be upset if I stayed?" he asked.

How quickly he could make her forgive him. She shook her head again.

He stepped nearer and slowly reached out his hand to take hers. Despite him being drenched by the rain, his skin was warm, and it felt good. She let him pull her closer to him.

"I'm sorry, Salara," he breathed. His nearness made the world fall away. He pulled her even closer. "Would you be upset if I kissed you?" he asked.

She would be upset if he didn't. She lifted her chin to him.

His kiss wasn't the hungry force it usually was. He kissed her softly, as if unsure—asking, searching, seeking her forgiveness.

And she gave it to him. She sought forgiveness herself. He wasn't the only one among them with fault.

"You were right to be angry," she said as she broke from their kiss. "I'm sorry I lied. Two times I've kissed Alexander, and both bring deep regret. It's not something I want to talk about, but I will if you ask me. And yes, I didn't want you to read Phillip's letter. His tone toward me is not one you'd take kindly to, and it worried me. But I'll recite it word for word; the worry has burned it into my mind. I just... I don't want secrets between us. And I want to rid you of this doubt."

Norah reached up and ran her fingertips through the short crop of his beard. "And I want you to let me in. I want you to tell me what worries you." She pulled his lips back to hers. "Will you talk to me?" she whispered, then kissed him softly with her own plea for forgiveness.

She pulled back and looked up at the darkness of his eyes. Slowly, he nodded. She dropped her cloak on a chair by the door.

"Come, then," she said, taking his hand and leading him to the bedchamber. Inside, she turned to him. She pulled his wet cloak from his shoulders. He stood as she took her time draping it over a chair and turning her attention back to him. He was soaked through, and needed dry clothing.

"What did the seer show you?" she asked as she pulled his shirt out from his breeches, one side and then the other.

"I've failed," he said. "I've failed to change my fate."

She swallowed as she drew his shirt up. He bowed his head and lifted his arms, letting her take it from him.

Norah dropped down, pulling at the heel of his boot, and he let her take them, the left and then right. She rose again, and their gazes locked as she pulled loose the ties of his breeches. "How does the seer know?"

"Because fate can't be changed. But I already knew this."

She pulled down his breeches, then stooped as he stepped out of them. "Then why did you go?" Rising back up, she met his eyes again.

"It's the curse of the seer—to draw a man into obsession."

Norah stepped to the armoire and pulled out a clean linen tunic and breeches. "What else did you see?" she asked as she moved back to him. She knew he'd seen Alexander. He'd already told her so.

He hesitated. "I saw the Bear." His eyes were filled with sorrow. "He came to your bed in the night, and you took him."

She said nothing but cursed the seers in the depths of her soul. She cursed the visions. They did nothing but cause pain, and for what? She unfolded the clean breeches, and he took them and stepped into them. He drew them up, around his waist, and she pulled tight the ties, slowly looping them closed.

"Many things are not as they seem in these visions," she said finally. "You know this."

"Some things aren't. Yet some things are exactly as they seem."

She shook out the folded tunic and raised it, and he complied, bowing his head for her to put it on him. She swallowed again. "I don't know how else to show you that I choose you," she whispered. "That I love you and that I'm beside you. I would never betray you."

She spread her hand over the fabric of the tunic against his chest. His warmth permeated through it.

He reached up and put his hand over hers. "I know." He brought her chin up so that their gaze met again. "I know you choose me, Salara."

She gave him a small smile through the wave of emotion. That was what she desperately needed to hear. She did choose him, and she needed him to know it, to feel it, to believe it.

"While I'm still here, you choose me," he added. "But it's not betrayal when I'm gone. And this has made me realize I must help you prepare."

A sickening fear seeded in her stomach, vining up into her heart. "For what?" she breathed.

He brought up his other hand and brushed her cheek. "To rule without me."

"No." She shook her head, denial rippling through her. "Don't say that."

"I have to. You have to be ready."

"No!" She tried to pull her hand away from under his, but he held it.

"Salara," he said as she fought against him.

"I won't hear it!" Talk of defeat meant he accepted his fate, but she didn't. She fought harder.

He gripped her sternly. "Norah, stop!"

Her struggles weakened.

"You'll listen to me," he said, softer now. "When I'm gone, you need the alliance with Aleon. You'll take his offer of marriage. Then, with Soren and the Bear beside you, and the power of the empire, no one can stand against you."

She would never do that. "Stop!"

"I'll stop when you acknowledge it. I *will* die, Salara. And soon."

She shook her head again, and a cry escaped her.

"You'll have Soren and the Bear by your side, regardless of what happens to Kharav. They bring with them the loyalty of both our armies, and I know they'll do whatever's necessary to keep you safe. As I must do. It's why I'm sending you back to the North."

Norah's mouth dropped open, and she pulled back again. "What?"

"Cyrus grows a vast army, which he's already moved into Japheth. If it's Gregor's intention to march against me, which I'm certain it is, I don't want you here."

He couldn't possibly be sending her away. Her place was by his side. "I can't leave you!"

He brushed her cheek again. "Salara, you have to go. Go to the North, where you're protected. And if I should fall, you won't be alone. You'll have the Bear. And Aleon will stand beside you."

He was right in that Phillip would be hesitant to come to her aid in Kharav, but he would readily join her in Mercia to march against anyone who opposed her, especially if the opposition was Japheth. But she would never wed the king of Aleon. And she wouldn't leave Mikael. She hadn't weathered this madness only to lose him again.

"I'm not leaving you," she insisted.

"Salara, you have more power in the North. You'll be able to help me more there."

Yes, she would have more power in person than trying to influence her council from afar, but that wasn't enough to pull her from him. "We'll get through this. I'll stay, and we'll get through this. You don't even know these things will actually happen."

"And if they don't, you'll come home. And everything will be as it was. But I can't manage this and fear for you at the same time."

"You don't need to fear—"

"I'm breaking!"

She stilled as he gripped her.

"I'm breaking," he whispered. "And I know I have your love. I know that now. I know you choose me. But it's not enough—I need to know you're safe. Go to the North. Let me focus on Gregor and Cyrus. Will you do this?"

She couldn't answer.

"Salara, please. Help me." He cupped her face in his hands, begging. "Salara. Please."

Norah drew in a ragged breath, and she nodded, relenting.

He pulled her close to him, then drew her face up to look at him again. His eyes glistened. "I need you," he whispered.

The sudden need to escape their clothes overtook them. Fabric tore as Mikael shucked his newly donned tunic and breeches, and Norah clawed off her dress, but neither of them cared.

They didn't come together in a sudden heat. It wasn't a wanton need. It was the need of touch, of the warmth of skin against skin. Mikael carried her to the bed and lowered himself to bury his face in the corner of her neck and breathe in her being. He simply held her. Tightly. And she held him, clinging to him like life, scared she might not be able to again.

CHAPTER FIFTY-FOUR

Calla's face wore a firm frown. She wasn't one to hide her feelings. Norah knew she wanted to come to Mercia, and so did Cohen, although he was much more discreet with his disappointment. And Norah had wanted to bring them, but they would remain at the castle with their grandparents, who had finally come, at Norah's insistence, until threats against Kharav had passed. Norah needed them all safe.

The Crest stood in the courtyard, all of them ready and prepared to depart. Mikael would keep none of the warriors for himself or the castle, despite Norah's insistence. And, of course, Soren would go with her, as would Adrian. Norah had wanted Adrian to stay with his son and Sevina, but Mikael was firm. He even sent the dogs.

"You send too much," she told him as he placed a gentle kiss on her head. "You'll at least need the commander of your armies."

He feigned offense. "You think I don't know how to command an army?"

But she wasn't in the mind for jokes. Emotion overwhelmed her.

His face grew more serious when he saw it. "I need him to protect what's most important to me," he said.

Norah reached up and clasped the side of his face. "And who will protect what's important to me?" she said through her tears.

He pulled her hand to his lips and kissed her palm. "We've both seen my end, and it's not here. You don't need to fear for me."

"I still do." She stood up on her toes and kissed him. Then she climbed atop Sephir under the warm rays of the sun.

"Keep her well," he said to Soren as the commander mounted his destrier.

Soren nodded his oath.

Norah looked back at Mikael as they rode out of the courtyard. She felt like she would fall apart in the wind, like this was the last time she would see him. What if it was the last time?

The journey to Mercia was longer than she remembered. They traveled slower with so many men. The time was agonizing.

They passed through the Uru. Norah tried to enjoy her visit with Tahla, but all she could think about was Mikael. So many times she almost turned back. It wasn't too late, she told herself. She was so afraid—afraid she wouldn't see him again, afraid she wouldn't hold him again. She desperately wanted to run back to him, but she knew Soren wouldn't let her.

She tried to focus her mind on something else.

Adrian traveled silently, which was unlike him. He had started their journey with excitement at returning home again, but as they drew nearer to Mercia, he became quieter, worried even.

"Are you all right?" she asked him one evening after they had set camp.

He gave a stiff nod. They sat under the stars, and he rubbed the marking on his forearm. "He's going to be upset with me," he said quietly. He was worried about Alexander's reaction to the ink on his skin. It would be a challenging conversation, no doubt.

"Wait for the right time," she said. "Then explain it to him, privately. You just need to help him understand."

He nodded again, but her words obviously did little to allay his fears.

"He loves you, Adrian, and he'll be proud of you. He just needs you to talk to him."

Her own heart broke for him, but she knew the brothers loved each other deeply, and she was glad they would be together again. Alexander would be surprised when he saw him. Adrian didn't look like the same man that had come to Kharav. He was even taller now, broad shouldered, and cloaked in strength. He had the hardened look of a warrior. It was easy to forget he was so young. He'd taken on the lord commander's solemn countenance. Or perhaps it was Alexander's, she mused.

Adrian had become close friends with Cohen, she noticed. The two were inseparable, often exchanging silent words between them. Norah had worried about them both, that they might find life in Ashan difficult. But they seemed to thrive with every challenge, every trial—to relish them even. And with their resilience came the respect of the earlies and even the lord commander, although he didn't show it.

Calla had proven herself as well. Norah loved to watch her on the sparring field. While proficient in combat, the girl was quick-witted and clever and made up in intellect for what she lacked in physical strength. And she was a master with a bow. Norah was excited to one day take her to Mercia—home to the greatest bowmen in the world—to hone her skill even more.

Finally, after almost three weeks of travel, Mercia came into view, white and radiant in the light of the sun. Its towered turrets and spires rose high against the sky, adorned with arched clerestories and elegant tracery. It really was beautiful. But seeing her kingdom brought a deep and growing angst within Norah. With the news of Japheth breaking from Kharav, everyone would be looking to see what she would do now. Her grandmother, the council, Alexander—they would be waiting, watching, judging how she would handle Japheth and Rael, if she would drive Mercia to support a king they didn't even recognize as king. And she worried about how she would manage them, because that's exactly what she planned to do.

Norah looked at Adrian as they drew nearer. "Are you ready?"

He smiled, but she could see his anxiousness underneath.

She shifted her gaze to Soren. "Behave yourself," she told him. Then she eyed the dogs that trotted alongside the horses. "And don't let them eat the cat."

They crossed the bridge, then continued through the gates and into the courtyard of the castle. Norah saw Catherine waiting for her by the fountain, and a smile came to her lips. She had missed her grandmother. She had last parted Mercia with a rift between them, a rift she hoped had been forgiven.

Had she been forgiven?

Norah slid down from Sephir and paused just before she reached Catherine. She couldn't read her grandmother's expression, and angst twisted in her stomach.

But Catherine's eyes welled, and she smiled, then she stepped forward and hugged Norah tightly. "Welcome home, child," she said through her tears. She pulled back. "Oh, let me look at you." Her eyes were misted in happiness, her lips pursed to hold them from trembling. "I'm so glad you're home."

But this wasn't home. Still, Norah smiled as she stepped back, until another caught her eyes, and her smile fell.

Alexander. Her heart quickened in her chest. To see him again brought a heartache she'd thought long gone.

He approached with a gentle smile. "Queen Norah," he said softly.

"Lord Justice."

His eyes burned a brilliant blue, eyes that still held her.

"Lord Justice," came Adrian's voice from behind her. He grinned as he stepped forward and bowed his head.

"Brother," Alexander said in surprise. He let out a hearty laugh as he reached out and clasped his shoulder, then pulled him into an embrace. His face filled with emotion. They were the same height, but Adrian was larger now. Alexander still held him close, his hand on the back of his head as he embraced him, like he would a small boy. Pushing Adrian back slightly to look at him, Alexander scoffed, "What are you eating? And what have you done with your hair?"

Norah shifted. The Northmen kept their hair cut short, one of the many things they did differently than those in Kharav—as Alexander would surely find out.

"I'm letting it grow," Adrian replied with a grin.

Alexander's brow creased. "Why?"

Adrian shrugged. "Because I like the way it looks."

"His training is coming along well," Norah interrupted. "I know he's excited to tell you about it."

"I've earned my sword entitlement. And a blade," Adrian grinned, pulling the sword from his scabbard and holding it for his brother.

"It's a high achievement," Soren spoke out, surprising everyone around them. "One of the highest in the Kharavian army."

Catherine gaped at the lord commander and then looked back at Alexander.

Alexander stiffened at Soren speaking for his brother, but his pride was evident, and he gave a nod to Adrian. "Well done, brother."

Adrian let out an excited breath.

But then Alexander paused. "What's that?" he asked, his eyes on Adrian's forearm peeking out from under his sleeve.

Adrian glanced at Norah, and she gave a small shake of her head. But it wasn't unnoticed. Alexander grabbed Adrian's arm.

"Alec," Adrian pleaded as Alexander pushed back his sleeve to reveal the patterned black ink.

"You marked your skin?" Alexander asked, pained.

"By the gods," Catherine breathed.

Norah blinked slowly as a murmur rippled through the people around them.

"I told you, I earned my entitlement," Adrian said quickly.

"You're Mercian." Alexander's voice was low but tinged with anger. "We don't mark our skin."

"Alexander," Norah said quietly, trying to calm him.

"Did you know about this?" Catherine asked her.

Norah eyed her sharply. Her grandmother wasn't helping. She turned back to Alexander. "We'll discuss this privately."

"How could you allow him?" he said angrily. He turned to Soren. "This was you. This was your influence," he seethed.

"That marking is one of honor," Soren cut back. "Men die trying to achieve it. And he's not a boy; he can make his own choices."

Alexander's rage pushed him forward, but Norah stepped in front of him. "That's enough," she told him. "Walk with me. Alone." She needed to get him away, right now.

Alexander's eyes burned with anger, but she knew he would follow. Norah headed for the library. She felt Alexander's wrath behind her, but she didn't dare turn before they were away from prying ears, for fear of an argument. Once inside the library, she turned to face him.

"How could you allow this?" he seethed. "My own brother?"

Norah let out a long breath. "I wasn't aware until after."

"And you didn't want him to tell me?"

This was exactly what she had feared. "I wanted him to wait for a more opportune time, a more private time. It wasn't fair to you to find out that way."

His voice came sharp. "You should have written me."

She shook her head. "That's not the kind of thing I'd write to you about." She sighed. "Don't be angry at him."

Alexander's eyes stared right through her. "He would have known it was against Mercian custom and how I would feel about it, and he still did it."

"No," she argued. She couldn't let him think that. "He got carried away in the excitement. No other Northman, and very few Kharavian men, have accomplished what he has. It wasn't until he saw my reaction afterward that he thought of what it would mean when he came home, what it would mean to you." She let out a saddened breath. "The whole journey, he's been consumed with the fear of your disappointment. I'm surprised he didn't flay the skin from his arm to be rid of it."

Alexander sank onto a bench along the hallway of stone and glass. She could see it pained him to hear that, and she sat down beside him. "All he wants is for you to be proud of him." She could tell he was listening to her words, and she let him sit for a moment and soak them in. "He drew the lord commander's ire, showing off what you had taught him."

Alexander let out a faint snort.

"It made Soren hard on him. Perhaps too hard. There were days I feared for him. But he was strong, determined. Relentless." She smiled, remembering. "And then he began to rise." She paused. "Alexander, I wish you could have been there. I wish you could have seen him. There must have been a hundred soldiers beating their swords on their shields, calling for his entitlement. They were cheering him, they were *all* cheering him. He's respected by those who were once enemies. He's finding his way in two opposite worlds where most struggle in one. You should be proud, incredibly proud."

He was quiet for a long time. Then he said, "I am proud."

She put her hand on his arm. "Then let him embrace all that Kharav offers him. Think of what he can accomplish between our two kingdoms."

His blue eyes stared up at her, piercing. "When did you become so wise?" he asked.

She smiled.

He gave a small sigh. "I suppose you're also going to tell me to leave him alone about his hair."

"I think it looks good on him. You might want to consider it yourself."

He snorted.

"You should go talk to him," she urged.

"I will."

Norah stood to leave.

"Norah," he said, stopping her. "I don't ever want him to be anxious about returning home."

"Then you should tell him that."

Alexander found Adrian in his chamber, settling back in. His brother turned in surprise when he knocked on the doorframe.

"You didn't bring your son?" Alexander asked.

"Sevina wants to wait until he's a little older, and when we aren't on the brink of war."

Alexander could understand that, although he would've liked to have seen the child. It was hard to imagine Adrian, who was still so young himself, with a son. Alexander had been upset by the news of Adrian marrying a Kharavian woman, extremely upset. But not of the news of the child. Far from it, all he felt was... joy.

"How is the child?" he asked.

Adrian grinned, nodding. "He's good. Strong. Fat."

Alexander chuckled. Adrian had been a fat baby. "How is your wife?"

Adrian's eyes lit up at the mention of her.

"She's well. You'd like her. She's smart and thoughtful. She cares for me a great deal." His grin grew wider. "She tells me not to do stupid things. Sometimes I hear you in her voice."

"Does it keep you from doing them?"

Adrian shook his head with a smiling frown. "No."

He laughed.

Adrian's face grew serious. "I know you're disappointed."

Alexander let out a long breath. "I had thought that you would hold our customs, hold our values. I'm disappointed you marked your skin."

Adrian nodded, his eyes falling to the floor.

"But I'm also proud," Alexander continued.

Adrian's head jerked up in surprise.

"You're the son of Beurnat the Bear, and you have the respect of the Destroyer and the army of the Shadowlands. You bring our kingdoms together. I'm proud that you're my brother." Adrian's lip trembled, and Alexander clasped the side of his neck affectionately. "Now get your sword. I want to see what you've learned."

Adrian nodded, smiling through his tears.

Norah knocked lightly on Adrian's chamber door. After the reunion with Alexander, she wanted to make sure he was all right.

She heard a small shuffle, but there was no reply. She knocked again.

"Not now, please," he called.

"Adrian?" she replied. "It's Norah."

More shuffling came, then the latch released and the door opened slowly, revealing Adrian with a half-cut head of hair.

"Norah," he greeted her as she gaped at him in surprise.

"What... what happened to your head?" she asked.

He smiled sheepishly. "You've caught me in the middle of cutting my hair."

She shook her head in confusion. "Why? I thought you were letting it grow long?"

He shrugged. "I was, but..." His words trailed off.

She sighed. The conversation with Alexander must have gone poorly, and by the looks of it—very poorly.

He opened the door wider, inviting her in, and she winced at his handiwork as she got a better look at his head.

"Thank you," he said, surprising her further. "I know you talked to him. He found me after, and he was... different. Understanding."

"Then why are you cutting your hair?"

Adrian inhaled deeply. "I'll continue to get ink markings if I earn them. It's who I am now." He paused for a moment. "But my hair, it means nothing to me. It means something to him, though, so I'll cut it to show that he's still in my heart and what's important to him is important to me."

Norah smiled through the emotion that had so suddenly overtaken her. "You're a good brother, Adrian."

He smiled bashfully.

"Would you like some help?" she asked.

"Very much so." He sighed in relief, and she laughed as he handed her the shears.

CHAPTER FIFTY-FIVE

Time passed quickly in Mercia, more quickly than Norah thought it would. While the nights were long without Mikael beside her, the days were filled with challenges that kept her on her toes.

The first thing she'd done when she reached Mercia was redirect steel-good shipments to Kharav, much to the council's dismay. They had somewhat valid arguments: promised shipments to trade partners, low inventories, slow mining times. But promises to Kharav were most important—Mikael came first.

Getting settled into Mercia's affairs proved more difficult than she'd expected. She was surprised at how much the council had so freely taken upon themselves to adjudicate things—things well within her authority, within Catherine's authority as regent in her absence. She tried not to jump to judgment. She'd been away in Kharav for quite some time, and Mercia needed strong leadership.

The attacks on the villages in the outer reaches had mostly stopped, thanks to the coverage the Aleon legions provided. Norah was thankful. Phillip wrote to her often, mostly with updates for Alexander and her forces, for which she was also thankful.

The days came easier as she gained her footing, but she still fought the unease of returning to the North. She did love Mercia. It just wasn't her home anymore.

Norah walked briskly to the judisaept, with Cusco and Cavaatsa trailing behind. She took the dogs everywhere, even to address state matters, under the council's disapproving eye. But they said nothing. She dared them to.

Another letter had come from Phillip. She hoped it brought news of his plans to advance on Japheth. He'd been moving his forces to the southern border of Eilor and stretching them across to Bahoul.

Mikael had sent the Kharavian forces northeast to the Canyonlands, heavily manning the eastern pass, and was doubling armies at Kharav's only two seaports. She worried for him. Not because she thought Kharav was unsafe but because he was alone. And she loved him.

Norah stepped into the judisaept. As usual, the council had already arrived and was waiting. Did they ever leave? Sometimes she thought they slept there.

Soren took his usual place beside her, resting his axe between his feet. Catherine had urged her to keep him from bringing weapons, but Norah would save her arguments with Soren for things that really mattered.

Alexander handed her the sealed letter and then took his place at the opposite head of the table. She broke the wax and opened it.

"Queen Norah," she read Phillip's words aloud. "I trust you remain well and safe in Mercia. I write with urgency, for I've discovered the army of Rael is larger than we understood before. Much larger, in fact…"

She couldn't speak the words anymore, she only read. Her heart hammered in her chest. She handed the letter to Soren, who read it over.

"What does it say?" Edward asked.

"Aleon's not going to march on Japheth," she said breathlessly.

Soren tossed the letter onto the table for Alexander, who picked it up.

"So, a delay in war," Councilman Alastair said. "That's not necessarily a bad thing."

Norah snapped her head up with fire on her lips. "It most certainly is a bad thing. Mikael needs Aleon to attack, before Gregor acts against Kharav. It's what we were counting on."

The letter passed around the council, each member reading its news.

"The largest army they've ever seen," Councilman Henricus read with a frown. "Even larger than Aleon's."

"That's not possible," Edward scoffed.

"The Aleon king admits it with his own pen," Soren said with a slight snarl, his patience clearly gone. "It should come as no surprise. Cyrus's army has the freed slaves of Serra. Now others flock to him, fleeing their own kingdoms to join him."

"Slaves are not warriors," Alastair countered.

"What about the thousands used as blood sport fighters?" Soren snapped back. "Each one would kill ten of your Northmen."

Norah swallowed the bile building in her throat. "Kharav needs us," she said. "We'll send more Mercian steel—swords, shields, polearms."

"This will take time," Edward argued.

"Then send the mined iron. We'll build a Mercian forge in Kharav, with smiths."

"Queen Norah," he gasped. "You cannot give the Shadowlands the ability to forge Mercian steel. They could dilute our trade value in the market, forge weapons against us."

"They *are* us!" she snapped. "I am queen of Mercia *and* Kharav, and I'll use all means to protect both. And no more talk of delay. If it's not ready, I'll have every man mining until it is, including everyone in this room."

Her councilmen stiffened but offered no further argument.

"We need more to show Japheth that Mikael's not alone." She looked at Alexander. "We'll send an army of five thousand."

"You cannot send our forces when we battle unknown attacks on our own lands," Henricus argued.

But Norah ignored him. Still looking at Alexander, she said, "The lord justice will take the legion himself. I want Gregor to know how serious I am."

Edward gaped at his fellow councilmen around the room. "Queen Norah, you cannot send our forces *and* our justice to fight the Shadowland's war!"

"It's *our* war!" she said angrily. She looked back at Alexander. "We still have Phillip's ten thousand men?"

He nodded.

"Take five thousand of them as well," she added.

"If Rael's army is larger than Aleon's, ten thousand men won't matter," James said, finally speaking.

"I'm not trying to match their number," she countered. "But if we show that Mercia and Aleon stand with Kharav, it makes for a strong deterrence."

"And how do you know Phillip will agree to sending his men to aid the Shadow King?" Edward questioned.

"I'll write to him and ask," she replied.

Henricus snorted. "After you've already sent his army?"

"I only return the favor," she said shortly.

Crossing into the Shadowlands brought a rare air of excitement, a much different feel than the loathing that normally pulsed through Alexander as he made his way through the lands of his enemy. Perhaps it was because the Shadowlands were starting to feel less like the enemy. They were now home to his infant nephew, whom he would soon meet for the first time.

Adrian's face carried a broad grin, as it had ever since they'd passed through the Canyonlands. Alexander couldn't help a smile of his own. He'd been angry before—angry that Adrian had been so excited to leave Mercia, like he no longer belonged to his own kingdom. But as Alexander let his brother take the lead in driving the legions south, he could only watch with pride.

Adrian moved between the ranks with confidence and command. He checked on the forge equipment often, their precious cargo, knowing it was even more important than the ten thousand men they brought. He moved them along at a fast pace, but not too fast to exhaust them. Mercia, Aleon—it didn't matter—the men listened to him, respected him. All of them, even the Crest guards that Norah had sent with them.

While Adrian's charismatic grin could make any heart feel light, Alexander realized he was no longer a boy. He was a gentle soul, yes, full of fun and adventure. But he was also a natural leader, skilled in all the ways Alexander had taught him. And although Alexander loathed to admit it, Adrian was made even stronger by his time with the Destroyer.

Adrian exceeded what either kingdom alone could have made him, and he belonged to so much more than just Mercia—he was destined for even greater things beyond.

"What?" Adrian said, pulling him from his thoughts.

Alexander hadn't realized he'd been staring at him. He shook his head. "Nothing."

They marched through the capital city, rounding the legions toward the soldiers' barracks and into the provisioned overflow housing. After turning command over to the field captains to settle the army, Alexander and Adrian broke away to the courtyard, where Alexander knew the Shadow King would be waiting. He'd seen him on the wall.

His core didn't roil as it usually did on the way to the king, perhaps because his hatred for him had died somewhere along the way. Alexander wasn't sure when. Perhaps it was when he realized how Adrian had grown in the Shadowlands. Or maybe it was well before the journey, when the king had sent Norah to the safety of Mercia. He could have kept her, forcing Mercia and Aleon to his side to help him stand against the threat of Japheth and Rael. But he didn't.

Alexander still didn't like him, but he no longer hated him.

They entered the courtyard, where the Shadow King now stood, and brought their horses to a halt. Alexander slid down from his mount and gave a stiff bow of his head.

"You bring forces of Aleon to aid me?" the king asked, his voice laced with disbelief.

"They were given to the queen," Alexander said, "and she gives them to you."

"They will follow Kharavian command?"

Hardly. "They'll follow Mercian command. I also bring forge equipment, with smiths. We'll teach you how to work Mercian steel. If you can do the ironmaking and casting here, it will quicken the time it takes for us to get it to you."

The king shifted in surprise. He hadn't expected that either. This man didn't know how fortunate he was.

"She sends you everything she can," Alexander told him.

"Including you."

Alexander stilled. Was he rubbing it in? His blood heated under his skin.

"I'm grateful," the king said. "I know she wouldn't take sending you lightly."

Alexander eased.

The king pushed his gaze to Adrian. "The lord commander remains with her?"

Adrian bowed his head and pulled a letter from his jacket. "He does. And he sends this for you."

The Destroyer had entrusted Adrian with a letter to the king? Adrian had said nothing of it.

The Shadow King took it but didn't open it. His eyes met Alexander's again. "I need you to return to her."

Alexander straightened. He'd half expected the Shadow King to cast him from the Shadowlands, and he imagined it in all forms—ordering him to leave, driving him out, or even just killing him. But never had he imagined the king would tell him to *return* to her.

"You'll depart tomorrow."

Tomorrow? *Tomorrow?* "She sent me with two armies to aid you. I can't just leave."

"You can and you will."

Alexander stumbled over his words, caught between astonishment and disbelief. "You *need* me. There are ten thousand men who await my orders." Was he really arguing with the Shadow King to stay in the Shadowlands?

"Take them back with you."

Alexander snorted. Was this man mad? He needed all the help he could get.

The Shadow King stepped closer. "You and the lord commander are the only ones I trust with her safety. You have to return to her."

Alexander stilled, sobering. This king would deny himself aid to keep Norah safe. He'd send the man he hated most in the world safely home, to protect the woman they both loved. Alexander glanced down, gathering his thoughts. Norah expected him to keep this man safe too. "I'll go then. But I'll leave my brother in my stead."

From the corner of his eye, he saw Adrian's head jerk toward him in surprise. But this was what Adrian had prepared for his whole life—to serve, to lead. And the men would follow him.

The Shadow King nodded. "Depart before dawn." The king glanced at Adrian and gave him a small nod, then he turned and strode into the castle.

Alexander turned to Adrian. "Are you ready for this?"

"Ready as I can be. I won't disappoint you."

Alexander gave a small smile. "I know." He drew in a long breath. "There's only a little left of the day. Take me to my nephew."

The grin returned to Adrian's face, and they turned from the courtyard and strode toward the city.

Evening had turned into the full of night as Alexander stepped from the grand statehouse. Adrian followed him out. The hours had passed too quickly.

Adrian's son, Theisen, was everything Alexander had imagined him to be, and more. With a head full of black hair and blue eyes, the child was beautiful. He could steal a heart at first glance. This child was family, immediately loved. As Alexander held him in his arms, he felt what every man feels for those he loves—he'd give his life for this child.

And Sevina—Alexander knew instantly she was perfect for his brother. While she was the image of quiet beauty, Adrian responded to her every touch and followed every gentle word. Alexander watched in shock as his brother minded things that Catherine had never been able to get him to do: not setting his sword on the table and using his silverware properly at dinner. And Sevina looked at Adrian with eyes of a pure heart. Alexander found himself grateful his brother had found such a love.

As the evening drew to a close, Alexander said his goodbyes. He'd be leaving before the sun rose to return to Mercia, and he wasn't sure when he'd return. Adrian walked him to the door, then down the stairs and to the gate of the walk, where they paused.

His brother shifted uneasily. "There is something I wanted to talk to you about."

They'd just spent two weeks traveling together, what had not already been said?

"Mercia will always be in my heart," Adrian said. "But Kharav is where my son is, where my wife is. Where my home is."

Alexander took a step back.

Adrian swallowed. "And I'd like to provide for my family here." He paused as he looked back over his shoulder at the statehouse. "Sevina is accustomed to a very different life than that of a mere soldier's wife. And her father can and will provide, but... I'm her husband..."

Alexander knew what he was asking, and he didn't hesitate. "I'll sell the manor in Mercia, and you can use the money to establish a life for yourself here."

"No, not the manor." Adrian shook his head. "It's too much. The city house on the isle is sufficient. And you should keep the manor for your son one day."

Alexander smiled sadly. "You know I'll have no need of it."

"The manor was our home."

The manor had been *Adrian's* home, with their mother. But to Alexander, it was only a memory of the pain. Still, it was the house of his father, and his father's father. But this was the dawn of a new era, a new generation, and if Norah had taught him anything, it was that some things had to change to move forward. His next generation would be in Kharav, and Alexander would see them provided for.

He nodded. "The city house then. I'll arrange it and send the proceeds for you to purchase a home here."

Adrian's eyes welled. "Thank you, brother."

Alexander pulled him close and embraced him. "Stay well. Until we see each other again." He gave his brother a final cuff on the shoulder, then pushed open the gate and started back toward the castle.

When Alexander reached the mainway, a familiar face was waiting for him. He couldn't help but smile.

Katya was leaning against a gas lamp post. She wasn't wearing her wrap, and her long hair hung around her shoulders. She was beautiful.

"When they told me the Bear had brought the Aleon army to join us, I almost didn't believe them," she said.

He smirked. "I like to be beyond belief."

"As you always have been."

They stood in the light of the lamp post.

"Can I offer you a drink?" she asked.

It was late, but this wasn't an offer he could refuse. He glanced around for a tavern.

"My house is just a few streets up," she added.

He paused. "Ah." Her eyes held a welcome smile, and he smiled back. "I'd love a drink."

They walked the cobbled streets under the gas lamps. Alexander had never realized how peaceful Kharav was at night.

"You saw your nephew?" she asked.

"I did. He's beautiful."

"Not surprising. Look at his family."

Alexander chuckled, and a warmth came to his cheeks.

They reached a well-kept rowhome, and Katya led him through the front door and foyer and back into a kitchen.

Alexander glanced around. It was a nice home—nicer than he'd expect a soldier's home to be, even for a captain. Kharav paid its army well, and it showed. The high ceilings had simple but elegant trim, and the furniture, while not lavish, was beautifully made and well situated. The kitchen was large, with enough space to employ a castle's staff.

"You live here by yourself?"

She smiled as his eyes wandered around the massive kitchen. "With my mother. She loves to cook and always wanted a big kitchen. When I made captain and was able to buy her one, I did. She's at her sister's now. I would have liked for her to have met you."

Alexander would have liked to have met Katya's mother.

She pulled out a pitcher of ale and poured two glasses. Then she led him to a round table, and they sat.

"It's good to see you, Bear."

He chuckled.

Her brows dipped. "What?"

"I like to think we know each other. Perhaps we might move to a first-name basis." He stared at her: her eyes, her nose, her lips. He'd almost forgotten how beautiful she was. *Almost.* "Katya."

She pressed her lips to hold her smile as she stared back at him. "Alexander." She took another drink of her wine. "I've thought a lot about when I might see you again."

He had too. "And what did you think about?"

"How I'd invite you for a drink." She stilled as her eyes caught his, and they sat in the quiet of the moment. "And then I'd invite you to stay."

His pulse quickened, and the groin of his leathers grew tighter, but he settled himself. He couldn't give in to the wants of his body. It wouldn't be fair to her. "I wouldn't take advantage of you this way. I can give neither my hand nor my heart."

"*You?* Take advantage of *me?*" She gave a light laugh, then her face grew more serious. "I don't ask for your heart, and I don't want your hand." She tilted her head to the side. "But I do want you to stay."

Stay. And be with her. Gods, he wanted to. He'd thought about Katya a great deal since he'd last seen her. He'd thought about her eyes, and the line of her jaw, and the fullness of her lips. He'd thought about her skin, and the feel of it against his. But he couldn't stay. While she'd said he wouldn't be taking advantage, he couldn't help but feel...

She leaned back slightly. "I'm sorry. I've misread you, misread what's between us."

He caught her hand, stilling them both. "Katya." Her eyes stared at him, dark and deep. He felt like he could fall into them. "You've misread nothing." He shook his head. "But I leave tomorrow. What if we never see each other again?"

"Exactly," she whispered. "What if we never have the chance to be with each other again? To take peace in each other, enjoy each other. Is this time not precious?" She leaned closer. "Stay."

She was beautiful, but it was more than her beauty. Katya had come to know him well over the past months. He'd come to know her. Slowly, he brought his hand to her cheek, brushing her skin with his thumb, and he pulled her lips to his.

And he stayed.

CHAPTER FIFTY-SIX

Norah walked through the courtyard. Nearly a month had passed since Alexander had taken the legions to Kharav. She knew she was pushing her council to their limits. Even Catherine urged her to bring him back, but she couldn't. Mikael needed the best men. There were only two best men, and Soren wouldn't leave her.

It had been Alexander's idea to take Adrian with him. He and Soren had agreed, to her astonishment. But she supposed she wasn't too surprised. Adrian was perhaps the rarest of gems—as a Northman for their Mercian forces to follow, as brother to Alexander, who the forces of Aleon were committed to, and as an accepted warrior of the Kharavian army. Norah missed him, but she was happy for him to help Mikael, and she knew Sevina was happy to have her husband home. And Norah was happy Alexander would have the opportunity to meet his nephew while he was there.

Footfalls interrupted her thoughts, and she looked up to see Soren and Caspian approaching.

"Queen Norah," Caspian said, "you need to come to the judisaept. Urgently."

"What's happened?"

"It's the lord justice. He's been taken."

A weight hit Norah in her chest. "What do you mean *taken*?"

Caspian waved to a soldier behind him to come forward. The man's armor was crusted in dirt and blood. He bowed. "Regal High," he said. "We'd just left the Shadowlands to return to Mercia. But they were waiting for us."

Her pulse rose in her throat. "Why would you be leaving the Shadowlands, and who was waiting for you?"

"The Shadow King ordered the lord justice to return to you."

Mikael had sent Alexander back to her?

"But as we left the Canyonlands, the Horsemen were waiting. Their king—he said his name was King Abilash and that you have something that belongs to him."

Her eyes widened, and she looked at Soren. He returned her gaze, dark and angry. And it hit her—*the mare*. Mikael had taken the mare from the Horseman king at her asking. And now Abilash sought to get it back. It shouldn't have surprised her—Tahla had told her that anyone with mastery over a horse of the Wild could draw other tribes to follow them, and Abilash was an ambitious king. He could grow his power with the horse, grow his kingdom. A deep and burning fury grew inside her.

His ambition would cost him.

"The councilmen are assembling in the judisaept," Caspian said. "You need to come."

Norah strode quickly toward the castle, her anger building as she went, with Caspian and Soren following behind.

When she reached the chamber, the councilmen were already there. They surrounded the table but didn't sit, and their voices rang over one another with the details. Catherine stood to the side. When she saw Norah, she moved to her.

But Norah didn't waste time with greetings. "As I'm sure you've heard, the lord justice has been taken," she called out, drawing the room quiet.

Edward was the first to speak. "I knew it was a mistake to send him," he said angrily.

"What are the Horseman's demands?" James asked. "What is it that belongs to him?"

"He means the horse of the Wild," she said. "And she does *not* belong to him."

"This is over a horse?" Edward's voice was shrill, and it only angered her further. "By the gods, just send it!"

Just send it? Norah pushed out a furious breath between her teeth. Abilash had made a devastating mistake. And now she'd take everything from him. She turned to the messenger, who stood behind Soren and Caspian. "Where is he?" she demanded. "Where is he keeping the lord justice?"

"King Abilash has taken the ruins of Aviron for his own. They've somewhat rebuilt the destroyed castle. The lord justice and three other Northmen are being held in the dungeon as he awaits your reply."

"Get the horse," Edward said. "Send it to him."

"He'll get nothing!" Norah snapped, drawing all eyes to her. Her skin was on fire. This man dared to take something from her, something very dear. He thought he had power over her—the Shadow Queen. She looked at Soren. "Ready an army, one large enough to bring Aviron to the ground."

"You would march against Aviron?" Edward gasped.

Aviron—the kingdom that had tried to kill Mikael so long ago, the kingdom that Soren had destroyed.

"There is no Aviron!" she spat back. "Abilash is a pretender king in the bones of what used to be a wretched and wicked kingdom!"

Edward shook his finger at her. "You've already sent five thousand of our Northmen to the Shadowlands, as well as half our forces from Aleon. It's well within this council's authority to veto a march to war, which I recommend we—"

Surprisingly graceful for his size, Soren leapt onto the table, interrupting the councilman and forcing the room silent. He walked the table's length, toward Edward, dragging the edge of his axe along the wood and carving a trail of warning.

How she loved this brute. "If there's any councilman who doesn't support the retrieval of my lord justice, let him speak now," she challenged.

"Norah," James said. "You cannot mean to influence this council by force."

She looked around the room, her eyes ablaze. "Does anyone feel forced?"

Soren rolled his gaze over each one of them, awaiting the smallest objection. The room was silent. Even James.

"Norah!" Catherine whispered harshly. "I want Alexander back as much as you do."

Norah caught her with a look that silenced her. "That's not possible."

Soren dropped down from the table, shaking the room like thunder, and stood before her.

"If he's been harmed..." she let her words drop off, her silence speaking for her. She raised her eyes to his. "Go, Destroyer."

Water dripped from the stone of the ceilings to the stone of the floors. Alexander sat with his men in the cold, dark dungeon cell. They were starving. They'd been given two loaves of bread and a bucket of water a day for four men. It had been three weeks since the Horseman king had sent his demands to Norah. The horse of the Wild was what he wanted. It shouldn't be long now. Norah would send the mare, he was sure of it—she wouldn't accept his capture, but she'd resolve this diplomatically. He was grateful she was in Mercia, not the Shadowlands. Otherwise, she might be convinced to use more violent measures.

The Shadowlands. He didn't know what to feel about the kingdom anymore. He'd hated it. With every fiber of his being, he'd hated it. *Had* hated it. It had taken Norah from him, taken his brother. It had upheaved Mercia's political safeties and spit in the faces of tradition. But now it was home to his nephew, the small joy he'd been able to hold in his arms just a few weeks ago. It was where Adrian would build his life. Alexander had decided to sell both the city house and the manor when he returned to Mercia. He didn't have need for either of them and would see his brother had everything to support his wife and child.

His mind shifted to Katya. He'd almost lingered longer in the Shadowlands, for more time with her. He wished he had. It had been hard to leave her, even to return to Mercia. Even to return to Norah.

Outside the cell, footsteps approached. "Open it," a voice demanded—the Horseman king.

The heavy door swung open, and Alexander stood quickly. Relief rolled through him. His Northmen must have arrived with the horse of the Wild.

But instead of removing the chains around his wrists, a guard struck Alexander across the face, knocking him against the wall. Others held his men at bay with swords. Alexander spit blood as he tried to regain his senses.

The king's lips peeled back in a rage, flashing his decaying teeth. "Bring him."

The guards grabbed Alexander's arms and pulled him from the cell, down the dark and mildewy hall, and up a set of stairs to the outside. As he stepped into the light, the glare of the sun blinded him. He struggled to keep up and was forcefully pushed along. They took him up to the castle wall to look out to the east.

Leaning over the rampart, the Horseman king pointed in the distance. "You said she'd send the horse!"

Alexander squinted, still struggling to see. His eyes finally adjusted, and he could make out figures along the outer hills. But as he looked closer, he realized there were more men than required to bring a horse—many more. His pulse quickened. The council would have never sent an army. Then Alexander knew—he scanned the ranks and found him.

The Destroyer.

"Why is *he* here?" the king seethed.

Alexander pushed out a disappointed breath. "He serves my queen."

The color drained from the Horseman's face. "He is supposed to be in Kharav, with Salar!"

The Horseman king was expecting to capitalize on the separation of Norah and the Shadow King, Alexander realized, and on Kharav being distracted by war.

Alexander shook his head. "No, the Destroyer has joined the queen in Mercia." He looked out at the soldiers on the hills. "And he brings his methods of resolution with him. You need to release us."

"Do I?" the king sneered.

"If you know who he is, then you know he'll tear this castle to the ground," Alexander warned. "Not for me—he'll happily see me dead. He merely wants a reason. Don't give him one." Alexander looked out at the army, then back to the king. "I'm trying to help you save your people. You have families here."

The king ignored him.

Alexander sighed in exasperation. "If you care about your people, you'll let me meet him before he even reaches this castle, before he advances farther. He hasn't come to negotiate."

The king shook with anger. He turned to one of his warriors. "Ride out. Tell the commander all I want is the horse."

The Horseman warrior nodded and left.

Alexander shook his head again. "Why? Why do you provoke him? You know who he is. He's not going to talk. He's the *Destroyer*, and he's come to *destroy*."

The king glared at him. "I'm in here. He's out there. We'll see what he has to say." The Horsemen thought they had repaired the castle walls, but they knew nothing of stone foundations. They knew nothing of how to construct walls fit for battle.

"This is the man who originally destroyed this kingdom," Alexander pressed. "He's come to do it again."

The king said nothing.

"Are you mad?"

The king jerked his head back to Alexander. "I'm mad enough to throw you over this wall if you say another word."

Alexander's heart sank. He looked out over the wall as the Horseman messenger rode out to meet the army.

As the warrior neared the approaching army, the Destroyer dismounted and started walking toward him. The king smirked at Alexander. "Looks like he's willing to say a few words after all."

They waited. As the rider drew up his horse beside the commander, he appeared to relay the message. The commander stood for a moment, then faster than the warrior could react, he reached up and pulled the man from his horse. In a singular motion, the commander swung his battle-axe high and cleaved the man's head from his body. Then he shouted back to the army behind him.

Behind the ranks, a catapult was brought forward.

The Horseman king looked on in horror.

The army quickly readied the catapult, and the commander pushed the head of the man into the sling. With the catapult loaded, he released it, sending his message over the castle wall, amidst the screams of horrified people inside.

The commander turned and loosed his axe again, methodically loading pieces of the man's body into the catapult and sending them over the castle wall one at a time. After he sent over the body, the army loaded a boulder and took aim for the wall the Horsemen had repaired. It struck the stone with force that crumpled a large section to the ground.

Then the Destroyer mounted his destrier, and the army advanced.

"Do you understand now?" Alexander pressed the king. "Release us!"

Horrified and shocked, the king nodded his head, waving his men to release the Northmen. Soldiers removed the chains around Alexander's wrists and pushed him down the stairs and to the gates of the castle.

"If we release you, he will leave?" the king asked.

Alexander couldn't answer that, but... "If you don't release me, he'll kill you all."

The king swayed, seemingly unsure of what to do to stop the looming army. "Go!" he snapped finally.

Alexander and his men stumbled out of the gates and hurried toward the advancing army. He prayed he could stop the commander. The Horsemen had taken over the ruins, restoring much of Aviron and settling their families. Despite his anger at the king, Alexander didn't want harm to come to those families, a moral consideration he knew wouldn't concern the Destroyer.

When Alexander reached the army, he stopped to catch his breath, eyeing the commander before looking back at the castle. "Was that necessary?" he asked.

"Are you not released?" the Destroyer taunted, sitting on top of his horse and looking down at him. "You don't look as bad as I thought you would."

"Not as bad as you'd hoped?" Alexander cut back.

"There's still time."

Alexander ignored the jab and eyed the army. "What is your intent?"

A wrap covered the commander's face, but his eyes revealed his smile. "What Salara sent me here for—to see Aviron no more."

"Why didn't she send the horse, or at least a ransom?"

"Because then everyone would be trying to steal you away, with how easy it is."

Alexander shook his head. "What did you say to her? She wouldn't have been willing to destroy an entire tribe to release me."

"Had I said anything, it would have been for her to have left you," he snarled. "No, Bear, you're wrong. I don't imagine there's anything she wouldn't do to get you back."

Alexander stepped closer to his destrier, speaking low. "There are children in there. Families. If Norah has truly sent you, it's out of rash anger, but she wouldn't want them hurt. She wouldn't be able to bear it. If you care for her at all, you'll let them live."

The commander didn't answer. He simply urged his horse forward, closer to the walls of Aviron. "Abilash!" he bellowed, then waited. "Abilash!" he thundered again.

The king appeared on the top of the wall, looking down at them. Alexander knew the Horseman would be shaking in his boots.

"You are no longer king!" the commander roared. "I take from you your title, your lands, this very castle you try to squat yourself in, hiding like a coward. Everything you have is now Salara's. And you are no more!" He paused, letting his message sink in. "Anyone who seeks to leave will be given safe passage, but come tomorrow, Aviron and anyone in it will be destroyed."

The commander reined back his horse, toward the army. "Satisfied?" he sneered at Alexander.

Surprisingly, he was. It was more than he had hoped for.

"Where's your horse?" the commander asked him.

"Lost."

"That was a good horse," the Destroyer said angrily.

Of course the commander was more concerned with his horse. A soldier brought him another destrier, and Alexander mounted. He swept his eyes across the masses of Mercian forces that the commander had brought. He truly was prepared to destroy Aviron, and Norah had given him Northmen to do it. Alexander's attention shifted back to the commander, who growled out to the men, "I'll start back with the Bear. They have one day to leave the castle, then I want it torn to the ground. Every stone."

These were Mercian forces. Alexander's forces. But they looked to the Destroyer and nodded. Alexander's stomach turned.

"Every stone," the Shadow commander emphasized. Then he urged his mount north.

Anger knifed through Alexander, but he knew he couldn't stay. He knew he couldn't alter the task, not if Norah had sent the army. He cursed as he followed after.

The Destroyer looked back at the castle as they rode away. "I don't know which I despise more," he said to Alexander, "traveling all the way out here and being denied a battle, or seeing Salara absolutely consumed with your return."

"Is she well?" he asked.

"No, she's not well," the commander spat. "She had me march five thousand men to retrieve you. We lost more on the journey than we rescued from that flea-bitten castle. Now eat something. The only thing that could make this worse is having to explain to her how you died on the way back."

Norah paced her study as the sun set over the snow-packed mountains in the distance. She wrung her clammy hands, trying to force back the sickness bubbling in her stomach.

What had she done?

She had threatened her council with the very man they viewed as their enemy; sent Kharav all the steel trade bound for markets, even that in reserve; and stripped forces from a vulnerable Mercia to aid the Shadowlands. She'd sent an Aleon legion to Kharav, essentially forcing them to a side she wasn't sure Phillip would choose, and now her lord justice had been taken.

But all of that paled in comparison to the fact that she had sent Soren to Aviron. No, not Soren—*the Destroyer*. In her anger toward Abilash, she sent hell upon his people. She should have sent the horse of the Wild. She loved Sephir, but she would have sent a thousand horses. Ten thousand. She would have traded most anything for Alexander. But her rage hadn't let her. Soren would have no mercy, and now she'd have blood on her hands.

There was a shuffle outside. A guard's voice came. "You can't go—"

The door to her study swung open, and Soren stepped inside, followed by a few Mercian soldiers guarding the hall. Any other time, she'd have been amused. Some of the guards less acquainted with Soren still tried to stop him from going where he pleased.

But it wasn't the time for amusement. Norah stared at him, her mouth dry, her skin cold, her heart hammering so hard she thought it might burst from her chest. She was desperate to hear his news but feared what he'd tell her. She waved the guards away.

"I've brought him back," he said after they stepped out.

Her eyes welled. Alexander was safe.

"And I've removed Abilash as king."

"What about his people?" she breathed.

"Given safe passage to join another tribe, or form a separate one, I don't care, so long as it's not under Abilash."

Norah rushed forward and threw her arms around him. He hadn't killed them. *She* hadn't killed them.

He stiffened but let her cling to him until her emotion passed. Then he pushed her back so he could look her in the eye. "The Bear's cleaning up, then he's coming here. Don't let him see you like this. Pull yourself together."

She nodded. "Thank—"

"Don't," he said as he stepped back from her.

Norah swallowed back the rest of her words. She only nodded again, and he took his leave. She wiped her face and raked her fingers through her hair, then set back to pacing the room. Alexander was safe. Her relief threatened her with emotion again.

Years seemed to pass before a knock came to the door, and it opened. Alexander stepped inside. She could only look at him. It hadn't even been two months since he'd last left Mercia, but he looked older. He looked tired.

"Queen Norah," he said finally.

She crossed the space between them. His eyes were filled with an emotion she couldn't read—worry? Sadness? She wanted to hug him, she wanted to touch him, but she didn't. His eyes didn't hold the same softness toward her, they didn't beg her nearness the way they usually did.

"You sent the Destroyer?" he asked. There was judgment in his tone. His expression was clear now—disapproval. And it angered her. "Why didn't you send the horse?" he asked. "Or the ransom?"

"I sent what was required. And I will *not* negotiate with someone who tries to force my hand."

"This isn't who you are." His voice was softer now, but it still held the sting of a cut.

"Then perhaps you don't know me," she knifed back.

"There were families there, and you sent the Destroyer and a legion! For a few men!"

Anger radiated through her. "Who are you to judge me? You marched the entire Mercian army across the Tribelands, for one!"

"You're queen!" he thundered. "I'm nothing!"

But he wasn't nothing.

"And I would do things very differently now," he added.

What did that mean? He'd do things differently... He was different... now.

Silence came again. They stood in the quiet of the candlelit room, with only the sound of their hearts beating. What was this strangeness between them? Was it only his anger?

She let out a long exhale. She couldn't resolve it tonight. "The council will want to speak with you in the morning," she said, shifting the conversation away from one of emotion. "They're not very happy with me."

The air between them calmed, and the heat dissipated. His lips tightened in frustration still, but he nodded. "I'll help smooth things out."

It wouldn't be an easy task, to settle things with the council, but Alexander held their respect. Norah would talk to her grandmother too.

"Then I'll see you tomorrow," she said. What else could she say?

"Of course."

"Goodnight, Alexander."

"Goodnight."

CHAPTER FIFTY-SEVEN

With Alexander's political savvy, the council seemed to calm over the next few days. Norah kept Soren away, busy with what she was sure he felt were trivial tasks—assessing arrivals and risks from the ports, combing the isle for weaknesses—but there was nothing trivial about keeping busy and keeping the peace.

She walked the great hall with the dogs trailing behind her, her frustration growing. She felt chained, unable to move, just waiting for war. How long would it be like this?

Footfalls sounded from her left, and she turned to see a Kharavian soldier approaching—a messenger—with a letter in his hand. When she saw the black seal, she smiled—a letter from Mikael.

"Thank you," she said as she took it and broke the seal.

Mikael's words came as they usually did, wanting to make sure she was well. She had a small painted portrait that she planned to send with her next letter. Her smile widened as she thought of him receiving it. But as she read his letter, her thoughts of the portrait fell away.

Mikael wrote that Aleon had sent him a warning, advising him to close his ports. A fever was rumored to be sweeping through Nestrana, along the port cities, and down to Pryam—the kingdoms across the Aged Sea from Kharav.

Phillip hadn't responded to the matter of her sending Aleon forces to Kharav. She assumed he wasn't happy about it, but he hadn't called to withdraw them. Now, with his helpful warning of potential danger, she hoped she was seeing the beginnings of cooperation, even if reluctant.

With Phillip's letter to Mikael, there would have been one sent to Mercia as well. She caught a nearby servant. "Have the council meet me in the judisaept."

She made her way through the halls to the council chamber. Surely Aleon's amicable actions toward Kharav would help with the council's own feelings toward Mikael, or so she hoped.

For once, she was the first to arrive, and she waited as her councilmen each reached the judisaept. They filed in stiffly. Soren came with Alexander.

"Any news from Aleon?" she asked when they had all gathered.

"Not recently," James said.

She held up the letter from Mikael. "Phillip sent a warning for Kharav to close its ports. A fever spreads from Nestrana to Pryam. We should do the same."

Henricus scoffed. "James and I have just come from Damask. The ports are fine."

"Perhaps for now," Alexander said. "But if the fever travels from Nestrana, it will likely reach Tarsus, which means it could be in our harbors now."

"Unless there is no fever," Alastair said. "We've heard no word of this from anyone else."

"Then why would Phillip send a message to Kharav?" Norah asked, her irritation growing. "There's absolutely no benefit to Aleon for Kharav closing its ports, and no hardship to Kharav for doing so. It has only two, and other means to export trade."

"Why wouldn't Phillip send word to Mercia, then?" James asked.

That didn't make sense to Norah either, but there could be a number of reasons. "Still, we should be cautious, and close our ports as well."

"That's no small feat," Edward said. "We'd be closing trade to thousands—tens of thousands—on the basis of nothing. We don't even know how serious this fever is, if it even *is* at all."

Norah couldn't argue with that. She didn't know the consequences of the fever, although she couldn't imagine Aleon advising Kharav to close its ports if it wasn't serious. And while she didn't trust that her council would put the well-being of the people over profit or political gain, she also couldn't overrule them on everything.

"We'll leave them open, then," she said, relenting. "But have guards ready to close them down at the first sign of sickness."

The council grudgingly agreed.

Morning came, and the port situation still needled in Norah's mind. She'd write to Phillip and ask him what was happening. Serene helped her dress, and she made her way to the dining room for breakfast. Caspian picked up alongside her as she walked, like he usually did in the morning, briefing her of news and activities.

As she passed through the great hall, she saw Catherine and Edward in a seemingly heated conversation.

"What's going on?" she asked as she approached.

"Henricus has fallen ill," Catherine said.

Norah darted her eyes between her grandmother and Edward. "Does he have the fever?"

Edward held up his hands. "We can't jump to conclusions."

"He was just in Damask at the ports," Norah said, her pulse quickening.

"So was James," he argued, "who's perfectly well. This could be anything."

Norah shook her head. "But it's not just anything. I knew it." She turned to Caspian. "Send word—close the ports."

"We must assemble the council first," Edward stressed.

"The council has already agreed—the first sign of sickness."

"*At the ports,*" he said, his tone rising. "For all we know, Henricus might have eaten something that didn't agree with his stomach."

But Norah wasn't willing to take that risk. "Go," she told Caspian.

Edward's voice pitched higher. "You cannot make unilateral decisions that affect Mercia's trade and economy."

"Why not?" she snapped back. She was near breaking with this man. "Am I not queen?"

"You have a council—"

"Who's failing! If you were doing your job, you'd put aside your differences and help me build a stronger alliance between Mercia and Kharav, and stand beside your king! You would help me help our people. You wouldn't undermine me at every turn—don't think I haven't noticed." Her cheeks were hot with anger. "We'll stop all trade until we know just how serious this is. Lives mean more than money. We close the ports."

Things went from bad to worse. The sickness was as Norah had feared, and two days later, more men were showing signs of illness. They had all visited the ports or interacted with those who had done so.

She stood in her study, looking out the window over the castle. Caspian knocked on the door and entered.

"Norah," he said gently. His reluctant tone brought a chill to her spine.

She turned.

"Henricus is dead."

Her blood ran cold. "What?" she breathed.

"He died this morning."

"Of the fever?"

He nodded solemnly. "It appears so. Deaths are being reported through Damask and into the markets of the Free Cities."

Deaths. It was like a blow to the stomach. Her mind shifted to Mikael. Had he closed the ports of Kharav in time?

"There's more," Caspian said. "The lord commander has taken ill."

Norah's chest tightened. "What? How?" She needed to see him. She darted from the chamber before Caspian could answer.

"Norah, you can't see him."

"How is he sick? He didn't even go to the ports! He—" she stopped, and bile rose in the back of the throat. She'd sent him on miscellaneous tasks to keep him busy, which included assessing risks at the ports. And now he'd caught the fever. She turned and raced toward his chamber.

"Norah, you can't," Caspian called after her. But she ignored him.

As she neared Soren's chamber and reached for the latch, Caspian caught her arm. "Norah, you can't see him."

"Soren," she called from outside the door.

"Leave!" he called angrily from inside. "You can't be here."

She rattled the handle, but it didn't give. "The door's locked."

"Because I knew you'd be foolish enough to open it," Soren hurled back.

"You can't go in," Caspian told her. "You can't risk catching the fever. The healer says it can be passed easily: through touch, eating after one who has it, through the air when you cough."

She stepped backward, the devastation of the situation creeping in. It could pass so easily from one to another? That meant it would spread through Mercia like fire. How many would catch it? She turned her focus back to Soren. "I need to know you're all right."

"I'll be all right when you leave," he rumbled back.

"I'll be back to check on you," she said.

"Don't let her come back!" he bellowed, speaking to Caspian now.

"Queen Norah, you have to leave. Serene and Vitalia are preparing an isolation chamber for you now. You'll remain there with them, and I'll personally serve as your guard at all times to reduce your contact with anyone. Alexander will be down the hall from you, and members of the council will each stay in isolation in their separate chambers. The same with your grandmother."

"How long?" she asked.

He shook his head. "I don't know exactly, but it appears that as it spreads quickly, it also leaves quickly. For those who are surviving, they seem to recover after three days."

"How many recover?"

He grew quiet. "About half."

Serene stepped inside Norah's chamber with a tray of hot soup. It was the only food approved throughout Mercia—food that could be boiled. No bread, no fresh fruits or vegetables.

Norah was surprised at how quickly Caspian had put together a plan. Everyone was ordered to their chambers, and citizens were required to remain in their homes.

The castle worked at half staff, with each person contained within a specific area at all times. Caspian left food in the hall for Serene to bring inside after he stepped away. Messages were delivered through doors. Caspian kept her updated throughout the day. Alexander, her grandmother, the remaining members of the council—they were all keeping well, even James, despite his previous visit to the ports. Soren was still with fever, but Caspian said he continued to answer through the door, and the servants still found he was taking the food into his chamber after they left it for him.

Two days passed, with Norah's worry stretching the time even longer. She wished she had more books in her chamber. Had she been smarter, she would have asked to have been isolated in the library.

A knock on the door told her Caspian had brought dinner. Soup. Again.

"How is my grandmother?" she asked through the door.

"She says if she's served soup one more time, she'll throw it at me when she sees me next."

Norah smiled.

"The lord justice says to hold on. Hopefully this won't be for much longer."

"And Soren?" she asked.

He was quiet.

"Caspian?"

Still, he did not answer.

"Caspian?" she said, more urgently.

"I don't know."

"What do you mean, you don't know?"

"He hasn't taken his food, and he's not answering the servants at his door."

Her stomach twisted. *Half did not recover.* Soren had to recover—he was strong, he was the Destroyer. Why didn't he answer? Fear flooded her, and she swung the door to her chamber open.

Caspian stepped back, raising his arm to her. "Don't come out here."

But she wasn't listening. She tore from the room and down the hall.

"Norah!" he yelled, and tried to grab her, but he wasn't fast enough.

She ran by Alexander's door and to the hall of Soren's chamber. Two servants stood outside, and she pushed through them. "Soren!" she called, but there was no answer. "Soren!" She jerked at the iron handle, but it wouldn't open. "Soren!" she cried.

"Norah!" Alexander's voice came from behind.

She turned, her panic building. "He's not answering!"

"You can't be here," he told her.

Fear coursed through her. Why didn't Soren answer? She jerked the handle again. "Soren!"

Alexander caught her and pulled her back. "I'll see if he's all right and send word to you. But you need to go back to your chamber."

She shook her head. She couldn't. She wouldn't.

"You can't expose yourself."

Norah struggled to hold in her sob. She couldn't leave Soren.

"I'll make sure he's all right," he promised.

But she still couldn't go.

He gripped her shoulders and pulled her eyes to his. "I'll make sure he's all right. You have my word. Go."

Finally, she relented and backed away. Then she reluctantly turned and headed back to her chamber.

Alexander stood in front of the door to the Shadow commander's chamber. He looked at Caspian beside him. "You go too. You need to look after Norah."

"You can't go in there," Caspian argued. "I'll do it."

"No, you'll look after Norah. That's an order."

Caspian stood in the hallway.

"Go!" Alexander snapped.

Finally, the captain yielded and headed back to the hall of the queen's chamber. When he had gone, Alexander turned back to the door.

"Destroyer," he called.

There still came no answer. He put his ear against the door and listened. No movement inside. If this bastard was dead... he'd kill him.

Alexander pulled his sword and angled its tip into the crevice of the door. The latches were well-made and strong, but Mercian steel was stronger. He strained as he put his weight against it, prying it, forcing it. Finally, the latch broke, and the door swung open.

Soren lay on the floor near the window, stripped of his clothing. No doubt he'd been trying to pull the heat from his body with the cold stone. He lay still, his eyes closed, unmoving.

"Destroyer," Alexander called to him.

He didn't respond.

"Soren," he called again, stepping to the window and dropping down beside him. The commander's chest shuddered as a small gurgle escaped his lips—he was alive. He tried to cough, but only a choking noise came from his throat. He couldn't breathe. Alexander pulled him up to a sitting position. By the gods, he was a heavy beast.

"Breathe!" he ordered, giving Soren's back a hearty beat with the heel of his hand. The commander's body heaved and then let out a drowning cough. The thick warmth of blood ran over his own arm and down the commander's chest. Alexander hit Soren's back again.

The commander took a desperate breath and his body relaxed in relief. Alexander positioned himself against the wall behind Soren, leaning the weight of the commander against him and holding his body upright. The Shadow beast couldn't hold himself, and his head fell back against Alexander's shoulder. But he was able to breathe.

"Death is near," Soren's voice came in barely a whisper. "Let it come." His body shook with another cough, and Alexander held him forward as he purged more blood from his lungs.

"They say this is the worst—the third day," Alexander told him. "You need to stay upright. If you lie down, you'll drown in your blood."

"I don't have the strength."

Alexander shifted and positioned himself more firmly against the commander's back. "I know," he said.

And they sat.

Chapter Fifty-Eight

Nothing. Norah paced her chamber. There had been nothing—no word about Soren. Three times Serene had talked her out of leaving the room again, but she couldn't shake the crushing fear inside her.

She couldn't lose him.

Mikael needed him. She needed him. And he deserved to die in glory on a battlefield or ascend the earth as an immortal warrior of the gods, not broken by a port fever in a kingdom that wouldn't even speak his name. She'd never seen a vision of his end. Is that how it was for people with wretched deaths? Was their end not powerful enough to show their greatness to the seers?

He deserved so much more than this.

A knock on the door made her jump, and she raced over to it.

"Queen Norah," Caspian called.

"Tell me! Is Soren all right?"

"He's alive."

Norah leaned against the door and let out a shaking breath. She covered her face in her hands as tears came.

"The lord justice stays with him," he said. "He's keeping him upright and breathing."

Norah's heart stopped. "Alexander?" Alexander was with him, *inside*? "Yes."

She heard the gravity in his voice; she felt the weight of his worry, because it was her own. Alexander would surely have the sickness within a day or two. With only half those afflicted surviving, what were the chances of both of them making it through safely?

Norah cursed herself. She knew she should have closed the ports, and she hadn't. She was queen, and she was responsible for the suffering of her people.

Two more days went by, with Caspian delivering the news that Soren was recovering. The danger of death had passed. Alexander had been confined to a far chamber in the castle to quarantine while he waited for the sickness to come. Norah was desperate to see him, but of course, she couldn't.

It wrecked the heart—waiting to see if death would come for a loved one, or if it would mercifully pass over. Did she deserve mercy? Did the gods still curse her?

After several more days, the sickness appeared to have left the castle. Slowly, Caspian executed plans for a return to normality. Sections of the castle were opened, with only those that had quarantined allowed to associate with one another. To Catherine's horror, they still ate soup.

At last free from her chamber, Norah strolled between the great hall and her study. The library was still closed. On her return walk, Caspian was waiting for her. He held a letter in his hand. Two letters, actually.

She saw Mikael's seal, and she tore it open. Her eyes welled with relief as she read his words.

All was well in Kharav. Mikael had closed the ports immediately after Phillip's warning, and they had no reports of sickness. He'd sent food to the Uru and ordered them confined to the canyons—no contact with the outside world. They, too, had fared well. Of course, he asked about Mercia, and Soren. She was relieved she had good news to share, at least concerning Soren.

Her attention shifted to the second letter. It was a letter from Phillip. She would normally assemble the council before reading his letters, but she broke the seal and opened it.

Dear Norah,

I hope this letter finds you safe and in good health, and pray you received my last letter in time to close your ports. May you have fared the fever better than Aleon. It's with great regret I share that I've lost nearly one quarter of my men, with Tarsus hit hardest—I fear beyond recovery.

I'm grateful I didn't heed the words of your council and withdraw my forces from Kharav, for not a single man was lost there. If I'd not been so selfish, I would have sent more, and so saved more. Another lesson in humility from the gods.

Norah stopped. The council had written Phillip and told him to pull back the forces she had sent to Kharav? Anger pulsed through her.

But within the darkness, there comes a light. I've received reports that the armies of Japheth and Rael have suffered losses of almost half. And while I can't jump to war so soon after such devastation, I know that victory over Japheth is now within my grasp.

Write to me urgently, so I know you are well and safe.

Most anxiously, I wait,

Phillip

Phillip would be able to march against a weakened Japheth soon, and for that, she was grateful. But her face still burned with a rising anger. "I want to see the council in the judisaept," she said. "Now."

"I'll assemble them," Caspian replied.

"Where's Soren?"

"In his chamber still, resting."

"Time for rest is done," she said. "Tell him to come, and dress for blood. I may need it."

Caspian's brows dipped in concern. "Norah—"

"Do as I say."

Reluctantly, he nodded and left her in the hall, and she turned toward the judisaept.

Soren arrived before the councilmen, much sooner than she'd expected. She'd thought he would appear a little more just-coming-back-from-the-brink-of-death-like, not at all the full Destroyer that stood before her now. Perhaps the potential call for blood had breathed new life into him. It was the first she had seen him since he'd fallen sick, and she desperately wanted to hug him, but there would be time for merriment and thanksgiving later. Right now, she had things to address.

The councilmen came quickly. Of course, they expected her call would be in response to a letter. She doubted they expected what she had in store for them.

When Alexander stepped into the room, he surprised everyone, including Norah.

"Lord Justice," she said. She swallowed back her emotion at seeing him. Did this mean he was well?

"Queen Norah," he greeted back with a nod of his head. "The healer has said I'm beyond the window of danger. If I had the fever, I would have displayed symptoms already."

She let out a breath of relief, and the councilmen clapped. Even Soren gave him an indebted nod.

"Good news, Lord Justice," Edward said. "Praise the gods; they're merciful to their faithful subjects."

Norah's eyes narrowed. No doubt it was a jab at Soren. "Was Henricus not faithful?" she asked.

The room fell silent.

But she wasn't here to discuss the gods' mercy, or Henricus. "Where is the last letter from the king of Aleon?" she asked.

"Surely you have it," Edward said.

She eyed him suspiciously. "No, I don't. It never reached me."

"Then what makes you think there was a letter?"

"Because I know its contents. Phillip sent a warning to close our ports, the same warning he sent to Kharav." She kept her eyes on Edward. "But you didn't want to close the ports, Councilman Edward."

"I didn't take the letter, if that's what you are insinuating," he said, with an edge to his voice.

"I don't believe you," she challenged.

"That's a bold statement," Councilman Alastair warned.

"Not as bold as writing the king of Aleon and asking him to withdraw the forces your queen sent to Kharav."

Alastair looked around the table. "You cannot think anyone here would do such a thing."

She raised Phillip's letter. "I have the proof in my hand. Phillip shares how grateful he is that he didn't heed this council's advice and withdraw his forces, for not a single man was lost in Kharav. Meanwhile, the fever has taken nearly a quarter of his men across Aleon."

The council let out an audible gasp.

"I know you're not happy with my decision to close the ports and halt our trade," she continued. "I know you're not happy with many of my decisions, but perhaps you shouldn't have been so eager to put this crown on my head and call me queen. Well, now I *am* queen. I've forged an alliance that brings Mercia strength, one that's kept us from war. I've brought our people peace, provisions, security. But you don't want peace, do you? You work against me."

Her eyes moved around the table from councilman to councilman. "Do you know what that is?" she asked them. "*Treason*."

"This is your council," Edward said with wide eyes. "It's our duty to protect the ways of Mercia."

"The old ways are dead," she said firmly. "I'll bring a new Mercia—a Mercia that thrives on unity and peace and strength with Kharav. It's what's best for the people. That is *my* duty. It's yours. And I will find who betrayed that duty."

And she meant every word.

Norah paced the side hall that ran the length of the west wing. She didn't know what she would do when she found out who'd written Phillip to withdraw his forces in Kharav. What if it was more than one person? What if it came from her collective council? She didn't want to rule Mercia with an iron hand. She didn't want to rule by force, but she couldn't tolerate divisive measures from her own council. She had condemned Mikael for his violence; she couldn't do the same. Nor could she show lenience. Expulsion perhaps. Was she able to do that? She cursed herself—she didn't even know the laws of her own kingdom. Alexander would know.

She found him in the courtyard, talking with a group of men. They wore leather armor and open-faced helms. They weren't from Mercia.

When he saw her, he excused them and crossed the distance to meet her.

"Who are those men?" she asked.

"The council has brought in mercenaries to augment our forces," he explained.

"Mercenaries? Without me knowing?"

"Yes, I've already addressed that. I wasn't aware either."

"They can't do that. Send these mercenaries on their way."

He extended a hand to calm her. "They've stepped beyond their bounds, certainly, but hiring mercenaries isn't a far-fetched idea. Especially when we've sent so many men to Kharav, and the attacks on our villages could start again at any time."

Anger swelled inside her. "They should have discussed it with me."

"Yes, they should have. And with me, as lord justice. But"—he paused—"give some leniency. You are... bringing a wave of change that's difficult for them, all of them, even Catherine. Give a little."

Give a little. She'd already given. But maybe he was right—she was pushing the council hard. Perhaps now wasn't the best time to bring up expulsion, but when she found out who had written Phillip, there would be consequences. Severe ones.

They turned and walked through the gardens together.

"Has it been difficult for you?" she asked softly.

He was quiet for a time, but she could see his mind churning. "Do you love the Shadow King?" he asked finally.

"Yes," she answered. She had no hesitation, no reservation. She did love him.

"I see it in you," he said.

Good. He should. Everyone should see it.

"His darkness," he added.

She stopped as she drew her brows together. "What?"

"You're not yourself, Norah. He's changed you."

Anger burned inside her. "Or perhaps I *am* myself, I'm just not who you want me to be."

He halted, and his face dropped in sadness. "I know you better than anyone. This isn't you. The Shadow King, he's made you harsh, and dark."

"If you really believe that, then you don't know me at all. Mikael has made me strong—stronger than I ever thought I could be, strong enough to be a queen."

He stepped back at her words, whether surprised or upset—she didn't care. She remembered so long ago, seeing the vision of herself on the Shadow throne. She hadn't thought she could be that woman, that woman who sat so tall amid the darkness. Now she couldn't imagine herself as anything else. It was where she belonged. It was who she was. And she wouldn't let anyone tell her different, even Alexander.

"And you've changed too," she said.

He quieted. He cast his eyes down and swallowed. "Yes, I suppose we both have," he said finally as he looked back up at her.

557

And when two people changed, what was left between them? She drew in a long breath and let it out slowly. She nodded solemnly, then turned back to the castle, leaving him alone in the courtyard.

Alexander walked through the castle without intention, lost in his mind. His chest felt it would cave under an invisible weight—a weight that forced the air from his lungs and crushed his heart.

"Alexander," a man's voice called.

He stopped, not sure from where it had come.

"Alexander," it called again.

He turned around to see Councilmen Edward and Alastair walking toward him. He frowned. Edward had called him by his name only a handful of times over his life, usually when he was trying to convince him of something.

"Are you well?" Edward said with a worried brow.

He wasn't well. He would never be well. But he didn't answer. What did Edward want from him now?

"Will you join us?" Edward asked him, motioning toward a small side hall.

Alexander didn't want to join them. He didn't want to hear whatever it was Edward was going to peddle, but one didn't simply ignore an elder councilman, even a lord justice. And he knew where they were headed. The councilmen had a small library in the east wing, more of a shared study, not large—a good place for talking and thinking. He didn't want to talk or think right now, but still he followed.

"Perhaps you're concerned, as we are, regarding this morning's council meeting?" Alastair said as they walked.

The council meeting. He'd almost forgotten—add it to the list of things that weighed on his shoulders.

When they reached the council's library, Alexander unbuckled his sword belt and set the blade at the foot of the oversize chair by the bookshelf that stretched to the ceiling. He forgot all proprieties and sank down into the soft leather. He just needed to sit.

"Here." Edward poured wine into a chalice and held it for him. "Have a drink. Ease your mind."

Norah closed the door of her chamber and leaned back against it. Her heart started to slow as she tried to cool her anger. Everyone wanted to tell her who she should be, who she shouldn't, even Alexander. But she knew who she was.

She knew now.

"Salara, are you all right?" Vitalia said, coming quickly to her side.

She nodded.

"You don't look all right." Vitalia knew her well. She pulled Norah to the chair by the small table and sat down across from her, pouring them both a cup of wine. She pushed Norah's cup in front of her. "Is it those old bastards again?" she asked as she took a drink from her own cup.

Norah smiled appreciatively. "They are old bastards, aren't they?"

Vitalia smiled.

Norah let out a long breath. "I've decided to return to Kharav."

Her maid's face grew serious, and she swallowed. "Surely it's not safe, Salara."

"I don't know why it wouldn't be," Norah countered. "Mikael still has a full army. He lost nothing to the sickness, and he has the additional forces of Mercia and Aleon. The armies of Japheth and Rael have been devastated by the fever. They can't move against us, at least not now. I should return. And I want to go home."

Vitalia swayed slightly in her chair.

Norah knew the news would disappoint her. Vitalia would be upset to leave if Serene stayed, which was likely. They had become very close friends. "I'll ask Serene to return with us," she said, "but I'll leave it her choice."

Vitalia didn't respond. She *was* disappointed, Norah was sure. But Norah hadn't expected her silence.

"Would you... want to stay in Mercia?" Norah hadn't thought Vitalia would want to stay, given Mercia's narrow moral views and constant judgment. She didn't know what she'd do for a maid, but if Vitalia wanted to stay in Mercia with Serene, she'd allow her to.

Still, Vitalia didn't answer.

Suddenly, the chalice dropped from the maid's hands, but she didn't move to catch it.

"Vitalia, are you all right?"

Her maid swayed again and then fell forward out of the chair, hitting the table before collapsing to the floor.

"Vitalia!" Norah cried as she sprang down to her side.

Vitalia's eyes were open, but they stared blankly back at her. Norah clutched her face. "Vitalia!" Then her gaze moved to the chalice on the floor with spilled wine around it.

Beside her, Cusco whined.

Norah staggered to her feet. "Guards!" she screamed. But when she ripped the door to the hall open, it wasn't her guards looking back at her. They lay on the stone floor of the hall, dead.

The council's mercenaries blocked her way, their swords drawn.

Alexander took the chalice of wine from Edward and drank deeply.

"Lord Justice," the councilman said. "I'm sure you would agree that the queen's words and actions are quite troubling."

Yes, the council was troubled. And if he was honest with himself, Alexander was too. Not of Norah's intentions; in her heart, she truly wanted the best for both Mercia and Kharav, but things with the council were escalating. He took another drink.

"What she has done," the councilman continued, "what she continues to do—it will inflict great harm on Mercia." He refilled Alexander's chalice from the glass carafe of wine. "Our values, our customs, our way of life, everything we believe and everything we stand for. I'm sure you can agree, she is not the woman who left us those years ago."

No, she was not. What he wouldn't give to have that woman back. He grieved her, the loss.

"She's been corrupted by the darkness," the councilman said.

Alexander found himself nodding. There was a darkness. But Norah couldn't see it, and he didn't know how to make her see. And to make it more complicated, he didn't entirely despise the king who brought this darkness. Alexander's head hurt, and he drew up his hand and pressed his fingers to his temples. He was just so tired.

He took another drink.

"So, again, we appear in agreement," Edward said.

Perhaps. He lauded Norah's effort for peace, her relentless struggle to bring two opposite worlds together, but they were two worlds that should remain opposite. He set the chalice down on the side table, and Edward promptly refilled it again.

"This is why she must be removed," the councilman said.

Removed. Alexander's head snapped up. Edward's words seemed to sink in for the first time. "What?"

"She must be removed," Edward repeated.

Alexander surged to his feet. A rush of fog filled his mind, but he blinked it back. What was happening? His hand moved to where the hilt of his sword normally sat against his hip, but he'd taken it off. He struggled to remember where he'd set it. "She's queen. You can't just remove her."

"We have another with royal blood, the queen's second cousin, Evangeline, and Catherine will continue as regent until the girl is of age. As before, we are here to guide her."

His breaths came harder now. The room swirled around him, and he parted his stance slightly to keep his balance. "Those are treasonous words," he warned. Catherine would never accept that. He'd never accept it. He blinked again to focus his failing vision. What was happening to him?

The wine.

Alexander spotted his sword on the floor by the foot of the chair, but he wasn't sure he'd stay on his feet if he reached for it.

"We have done everything in the name of Mercia," Edward said. "Our consciences are clear."

Alexander's heartbeat grew in his ears, thrumming with the heat of fight. What did that mean? "Where's the queen?"

"Alexander," Edward said. "Your family has safeguarded Mercia for generations upon generations. Your blood can be traced back to the original protector of the crown. Your father sacrificed for this great kingdom. And now so must you."

"Where's Norah?" he demanded again.

"You should sit down, Lord Justice."

Alexander had no intention of sitting down. His eyes dropped again to his sword.

"Sit down, Alexander," James said, stepping into the doorway.

He whirled around. *Even James?* "Where is Norah?" he asked again, more desperate now.

James stepped closer to him, with his eyes full of sorrow. "We had no choice."

Alexander shook with a fury seeping into his heart at the man he trusted most in the world—the man who'd guided him his whole life, mentored him, believed in him. He lunged toward his sword, but his body failed him, and he dropped to his knees.

James caught him, softening his fall.

"We had no choice," came the words again, as the darkness closed around him.

Norah stared at the mercenaries looking back at her with intentions of death in their eyes. But Cusco and Cavaatsa growled and leapt forward, each downing a man, and she darted out of her chamber.

The sound of steel rang through the air. Suddenly, Soren crashed into the hall with a half-dozen mercenaries around him. "Salara!" he roared as he fought them back.

Norah desperately searched for a weapon, but there was nothing close around her.

Soren cut down another man, then he grabbed her and barreled down the hall to the side door as the dogs took down another two mercenaries. "We need to get out of here!" he snarled.

"No! Vitalia's back there! She's been poisoned!"

"You can't help her now."

"I'm not leaving her!" she screamed as she fought him. He pulled her closer for a better hold. She caught his chin with her elbow, briefly stopping their flight, but he grabbed her as she tried to jerk away.

"Let me go!" she cried.

Soren pulled her back to him and clutched her close under his arm, covering her mouth and stifling her screams with his hand. He pulled her into a connecting hall and down a stair. The dogs followed.

From behind, she heard the wisp of an arrow. A dog yelped. Then only Cavaatsa was beside them.

She managed to pull Soren's hand free. "Cusco!" she screamed.

But the dog didn't come. And Soren didn't stop.

More footsteps came behind them. Soren called out in the Shadow tongue, and Cavaatsa turned back to slow their pursuers.

Soren dragged her down another hall and to a small side room, where they nearly collided with Caspian.

"Caspian!" she cried. "You have to save Vitalia!"

Caspian stepped forward and gripped her in Soren's hold. "Norah, listen to me. The council—they're trying to kill you."

"I can't leave her!"

"She's gone," Soren said firmly.

But she shook her head. She couldn't accept that.

Caspian clutched her firmly, looking into her eyes. "Norah, we have to get you out of here."

A sob escaped her throat.

Caspian rapidly led them down another stair and through the tunnels under the city. They came up through a row building, out the back, and to a small side street on the mainland, where they found a public stable. Caspian quickly set to saddling a horse.

Soren shoved her up and then mounted behind her.

She looked down at Caspian in horror. "You're not coming too?"

He shook his head. "You have a better chance of making it out alone."

"You can't stay here!"

"Don't you worry about me. Keep yourself safe." He looked up at her, his eyes full of sorrow. "I'm sorry, Norah."

But she didn't have time to respond before Soren urged the horse forward and into the night.

CHAPTER FIFTY-NINE

The journey back to Kharav was the longest Norah had ever known. She rode in the silence of defeat. She didn't sleep when they stopped to rest. Soren didn't either.

Their mount wasn't a destrier, and when they reached the Horsemen tribes, Soren traded it for a larger beast that could better carry them both.

He caught rabbits and a few birds as they went. Despite their fleeing and his aversion to fires while traveling, he built a small campfire for her each time they stopped.

Her cheeks were constantly wet with tears, her stomach sick.

"Why didn't Alexander come?" she whispered on the fifth night. It was the first she'd spoken since they left Mercia. "What if they killed him too?"

"That's not possible."

Her lip trembled. "But he would have come. He would have come for me."

Soren clasped her by the arm. "Look at me."

She couldn't.

He near shook her. "Look at me!"

She lifted her tear-filled eyes to his.

"That bastard won't die. I know. I've tried. He'll be all right."

But she couldn't stop the tears.

"Come here," he said, and pulled her close, wrapping his arm around her.

Days passed in a blur. Even visiting the Uru, Norah didn't remember much, only a little of Tahla taking care of her—helping her clean up, braiding her hair, giving her another knife. She had left Alexander's dagger back in her chamber in Mercia.

Once they cleared the Canyonlands, the Kharavian border patrol joined them. Soren spoke to them in Kharavian tongue, and two soldiers split off and away to the capital, to Mikael. She still couldn't speak the Kharavian language well, but she understood a large amount now. They rode to tell Mikael of the Mercian council's takeover, of the attempt against her life, and that Soren was bringing her home.

Mikael stood outside in the courtyard as they rode in, waiting. Soren slipped her down off the horse. The tears came again, and she let out a sob as Mikael swept her into his arms. She clung to him as she cried.

He held her tight. Then he picked her up and carried her into the safety of the Shadows.

Norah sat on her throne in stoic silence, with Mikael beside her on his own throne, as the nobles entered. They didn't sit close enough to touch, their chairs too far apart for her to do what she needed most—to simply hold his hand. But she could feel his rage. He hadn't even given her arrival a full day before he urgently summoned all his nobles. At least she'd had time to wash and look put together, even if just for appearances.

Soren stood to Mikael's right, and Salara-Mae stood to Norah's left, back just into the shadows. As the nobles took their places, Mikael rose.

"I've called you here to discuss an urgent matter," he said. "A march against the North."

Norah's head snapped up, and she gaped at him. That wasn't what she'd expected. She thought he'd only inform them of the circumstance. They hadn't discussed going to war against her council. Murmurs rippled through the nobles, and even Soren shifted in surprise.

"We can't march against the North," Lord Narsing said. "We have no allies and are on the brink of war ourselves."

"I'll remove the North's council." Mikael's words came with venom. *Punish them*, he had meant. He glanced at Norah and then back out to his nobles. "And I'll reestablish the alliance."

"The North was never an ally," Narsing argued. "Not a true one. And if Aleon decides to stand with them after this?"

"We can get there before Aleon mobilizes, but we'd have to march now."

Narsing scoffed. "You can't be serious."

"Salar," Soren said quietly. "We should discuss this."

Mikael shot him a look in surprise. Soren never spoke against him publicly. "There's nothing to discuss."

"Apparently there is," Narsing said. "Even your lord commander thinks it's a foolish idea." Another murmur rumbled through nobles in agreement. "What do you say, Lord Commander?"

But Soren didn't answer. He only looked at Mikael.

Norah caught Mikael's eyes. She silently prayed that he'd relent. He couldn't march to war against Mercia, not when his nobles, and even Soren, were unsupportive. And certainly not before Norah could get her mind around it. Perhaps there would come the time when she wanted revenge, but that time wasn't now. Now she was just trying to get her mind right about what had happened. She begged him with her eyes.

"Get out," Mikael told the room.

They stared at him for a moment.

"Now!" he demanded. And they slowly filed out.

The room emptied, and relief filled her. But the conversation wasn't done. Mikael's eyes bore into Soren. "You don't agree with me?" His voice was cold and calm—the deepest of anger.

But Soren held his own calm reply. "I wish you would have discussed it with me before bringing it to the nobles."

"I don't need your permission," Mikael snarled.

Soren's eyes were dark, darker than the midnight they normally were. "I'm lord commander. I lead our army."

Mikael bristled. "*My* army! *I* am Salar!" He was too far from Norah for her to reach out to him, to touch him, to try to calm him.

"This is just what you wanted," Salara-Mae hissed as she stepped out of the shadows, making them all stop. Norah jerked her head toward the woman in astonishment. But then she realized Salara-Mae wasn't talking to her. The woman's eyes were on Soren. "You supported this marriage when you knew it would be his downfall. Then you broke us from Japheth by murdering Gregor's nephew." Her words dripped with hatred. She looked at Mikael. "He provokes your enemies to rise against you! And now even your nobles."

"He's had nothing to do with anything that's happened," Mikael said shortly, his anger at Soren now switching to defense. "How can you even blame him?"

Salara-Mae snorted in rage and disbelief, wrinkling her face in disgust. "No," she said bitterly. "Get out!" She spoke to Soren directly. "Get out!" she seethed again.

"Mother!" Mikael tried to quiet her.

"Salara-Mae," Norah breathed.

"No!" The woman pointed at Soren, peeling her lips back in rage. "I've watched you plot and scheme and claw your way closer to the crown. This is just what you wanted! Salar on the cusp of defeat! You wanted this!"

Norah gaped at the woman in horror. "How can you say this?"

Salara-Mae's breath came ragged, her anger taking all her energy. "He knows," she seethed.

Norah looked at Soren, who stood bewildered.

"Bastard son of Rhalstad," the woman spat.

Rhalstad, *Mikael's father*?

Mikael leaned back on his heel, with his brow creased in confusion. He stared at his mother.

"He knows," Salara-Mae said again. "He knows who he is."

Mikael shifted his gaze to Soren.

Soren shook his head. "You're mistaken. My father was Tyrhar Nazim, captain of the Crest and lord of Bahoul."

Her rage sparked through the air. "Rhalstad thought he could hide you away, his son of a whore! She wasn't even a wife! When he had his captain of the Crest take you both to Bahoul, I knew. I knew!"

"That's not true," Soren said, but Norah could see the fear on his face.

Salara-Mae stepped forward, pointing a long, thin finger at him. "I watched you!" she seethed. "Always watching him! Always close! You were always scheming, just looking for your opportunity."

Norah's mind raced. Soren's claim to the throne wouldn't be a strong one if his mother *was* a concubine, but he would have one nonetheless, and an even stronger claim if the nobles didn't support the current king.

Soren stumbled backward, shaking his head. "No, that's not true," he said again.

"I saw the way you looked at him. You envied him! You envied what he had! You wanted it for yourself."

But Soren would never betray Mikael.

"Enough!" Norah cried, finally gathering the strength to stand.

Soren backed up, toward the ash-wood doors, his eyes filled with sorrow and disbelief, then he turned and staggered out into the side hall.

"Soren," Mikael called after him, but the commander didn't stop. "Soren!" he called again. He looked back at his mother.

Salara-Mae stood smugly, with her face covered in hate.

"You have no idea your ignorance," Mikael snarled at her.

"My ignorance!" she snapped back. "You defend a man with a claim to your throne, who your army follows. He can take everything from you!"

"He's *given* everything to me!" he thundered.

"You're a fool," she said, and stormed from the hall.

Norah looked to the open doors of the hall, and her blood ran cold. Several of the nobles stood, watching them. They turned and left quickly.

Norah's mind reeled from the exchange she had just witnessed and the events of the past several weeks. What had just happened? Soren was Mikael's half brother? And now the nobles knew—on top of everything else—*they knew*.

Mikael stood. Lost.

Finally, he sank down onto his throne. She crossed the space between them and stepped between his knees, taking his face in her hands and drawing his eyes up to look at her.

"Do you think she speaks the truth?" he asked hoarsely.

Norah was hesitant. She didn't know. "I think... *she* thinks it's the truth," she said finally.

"But do you?" he asked. "Do you think Soren's the son of my father?" She pulled her bottom lip between her teeth. "We don't know that."

He let out a breath, his eyes rimmed red. "Don't we? Even *you* said a child of Soren could pass for my own. I didn't see it before, but..." His voice fell.

"We don't know that," she repeated softly.

"Why else would she hate him the way she does? Why else would she think he was after power? Even as the son of a concubine, he'd have a claim to the throne, a claim he could use to challenge me—a challenge that grows stronger with no heir." He looked up at her. "Why would she lie?" he whispered. "Do you think she lies?"

She ran her gaze over the darkness of his eyes and the strength of his jaw. The line of his nose and the shape of his brow. His black hair, dark like the night, with a faint curl. And his stature—how he stood, how he walked. All like Soren. She couldn't deny it, and she shook her head slowly.

Mikael squeezed his eyes shut and let out a shaking breath, and she pulled him to her.

Norah stood in front of Soren's chamber door. She raised her hand to knock. And stopped. She spread her palm against it. This news would have devastated him.

Finally, she knocked, but there was no answer. Slowly, she pushed open the door. Glass scraped against the floor underneath. She drew in a breath as she surveyed the room.

Everything was broken. Furniture, the mirror, the basin. Broken like Soren. Like Mikael. Like her.

"He's gone," a voice said behind her.

She turned to see Adrian—one of the few people helping her keep her sanity. Of course he'd been shocked and distraught over the news of Mercia, but he had jumped to support her and had promptly pledged himself, to which all five thousand Mercian soldiers in Kharav followed.

"I saw him as he was leaving the stables," he told her.

"When will he return?"

Adrian hesitated before shaking his head. "He's not coming back, Norah."

Not coming back? How could he just not come back? "Where did he go?"

He shook his head again. "I don't know. He said to tell Katya, and she would know what to do until Salar could appoint a new commander."

Her breath caught in her throat. A new commander? There could never be another.

"I'm on my way to find her now," he said. "I just wanted to make sure you knew first." He stood quietly for a moment. "Will you tell me if I can do anything?"

What could he do? What could anyone do? Her lip trembled.

He let out a sorrowful sigh and left her alone to the broken room.

Norah let herself sink down onto the edge of the bed, her legs weak beneath her. She covered her mouth as a sobbing breath escaped.

Alexander.

Vitalia.

Serene.

Her grandmother.

Mercia.

Cusco. Cavaatsa. Sephir.

They were all lost to her. And now Soren.

And once Mikael discovered he was gone, she'd lose him too. Soren's leaving would destroy him, like it was destroying her. They needed him. He couldn't leave.

Her silent cries turned to breathless rage—rage at the circumstance, her council, at the gods themselves.

She needed Soren back.

She needed her kingdom back.

And she needed blood.

Norah sat up as an icy fire burned over her skin. She'd get back what belonged to her, with the blood of recompense now owed. She'd take back what was hers. The Shadow Queen.

THE COMPLETE TRILOGY

Continue the journey with:

WAR QUEEN

Only blood can end it all.

ABOUT THE AUTHOR

Nicola Tyche is an American fiction and fantasy author writing romantic fantasy, paranormal, urban fantasy, and other women's fiction. Suspenseful plot twists, strong heroines, relatable villains, and melt-your-insides anti-heroes are ingredients for every book, and Nicola is a sucker for a happily ever after.

She lives in Vancouver, Washington, with her husband and three daughters. When she isn't writing, she enjoys tacos, traveling, gardening, exploring the great outdoors, and other creative projects. Visit her website at www.nicolatyche.com, connect on the Nicola Tyche Facebook reader group, or the platforms below!

nicolatyche